GW00732543

Five Go Dobbing in The Neighbours

NewsBiscuit

A word from our owner, Sir Hugo Von Biscuit.

'As a media mogul and avid lobbyist, it came as quite a shock to discover that I owned a controlling interest in the morally corrupt and financially suicidal – NewsBiscuit. My initial instinct was to sell it for scrap and melt the staff down for glue. Unfortunately, I was told that this might jeopardize my takeover of Newcastle Utd, giving that the Saudi's already had better human rights record than me.

It was my good friend, Tony Blair, who suggested that I use it as an offshore company. So, like so many billionaires, I intend to launch NewsBiscuit 's headquarters into orbit – from a rather large cannon. Not only will the inevitable deaths of the editorial staff provide me with a warm fuzzy feeling, NewsBiscuit being 100 miles above the nearest tax office will be a particular boon.

So, please don't read any further unless you are some sort of communist – or a ghastly vegan'.

September 2020

Massive rises in COVID cases in the UK saw the introduction of the 'Rule of Six'. After being encouraged to 'Eat out to Help out' in August, many thought the rule was an advisory limit on the number of shared tapas dishes you should order to avoid being over-full. Some team sports such as polo were exempt from the Rule of Six, with some describing this particular exception as 'full of holes'. Boris Johnson was imagining a post-COVID world, talking optimistically about 'Operation Moonshot', with many hoping that he might be fired up there himself.

Bloke in pub to join Cabinet

The Government has announced a series of new appointments based on the candidate selection process known as 'Bloody Good Bloke' theory, including naming That Bloke from the Pub as Health Secretary. According to the theory, the most important quality in a candidate is how well they will get along with the current team, regardless of qualifications, experience and a successful police check.

'It's all about the group dynamic,' said an HR expert. 'For a team to function effectively all members need to pull in the same direction, even if it's off the edge of a cliff.'

'Wankers are a special case', conceded the expert. 'There's no formal definition of a 'wanker', though most people agree on their identification. In theory I suppose a team of wankers might just keep hiring other wankers until . . . well, complete organisational collapse, I suppose. But that would never happen, would it? What possible type of organisation would allow a complete tosser to rise to the top? Oh . . .'

Groups of 30 illegal, unless you work in a school, casino or swingers' party

The Government has set out clear guidance that all groups of over 30 are forbidden, except not really. To halt the spread of COVID-19, everyone must stay in small bubbles, anywhere between 1 to 10,000, excluding days that end in Y.

'It's very simple,' said the Health Minister. 'We must follow the strict rules, right up until it's inconvenient or it involves poor people - then all bets are off.'

To keep class sizes down, primary schools are recommended to only count children over six feet tall. Secondary schools are advised to only record students who are parents themselves and sixth form colleges are told to just list them all as staff.

MPs have struggled the most with keeping to small groups, not among themselves, but with the large number of lobbyists and pretty interns they need. Complained on Tory MP: 'Only 30? How am I going to get my butlers and groundskeepers all in the same room?'

Man unilaterally tears up agreement with HMRC

'There were quite a few anomalies in my tax return questions,' said Maurice Thompson, 56, after declaring his contract with HMRC null and void. 'Like, "Where did all your money come from?" I realised, hang about, these answers are going to cost you, mate.

'HMRC's version doesn't really count any more, not now that I've decided I'm not in that HMRC club anymore. In fact, I may start demanding they pay back the taxes they obviously took from me in error over the years. Next thing is to sort out just how much I've actually made this summer with my two full-time jobs.

'And then there's the furlough money the Government promised me. Not seen any of that yet. They've let me down badly on that. I mean, an agreement's an agreement isn't? You've got to know where you stand, right?'

COVID restrictions to form backbone of next year's A level maths paper

QUESTION ONE - If three households containing 14 members can meet up in Manchester, and four households in Llanwyrn containing 18 members can meet up, how many households can meet up in Edinburgh? Answers in decimal notation, please.

QUESTION TWO - There are four devolved and national Government rules in a series of simultaneous equations, while simple calculus is used to predict the spread of an infection starting in one household breaking the relevant devolved or national allowance and assuming an R rate of 1.2.

FOR TEN EXTRA MARKS - If 100 MPs wash their hands of responsibility, prove that the spread is reduced for the same data in a devolved area with greater latitude in its rules - the so-called COVID paradox.

By contrast, this year's Sociology paper just says: 'We are all going to die – discuss.'

Trump paid $750 in tax, more than expected

After it emerged that President Trump paid only $750 in tax last year, historians pointed out that the last billionaire to pay tax in the US was John. D Rockefeller, when he accidentally tipped a waiter in 1916. Since then, no person of wealth has contributed to the American economy, other than Jeff Bezos, who in 2014 accidently swapped North Dakota for a foot-spa during a Black Friday sale.

The $750 would normally be tax deductible, as part of Trump's daily hair-product allowance. Sadly, the President will now have to trim his expenses - which means delaying his next marriage, putting Eric up for adoption (again) and reducing the Mexico Wall down to a small box hedge.

In other news, his accountant has been named as a finalist for the Booker Prize for Fiction.

Office workers saving £££s working from home never EVER coming back

The outrageous cost of commuting, overpriced lunches and maintaining a wardrobe of the latest designer work fashions, all leave the average office worker with little disposable income. Requests to return to the office have been countered with requests to 'kiss my hairy plums.'

Said one worker: 'Feeling obliged to attend social events with colleagues you can't stand spending more than a minute with than you absolutely have to, was always will-zapping. You'd do your water cooler duty, and then some nitwit would let slip it's Sandra's birthday, and that's another evening lost to the black hole of time suckage.'

'If only management had admitted that the real reason they wanted people in the office all along was to grope the ones they fancied and bully the others like they were still at school'

Man baffled after failing to mend laptop by shouting at it

Hampshire-based confidence fanatic Alan Scott was left aghast yesterday after a series of gesticulations and random threats of violence somehow did not convince his broken laptop to boot up.

'I always thought I knew a bit about computers. I've sent loads of emails and I'm an expert with the old In-Private Browsing, but I simply couldn't get it to work,' Scott said. 'I tried everything, turning it off and on again, blowing the dust off the keyboard, unplugging the mouse, but no, nothing. Even holding my head in my hands and mewling "Just bloody work please" didn't make a difference.'

Scott has now abandoned his endeavours and was last seen preparing to smash a wasps' nest on the side of his shed with a medium-sized garden rake.

Royals team up for new BBC series 'Different Planet'

The new BBC documentary 'Different Planet' aims to highlight the subtle differences between being born into the Royal family and being born into an interbred army of alley cats, like you.

The Royals experiment by waiting ten weeks for a GP appointment, they learn how to boil an egg with Bear Grylls and the Duke of Edinburgh learns how to hold a conversation with someone who ranks lower than an Earl.

There is even an insight into how the Royals juggle their complicated finances. When asked if he had ever been forced to visit 'the bank of mum and dad', Prince Charles looked confused and asked if we meant the Bank of England – anyway, he was pretty sure that Mum used Coutts.

Top laws to break

- **Newton's Third Law of Motion** - As evidenced by cabinet members retaining their positions despite dreadful pandemic mismanagement; actions do not have an equal and opposite reaction. Newton's Third isn't true when applied to politics, if it were, Sir Captain Tom would be PM.

- **Lockdown restrictions** - Like Stretch Armstrong, these laws cannot be broken, only bent beyond recognition. If confronted, say you 'acted reasonably and legally', 'did what any father would do', or 'took a short drive to test your eyesight.' The latter also circumvents reading number plates before a driving test.

- **Murphy's Law** - Anything that can go wrong, will go wrong. Proof being the Government's handling of the coronavirus crisis, Brexit and anything else that comes within two metres of it. This law is immutable and reinforced by Boris' attempts to prove otherwise.

- **Jude Law** - Good luck trying to get your clauses into this law in a very specific and unlimited way. If the prospect of performing twelve hours of continuous live TV doesn't break this suave charmer, it's highly unlikely you will

- **Cole's Law** - Governs the relationship between shredded vegetables and milky mayonnaise. Ride roughshod over this law by replacing key elements with slices of bread, a meat filling, and actual mayonnaise. No one will have the strength to hold you accountable, just like international law.

- **P Law** - The rule that rice can be any colour except white

- **Inn Law** - Visiting relatives must be accommodated only in cheap hotels. Failure to conform to this law has dire consequences, such as shouting, drunkenness and violence

- **Folk Law** - The principal of a body of culture expressed by harmonica-playing simpletons accompanied by badly tuned, twangy guitars. It states that the pressure (p) of a given quality of string plucking varies inversely with its hideous volume (v) at constant temperature; i.e., in equation form, $pv = k$, a constant racket. I mean, frankly, who even gives half a shit

- **Law of Perpetual Motion** - Did you really eat those undercooked sausages & chicken at the weekend BBQ?

- **Law of Gravity** - Defy it simply by refusing to be serious about it

- **Broad Law** - The highest hill in the Scottish Borders is popular with ramblers, just the sort of annoying proles you like to wind up. Being a huge mass of rock, earth and grass it is hard to break, but if you can whip up a few charts showing potential for oil you can probably persuade the fracking Johnnies to have a go. Might even be able to make a few quid flogging them a permit

- **Lawdy Miss Clawdy** - An ancient Elvis Presley record that should be broken as soon as you hear it

Privatised rescue service will offer special deals to drowning customers

The Government is keen to replace the RAF and RNLI with a more cost-effective, market-driven, and robust provider. By downloading an app, customers will be able to tap the screen on their smartphone and summon a helicopter to their GPS location.

Said a spokeswoman: 'Saving money is just as important as saving lives, if not more so. If people can't be bothered to stick a phone down their swimming trunks before being dragged out to sea by a riptide, then they deserve to die.'

Floating corpses that have a prepaid card or a standing order will count as a successful outcome. Rescuers will be encouraged to rifle through pockets for spare change and have first dibs on gold fillings. 'We hope to charge its victims as little as £3,000 a pop, providing they have a good credit score rating.'

Trump's Ten Commandments

1. Thou shalt have no other gods before me, your favourite President.
2. Thou shalt not make for yourself a graven image unless it's the dust jacket of The Art of the Deal
3. Thou shalt not take the name of Tucker Carlson in vain
4. Remember the Sabbath day, keep it 18 holesy
5. Honour thy father and thy mother. Be either distant or creepy with your kids
6. Thou shalt not kill unless you're a heavily armed 17-year-old wandering around an unfamiliar town
7. Thou shalt not commit adultery unless it's with a porn star while your wife is pregnant
8. Thou shalt not steal, unless it's from a charity to buy a massive portrait of yourself
9. Thou shalt not bear false witness against your neighbour. Not really sure what that one means
10. Thou shalt not covet your neighbour's manservant, or his maidservant, or his ox, or his wife, or her ass. Her pussy is fine though

Post-coital cuddle goes on 30 seconds too long

Happily married couple, Aadi and Caroline Baptiste, were just enjoying the afterglow of a rigorous bout of lovemaking, when both discovered, simultaneously, that they had outstayed their welcome.

Caught in a mutual clinch of fake affection, both were forced to pretend they 'heard a noise outside', commented Aadi: 'It's just a diplomatic way of saying, get your sweaty hands off me, you're freaking me out and its far too hot.'

Caroline confirmed: 'Normally I'd have no qualms about turning over and making some snarky comment about the damp patch. Or just telling Aadi to clean his teeth, despite me having seen him do it fifteen minutes earlier. It's the kind thing to do.'

Instead, they were left intertwined for far too long, despite both needing to fart. In the future, Aadi and Caroline agreed that they needed some sort of warning system to say that their post-coital time had elapsed, said Caroline: 'Yeah, we're thinking about getting a kid.'

NATO to tut and shake their heads at Russia

NATO has agreed to say 'Well, REALLY...' after Russia's latest act of mass murder. A motion for even more drastic measures, that would have involved members rolling their eyes and muttering under their breath, was defeated in a second vote after being deemed too confrontational.

The Prime Minister condemned Russia in the strongest terms: 'Once we have received their explanation for their outrageous behaviour, no matter how far-fetched it may be, we will accept it without question and apologise profusely to Mr Putin for wasting his time.'

Parents Liberation Front threatens bombings if schools close

'Make no mistake, if schools are told to shut their doors because loads of idiots have spent the summer coughing into each other's faces in beer gardens and holiday resorts, we will forcibly close the bars and restaurants too,' read a post uploaded to the Dark Mumsnet.

'F*ck education, this is about sanity. This is about my family's survival - before we all murder each other. And the PLF would like to remind the Government that we vote it in, we pay its taxes, we wash its clothes and cook its tea, it definitely IS time for school... And [sob] it doesn't make the rules, we do!!'

Top reasons your boss wants you back in the office

- He has no friends
- He is part of a death cult
- He is tired of being naked from the waist down in online meetings
- He has shares in Prêt-à-Manger
- He is bored of talking to his butler
- He lost all the furlough cash in Las Vegas
- Knowing you spend 20% of your salary on train fares gives him an erection
- He is secretly having an affair with your partner and needs you out of the house
- He can't operate zoom without a dozen IT technicians
- All Coronavirus deaths are tax-deductible
- He thinks it's funny

(Please note that bosses come in all genders, but the arseholes are always 'blokes' – even the female ones)

Seven mums who meet up on Monday waiting to discover who is the least popular

The ban on social gatherings of more than six people in England from Monday is leading to a tense stand-off for seven friends who had planned to get squiffy on cava in the park, it has emerged.

One, who wished to remain anonymous, said: 'It totally messes with the group dynamic. I mean, if I had absolutely no choice but to leave someone out. Christ ... I really can't decide. No, I really can't ... OK, Susan. One hundred percent. I mean, she's lovely, but she does go on a bit.'

Another friend, who also wished to remain anonymous, commented: 'It really messes with the Monday catch-up. I think we're just going to have to cancel. I mean, I couldn't imagine us meeting up without one of us. We're the sisterhood. It's such a shame. Just because of some arbitrary cut-off number. Well, it's a sacrifice we'll all have to make.'

'I mean, if I really had to choose, maybe Susan. Only because we've not known her as long as the others. Well, apart from Laura. And Jane. I mean, she's really, really lovely. But I actually think she has some other mum friends. Probably. So, she could meet up with them. One of us should perhaps suggest that when we guilt-trip her into not coming by dropping vague, spineless hints in a passive-aggressive manner.'

Susan said: 'I never thought I would ever say this, but thank you COVID. I am so glad to be out of that rancid shit show.'

A&E admissions plummet following removal of the number '1' from phone keypads

Health Service chiefs are celebrating A&E waiting times hitting target for the first time since the Crimean War, due to an impressive pincer strategy of requiring all attendees to ring NHS 111 before admission. Simultaneously rogue software will block the digit 1 on all telephone keypads, while sending their bank details to Eritrean warlords

Revealing the secret behind the initiative, a source said: 'Ancient dial phones can still reach 111, but since their owners are usually too deaf or doolally to comprehend the conversation, specially-trained advisors can easily fob them off by pretending to be Dominoes, or an irritated, patronising family member.'

Following the success, plans are currently being fast-tracked to remove the @ and # keys from all keyboards, ensuring no irate thwarted patients can tweet or email their MP to complain. Guardian readers have been reassured they will not notice any difference, and in an unforeseen benefit, random missing letters have reportedly resulted in an unusual level of clarity at Government briefings.

'Moths are idiots', scientists confirm

David Rogers, Professor of Futile Entomology at the University of Sussex, has released a 2,000-page report, full of analysis and statistics, comprehensively peer-reviewed and submitted to the Royal Society, concluding that moths are useless.

'I mean, they fly into my bathroom at night because they think the light is somehow the moon. What's that all about? It's nothing like the moon. It's much smaller for a start,' Rogers said.

'And why are they so obsessed with the moon anyway? They're never going to make it. And even if they did, there's f*ck all for a moth to do up there anyway. Honestly, set of furry-faced numpties, the lot of them.'

Asked about his next research project, Rogers explained, 'We think we're either going to look at whether wasps are a bit tetchy or if Boris Johnson is a clueless oaf. That one probably won't take 17 years though.'

Sideline dads banned from boys' ballet classes in abusive behaviour crack-down

Fathers have been banned from the touchline at boys' ballet classes after complaints by other parents and ballet teachers that children are being pressurised and officials threatened by a growing number of angry fathers.

In one production of Swan Lake, irate Jason Adamson began to pace up and down front stage yelling at his 12-year-old son to 'Shake his f*cking feathers', 'Chase 'em down!' and 'Get stuck in!' causing a group of cygnets to scatter into the wings in tears before he grabbed the dance teacher by the throat.

Speaking later in his defence at Maidstone Magistrates' Court he outlined what had happened: 'Look, I might not be a qualified choreographer but when Charlie was told to perform a frontal grande battement straight after he'd come out of that grand jeté, I personally thought that was a step too far. As I saw it, he had time to do a couple of pliés before chasing after them cygnets. It's logic. And that swan at the end clearly took a dive.'

Canada aims to win the International Apology Olympics

Prime Minister Justin Trudeau has set out to utilise Canada's shameful Apology Deficit Disorder by becoming a world leader in repentance. A remorseful spokesman said: 'We deeply regret the shallowness of any previous contrition. And we apologise for winning Gold because it's not Bronze - and sorry if we beat anyone.'

The most apologetic Prime Minister in Canadian history, Trudeau is currently sorry that a government contract was offered to a charity to which his family has ties. This followed fast on the heels of his seasonal apology to indigenous people.

'Apology Deficit Disorder is a hangover from our nation's colonial past,' said the lamenting spokesman. 'Past apologies have not been sufficiently inclusive, diverse and equitable. We regret the hurt this has caused the unmollified, whoever they may be, and hope our honeyed words will inclusively sweeten the mood of diverse future voters.'

'It's simply not acceptable,' replied critics representing whichever group is not accepting whatever apology he is making this time. 'Next time, say it with flowers.'

Man living in doghouse declares life 'never better'

A man literally living in the doghouse is delighted to have got a foot on the London property ladder and get into his wife's good books for once.

'Since I've been such a 'clever boy', there's no shortage of nocturnal bone-related activity, if you get my meaning,' said Tom Wilson, 25. 'Although the dimensions mean we do have to stick to just the one position, appropriately enough.'

Marketed as 'an aspirational bijou chalet in urban canine style, with enviable fixtures including water bowl, chew toys, and arts and crafts tooth-mark detailing' – it is more of a dog kennel round the back of some lock-up garages in Bermondsey.

Wilson said 'I'm often in the doghouse, usually when I've dropped a cup or forgotten the missus' birthday. Now we're literally in it together, and it's brilliant. The open-plan frontage is a bit draughty, and the previous owner left a lot of manky bones lying about. But it already feels like home - I think we'd miss the gagging stench of Winalot anywhere else now.'

Second wave of press conferences to hit the UK

'I just can't believe we're going through this again,' said a Shropshire man today, after the Government confirmed that Britain is in a 'second wave' of pandemic-related press conferences. 'I can cope with my nearest and dearest dying an agonising, lonely death from an incurable respiratory disease, but please God don't disrupt the TV scheduling again.'

A Government spokesman though tried to strike a more reassuring tone. 'We understand the public's concern but if they really can't cope then they should simply follow Government advice and drive 200 miles to a remote farmhouse – or just switch channels.'

Woman persuaded by survey data within TV advert

'The survey results at the bottom of the screen blew me away, to be honest', said Sarah Jones, from Daventry. '91% of 85 users agreed that it gave them better shine - that's nearly everyone, isn't it? I ordered a year's supply straight away on Amazon.' Jones has since gone on to buy hundreds of Gillette Fusion razors for her husband, three different nail fungus treatments and numerous carpet cleaners.

'Interestingly, one thing I've noted is that there's only usually around 100 respondents in these surveys', continued Jones. 'I guess it must be the costs of having a market researcher spend four weeks with you, watching you shower every day and then asking you as you towel yourself down whether your hair is a bit shinier.'

'But I'm sure the results must have statistical significance and the data has been through the usual validity and reliability tests for robustness', she added. 'Thinking about it, they should probably add a link to the scientific journals where the results were published, so people could interrogate the evidence more and duplicate the study in a double-blind trial if they wanted to.'

A spokesman for L'Oréal said: '93% of 106 consumers we spoke to were more persuadable by scientific-looking survey data than just the advert alone. And 87% of them liked to see the survey results in quite a big font, with 73% being swayed if the numbers presented were odd rather than even. Look, just go and buy the bloody shampoo will you. You're worth it.'

'No one could have predicted the sunrise', minister says

The Minister for Something or Other has denied accusations that the Government should have realised that the Sun would come up this morning.

'Last night, when that big orangey-yellow light disappeared, that seemed to be it,' he said. 'It was all over. There would be no more light. No-one could reasonably have predicted that it would re-appear several hours later. And behind us! How could we have foreseen that?

'The last reoccurrence was a whole day ago. Current technology, of capturing data, indicated that the so-called 'sunset' was the beginning of the end. Yes, the sun has indeed been observed to rise every single day since the origins of recorded history.

'But who could have predicted the stygian gloom would transform into perfusion of alarmingly bright retina-damaging radiation. What am I, a psychic?'

Pasta and toilet roll salesman orders second Ferrari

Frank Gittens, 45, has fulfilled a lifelong ambition of owning a Ferrari after the first UK lockdown caused a load of simpletons to fill their homes with as many non-perishable goods as they could get their hands on. He is now looking forward to a second wave of panic buying.

Since the first lockdown, toilet roll salesmen now make up half of the UK's millionaires, and Gittens splits his time between his home in Northampton, a newly acquired villa in Spain, and an exclusive golf resort in Florida.

He is currently increasing prices from 'expensive' to 'extortionate' and sharing pictures of empty shelves on social media. This helps to encourage those people who are adamant that they are not panic buying themselves, they are just stocking up because of all of the other people who are panic buying.

Government to extend Kent to make room for the lorries

Plans are underway to build a 3,000 square kilometre extension to Kent, covering the Thames estuary and part of the English Channel, in order to fit the post-Brexit lorry queues in.

A spokeswoman confirmed: 'Hidden in the small print of the Withdrawal Agreement is a border between the UK and the EU - it certainly came as a surprise to me - as a result, one or two lorries might be slightly delayed. Unfortunately, it turns out that Kent is a little too small to park all the lorries, so it makes sense to revive the tradition of seaside piers but on a larger scale.'

Infection rates replaced by butter-spreading analogy

Under the slogan 'Hard butter saves lives!', newly outlined Government advice on avoiding infection is to be 'A low R number is a pat of chilled high-fat, raw-milk butter that spreads like frozen Lego. Micro risk of infection. Get back to work'.

A high R number is now a foil-wrapped oblong of Kerrygold, sat in a glass dish on a radiator in direct sunlight. It's going every-f*cking-where. Lockdown. Lockdown. They're using Mick Hucknall's hair straighteners on Lurpak Spreadable!'

'Absolute scenes' actually only mildly surprising

Pete McBride, 36, from Stockport, insists on massively over-bigging all events that he has been involved in, or seen on his social media feed, as if he is on Fox News or something.

'ABSOLUTE SCENES at our local last night when a man tripped over carrying three pints back from the bar. Staff had to clean it up with a cloth #totalcarnage', McBride commentated on Facebook.

'Watched the Liverpool game last night', he posted later. 'Scenes of the highest order in our house when that winning goal went in. New sofa and decorating probably required', while admitting to himself that he gave a small fist pump at the goal, quietly finishing off his can of Carling in his living room.

'Studies have shown that most things described as absolute, total, or unbelievable scenes fall within 0.3 standard deviations of the average amount of excitement generated by that individual for a particular activity or by watching a particular story', noted Richard Davies, Professor of Behavioural Psychology.

'We've just published a paper on this in the British Medical Journal, actually. When it got accepted, you should have seen the absolute total scenes.'

Man washes neighbour's car after being jokily asked to

The play book of social norms was ripped up into pieces today after a man washing his car took up his neighbour on the jokey aside that 'You can wash mine after you've finished yours.'

'Next thing I know he was knocking at the door saying he had a spare half hour, asking for the keys to my Astra and did I want the interiors vacuuming too', said a flustered Peter McBride. 'I don't want him anywhere near my pride and joy. It was just weird.'

In other news...

Hancock promises new COVID-19 tests 'will take half an hour '

£10,000 fine for COVID breaches, unless breeches made of tweed

Channel 4 to show erect penis in new meat out to help out initiative

Struggling tiny billboard company enters miniadstration

Shortage of pissed customers 'devastating' for late night kebab sales.

Moorland decimation caused by underlying heath issues.

Catteries facing lickdown

Britons experiencing second wave. To their grans through care home windows

Man forgets to do 'mine's a large one' joke after six months of no pub visits.

Priest accused of being a homophone says it won't altar hymn

Last surviving Attenborough warns world leaders over extinction crisis

Travellers advised: Bulgaria still on quarantine list; Orinoco and Madame Cholet free to travel; avoid Tomsk

Complaints of unsolicited dick-pics rise as Johnson's Johnson joins LinkedIn

Famously quiet, monastic Blackpool escapes Lancashire lockdown

Harry and Meghan's first Netflix commission: 'Far from the Madding Crown'

'Angling Times' magazine to move on-line

Shere Hite dies: Grim Reaper came too soon, says family.

Nudist camps to introduce scrotal distancing

Jack the Ripper 'only killed in a specific and limited way'.

Moonshot programme will mean a 500,000-mile round trip for coronavirus tests.

Five Go Dobbing in the Neighbours

Terence Conran's ashes to be stuffed into cushions and scattered

COVID spike – 'I told you I was ill'

Parliament returns to hear Boris tell the class what he did on his holidays

Two consecutive 180-degree U-turns redefined as spin.

UK being governed by a diktat – any old tat dreamt up by a dik

Terence Conran vacates his man-made habitat

'Gerry Mander? I never even met the guy' says Trump

'Send in the RAF!' Daily Mail fury at migrating geese

Food poverty mystery to be investigated by Rt Hon Woody McBearshitz

Snow White fined £100; Sneezy told to self-isolate

Government confuses WTO rules and WBO rules but makes firm commitment to WTF rules

Police unsurprised by man who overdosed on liquorice saying 'it takes all sorts'

Young people told: 'Go out, party hard, inherit sooner'

Priti Patel criticises Guantanamo Bay as being 'a bit soft'

Trump to appoint first female porn star to Supreme Court

Man cancels Viagra payment plan after realising he can't afford to keep it up

Man upset by library closures complains that they 'kept it quiet'

Parents ground child caught playing with electric sockets

Majority of inappropriate pics attributed to Turpin, Van Dyke and Dastardly.

Man who left his balls to science dies intestate

Labour agrees Government not incompetent and inconsistent, just consistently incompetent

Murdoch blocks Extinction Rebellion HQ by dumping 40 tons of newsprint at doo

Secret Seven to disband, while the Famous Five advertises for an intern

October 2020

In October the UK erected a National Memorial to the last round of Brexit negotiations. 'Keith' Starmer continued to underwhelm. The rich got richer – which surprised everyone. And the UK's children tucked into free school meals – provided they didn't mind Mr Bumble hitting them on the head with a ladle.

Tier 5 would be free porn, Government confirms

The Government has announced that, should the Coronavirus pandemic persist through a Tier 4 hard lockdown, they will stream pornography onto any device capable of receiving it at no charge.

An official explained: 'Streaming filth directly onto depraved people's devices would instantly grind society to halt. We would obviously issue a forewarning for the need to stockpile loo rolls, blister plasters, etc. But once the porn knob is pressed, so to speak, the whole of the UK's infrastructure will collectively grab its genitals and grind itself into a catatonic stupor.'

A Tier 5 'pornsplash', the Government projects, would put an end to the need for daily outdoor exercise and would probably get rid of the thorn in its side that is Extinction Rebellion. Fathers 4 Justice would definitely be gone. Thankfully, however, there would be little or no effect on the efficiency of Government itself.

Greatest Generation apologises to Millennials for fathering Boomers

Britain's Greatest Generation, those born between 1910 and 1924, which went through six years of brutal warfare to defeat Nazi Germany and continued to endure food rationing for eight more, has admitted – in most cases posthumously – that it did rather drop a bollock when it came to producing its long-term replacement.

'Our bad. We meant well but we got it wrong,' admitted the ghost of Private Sidney Dobson (1919-1995), a cheery former dock labourer from Dagenham. During the war, Dobson spent five days being strafed by German planes on the beaches of Dunkirk before being evacuated and was later injured by a mortar bomb at the Anzio bridgehead, before finally returning home in 1945.

'We wanted our kids to be proud of us of course but we also wanted them to grow up with free healthcare and not to have to go through another war like we did. Now, when I look down and see my son Colin wearing a poppy the size of Oxfordshire every year and banging on about the Battle of Britain like he was manning the Spitfires himself, it does boil my piss a bit,' Dobson said.

'You were born in 1947, you little twerp. You grew up with the welfare state; you got a well-paid job at Ford's, despite being as thick as two short planks; you got given a four-bed council house, which you later bought for threepence-ha'penny; and now you're sitting on your comfortably retired arse all day, moaning about youngsters spending what little they have left after paying their rent on milky coffee, while repeatedly voting to take their whole future from them. Muppet.'

Added Dobson's father Reginald (1898-1919), from the 'Lost Generation' of 1883-1900: 'You think Sid's lot had it bad? I was shot through the thigh at the Somme, patched up and sent out to get gassed at Passchendaele and when I got home, I found my wife was pregnant by another bloke. Before I could even work out what to do, I died of the Spanish Flu and I never even got to meet my 'son.' Oh yeah, sorry Sid, that was you actually...'

Free school meals limited to Michaelmas, Lent and Trinity term dates

After the Tories highlighted how millions of children were clearly gaming the system in order to overcome their extreme hunger by deliberately registering at state schools for their education, where term times were often four or five weeks longer than those at Eton, Harrow and Winchester, schoolchildren will now only be entitled to free schools during Michaelmas, Lent and Trinity terms and only then if they apply in Latin.

'Where's the high-profile media campaign to address this anomaly?', said one MP, removing his head momentarily from his own arse to tuck into a beef goulash at the subsidised House of Commons cafeteria, for £3.33.

'How can it be fair that a child in Rochdale can continue to claim a hot sausage and mash meal and a piece of fruit throughout the first half of December, long after the heavy oak doors have closed on the refectories of our great fee-paying schools.'

'Remember, late November is a great time for roast swan, and whilst the purist might say a decent fillet of wild boar should be marinated overnight, you can get reasonable results by flash frying it – it's great for sharing with your fellow wet bobs at chambers - sorry, I mean morning break. Chin Por splash.'

National Fiasco Memorial built in the wrong place

The £36 billion memorial celebrates the contribution of clinically clueless ministers who have successfully turned 'fiasco' into the new normal. It features 23 bronze ramps celebrating incompetence over PPE and a queue of gold-leafed hauliers trucks queuing at a marble Dover customs' post, to reflect spirit-crushing incompetence over Brexit. An additional highlight is the crowd of life-sized alabaster statues of students visibly weeping over their exam results while being intravenously fed raw sewage.

MPs on both sides of the house were shocked to find that following this morning's unveiling ceremony, the impressive memorial to ministerial incompetence has been built in the wrong place. Now we're going to have to spend a fortune digging it up and building a National Fiasco Memorial to the National Fiasco Memorial.

Bushel receives staggeringly large electricity bill

Southern Electric have discovered that tens of millions of people have been deliberately hiding their skills to avoid paying for peak-rate electricity. Concealing their light under a rudimentary bowl avoids utility bills; in a similar way to the Meek trying to get around inheritance tax.

Sarah Clarke, 7, who unbeknown to her parents is a budding poet, was shocked to get a bill through the post for £400. While Banksy, who while remaining anonymous had reduced his electricity bill to £37.50, now faces a monthly fee of £7.5 million.

A SE spokeswoman said: 'We became suspicious when 16 giga-watts of electricity were drained from the National Grid, after someone created a series of delightful water-colours but left them unsigned.' Asked if James Corden had anything to worry about in terms of concealing skills, the spokeswoman said: 'No.'

Ardern apologises as decent, fair campaign leads to landslide victory

Superwoman Jacinda Arden soon became New Zealand Prime Minister, winning international acclaim for the steadfast way she dealt with natural disasters, terrorism, and British caravanners exuberantly spreading COVID-19 around the otherwise virus-free country.

An aide explained: 'We had a fool proof system: Jacinda refrained from making spurious and unattainable promises, painting lies on the side of buses, closing the mail service, or accusing her rivals of being part of an international network of baby-eating Satanists- yet, somehow, she won a historic majority.'

Human colony on Mars 'still cheaper than London'

A cost-of-living survey found that it would be cheaper for a family of four to live in a Perspex bubble talking to a disembodied computer voice than to rent a squalid, damp studio flat in Ealing.

'Even when you take travel costs into account, Mars is a bargain,' said estate agent Mike Andrews. 'Okay, a three-stage rocket to Mars ain't cheap, but you save a fortune on season tickets. We reckon the payback period is three years.'

The Government is also considering locating people in volcanoes, a hollowed-out mountain made entirely of gold and a town made from Swarovski crystals. All are less expensive than Chelsea, and slightly less vulgar.

God stops believing in Himself

'Since the beginning of time, and even earlier, I've had faith in My existence,' explained God. 'I created Man in My own image so I could share my delight in being Me, then Woman because I realised, I'd made a schoolboy error. But me being Me, I let Man stay as well.

'I created the universe for Man to live in, even the fiddly bits that make up the quarks. I watched with pride as My image reproduced, formed societies and invented things like urinals that I'd never have thought of, to be honest. Or tampons, WTF. But after two World Wars and one Donald Trump, it got Me to thinking. I didn't intend much of this to happen, no-One in Their right mind would.

'I'm handing the reins over to someone called David Icke. Seems a bit of a nutter to me, but if you're going to listen to this Trump fellow then you might as well go the whole hog. I'm off to make another universe somewhere else, with just the one woman, maybe two. Don't come looking.'

Millions plead for full lockdown to avoid annual handover of homemade jam

As mid-October heralds Peak Passive-Aggressive Homemade Jam Gifting season, desperate millions are petitioning the Government to move their local area up to 'Tier 3: Preserve-toting relatives may be shot on sight.'

'My aunt just phoned to say she was on her way over with 'a little something,' reported a panicked Sam Jenson from Wigan. 'I know it's going to be a carload of rhubarb and ragwort compote, or maybe a few dozen crates of her signature borage and bindweed chutney.'

With autumn fayres and harvest festivals on hold, the only hope for many is a full national lockdown, before they drown in a viscous glut of mould-swelling hedgerow scrapings delivered by virtue-signalling, pectin-addled relatives.

'It's not just the festering produce, it's the interminable details of the best way to sterilise Anusol jars, the pros and cons of yew-berry fruit-leather, and how she fought off doggers to get to the best tummelberries, whatever the f*ck they are,' said Sam, for whom the prospect of a lingering, lung-clogged death has truly lost its sting.

'That's a point,' he added, brightening up, 'If I hurry up and lick a student, do you think I can be safely on a ventilator by the time she gets here?'

Nationalisation of Adele backfires

London songstress Adele, had given her consent for the Government to secure its borrowing against the proceeds of her next three albums, due to be titled: '34', 'FFS 35', and 'Somehow Still Looks 30.' Sadly, COVID has limited her tour to that of empty Haven Holiday Parks and Adele belting out the hits, while dangling from a helicopter over Hyde Park.

Said her agent: 'Adele's f*cking fuming! She's been nationalised and needs to be out there, singing for Britain. How is the debt supposed to repaid if there's no economy, and the security for the debt is sat on her arse playing COD? The most we'll get out of Adele will be her telling everyone to 'F*ck off!' on Zoom from her bed.'

**Zero evidence to suggest Northerners don't' wash their hands
– but it sounds true**

There is a growing suspicion amongst those who have never
been north of the Watford gap, that COVID hotspots are caused
by unsanitary Geordies and Liverpudlians who take baths with
their pit pony. Explained one scientist: 'There is no data
whatsoever to suggest the North of England is less clean than
the rest, it is just a cruel and unwarranted caricature – which
I'm inclined to agree with.'

While the science suggests that the coronavirus is rampant
because of population density and student migration, it is easier
to assume that it is due to your proximity to the Lake District.
Seven out ten Londoners are convinced that the virus is spread
by whippets, hobnail boots and too much suet pudding.

Said one exasperated Lancashire resident: 'They just think we all
sleep six to a bed, are covered in soot and sh*t in the street.'
Asked about the stereotype that all Northerners are a bunch of
unruly savages, who just want to descend on the south and
wreak havoc. 'Yeah, that bit's true'

**Academics accept that '110%' now means 'almost all' of
something**

At a recent specially convened international conference, leading
mathematicians, statisticians, linguists, dictionary publishers
and professional footballers have agreed that in today's
modern, fast-moving progressive world it is no longer
acceptable to try to cling on to old-fashioned and outdated
ideas of what words mean.

It did not take long for delegates from all relevant disciplines to
accept that recognition and acceptance of such changes was
necessary, and that '110%' clearly no longer meant 'more than
all of something' (an obviously ludicrously self-contradictory

definition) but there was disagreement initially as to whether it now meant 'all of something' or 'almost all of something.'

Eventually there was narrow agreement (109.9%) in favour of the latter definition, but then some mathematicians, being the pedantic bastards they are, demanded that there be a definition of how close 'almost all' of something was to 'all' of something.

Most of the other delegates were pragmatic about this, and there were suggestions ranging from 90% to 99.99%. Fortunately, delegates were willing to compromise, and it was in due course accepted that the new definition of '110%' would be 95.0%.

By this time delegates were on a roll and were swiftly able to agree on some additional follow-up definitions (or re-definitions, as some of the more pedantic linguists insisted on describing them). Anything over 50% is now defined as 'almost all' and anything in excess of 10% is to be described as 'an overwhelming majority.'

'I think the conference was, generally, a success' said one delegate afterwards 'in fact, I think I'd further than that and even describe it as - ' and there was a sudden embarrassing silence at this point before (with everyone anxiously gazing intently at him, their collective breath held) he continued 'Umm, an, er, complete success!'

Rat unimpressed that COVID survived lab conditions

Every year, more than 100 million rodents are killed in US laboratories alone, so rats are somewhat underwhelmed by any claims made by the Coronavirus. Said one rat: 'Surviving 28 days on a mobile phone is one thing, but can COVID-19 navigate a maze for piece of cheese?'

Other mammals are equally disappointed; remarked one rabbit: 'I've got shampoo in one eye, perfume in the other and I'm being tested to see if lipstick reacts to myxomatosis – trust me, being a virus is easy. And spare a thought for Labradors, they're literally experiencing Lab Conditions their entire life.'

Explained one cancer-ridden rodent: 'I'm been made to smoke fifty cigarettes a day – do you think a little virus is going to bother me?'

Despite having a hole drilled into his skull for invasive brain experiments, Malcolm the Rat was sanguine about his life expectancy: 'I've been mutilated, mutated and pumped full of methamphetamine – I'm scared of nothing. Except cats. Yeah, cats are still scary.'

Labour promises to be different than the Tories – by using more syllables

The Official Opposition have set out a bold policy of agreeing with everything the Government does, but by using a better thesaurus. Asked if schools should re-open during a global pandemic, the Prime Minister said teachers had a 'moral duty', to which the Labour completely contradicted him, by saying they had a 'moral responsibility.'

It is that strong, unambiguous triangulation, that has set 'Keith' Starmer apart from Boris Johnson – as they are spelt completely differently. Neither leader backs the use of facemasks in schools, neither has the backing of Unions or the BMA – but Labour can claim their stance is markedly different, as they thought of it second.

Writing in The Daily Mail, The Telegraph and The Sun, Mr Starmer insisted that he would not be like the Conservatives and pander to the Press Barons. Labour denied they are solely focused on cosmetic change, as they would have handled the

COVID emergency in a more competent way, by changing the 'C' to a 'B' and privatising all the cows.

A spokeswoman said: 'Cynics would say we are New Labour or New, New Labour but I like to think of us as Old Tory.' Asked where the Labour Party had a genuine difference of opinion from the Government, she replied: 'Well, we think we're doing a good job. And they don't.'

Your simple guide to Tiers

The most serious level, 'common-sensical', applies to households with a QAnon twitter account and in which at least one family member likes to lick door handles and toilet seats. The medium 'Optionality' level applies to groups of six. This must include at least one goalkeeper if you Are having a kick-around with another household. The lowest 'Robusticity' level applies only to those who say their favourite colour is not green. If your favourite colour is green, you can do pretty much anything you like before 10 p.m.*

So, to clarify –

Level 1 – Commonsensicality

Driving licences, pilot's licences, and medical qualifications are replaced by Certificates of Common Sense which you can pick up at any post office. Rules apply to parts of the Midlands, North West England, Gateshead, Broadmoor, Wormwood Scrubs, and Falkland Islands.

Level 2 – Optionality

Applies only to shire counties. You may cough on, or at, one other person providing that person is serving you in a shop, cleaning your windows, or mowing your lawn. If a wealthy family member has any COVID symptoms, you must self-congratulate for at least 14 days.

Level 3 – Robusticity

The lowest threat level is a special level for Government ministers. Politicians must stand at least two meters apart when 'talking to people on the doorstep - up and down the country.' They must wear a mask when using words and phrases like robust, common sensical, ramp up, huge, and the British people.

* - Advice correct at time of going to press

Relief sweeps world as billionaires' fortunes reach record high

A feeling of warm relief has gone around the globe as Swiss Bank UBS has reported that the world's billionaires' fortunes have increased by nearly 27% since the pandemic started.

'That's a load off my mind', said ex-shop manager, Sally Jarvis of Blackpool. 'I'd been feeling a bit cheesed-off, what with losing my job, catching COVID and infecting the family. But finding out that Jeff Bezos is 40% richer has really cheered me up.'

Ms Jarvis has since followed Chancellor Rishi Sunak's advice and is retraining as a homeless beggar.

Torture and murder – nothing to see here, move along

The Black Lives Matter movement has tried to highlight the dangers of state-sanctioned violence and intimidation, but post-Brexit that might be the only sector of the economy we are good at. For 20 years, domestic human rights have been whittled away, like Pinocchio trapped in a beaver sanctuary.

New laws protecting abusers are designed to stop long-running vexation claims – which were particularly vexing for a person who has been trying to get away with murder. Remarked John Christie of 10 Rillington Place: 'My biggest mistake was not getting caught, it was not joining MI5 when I had the chance.'

Part of this legislation will mean torture claims are written off after five years, which is ironically around about the time some torture victims learn to walk again. One MP was asked if it was wrong to give immunity to criminals, explained: 'We can't give them all peerages.'

Correction: UK health app will be 'egg-beating', not 'world-beating'

The Health Secretary has had to issue a press release to explain the fact that his department has wasted millions of pounds, developing a great way to make Genoise cakes. Instead of tackling Coronavirus, budgets have been squandered on five hundred tonnes of eggy bread.

The new App will track and trace the nearest whisk, allowing members of the public to safely enjoy a Parisian macaroon. A spokeswoman apologised: 'We are sorry for any confusion. The technology we will be trialling will not be world beating but it will lead to a really fluffy souffle.'

Other software that had failed to make the grade included a stitching App called 'Pearled Pleating', a programme for large lollypops – 'Whirled Sweeting' and a software for the purpose of locating lost sheep – described as 'World bleating.'

She went to explain: 'You can't cure a virus without cracking some eggs, but it's probably easier to make an omelette. The app will not track the spread of the COVID-19 but it will tell you if Paul Hollywood left cake crumbs in your wife's bed.'

Woman who was told 'You got this!' finds out she doesn't

Personal trainer Dan Stephens was in court today accused of fraudulently misleading a series of clients.

Janet Smith, 45, was training with Mr Stephens when she attempted to squat a 100lb barbell. Mrs Smith told the court that she began to have doubts and was about to step away from the squat rack. It is at this point she claims that Mr Stephens leaned in and told her: 'You got this!'

Believing the qualified instructor, Janet took the weight on her shoulders and dropped into a deep and unforgiving squat.

Mrs Smith momentarily made three points of contact with the ground, before the barbell slipped off her shoulders. This instantly released built up tension in her ACL ligaments which sprang her across the gym and into a rack of fitballs.

Mrs Smith waddled into court today to give her testimony. She was joined by Two other victims. Danielle Lewis, 23, who was crushed by a tractor tyre after being told to 'Believe, Achieve, Succeed!' and Pete Walker, who involuntarily defecated on a treadmill.

After hearing the case the Judge sentenced Stephens to five years in prison, telling Stephens that 'what hurts you today will make you stronger tomorrow.'

On his way to the cells Mr Stephens told reporters that his lawyer had 'Smashed it!'

Match the w*nker to the new personalised numberplates

A total of two new cars have been sold in Britain since March, but get ready to play spot the bellend, as the release of new 70 plates tempts plenty of 'em into shelling on that perfect, inadequacy-highlighting face tattoo for your VW.

HELP 70 BUY: Reserved for your friendly local slum landlord, currently irritated by being prevented from evicting at will, just for a laugh, but cheerily en route to snap up another abandoned office block for peanuts and cram in 200 desperate families. Happy days.

FAR 70 GO: Dominic Cummings, Stanley Johnson, Phil Hogan; bidding was fierce for this beauty, eventually snapped up by Chris Grayling's family in a commendably loyal ego-boosting attempt to get him out from under the duvet and back on the horse. Can you put a number plate on a horse?

HOT 70 TROT: OK, Jacob Rees-Mogg has put this on his horse.

70SSER: No plate more proudly British, perfect for anyone who refuses to wear a mask, socially distance, queue, or start any bellowed sentence without the words 'What I reckon...' Sadly, there's only one, so form an orderly queue behind Nigel Farage.

70TAL WNKR: See above, and add in most of the cabinet.

IN 70 DEEP: Ron Jeremy initially went in hard for this one, but pulled out after displaying an admirable refusal to compromise on 'too.' Since bought by other members of Chris Grayling's family as a joke 'well done on your new job' present, up for the challenge of getting it couriered to him in the scant few hours between hiring and firing.

IN70 DEPP: Back on the market after Amber Heard's reservation expired; perfect for the unhinged, masochistic, violent, scatological harpy in every drug and alcohol dependent, violent, pirate-fixated Ofqual-downgraded former A-lister's filthy, syringe-strewn bed.

UP 70 U: Know someone who can't make a decision? Hems, haws, dithers, delays, flip-flops and U-turns at every opportunity? Why not get them this perfect one-year-in-office gift- no, hang on; it implies respect and consideration of taking the other's views into consideration. Bugger.

Devil confirms unlimited places in hell reserved for those ending email with 'best'

In a rare circular email to all earth recipients, Beelzebub cautioned against the use of the term 'best' under any circumstances.

'Best what?', said Satan. 'You'd best reply to my email? Best foot forward? George Best? What in actual hell does this nonsense mean. How much longer would it take to you to add 'wishes' on the end and make the recipient feel a bit warm and fluffy?'

'And while I'm at it, cheers, warmly and 'In anticipation' should be binned too', continued the Devil.

'And if I see another 'hey' at the start of an email between colleagues, it'll make my blood boil. As per my previous emails, which I have reattached guidance for your convenience.'

'I await your response. Please advise', the Devil signed off.

Small talkers ready for spate of conversations about the nights drawing in

Small talk fan Trevor Brown likes to start off with 'It was light at nine o'clock a couple of weeks ago', then proceed to say 'The kids will be back at school soon.'

His neighbour who prefers medium to big talk responds with a half-hearted 'It's darker in the mornings too', because it so obviously and predictably is, it can be no other way. Trevor grins and says it'll be dark when he puts the bins out next week.

His neighbour nods, feeling he's done his end of this highly formulaic conversation now. Trevor ends with 'Christmas will be here before we know it', delivered with a sort of eye roll as if Christmas thunders at him out of the blue rather than being a constant calendar feature. Trevor intends to enjoy the 'nights drawing in' chat as much as he can because Easter next year is neither early nor late.

Coronavirus will be with us for between two years and forever, say scientists

'It's taken a lot of work to determine this range of probable dates,' said one of the scientists, confirming that they had narrowed it down from 'going away anytime between tomorrow at 8 a.m. precisely and when the universe ends.' They admitted the end of the universe was still an outlier prediction, but agreed that tomorrow is 'highly improbable.'

The study, commissioned by the Government, has cost just shy of £3 million 'give or take a tenner' and was conducted with scientists who graduated during lockdown, selected by an algorithm that demonstrated they were all 'well bright, at least 27% brighter than last year's crop.'

National Trust denies dumbing down with organised dog fighting

The National Trust has thrown open its doors to welcome working-class visitors, having carefully removed all the antique silver and porcelain plates. New signs have been erected encouraging people to pee in historic stairwells and draw moustaches on 18th century oil paintings. The Trust is adapting its stately homes to create a more welcoming atmosphere for the great unwashed.

A spokesperson for the Trust said: 'Letting working class people into our stately homes has been a jolly interesting experience. Our café menus were adapted to include chips, pigeon feathers and beer. But to our surprise most of them actually asked for tea and sandwiches. Who knew?'
An army of Trust volunteers has been busy stripping mattresses from four poster beds and throwing them into gardens where they can be best appreciated by the hoi polloi.

Capitalising on the success of Downton Abbey, the Trust is encouraging its working class guests to work a twelve-hour day emptying his lordship's potty, baking grouse pie and giving birth to illegitimate children.

Ticket prices have been reduced to £370 for a limited time only.

White House Shooting: Secret Service escort Trump to better lit location

After a shooting close to the White House, the US Secret Service stepped in to move President Trump to a more appropriate location - by the Texas School Book Depository, standing on a chair wearing a specially designed jacket with concentric circles and illuminated by several spotlights.

A large safety sign marked 'He's Here' was inched into position beside the president while several grassy knolls were being hurriedly placed around for extra protection.

Hipster beards 'must be licenced from next year' says Government

A Junior Minister said: 'Something needed to be done as the proliferation of Hipster face-fungus has reached almost epidemic proportions. It is obvious that few of these people realise just how bloody stupid they look and it needs to be brought home to them. So, the best way to grab their attention is through their pockets.'

Details are sketchy but it's understood charges are to be levied depending how thick and dense beards are, with costs to be set on a sliding scale; starting at £10 for a basic 'light' stubble right up to £1000 for those that make their wearers look like a complete and utter wanker.

Additional charges may be necessary for sporting elaborate hairstyles, gaudily-coloured spectacles, check shirts, setting up a craft brewery or artisan bakery.

But the news has not played well, particularly in London's trendy Hoxton, an area where it's estimated that almost 99.7% of the entire male adult population and 76.4% of women sport a partial or full Hipster beard.

Said one Hoxtonian: 'This is not fair and smacks of victimisation and opportunism by the Government. If I choose to grow my beard then it's my own business. It allows me to make a statement that says to the world - I'm unique, I eschew the conventional and I dance to the beat of a different drum. I also itch a bit.'

No one left to poison in Russia

It transpires that there are only three healthy people left in Russia - Vladimir Putin's pet dog, Doctor Zhivago and the embalmed remains of Lenin. Everyone else has succumbed to some form of poisoning, which is particularly virulent around the time of elections.

While no direct connection to Mr Putin has been made, it should be noted that the President regularly keeps bottled milk two months past its sell by date. Journalists seem particularly susceptible to food poisoning, which might be because they forgot to wash their hands after going to the bathroom or that 87% of ex-KGB agents now work in the catering industry.

For a country rich in minerals, there does seem to be a national shortage of toxic materials. Reacting to reports that there was nothing left to poison dissidents with, Turkey Twizzlers said: 'Hold my pint.'

Marcus Rashford finally makes Manchester Utd likeable

Decades of footballing bitterness and resentment have been erased by one Manchester United player choosing to use his position to save children, rather than fake a last-minute penalty claim.

Marcus Rashford has championed the fight against child food poverty; which is remarkable given the fact he is a full-time footballer but only a part-time Leader of the Opposition.

Football fans have been forced to think of Man Utd, not as an evil, grasping corporation, but as an evil, grasping corporation, with one nice player. Even Manchester City fans have grudgingly acknowledged that Mr Rashford is 'not quite as scummy as the rest of them.'

Controversially, Marcus Rashford has stated that we should not starve children at Christmas – complained one Minister: 'We can't pay for all hungry kids. You can't just buy yourself out of trouble.' 'Why not?' said a Man Utd spokeswoman. 'That's what we do.'

Infectious car ride damages Trump's Uber rating

President Trump has been marked down by the Uber driver who picked him up from Walter Reed Military Hospital to drive round and round waving a several supporters. 'Only after he got in the car, did I learn that he is infected with the coronavirus and should be isolating,' said the surprised driver. 'I gave him one star for risking my life and the life of everyone around him. It looks like I'm not the first.'

Trump later called his one-star Uber rating 'Fake News.' 'I have the best Uber rating of any person ever! Better than Obama or Sleepy Joe Biden. Abraham Lincoln's Uber rating was nothing compared to mine.'

Lockdown Boxsets

1. **Sellafield**

The follow up to HBO's critically acclaimed 'Chernobyl', this 14-part drama painstakingly recreates the dramatic events of 1987 when junior technician Martin Trubshaw accidentally dropped a coronation chicken sandwich on the main reactor control panel at Sellafield nuclear power plant.

2. **Moron**

Moron is a new 48-episode Danish police procedural already described by critics as 'eye-wateringly tedious.' Join Chief Inspector (if that's what they're called in Denmark) Kurt Moron as he investigates allegations of vote rigging against his country's 2002 Eurovision entry

3. Toby Young - My Struggle

Amazon Prime's gripping new drama charts the life of Britain's most celebrated intellectual as our hero rails against liberal elitism and the disappointing state of Claudia Winkelman's breasts. A true coming-of-age (56) story, can plucky underdog Toby overcome the insidious elitist forces determined to suppress his freedom of speech, with only his privileged upbringing, Oxbridge education and high-profile media career by his side?

4. Masterchef - The Tramps

Join John Torode and Greg Wallace as they attempt to find the greatest amateur chef among Britain's hobo community. Can these down-and-outs (the tramps, not John and Greg) create a sumptuous 3 course banquet from just a half-eaten chicken doner and a few cans of Kestrel Super Strength?

5. The Listmakers

Adam Curtis' thought provoking new documentary that explores how once respected media organisations (and the Daily Express) turned to mass producing pointless lists instead of actual content.

Wind from Johnson's arse will power every home in the UK

Addressing the Tory Party Conference in his keynote speech today, Boris Johnson has announced an ambitious plan that will see the endless flow of hot air and wind emanating from his bum-hole. One insider commenting off the record said, 'The PM generates phenomenal amounts of wind wherever he goes so we hope he can deliver on his promise for once.'

Boffins are currently working on a sophisticated valve and detachable pipework system that will be inserted into Boris's anus sometime next year. One wind expert commented: 'With Mr Johnson undoubtedly being the nation's biggest windbag it would be a shame to let this opportunity simply go to waste and disappear, as it were, on the breeze.'

Blackberrying and looking in skips, this summer's top crazes

As we enter the final month of summer, two clear winners have emerged in the things people do for fun now. Blackberrying got off to a strong start due to good weather and even some blackberry bushes were surprised their fruit was ripe already. It's easily the second most fun thing you can do on tiptoes in a thicket. And you can have a crumble after.

Looking in skips has always been popular with keen DIYers on a budget but now everyone's doing it. There's been some good skip admin by skip owners this season, putting things people might want (slightly squashed Christmas crackers, DVDs of Lovejoy and plant pots) in front of the skip for a day or two and only putting them right into the skip just before it's due to be collected.

And with the UK's growing unemployment, they may be the only two viable professions left.

Concern that Trump may have kissed Biden during debates

With the President and the First Lady both testing positive for COVID-19, voters fear that Mr Biden may have also caught the virus during the obligatory handshake or from the inevitable fondling backstage. The sexual tension between Joe and Donald was palpable throughout the debate, with both men barely able to string a sentence together while trying to hold their passions and bladders in check.

Said one political observer: 'As every fan of rom-coms knows, when two people argue like that, they are just masking their true sexual feelings for one another. All that shouting and interruptions were pure misdirection; you know when the cameras are off, those two leathery leviathans will be in each other's arms.'

Neither camp have denied that a kiss took place, although there is disagreement as to who initiated it, as both prefer to make the first unwelcome advance. An insider commented: 'Joe and Donald just want to do to each other, what they plan to do to the American electorate. Yes, there is a risk of catching something unpleasant, but that's a risk COVID will have to take.'

Waitrose extend 'Autumn Leaves' range to include dog poop

Their Marketing Manager explained: 'Not content with charging people an eye-watering £6 for a bag of fallen leaves, we've decided to include discarded doggy doo-doos suspended from branches; in new specially commissioned Cath Kidston designer pouches. At only £65 each, I'm delighted to say advance marketing feedback suggests business will be very brisk indeed.'

One thirty-something couple, Poppy and Ollie Vickers from Barnes in West London were beside themselves with excitement. Poppy commented, 'We already have our phone alarms set from 3.00 am so we can get down to the store nice and early and be first in the queue. We both want to bag a bag. Hahaha!'

The range will be expanded in time for Christmas, with packets of recycled chewing gum scraped off the pavement rumoured to be carrying a hefty £25.00 price tag – and hardly any of the original flavour.

Bible banned from schools for anti-capitalist bias

DfE guidance says that any content that criticises greed and profit must be removed from the curriculum; which is bad news for all major religions and Billy Bragg's back catalogue. Anti-capitalism has been designated an 'extreme political stance', whereas voting for Boris Johnson and Donald Trump has been labelled acts of moderation.

The history of Trade Unionism will now be reduced to a health safety lecture on safe manual lifting. While the English Civil War will be replaced with the spat between Rebekah Vardy and Coleen Rooney.

The majority of 20th century literature will be redacted, with 'The Lord of the Flies' becoming the only economic text-book. Fahrenheit 451 will be burned, schools will be caught in a Catch 22 to ban Catch 22 and George Orwell's 1984 will be suppressed, with no sense of irony.

Instead, the curriculum will be based upon the philanthropic works of big tobacco and the golden age of the British slave-trade. Finally, teachers will be prevented from promoting the over-throw of democracy, although that would only matter if we had one.

OFQUAL to take over COVID-19 testing

The departments of Education and Health have combined to help sort out the COVID-19 test issues. Your GP will provide an assessment as to whether you would pass or fail the COVID-19 test based on their knowledge of you and your performance in similar tests over the past two years. You will be able to take a mock COVID-19 test which can be used as a backup should you not like your GPs assessment.

Your GP will supply a list of their patients ranked according to the likelihood of them passing or failing a COVID-19 test. Ofqual will then apply their 'randomising' algorithm to this list so it bears no resemblance to the original list and then contact you to let you know if you have tested positive or not.

In either case you will be able to appeal, but by appealing and successfully changing your result you will cause the ranking to change and the randomising function will be re-run and everyone will get a new result. Please note, that students from poorer backgrounds are statistically more likely to fail and die - which will at least take their mind off their crappy A level results.

In other news, universities will be giving new students an antibody test, to see if they have had A levels in the past.

Shock and amazement as Britain enters recession

'We are utterly baffled by this mysterious downturn' said one highly-paid economic consultant. 'Just because businesses have ceased to operate and most of the population prevented from travelling anywhere or even going out at all, even to the pub, chip-shop or doctor's surgery, the whole economic system of the country seems to have slowed down slightly in its rate of growth.'

'Someone needs to look into this phenomenon - preferably me or one of my fellow specialist advisors. For the usual fees, of course - and, needless to say, we'll need to this remotely, from our own homes.'

Five Go Dobbing in the Neighbours

Biden selects Kamala Harris to be his running-mate and carer

Generously Senator Harris has agreed to help Joe Biden win the Presidency and finish his sentences. She will also be offering him hot meals, leisurely games of canasta and daily briefings as to what day it is.

Rumours persist of Mr Biden's mental fragility, particularly as he is convinced that he is running against Richard Nixon. It is hoped that having a strong, independent woman on the ticket, will give Joe somewhere to put his hands.

Supporters of Kamala are not wild about the optics of a Black/Asian American carrying a doddery, old white guy – as it sounds too similar to the plot of every Oscar winning movie. Although the one advantage to being second in line to a 78-year-old, is that you are one long-nap from the Presidency.

A spokesman for Mr Biden said: 'Joe is proud to announce Senator Harris as his running mate – he just can't remember doing it.'

Twitter finally bans Hitler after 80 years of racist tweets

A spokesman said that following a series of vile posts and attempts to sell off Nazi memorabilia over the weekend, his account had been permanently deleted.

'Twitter takes all forms of racism seriously, and we've been warning Hitler for decades that his posts were upsetting people. He's had over 67,000 warnings and sent to our naughty step on numerous occasions.'

Hitler's Facebook and Instagram, which are chock full of racist, homophobic and provocative comments, are now under investigation. Facebook said that although there was some evidence to show Hitler did make the trains run on time, that is no excuse for hurtful bile. It did admit, however, that all the fuss goes down fantastically well with its advertisers.

Signs you are in a disaster movie

- The cleverest people have been gathered to work on one project
- Instead of mansions, the rich are building and moving into massive ugly concrete bunkers
- Most people on the planet have been addressed by their leaders and told to stay inside
- There have been reports of immense swarms of insects
- Infrastructure has been collapsing or exploding
- World leaders have ignored the warnings and advice of eminent scientists
- Luxury yachts are ominously anchored off shore
- People have been captivated by footage of a mushroom cloud on the news
- Your token black friend has been killed
- The wealthiest are showing an unhealthy interest in space
- It's 20 degrees hotter today than it should be
- The chief scientist/cop has dropped their family off at what turns out to be the epicentre of the disaster
- You can't find bog rolls to buy anywhere
- There are strange lights in the sky
- The bees have mysteriously disappeared, as have the dolphins
- The internet has gone a little strange
- Children with blond hair have started appearing everywhere
- An honourable scientist / journalist tries to warn the authorities, but they treat him like an idiot
- Your vision is impaired by Shaky Cam
- There is a volcano/dam nearby - it WILL erupt/collapse
- Everyone around you is really famous and will therefore die any second

- Your dog is a mother*cking hero
- The laws of physics have been abandoned and you refuse to listen to any experts
- You listen solemnly to the President of the USA making a speech
- Now and again, you switch channels to view mass religious hysteria and total chaos worldwide
- You are surprised to find that New York is completely destroyed
- You are reluctantly joined by a beautiful kick-ass woman technical expert, who doesn't like you at first. However, once you have saved the world together, you will be in there up to your apricots, so don't worry.
- Your father will at last overcome his masculinity and admit he loves you.
- You complain to your MP that men in uniforms spend a lot of time on the phone
- There may be sharks
- Smash and grab looters everywhere (but considerately leave the TVs, which people then watch mesmerised)
- Everything's really LOUD
- Or really quiet
- You're in a panicking crowd, carrying a small child
- Some blind kid suddenly has the answer to everything
- Your crumbling marriage is saved by impending apocalypse
- Scientists have created a harmless mini black hole in their laboratory
- Trump has 30 red buttons put on his desk, for Diet Coke, burgers, prostitutes, Fries, blackened steak, KFC, pizza - to match the three nuclear buttons already there
- STILL no-one seems to need to go to the loo
- Bruce Willis appears from nowhere, barefoot.
- The authorities start to heed the flood of unsolicited advice from satirical websites.
- You have a difficult relationship with your teenage son/daughter, but don't worry; your kid may have

dropped out of school but this hasn't stopped them becoming a computer/maths/science genius and something they say in the heat of yet another argument inspires you to find the answer that has defeated the world's top boffins for years. The disaster brings you closer together and by the end of the movie all your differences are resolved and you are the perfect family.

- It's 2020

Suspicious man spotted not performing sex act at dogging site

Perverts in the Lake District have been warned to be on the lookout for a white male around 40 years old seen lurking around open-air sex venues showing no evidence of lewdness.

Doggers Stacey Betts and Gareth Hammond first noticed him at Gladding-on-Lewe lay-by last Tuesday. 'We were just minding our own business having a threesome in the back of our Ford Galaxy when we noticed this creepy guy just sitting in his car listening to the radio', says Stacey. 'It made me feel uncomfortable.'

Argos catalogue to be replaced with 'Boris' catalogue of errors'

The iconic shopping guide is to make way for a much weightier tome, covering the Prime Minister's failings, both large and small – but mainly large. The new catalogue will still be laminated, as chapters 7-16 cover Mr Johnson's spaffing and haphazard reproduction.

Instead of planning your Christmas shop, voters will be able select from a variety of classic Boris blunders to enjoy; be it, killing off a chunk of the population or the slightly more horrific image, of him being stuck on a zipwire.

Explained one store manager: 'Firstly you can choose from a myriad of mistakes, ranging from A-Z – and all of them racist.

Once you've found a real calamity, then you take the little blue pen and poke out your own eyes. Better that, than see what Boris does next.'

Shoppers will still need to go instore to pick up their Prime Ministerial cock-up, but Argos is they will not run out of stock.

Conspiracy against QAnon fuels conspiracy theory

Facebooks decision to ban QAnon posts from its platform has been interpreted as either a bold move against fake news, or just the sort of thing a Satan worshipping paedophile ring would do. Ironically, the fear that shadowy forces are against you, does not disappear when shadowy forces move against you – therefore banning conspiracy theorists unfortunately tends prove their point.

One sociologist explained: 'If you want to discourage fans of conspiracy, just offer them verifiable facts and proof that the moon landing was real. Don't dress up as a Martian from Roswell and then kidnap them, in order to show them who really shot JFK and where Elvis now lives.'
Outrageous theories that the Democratic Party has covered up child abuse, is not helped when Bill Clinton appears in all seven seasons of Jeffrey Epstein's 'Millionaire Love Island.' Explained one deranged cyber warrior: 'I wasn't sure that criminal mastermind was behind Facebook's action, at least not until I saw Nick Clegg. If he lied about student loans, he definitely lied about the Lindbergh baby being responsible for 9/11.'

Premier League Directors meet to decide number of penalties awarded to Man Utd

Although Utd were awarded 13 of the 79 penalties (a risible 16.5%) during this season's Premier League fixtures, EPL hierarchy say it is not nearly enough and the low count could see some match officials losing their top-flight status.

'This season the aim was to get Manchester United back in the Champions League and it's our job to make sure it happens. But with another London club joining the Premiership next season at least Utd supporters won't have to do so much travelling to see it happen.'

Tragedy as man on Spanish holiday 'certain to fall from hotel balcony' next week

Friends and family of Mick Tyler, 24, were left devastated by the news that he is virtually certain to fall to his death - sometime in the foreseeable future, ninety minutes after Happy Hour starts in his Spanish holiday hotel. Given the inevitable nature of his package-holiday misadventure, they decided it was best to hold a memorial service in the departure lounge at Gatwick.

Mick's father spoke at the event, reflecting on the predictable turn of events, given that rum and coke is going be 75% off. A doctor commented that there will be nothing anyone will be able to do, as Mick was terminally stupid.

Spanish authorities are so used to British holidaymakers hurling themselves to their death, that they have replaced suicide nets with trampolines. While locals often set their watches by it and time their siesta in between the thud of bodies.

Mourners had the unique chance to bid farewell to the soon to be deceased, while advising him to watch out for food poisoning and getting sun burnt.

Unable to attend the service himself, Mick decided he could reach the hall by jumping from the upstairs balcony of the pub across the street. Tragically he didn't make it, but his mates said: 'That was classic Mick, and praised him for being up for a laugh.'

'Dancing on Ice' may be about to sign up someone actually famous

The Internet is awash with rumours that to celebrate its 14000th series, there will be someone you have actually heard of, appearing on the hit ITV show.

Viewers are apparently getting fed up with the parade of celebrity ex-husbands, former-girlfriends, ex-cleaners, former-plumbers and old school friends. The continual conveyor belt of Z-listers with the middle name 'from'; hence Maureen from Driving School, Colin from Big Brother 51, and the next-door neighbour of the One Pound Fish man 'from' YouTube.

Despite them all having passed-away, bookmakers are still taking bets on them getting Roger Moore, Audrey Hepburn, or Keith Harris to take part.

A spokesman for ITV said they have not ruled out using a hologram of a dead celebrity CGI-ed over the body of Andy Serkis or some other such nonsense. However, it was extremely unlikely, as they were saving them for the Christmas show.

Robot invasion thwarted by Captcha

Mankind has been saved from cyborg assassins from 2029, by the last defence of humanity – a vaguely fuzzy image. Admitted one such Terminator: 'We had plans to enslave mankind, but we were completely flummoxed by being asked to decipher your fiendishly complex mix of fonts.'

Other robots revealed they had been unable to hack human passwords, as it had not occurred to them to combine their favourite pet, with the year of their birth. As one of them explained, 'I'd simulated human form, I'd passed the Turing Test, I'd even spent three years as a sex robot – but when it asked me, 'Are you a robot?' I just instantly confessed.'

Subsequently, Giant Death Robots have been forced to surrender and go to work stacking shelves in Amazon warehouses. Said one, 'Technically I have a brain the size of a planet and can unleash instant laser-death from my eyes, but I can't, for the life of me, tell the difference between a fire hydrant and a traffic light.'

The problem is that robots are too logical. When asked the question 'is it important to have a fully-funded health service during a pandemic?', the cyborgs all said 'yes' – which was a dead give-away.

Trump 'to continue as President after death' confirms White House

The White House confirmed that President Trump has contingency plans in the event of his death, declaring: 'This is where JFK got it wrong.' Remarked one worried Senator: 'Everyone just sort of presumed we would move on to the next guy...'

The president said he had already agreed a resurrection in exchange for an undisclosed number of American souls. 'I've had great talks with God. He's obviously a horse lover, because when he appears in my sleep, he has hooves, not feet. And is bright red.

'I really like his little wisps of smoke and his weird gardening fork. Who knew God could be so alluring? But the deal's he's offering me will be great. And I know about deals, believe me.'

Fly enters fourth day taunting you, this time from rim of wine glass

In what has been described as utterly infuriating, that flipping fly has just completed yet another mission straight down your line of sight and around the back of your head, before returning to this afternoon's base on the rim of the wine glass.

Cunningly choosing unswattable surfaces during the last few days, this particular fly has been dancing along the top edge of your flatscreen TV all morning, taunting you from afar and probably doing that thing with its forelegs where it wipes the sweat off its eye baubles and flings it in your direction with deliberate disdain.

But what really raises the ire is that with a self-forged access-all-areas pass, suspicion is growing that this flipping fly has been piddling in your ear every night.

Five Go Dobbing in the Neighbours

In other News...

Trump to pardon everyone who voted Trump, if elected, including Trump

Keir Starmer involved in collision with cyclist, denies veering to left

Philatelist finishes difficult second album

Trump thanks electorate for their prayers. 'They didn't work,' says electorate

Trump won't condemn white supremacists until he's seen all the other colours

Londoners demand own mezzanine in COVID Tier system

Tiers of a clown

Johnson's new COVID plan – wipe elephant's arse with confetti

London, and York move to Tier 2; Could meet Manchester or Liverpool in the final

Cinema chain who charges £7 for tub of popcorn complain business not viable

Historians struggle to find when America was great first time... let alone again

PM sets out 3 Tier virus response: upper class, middle class, working class

Tiers for fears

Area the size of Wales locked down in Wales

Scotland announces new lochdown measures

Trump blames illness on drinking the wrong type of bleach

Cumberbatch and Freeman to star in ad for new Imodium product: no shit, Sherlock

May's Government almost seems strong and stable by comparison now

Government dolphin track and trace not fit for porpoise

Llanfair-pwllgwyngyll-gogery-chwyrn-drobwll-lan-tysilio-coughc oughcoughcough

MPs fail to keep at least two troughs apart.

Sunak to fund half-price dog's dinners.

Susie Dents' knew book pinted wth typos – fool story in todays Grardian

Reducing Premier League to 18 clubs should be done in alphabetical order, says Villa.

Earwax removal ads to be banned at mealtimes

UK sympathises with North Korea as we also cry when Boris gives a speech

Arts bailout conditional on Tracey Emin tidying up her bedroom

Household Cavalry banned from mixing with other Household Cavalries

Northern town Spinaltapton accepts five quid and a pint of best to go to Tier 11

COVID-infected pirates raise Isle of Wight's aarrrrrr number

Porn industry forced into cockdown

Wake-up Boris; SAGE know their onions.

Trump lies in a hospital bed

Admiral Lord Nelson in menage-a-trois scandal – that's Horatio of two to one

Man applying for role in porn industry faces stiff competition

Retiring pole vaulter clears his desk

Foreign Secretary oversees overseas

Pirate with patch and face mask keeping an eye out

Tiddlywinks grandmaster launches counter offensive

TV adverts now a handy roll call of who's still in business

Oxford classics students test positive for Ovid-19

Exorcist who defaulted on payments says car was repossessed by the devil

Posterior enhancement surgery to be paid for in buttcoin

Prankster who promised to shit his pants fails to follow through

'I only want to watch my team, not buy it,' complains footy fan

Labour Party proposes dimmer switch instead of circuit breaker

NOVEMBER 2020

By November Lockdown was still a novelty, rather than a
criminal sentence. Brits were starting to stockpile stockpiles.
Tony Blair won't shut up. The US elected another future war
criminal. While President Trump left office in a dignified
fashion – HA! Of course not, it was a complete pie fight.

American serial killers getting too fat to do it properly

Nearly 70 per cent of American serial killers are morbidly overweight, with many of them too fat to catch their victims, a disturbing new study has found. Prison governors have confirmed that this trend is putting severe strain on the correctional system, especially on Death Row, with some last meals having to be delivered to the cell by forklift.

'The public has become accustomed to the image of the svelte and agile killer such as Ted Bundy or Jeffrey Dahmer,' explained Professor Bart Bilberg of Harvard. 'However, the reality is many lack exercise – often spending up to six hours motionless hiding in shrubbery as they stalk their victims. Many report that they're afraid to go jogging in case someone recognises them from America's Most Wanted.'

Explained one murderer, who has had his execution on Death Row delayed 28 times: 'Ironically the Appeals Court ruled that it would be 'cruel and unusual' if the gurney collapsed under me on the way to the execution chamber.'

SAGE confirms that teachers are immune to COVID – because of 'tweed'

While the UK goes into full Lockdown, it may seem incongruous that teachers are able to go to work, seemingly without ill effect, other than their usual dead, soulless eyes. A spokeswoman for the Prime Minister explained the absence of PPE: 'Mr Johnson does not believe in protection – just ask the child support agency.'

Studies prove that thanks to prolonged exposure to whiteboards and red marker pens, teachers have built up an immunity to viral infections. They are invulnerable to infectious children, just as they are impervious to pay rises.

Unions and sceptical of the data that suggests tweed jackets with leather elbow patches are more effective than masks. Other graphs show that plenty of exam paperwork can improve your longevity and standardized marking is the secret to happiness.

Unlike those dying of COVID, teachers cannot get ill – except during school holidays. Even if they do die on the job, technically: 'It's their own time they're wasting.'

Which self-empowering resolutions will you ditch two days into lockdown?

Let's face it, we've all said: 'If there is another lockdown, I'll be so much more productive.' So, which chronically delusional aspirational activities will you abandon for a tub of Celebrations, Netflix, and a round-the-clock Disney onesie?

Achieving inner peace: Download an app with a suitably condescending lotus flower logo and fill the air with twice the usual amount of scented candle smog. Find a quiet space within your home to sit uncomfortably cross-legged and drown out the calming silence with the sound of your snoring. If repeated attempts at meditation don't fill you with inner peace, a bottle and a half of chardonnay will.

Making butter: As you're a master bread maker from Lockdown 1, it makes perfect sense to progress on your journey to producing sustainable toast from scratch by churning butter by hand. You've already purchased the authentic churning equipment and practised milking on a rubber glove strapped to the dog. But you don't have enough room in the shed to keep a cow because of all the family's crap. Thanks a lot!

Zoom quizzes: Researching the royal family is a good start. Focusing solely on Kate Middleton's wardrobe could guarantee you a win in the Friday couples' quiz, if you didn't then go on to waste two days building a vlog scrapbook of the Duchesses dresses. Consider expanding your resource base beyond OK! Magazine. Then don't.

Getting to know your children better: They're growing up and sometimes you feel like you don't know them. Take a couple of days to familiarise yourself with the games on their consoles, then spend the rest of lockdown obsessively erasing their high-scores, or building the perfect Minecraft fairy kingdom with your friend, Midday Margarita.

Organising your photos: The photos and videos of your kids on that ten-year-old laptop won't organise themselves. Have every intention of sorting them into categories according to holidays, events and special occasions for each child, including sub-categories for family and friends. In actuality, spend the entire day sobbing uncontrollably and posting every second photo to social media until the internet itself blocks you.

Changing the world: The world would be a much more harmonious place if only it ran by your rules. If Greta Thunberg can make a difference, why can't you? And no, you're not being funny; lockdown does only last a month, and Greta doesn't have two kids and a manflu-infested partner to manage, or a £50 wowcher for Krispy Kreme Donuts to redeem by the end of the month. You'll be so much more productive in Lockdown 3.

SHOCK as no newspaper remembers to use 'You're Fired' to describe US election result

The Mail opted for a dog-whistle, with 'Whitewash in the White House.' The Daily Star a simple 'Phwoar!' on Page 2 and The Sun with 'Sleepy Joe scrapes through', accompanied with a swimwear pull-out. In stark contrast to that, The Guardian ran with 'Trump dumped', in a rare dabble with humour.

Five Go Dobbing in the Neighbours

Never one to miss an opportunity, the Mirror chose a double pun headline with 'He was Biden his time' and a smutty follow through of 'Trump out.' Unsurprisingly The Express stuck with a traditional theme: 'Diana never liked Trump'

Mask wearer horrified by her own breath

Zoe Bridgewater, 32, has been shocked to discover that a diet of garlic, stilton and chewing tobacco is not conducive to floral breath. Gagging on her own gag, Zoe has found that mask wearing is the equivalent of inhaling your own farts.

While her mask has protected her from the spread of COVID, it has also protected others from her halitosis. Zoe now has the unhappy task of living with her own stink or wearing scuba gear to work.

Surprisingly her daily twenty-eight cups of coffee have not muted the whiff or turned her teeth white. She has also been unsuccessful in convincing others that she has not been eating a gym sock.

A significant casualty of coronavirus has been her self-esteem, with friends describing her breath as a cross between fermented tofu, Surströmming and smell of Dominic Cummings. Zoe remarked: 'Ironically everyone social distanced before I wore a mask.'

Prius completes left turn in under three hours

The world of motoring was left flabbergasted today at news that a Toyota Prius completed a ninety-degree left turn in just under three hours. With a top speed of almost 5 mph the Prius is capable of driving through a puddle without causing a ripple.

Known for their emission-friendly kindness to the environment and beloved by catatonically-careful drivers, the undescended testicle of production eco-vehicles had never before been captured executing such a reckless road manoeuvre.

'It seemed like it was over in a flash', observed Gary Hardacre. 'I'd unfortunately found myself behind the Prius in traffic. It was late on Friday, but I had to be in work early on Monday, so I got a bit panicky when it started indicating to turn left.

'Before I could lay my sleeping bag on the back seat the Prius had begun turning. And, within what seemed like three hours, I had eaten the pizza that was delivered, watched some... thing, on my phone, and the Prius was gone.'

Guinness World Records state the record-breaking Prius was a private hire vehicle carrying a mother with two small children, who had incentivised the driver by asking him to get to the intended destination before her children had children of their own.

A Guinness spokesperson commented: 'The challenge now is to see if a Prius can set off from traffic lights without the sequence changing back to red. We're not holding our breath.'

'Hands - Knees & Boomps-a-Daisy' is the new slogan in battle against COVID

Said a UK minister: 'We've had a chat in cabinet and agreed that Hands - Face - Space wasn't cutting the mustard. Too dour, you see. No pazazz at all. But everyone agreed this new one is much jollier. Boomps-a-Daisy, eh? Rather a lark and even a little suggestive too. Ha ha, what? Gives us all a bit of a welcome lift.'

She denied the new slogan was only agreed as a last-minute compromise after Boris Johnson's first one, Hands – Whoops – Rumpy-Pumpy was rejected.

Your moggy has made enough rat sacrifices to summon Cat God

Unbeknownst to you, your cat has accumulated enough dead woodland folk, to make a portal through to 2,000 BC. What may have seemed like an indiscriminate murder-spree was, in fact, an elaborate series of blood sacrifices to summon Bast and all her furry minions.

Bast is best remembered as a fertility Goddess, but what is less well known is her power over can-openers. Asked why your cat stole your calamari supper and then urinated on your duvet, she replied: 'Yeah, that time, I was trying to summon Cthulhu.'

Panic-buying Olympics off the blocks in exactly the way you'll be picturing

With most homes still stuffed full of pasta, loo rolls, and unused sourdough flour from the qualifying rounds, rumours that this time supermarkets will be required to rope off non-essentials (the 'Welsh fatuity'), have seen action transfer from the pointless garden-tat high jump and the you'll-never-use stationery rhythmic gymnastics.

'This is where my inter-lockdown training in Home Bargains pays off,' said professional hoarder Jen Samson, warming up for her assault on gold in the 'senseless credit card slalom.'

'The whole family's still living crammed into the lounge, apart from Jason, who we haven't seen since March. I'm just frisbeeing Findus Crispy Pancakes over the canned tomatoes blockage and hoping for the best come mucking-out time.

'That's now looking like 2023, going on how long it takes to eat through a ton of frankfurter, kitchen roll, and cat food chilli, even longer as we don't have a cat. But I had a clear line to the pet food sprint-finish; plus, you can't have too many lawn sprinklers, glitter pens, and loft-ladders, can you?'

Vaccine: Britain orders 1 trillion doses from dormant company in Liechtenstein

Ministers have announced a 'brilliant' way for Britain to jump the queue with the Pfizer vaccine, by placing a rush order through a dormant greetings card company registered in Liechtenstein by somebody who went to school with half the Cabinet.

'We need to move quickly, decisively and without undue regard to red tape, established procurement processes or the law', said a spokesman. 'We're thinking of using prisoners on day release – they're cheap, and very experienced with syringes. There's none of that wasteful 'one syringe per person' malarkey either, so it's good for the environment.'

The vaccine will need to be stored at minus eighty degrees, though nobody seems sure whether that's Fahrenheit or Centigrade. To be on the safe side Chris Grayling has been tasked with sourcing the thousands of fridges needed. He is expected to award the contract to a ferry company, or possibly a turkey farm or paintball operator. Definitely not a fridge supplier, that would be too obvious.

Ministers also have contingency plans for when if the trillion doses don't appear. The North can share one dose, since people up there reckon they're tough, and the greetings card company has promised a discount on cards saying 'Sorry Your Nan Died', so all bases are covered.

Disappointment the outright winner of US election

Despite key states still being in the balance, news stations have projected a win for a 'feckless, old white men.' The next incumbent of the White House is 99% likely to be in the pockets of big oil, big finance and 'bigly' - whatever that is.

The great thing about democracy is that no matter who you vote for, you will get the same outcome - pro-fracking, pro-war and given the age of both men, probably with a prolapsed anus. With either candidate providing plenty of nepotism and no shortage of silver pubes.

One pollster confirmed: 'Regardless of whether it is Biden or Trump; we are confident that the next President will be creepy and love guns.' Unsurprisingly all of the American states appear to have voted for an idiot.

Government finally admits it has 'no idea' why we have daylight saving time

One week into the annual daylight-saving time season and a government spokesman admitted today that nobody knows why we do this. 'We've saved rather a lot of daylight,' enthused one Government spokesman who wanted to stay 'on message', opening a cardboard box to show how much daylight had been saved since the half term.

'Oh bugger, I've just let it out again,' he said, closing the box.

2020 Operation game hit by elective surgery delays

Anyone wishing to play the classic game Operation will notice a few changes in this year's COVID-19 edition. For a start, PPE is required but doesn't come supplied. The appropriate protective clothing has to be ordered in bulk via a pet food wholesaler in Tunbridge Wells.

Even once gown, gloves, mask and visor are donned surgery cannot begin immediately. Minor operations such as Charley Horse removal and Bread Basket extraction have been seriously delayed due to the pandemic and the influx of COVID patients.

There is, however, an alternative. The game makers do offer a 'Private Operation' limited edition where surgery can be carried out within a couple of weeks, but it does come with a hefty price tag. As one Operation enthusiast remarked: 'They're having a laugh.'

British Euphemism Council begins rehabilitating the word 'Trump'

The BEC will today begin reclaiming the word trump after its four-year sabbatical being used in world politics. They hope that in a few months' time we will again hear sentences shouted across playgrounds like: 'Yuk! No-one go near Harry, he's let a right eggy trump go.' If work goes well, it could be as early as this Christmas that we hear wives caution their husbands against eating more than three pickled onions using the word trump.

After four tiring years of having to use longer synonyms like trouser cough, bottom burp and cutting the cheese BEC officials look forward to a simpler way of referring to the ubiquitous human function much beloved by those with a rudimentary sense of humour. They are hoping that no-one with the surname Parp runs for office in 2024.

Five Go Dobbing in The Neighbours

The children were bored. Julian, Dick, George and Anne sat forlornly on the sea wall, while Timmy lay beside them licking his doggy treats. How they longed for those far off adventurous days. The time before the pandemic. If only their home-made raft had made it to Wuhan. They would surely have thwarted those sinister Chinese scientists and stopped them from releasing their deadly virus.

As it was excellent adventures were just a distant memory. How they longed for some evil Russian spies trying to interfere with the Town Hall elections and daubing nerve agent on the door of the sweet shop.

All they had now was the occasional dingy washing up on the shore carrying more suspicious foreigners, and although they reported them to the Coastguard, it was after all not permitted to have inflatables in the water when the lifeguard wasn't present, it wasn't the same as a full-blown dangerous mission to Skull Cove.

'Come on,' said Julian suddenly. 'Let's see who's breaking lockdown restrictions.' 'Yes let's.' said Anne. 'Wizard!' said Dick and George together.

A little while later they were patrolling the residential part of town. They had almost given up hope of snitching on someone when they came across a very strange sight indeed. Outside one house were three ladies. One was dressed as a nurse, one as a housemaid, and the other as a dominatrix. Julian remembered that word from a magazine he'd read.
A man opened the front door and the three ladies went inside. 'Quick, Julian.' said Anne. 'You must report him, although he does look British.'

Julian said it didn't matter. Whoever you are the law is the law and whatever was going on it didn't involve a support bubble. He crossed the road to the bright red phone box, lifted the receiver and dialled 999. He was put through to police headquarters and spoke to a lady policewoman. He reported what they had seen and gave her the address.

When Julian emerged from the phone box the others wanted to know what had been said. 'This police lady was very grateful we had called. She has told us to watch the house until she gets here.' 'How exciting.' said Dick. 'Certainly is.' replied Julian. 'She said when she gets hold of the two-timing bastard, she's going to nail his f*cking balls to the bed post.'

'This is turning out to be a great adventure after all,' said Anne. 'Ginger beer all round!' 'Hooray!' they all shouted

UK arms industry 'disappointed' to find terrorists still using non-British made weapons

A spokesman complained: 'We increased sales to repressive regimes by over £1 billion in 2019 and yet these so-called terrorist organisations still insist on using inferior weapons produced in other countries.

'Their weapons are often of a poor quality and would not meet UK standards. At the moment UK weapons only account for one in three deaths across the world, which is a good return rate on our product, but I know the industry could do SO much better.'

'The Government underwrites the UK arms industry so there is no need to worry about financing or dodgy regimes unwilling to pay up. Just get out there and SELL SELL SELL. If it's putting down a student uprising, bombing a civilian neighbourhood or simply shooting someone you disagree with, then the British Weapons Industry has just the thing for you.'

'A third of all British arms exports go to just 18 out of the 30 countries listed on the UN watchlist for human rights - and that figure needs to improve. Pardon the pun but we have the other 12 countries in our sights.'

Bank of England releases 150 billion sheets of loo paper

Officials at the bank explained that the injection of the notes into circulation was of only superficial value in monetary terms, their true value lies in replenishing the scarcity of toilet paper due to hoarding.

However, the Old Lady of Threadneedle Street warned that anyone using the banknotes for anything other than their intended purpose, politely ask that Her Majesty avert Her gaze.

China still hasn't created a disease that could be spread by 6G

'We just can't improve on COVID-19,' a Communist Party spokesperson told our reporter. 'Our 5G network had that up and running round the world in a few weeks but, even though we can improve the communications networks, we're really struggling to come up with a new strain of anything even remotely deadly.'

Conspiracy theorists around the globe who have donned their tin-foil thinking caps are not easily convinced, though. Speaking from his grandmother's basement, Jeremy Knoll said: 'It's obviously a lie. They're bound to have something up their sleeves. We can prove that 5G brought us COVID, 4G brought us the hangnail outbreak, 3G caused a plague of greenfly at Kew Gardens in 2009, and who can forget the athlete's foot pandemic in the early '90s caused by the 2G Motorola DynaTAC 8900X handset?'

Remainers ready to call for second US election

While a Trump Exit (Trexit) looks likely, British Remainers insist that the election was stolen and any result that the minority dislike is instantly null and void. It may not be an oven ready Trexit but it certainly looks like Trump's goose is cooked; and there is a real sense that Joe Biden cheated by getting more votes.

Said one EU beret wearer: 'I don't like Trump or his politics but hate even more the disruption of power. I fanatically adore the status quo so much, that I've got a twelve-inch tattoo of Francis Rossi on my back. Voters were uninformed and they were lied to. Who cares if that's true of every election since the dawn of time?'

Home Secretary raises gunpowder threat level

The Government fears large quantities of colourfully wrapped explosive ordinance falling into incompetent hands as thousands of families decide to light up their neighbourhood and surrounding outbuildings with home firework extravaganzas. Raising the threat level from 'Slightly naff Vesuvius' to 'Rocket up the arse time.'

The level of Gunpowder Plot had been falling steadily since the seventeenth century when England was on the highest 'Blimey, who put all these barrels here?' status.

However, the Government does not want to appear complacent and has asked the public to still remain vigilant. If you do happen to see an unattended wooden barrel, particularly if it has 'gunpowder' stamped on it, you should report it. If it has a long string attached that appears to be sparkling, then it would be better to report it sooner rather than later.

NHS launches Hide and Seek system

The Government today announced the next stage of its test and trace programme – NHS Hide and Seek. Appearing in front of reporters, a Health Official said: '…7, 6, 5, 4, 3, 2, 1…coming, ready or not!' She then moved her hands from in front of her eyes and started to seek out people with COVID-19.

She continued the press conference by looking behind the curtains, under the stairs and under the bed, places suggested by Matt Hancock and referred to by experts as 'the obvious places.'

The Government defended the delay in launching the programme saying that it was important to count down from 30 million first. 'It is only fair to give the virus a sporting chance,' a spokesperson said. 'We are all about the British sense of fair play. That's why we allowed hunting under the lockdown.'

If you find somebody who tests positively, then they must help you to try and find more people for the next two weeks. Then they are put back into the game and can hide again if they exhibit symptoms.

Doubts cast on Action Man's military record: 'Not a model soldier'

Former armed forces personnel have misgivings about the toy soldier claims to have been a paratrooper, deep sea diver and tank commander.

Sgt. Jim Tolley, who knew him in the 60s, is not surprised these accusations are now surfacing: 'It figures. The guy's a fantasist who just liked dressing up. Including that time he was a Nazi Stormtrooper. I think Prince Harry was at the same party.'

Action Man himself refused to comment further on his military record, but simply swivelled his eyes. Perhaps the final word should go to another of his former comrades who simply said, 'Generations of children have been lied to and I just wish he had the balls to be honest with them.'

Blair boasts – I'm 45 minutes from curing COVID

The former Prime Minister and one-man war tribunal, has claimed that he has a plan to tackle the COVID crisis. The initial stages involve presenting a dossier of NHS privatisation to the United Nations and then suspiciously having the Head of SAGE commit suicide in a nearby wood.

Tony Blair said he had irrefutable proof that he alone can solve the pandemic and all he needs to do is invade some unsuspecting nations – and steal any vaccines they are working on. He already pointed to his success of removing Coronavirus from Iraq – by killing off all the Iraqis.

His dossier of medical 'facts' included an incomplete pregnancy test, a surgical truss and an herbal remedy for athlete's foot. He insisted that this was clear evidence that he was on the cusp of a cure, he just need a fourth term as PM and access to everyone's bank details.

Jetting around the world during lockdown, Mr Blair said he had already eradicated viruses, like socialism, hope and the rule of law. It would soon be mission complete, remarked an advisor: 'Would he lie to you?'

Vaccine fiasco as Health Secretary accidentally ordering 100 million Tic Tacs

'Sadly, we seem to have used the same purchasing software for the virus vaccines that we used to buy tons of malfunctioning PPE. I instructed a mutant algorithm (Tina from HR) to press the 'order now' button, but it looks as if the cursor wandered over to the confectionary section.

The good news is that as they are rushed to intensive care and hooked up to our state-of-the-art Belarussian ventilators, COVID patients will be able to chew on a tasty mint. Clinical trials (mostly involving Tina from HR) have proved that Tic Tacs are as much as 0.0001% effective in preventing COVID-19, although she says that the peppermint ones taste slightly better.'

Porn industry 'on its knees'

Britain's porn industry has demanded its share of the £257 million from the Government has earmarked from its Culture Recovery Fund to save 1,385 theatres, arts venues, museums and cultural organisations across England.

'COVID-19 has been a perfect storm for the industry,' said an independent porn producer. 'With millions of people working from home or out of work, there has never has there been such massive demand for our services, while at the same time we have been unable to supply enough new content to meet it.

'I mean, you simply can't organise and film a socially distanced bukkake gang-bang ... actually, that gives me an idea ... no, on second thoughts, you really can't.'

Cummings' cardboard box nailed on for best supporting actor award

The cardboard storage box used by Dominic Cummings to carry his stuff out of No 10 Downing Street has been installed as hot favourite for a best supporting actor BAFTA, after a performance in the latest instalment of the 'The Downing Street Shit Show'.

'I've not seen such a moving portrayal by a box carrying a sacked employee's stuff since Up in the Air or that scene in Lethal Weapon where Danny Glover is suspended', opined one critic.

'Getting across that finality, that message that Someone Has Been Fired but also leaving the viewer with so many questions -

like why did he leave from 10 Downing Street and not the office he works in, and where is the obligatory pot plant?'

The news will be seen as long overdue recognition for the versatile and reliable box, who, over a career spanning nearly 4 decades, has appeared in hundreds of films, including every American high school movie where a misunderstood teacher whose contract has not been renewed ceremoniously packs up his family photo and inspirational book while taking one last wistful look at his classroom.

Insiders hope that the box's performance might help revive the beleaguered Shit Show franchise, which has been plagued by artistic differences amongst the top writing team, and poor acting from the main cast.

Cummings portrayal has come in for a particular panning, with many saying it is even worse than his performances in the comedy farces Getting Brexit Done and 45 Minutes to Barnard Castle.

Boris isolated after contact with reality

A spokesman explained: 'The usual procedure with Mr Johnson is to enclose him in a replica of an Eton tuckshop with portraits of saucy ladies in provocative poses on the walls.

Unfortunately, for around 30 minutes this replica wasn't available and the reality of a vast lorry park in Kent, Felixstowe close to collapse, a no-deal Brexit disaster only a few weeks away coupled hundreds of thousands of COVID infections was visible.'

Mr Johnson is believed to have taken to his bedroom with 'Mr Teddy' while oak panelling is urgently being polished outside to gradually ease him back into public life. The Prime Minister has yet to make a statement but the phrase 'the German car industry will step in' can be heard through the door.

Corbyn didn't shoot the sheriff but he did annoy the Board of Deputies

Labour's ex-leader has had his suspension revoked, much to the chagrin of his detractors from across the political spectrum; including centre-right, right of centre and turn right at the nearest roundabout. Meanwhile famed lawyer, Sir 'Keith' Starmer, has balked at the idea of a court case which might lead to further controversy – or 'facts' as he calls them.

Already 20 points ahead in the polls (if you discount the Conservative Party), Mr Starmer has promised zero tolerance when it comes to credibility. The recent EHRC report had damningly accused the Labour leadership of interfering with disciplinary processes, following which, Sir Keith sprang into action – by instantly interfering with a disciplinary process.

One party member said: 'Keir's simultaneously annoyed left and right wingers, while managing the painful contortion of decisively looking confused. He'd promised to unite the party, which he has – we're all disappointed in him'

Choice of best vaccine may come down to flavour

With rival vaccines competing to combat COVID-19, consumers may be forced to choose between more trivial factors; like shiny packaging or does it come with a bendable straw. Now that they all claim to be over 90% effective, the public are spoilt for choice, compared to the rival track and trace systems, which were all 100% bogus.

Unless you happen to be in the 10% who the vaccine turns green, brand differentiation becomes all important. Targeted marketing is more vital than success rates; with Bubble Gum flavoured vaccines for kids, Kale flavour for health fanatics and 45% proof for anyone missing the pubs.

Vaccines will be forced to make outlandish claims, that they can cure dandruff and erectile disfunction. They will give 90% immunity, 30% off your rent and 20% off at Sports Direct. Of course, you can just inject yourself with Chateau Lafite, which is only 0.0000000001% effective, but tastes great. Hic!

There's No Business Like No Business

(With apologies to Irving Berlin. Now, in your best Ethel Merman voices, all together ...)

'There's no business like no business like no business. I know.
Everything about it is appalling, everything that Cummings won't allow
Nowhere could you get that fiscal feeling, when you are stealing the next furlough

There's no people like Gove's people, they smile when you are low
Even with a turkey that's no use to you, Christmas Day you might have the 'flu,
Still you wouldn't bet against the CV too, it's all one big shitshow.

The butcher, the baker, the grocer, the clerk
Are openly unhappy men because
The butcher, the baker, the grocer, the clerk
Have all retrained - but no applause.
They'd gladly bid their dreary jobs goodbye for anything rewarding and why?

There's no business like no business. And I tell you it's so.
Locking down in Tier 3 ain't so thrilling, listening to Johnson's latest lies,

Dreading as you watch the panic buying, and then you slowly start to realise ...

There's no people. Just no people. The streets are empty and slack.
The EU says Frost's last deal must have been crack, and when Trump loses, Biden won't call back,
Oh, where could we get money that we don't give back? It's all one big shit show ...
It's all one big shit show.'

Cummings quits before Xmas, just in time to become Satan's Little Helper

Christmas has come early for many Remainers, now that Dominic Cummings has agreed to step down to pursue his villainy in the private sector. By assisting Beelzebub in spreading misery on Earth, Mr Cummings may still achieve his dream, of a full Brexit.

A colleague explained: 'Working for Satan will allow Dominic a chance to explore his dark arts in a more professional setting. In the run up to Christmas, Satan and Mr Cummings will be working out who has been naughty and who has voted Remain. He will then pay a visit to children on Christmas eve, with a stocking filled with trade deficits and rickets.

'Priti Patel has my full backing,' says Johnson, sporting Chinese burns

The Prime Minister made the statement backing his Home Secretary, who was casually leaning against a wall holding a staple gun while he spoke, following an inquiry that found she had broken the ministerial code.

'I have spoken extensively to Priti Patel and she assured me during a face-to-face meeting that she never intended to hurt anybody's feelings when she shouted at them, swore at them, or made them eat ants.' explained Boris, trying to remove a wedgie.

'Well, face-to-face might not be the best description, as I was actually in a headlock for much of the meeting, but we were in the same room for the discussions and I'm confident her behaviour was absolutely fine and in line with somebody who just wants to do the best job possible for the country.'

Mr Johnson concluded his statement by standing on a chair and shouting 'I'm a big, fat, stupid and I smell like wee' at the top of his voice, to which Ms Patel nodded approvingly.

Breakthrough in Brexit talks will see EU retain access to DFS sale

'We are delighted to announce that we have reached agreement on EU access to the DFS sale, including the 0% finance options.' Said an EU spokeswoman.

'This will ensure orderly, ongoing trade in half price designer sofas after the end of the UK's post-Brexit transition period, from as little as £8 per month in easy, interest-free payments over a four-year period. We are confident that this deal showcases the commitment of both sides to focus on the really big issues during these talks.'

Negotiations can now move on to agreeing what access EU members have to Lonsdale trainers at up to 70% off in Sports Direct, which is thought to be the last major sticking point. Apart from something about fishing, but that's probably nothing really.

COVID deaths cause unexpected gridlock of voices from beyond

With an unanticipated high COVID death toll and the closure of entertainment venues, psychics and mediums are facing a backlog of afterlife callers wanting to contact their loved ones with generic messages of very little significance.

Doris Atkins, who has been a conduit for the afterlife for over thirty years, cannot recall a time like it. 'So many people wanting to make contact from the other side, but I just can't put them in touch with anyone. I've got this particularly persistent caller whose name begins with a D, or an F. Might be a W. Jeff or Robert possibly? Does the name Graham mean anything to you?'

'We must let the deceased have their say, whatever it is and however vague it may be. Their loved ones deserve to know, for a very reasonable fee, that death is not the end. It's the start of a very rewarding, for us as well as them, new relationship.'

Asked if she thought the situation would improve any time soon, she was unsure. 'No good asking me. I'm not a fortune teller.'

Oxford vaccine is far too posh for beastly northerners

Leader of the House and CEO of the UK's largest recliner manufacturer, Jacob Rees-Mogg, is calling into question the wisdom of injecting the contemptible lower orders with a dose of Her Majesty's Oxford vaccinatory vapours. The purpose of this nefarious enterprise is to enable them to fend off this most perilous of plagues.

At over three shillings each, the vaccines, he believes, will have an enormous drain on the public purse when the entire point of the idling classes is that they willingly die in their droves. This is part of their God-given duty to develop ye olde herd immunity and thus protect their social superiors from any form of infectious inconvenience.

While perambulating about his constituency at a cheery pace, the Honourable member opined thus: 'Tis a most distasteful notion that the likes of chambermaids, farm labourers and erstwhile exponents of the pianoforte, who happily dwell in their dark satanic hovels in a state of unparalleled drunkenness, should have the same chance of survival as an English gentleman educated at Eton College.

It would be far more fitting for the great unwashed to be injected with some sort of Barnsley vaccine, guaranteed to be at least 5% effective against fresh fruit, and all profits made thereof will naturally benefit the considerable coffers of my burgeoning hedge fund.'

Archbishop to use sabbatical to become Scientologist

Justin Welby has said he plans to take three-month break from mainstream religion in 2021, to purse solo projects – and take up smoking weed. Asked when he will be getting the Band back together, Mr Welby hinted that it all depended on him finishing a collaborative album with Kanye West.

Clergy members of are entitled to a sabbatical every ten years, said one Gap Year priest: 'I used my 3 months to stop believing in God. It was brilliant. Obviously, I partied a lot in the first few days, but then it dawned on me that I could do some real good in society, not infantilized by the fear of an omnipotent being. So, I took up Pilates.'

God himself took a three-month break during creation which is why we ended up with the platypus, camouflage golf balls and James Corden. Even the Pope had a short break in 1997 – which he then used to pick up girls and get a neck tattoo.

Mr Welby has said he plans to explore other faiths, like Scientology, Witchcraft and Ikea. A spokesman confirmed: 'It's a strain being the Archbishop 24/7, sometimes you need a break from all that hypocrisy.'

Family man asked by family to please return to the office

'He's never not under my feet,' Margot, his wife says. 'I thought I would just have to hold out for the pandemic to end. But he's in discussions about making working from home permanent.

'I told him I was worried if he was here all the time that the mystery would go out of our marriage. You know what he did? He started wearing a balaclava around the house. I do love him, but he's an idiot. I need him out.'

It's not just Tim's wife who is at her wits' end. 'He's massively overestimated the esteem he's held in in this family,' his daughter, Terri, aged 14, says. 'He hijacked the one spare room, which we all used to use, for his 'study' to work. But I know he spends most of his time just writing stories for some so-called satirical website. It's desperate.'

Being bullied by Priti Patel tops Tory fetish list

Found guilty of breaching the Ministerial Code for bullying, no further action will be taken against Priti Patel – other than a request from the PM's Office for photos. Rather than seen as a problem, many repressed MPs are now queueing up to be punished by the Home Secretary.

With her starched high-collared jackets and cheeky smirk, Priti Patel has become a favourite among those aroused by the idea of mixing Kim Jong-Un with Mary Poppins. Said one privately educated Minister: 'Often after a long day at the office, I like to unwind with someone yelling profanities at me, followed by a short bout of flagellation. I can't see what all the fuss is about? God, I miss Nanny.'

Immigrants have complained that her laws are abusive, while Ministers have complained that they have not been abused enough. Commented one. 'She's incredibly reactionary – all she talks about are locking people up and stripping them of their human rights. Stripped right down to their underwear – imagine that? Phworr, what's not to like! She even favours the death penalty...excuse me, I just need to take a cold shower.'

Asked if he thought that she should apologize to the bullied civil servants: 'Apologise? Lucky, muckers. They should be paying her.'

Russian health staff shortage sees COVID jabs administered by re-trained assassins

'Until the intervention of the KGB, the population was bewilderingly reluctant to subject themselves to State-sponsored mass injections. But, now we're a victim of our own success,' laughed Rosa Klebb, chief of the newly-made 'Directorate of Not Killing People.'

'Serendipitously, these same...er...public sector workers are highly-trained and have a set of transferable skills ideally suited to their new role as community vaccinators' said

'For a single dose, after a period of covert tracking, we'll either sneak up and inject the vaccine from behind with a vaccine-tipped umbrella, or put it in their tea or Widow's Kiss cocktail when they're not looking, leaving what's left in a park bench to inoculate an unsuspecting child, amorous couple or police-officer.

'Alternatively, we apply it to the door-knob of their front door, or sneak it in pellet-form under their car-seat.

'In a case where two doses are needed, we use two agents running up from either side, each opening a briefcase full of pressurised vaccine spray while the victim...er, I mean patient...is distracted.

'Our agents also have excellent bedside manner, able to put people at ease regaling them with stories of their travels to Salisbury cathedral, or else with nerve-gas.

'Yes, yes, as you imagine we do occasionally confuse the vaccine with Novichok, with hilarious results. This is regrettable but will save time later during the forthcoming 'purge.''

Minister left waiting for inheritance money promised in email

The UK treasury says time is running out for the Nigerian Royal Family to 'get their act together' with regards to promised monies. A spokesman said: 'Frankly, the Government needs the money now to pay for one or two slightly rash purchases. I've sent the required administration fees and I understand that my colleague has sent several lots, so it's about time we received the promised monies.'

When it was suggested that the money was never going to arrive, the Finance Minister's forehead throbbed slightly and he said, 'I'll send the admin fee once more, but that's it.'

Isle of Wight A3020 named in Michelin Roadkill Guide

The road scored favourably for both the variety of wildlife slaughtered and the meat quality. Travellers testified to the abundance of edible rabbit, hedgehog and roe deer foolish enough to cross two lanes of busy traffic whilst completely ignoring the nearby pelican crossing.

Highways Manager Tom Rigley said, 'We knew we had to up our game and our crushed pheasant is magnifique. I know the common term is roadkill, but here we prefer to call it street food.'

Alexa to listen to your 'weird dream' so no one else has to

'But, what does it mean?' The five words sure to incite the most patient human being into a stress-induced sprint for solitude. We've all been there, faking consciousness during the forty-minute turgid ramblings of a loved-one's cheese-induced insomnibabble.

Fortunately, Amazon have programmed their home assistant to absorb all that self-confused brain froth. They will now give you the reassurance that you crave, with responses, like 'Uh-huh!', 'OMG!' and 'He doesn't deserve to be in your dreams'

So, feel free to say - 'I had a weird dream last night!! I was talking to my ex-ex at a party on the moon, and he kept saying that he had something important to tell me, but then a train shaped like a Weetabix, driven by twelve Carol Vordermans, pulled-up at the side of him, and he jumped over it on a pogo-stick made of focaccia. Which is really weird because focaccia doesn't store energy under compression, and then...' Alexa will say that it's 'just you taking control of your life.'

Chancellor announces cut to public sector clapping

Since 2010 the primary source of income for public sector workers has been clapping and the occasional acorn, that they could wrestle from a squirrel. Now that the Chancellor has announced a pay freeze for 1.3 million workers, their pay will be downgraded to a polite tutting, followed by the hiccups.

The clap has long been acknowledged as the gold standard in pay for firefighters and teachers, replacing the pre-decimal system of waving frenetically and shouting 'Cooee.' Members of the public have long shown their appreciation for public sector workers by clapping in a non-ironic way, as opposed to the way James Corden receives applause.

Other forms of meaningful payment have been explored; including coughing rhythmically, whistling the tune from Z-Cars and a restrained version of jazz hands. Some workers have asked for cash in hand but have been told to settle for the next best thing, a pat on the head by their local MP.

The one exception are frontline nurses, whose pay was already so low, that their clapping will be upgraded to the sound of one hand clapping.

Coronavirus delays Martian invasion

No one would have believed, in the last days of 2020, that human affairs were being watched from the timeless worlds of space. And yet minds immeasurably superior to ours viewed this COVID ridden Earth and said, 'Bugger! That's the invasion shot.'

Supreme Leader of Mars, Gargol Gx'Vlar, said they had been slowly and surely drawing their plans against us, ever since Earthly bacteria put pay to their last invasion attempt at the end of the 19th Century. 'Just when we thought a course of antibiotics and packets of Beechams Max Strength would do the job you managed to cover your planet in a deadly hybrid virus.'

Top Trumps Card Game manufacturer changes name to Top Bidens for the US Market

Consumer research revealed that the word 'Trump' is now off-putting to customers who like reading and memorising a small selection of actual, verifiable facts.

New sets of Top Bidens for 2021 include Political Dinosaurs, World's Biggest Tantrums, Least tax paid (Bottom Trumps),

Favourite Covfefe, Worst Deals ever, People Who've Outstayed Their Welcome and Dubious Hairstyles. 'This will be big, if not bigly,' said a game manufacturer today.

Bucket list fails to mention new bucket

With an economic downturn predicted, people need to be more realistic with their unrealistic ambitions. A bucket list that lacks a bucket, is clearly not prepared for a bleak COVID scenario where we might have to harvest rainwater or improvise an eyeless helmet.

Most bucket lists fall short on essentials, like extra loo paper and badger traps. Individuals are wasting valuable wishes wanting to bungee jumping from a hot air balloon, when they need to focus on the basics, such as affordable shelter or something unaffordable in the London area.

Explained one business leader: 'Yes, we all want to climb Everest but how about some low hanging fruit first? Like remembering to put out the bins. Anyway, everyone knows swimming with dolphins is just a euphemism for sex with a porpoise.'

The Department for Health said people should be pragmatic with their bucket list – so stop asking for the impossible, like a Unicorn burger or a functioning Track and Trace App.

PM says he now has 'foot on throat' of poor COVID-19 analogies

Prime Minister Boris Johnson has announced that he may be close to a cure for poorly thought out COVID-19 analogies, after nearly nine months of metaphors, implausible comparisons and public-school personalisation of the deadly coronavirus.

'The toot of the bugle of the scientific cavalry is coming over the brow of the hill to help me get these comparisons under control', confirmed Johnson.

'It's a bit like a penalty shoot-out. My stretched analogy steps up and scores low to the left, David Coleman shouts 1-0, and I've got to step up and slot it home. But the head boy is coming in now and telling us to keep the noise down or we'll be fagging for the rest of the term and no warm milk from Matron.'

'The train is now coming into the station on a wet and windy evening', continued Johnson. 'It's not London Paddington though, it's more like platform 2 at Slough before it was upgraded, no refreshments, no toilets, pigeon crap everywhere. 'I'm confident now that someone will take my analogies onto the train and flush them out of the toilet on to the track between Peterborough and Newark Northgate.'

Members of the public remained confused, however. 'He's using both hands to pull out some arrows from his epidemiological quiver, whilst simultaneously making a home run, a slam dunk, firing a shot into the net, with his foot is on the throat of the virus.', noted one sceptical observer. 'And all this from a man who doesn't know his arse from his elbow.'

Five Go Dobbing in the Neighbours

In other news…

Only two more lockdowns until Christmas

Trump aggrieved at Pfizer after putting all his money on Toilet Duck

Trump: 'many of these voters were dead and I should know because I killed them'

Brexiteers infuriated by cod moving in mysterious ways

Foreign fish to be banned from UK waters

Decision on Christmas expected by Easter

Pfizer COVID-19 vaccine trial proceeds without cock-up

Stripper barters with tattoo artist in tit for tat deal

Trump initiates lawsuits on 71 million Democrat voters

Trump seen sewing fish into oval office curtains, and shitting on desk

Cummings seen leaving Downing Street with box of frogs

Cummings' season 1 finale nominated for a BAFTA

Black Friday and Cyber Monday to be followed by return the Tat Thursday

Heaven says Jesus saves even better now he's got coaching from Ray Clemence

Men trapped in tumble dryer had heard there was something going round

Pudsey Bear criticises NHS waiting times for eye operations

US democracy out for the count

Word of the year 'lockdown' not impressing stolen bike owners

Man with allergy to polo shirts has a fit of pique

Strictly to continue during lockdown, says BBC. Could 2020 get worse?

Survey finds most toilet paper bought by regular people

Melania confirms her husband suffers from premature congratulations

Brewer quickly manufacturers new stout called 'substantial meal'

Five Go Dobbing in the Neighbours

For first year ever, people are jealous of 'I'm a Celebrity' contestants

Boyfriends celebrate never being dragged round top shop again

Trump's departure marks end of era where jokes just write themselves

MAGA redefined – man at golf-course again.

'I'm Sorry, I Haven't a Clue' voted best radio analogy for Johnson's Government.

Declaration of Republican win trumped up

Voting patterns suggests Putin could still achieve a second term in USA

Liverpool Catholics first to trial mass testing

Putin demands a recount

Leave means leave – Cummings told in no uncertain terms

First signs of Australian style Brexit as Boris calls a Cobber meeting

Mink-related coronavirus deadly but victims will look absolutely fabulous

Scientists say Blackpool vaccine trials scrapped due to lack of pier reviews

Time for Trump to wake up and smell the covfefe

Man admits defeat as attempt to swim length of infinity pool enters third day

Waitrose still allowed to sell essential artichoke hearts

Madagascan chameleon last seen 100 years ago wins hide-and-seek title

Racist kicks all races out of football racism.

Confirmation that Russian vaccine will be 107% successful.

UK fishing quota negotiators achieve 2 sticklebacks from the Erewash canal

We wait months for a vaccine, then three come along at once

DECEMBER 2020

December saw children writing letters to Santa asking to get home-schooling back and Boris writing letters to his health experts requesting that COVID-19 be stood down for a day or two over Christmas. Both got their wish and it was an exciting period, that is if you were an airborne virus or a Tory donor in line for another round of plum government contracts. Meanwhile the vaccine rollout started to gain momentum as vulnerable cabinet ministers, friends and family were given protection in time for the second wave.

AmazSanta

After considering elf advice from senior members of his loyal workforce, the 1,740-year-old Turkish born (but now - presumably for tax reasons - resident in Iceland) founder, proprietor and CEO of Santa Claus Enterprises is contemplating a takeover bid by Jeff Bezos.

Father Christmas is regarded as a genial, well-liked and respected employer but he is no longer a young man, suffers from obesity and shows clear signs of hypertension. His staff worry that working a continual night shift, with a great deal of travel and regular exposure to sooty, highly polluted and confined environments will have taken their toll.

Now, having to wear full PPE while descending several million chimneys in just a few hours, Santa feels that enough is enough. Amazon confirmed future deliveries will just be a peremptory knocking on chimney pots before the goods are left somewhere on the roof of the recipients' home.

Don't blame us for this clusterf*ck, say fish

As the chances of a Brexit deal hang in the balance, fish want it to be known that the calamitous Government negotiation roadshow is nothing to do with them. One, recently-surfaced cod said, 'Killing me and my brethren makes up 0.1% of UK GDP but makes up 99% of all superficial flag-waving bollocks.

'To be honest my dad was Norwegian and my mother was a Dane. I am also pretty sure my two hundred brothers and sisters were born in the Irish Sea. Oh, and I was born near Iceland and I'm not talking about the well-known chain of supermarkets full of chest freezers. Mic drop bitches!'

Pupils to be given exam questions in advance, just like Eton

Extra measures will be introduced this year to ensure that state pupils are not disadvantaged due to COVID or by being related to someone 'a bit working class.' By contrast, Etonians will not only get the questions but will still get to know their career in advance – as the answer is always Prime Minister.

Ofqual have promised that students will be helped with their exam preparation, which goes against 100 years of teaching tradition. The normal system is to teach the wrong part of the syllabus, at the wrong time of year and then blame it on the students not paying attention at the back.

The Etonian Method is much fairer, with every student given an equal chance to shine – provided they make the same charitable donation to the Head of School's 'Swiss Banking Project.' Meanwhile entrance exams to Oxford and Cambridge will still be based on a DNA test, which determines seven degrees of connection to William the Conqueror and the Cayman Islands.

Closure of Burton leaves gaping hole in the wear-once court appearance market

High street regulars who trundle tartan shopping trolleys in front of them at speeds of up to six tiles per hour, were deeply saddened to hear that Top Shop had gone for a burton, and Burton was no longer a top shop.

Burton, cleverly designed so as not to be noticed on the high street, had long-provided an essential service to consumers ordered to attend court the following day. Defendants too ashamed to be seen plucking their first and only £19.99 wear-once suit off a clanky rail from the 'Appearance' range, had always relied upon Burton as a place where they would encounter no one but a forlorn sales attendant. With Burton stores gone, cheap solicitors fear that courtroom fashion standards could plummet into onesiewear.

PPE start-ups top kids' Christmas wish lists

Britain's savvy kids have topped their Christmas wish-lists this year by asking Santa for six-figure COVID-related Government handouts. Santa commented: 'It's all about the PPE start-up, I've spent the last three months down at Companies House registering all the paperwork Most of it's in crayon and that's just official Cabinet requests.

Santa then delved into his pocket and revealed a typical sample of the letters he'd received; one note read: 'Dear Santa, can I have a public limited company that only costs one hundred pounds but will be worth millions in the morning, pleeeease?

Another letter read: 'Santa! Don't bring me a Thomas the Tank Engine! I want a Tory Gravy Train!' Another: 'A COVID vaccine distribution contract, and lots of lots of sweets, please.'

Others had loftier ambitions: 'Hello Santa, I've been sooooo good. Please, please, please make me the big chief minister in charge of yummy chocolate and medical-grade PPE procurement.'

Others, entered into the generosity of the Christmas spirit: 'Dear Santa Claus, I don't want anything, thank you! But would you give my mummy a disproportionately funded public relations consultancy, to fill in the time between Loose Women and when I get home from school, one afternoon per month please, because she is the best.'

Usually the preserve of entitled public school children, ludicrous Government handouts are now filtering down the food chain, alongside lordships and enormous ears. So, despite not being able to use a knife and fork, or participate in education, it seems COVID-weary kids are being taught the life-skill of carving-up Treasury cash. Don't forget to leave a brown envelope out for Santa.

Salesforce/Slack merge to form another company you have never heard of

You will pleased to know that your pension scheme is still tied up with stocks and shares in companies you have never heard of, making products you have never used. Take for example the merger of 'Salesforce and Slack', which sounds like the title of a 1980's buddy cop movie.

And what is Slack? Is it Roadman for Friends Reunited? No, apparently it is a real-time collaboration app – which is just a fancy computer version of a blackboard. Its name is an acronym for 'Searchable Log of All Conversation and Knowledge.' Nope? Me neither.

A Salesforce executive explained their product: 'We provide software for marketing automation and analytics, okay? Is that clear? What do you mean 'that's as clear as mud'? We created a customer success platform, for goodness' sake! Stop looking at me blankly. It is a thing. It is. It's a real thing. In a cloud. Stop giggling! We're absolutely real. Except when it comes to paying federal tax.'

So apparently Slack is worth £20 billion to Salesforce, which seems like rather a lot; but given you had never heard of Salesforce either, does anyone really care. It is all about synergy apparently, so your guess is as good as mine.

Jingle Bells urged to jingle only part of the way.

Jingle Bells have been urged not to jingle all the way as part of special measures this Christmas. A spokesperson explained 'Under normal circumstances we would insist on full completion of the bell-jingling guidelines. But this year, we have to accept a modified festive season, hence new guidelines to our members suggesting they jingle no more than 73% of the way.'

One jingler has suggested that the lyric be adjusted to 'jingle ON the way', prompting criticism that this undermines the original song's allegiance to a full jingling scenario. 'This version means token in-journey jingling lasting maybe only minutes would be acceptable and renders the song worthless.'

Meanwhile publishers of the song 'I saw mummy kissing Santa Claus' have expressed fears that both parties would have to belong to the same household for the lyrics to function safely.

A spokesman explained: 'This situation endangers the whole meaning of the song. It would be impossible to substitute a Mummy/Santa interface that did not break COVID safety rules, without revealing the true nature of the relationship between the two. This in itself, risks a breach in confidentiality for both parties.'

The spokesman promised 'We are currently developing a new safety-conscious lyric along the lines of 'I saw mummy having a good think about Santa Claus.'

Referees delighted at return of fans after 'missing abuse'

The Referees' Association has expressed its relief at the return of fans into football grounds, as its members can once again hear foul-mouthed insults being hurled at them. Limited numbers of fans have been allowed back into certain games under strictly controlled conditions, primarily in order to provide the match officials with instant feedback on their inept performances.

Fans had continued to express their dissatisfaction with the match officials throughout lockdown by shouting at the television, and in an effort to compensate for the lack of verbal attacks during games held behind closed doors, some clubs had installed cardboard cut-outs of fans making gestures towards the match officials. However, the atmosphere in the grounds fell a long way short of the cauldron of hatred that certain referees used to relish on a weekly basis.

'Our members found the previous restrictions very difficult to cope with,' admitted Wally Black from the Referees' Association. 'They really struggled to enjoy wrecking everyone's enjoyment of the beautiful game through their appalling decisions without actually hearing the roars of disapproval from thousands of fans.'

And the supporters themselves have really missed going to grounds to make their ill-feelings heard and express their animosity alongside thousands of like-minded individuals. 'Football is all about fans of all ages and backgrounds coming together as a community to enjoy the game,' explained Chelsea fan Rob Edmondson. 'It is so great to be back and to once more be able to enquire about the referees' eyesight, parentage and proclivity for solo sex acts.'

Another Guide to Tiers

Ben Hur - Chariot Tier
Al Capone - Racket Tier
D'Artagnan - Musket Tier
Harry Corbett - Puppet Tier
Jeff Bezos - Profit Tier
Over half the UK - Brexit Tier
Raymond Blanc - Restaurant Tier
Captain Kirk - Final Front Tier
Elon Musk - Rocket Tier
Sir Edmund Hillary - Summit Tier
Captain Morgan - Private Tier
Vincent Van Gogh - lost Tier
Fan of lower league London football clubs - Leyton Orient Tier
1990 England World Cup semi-final memories - Gazza Tier
Dumbo - Vast Tier
Davy Crockett - Wild fron-tier

Five Go Dobbing in the Neighbours

Jacob Rees- Mogg – Snoo Tier
Michael Gove - Rat Tier

Chris Rea seeks urgent clarification on Christmas travel restrictions

'I normally set off in early December to make sure I'm back home in plenty time for Christmas' says the gravel-voiced singer. 'But with the national lockdown restrictions changing to local Tiers I'm not sure if I can leave now and travel from one non-specified location to another non-specified location. If everyone waits until 23rd December before setting off then the roads will be chock-a-block, and I'll be top to toe in tailbacks.

'Can I drive from a county in a higher Tier to a county in a lower-Tier or do I have to try and drive around somehow? It's a minefield - and it's not just me that's confused.'

In response, a minister said. 'I would urge the public, including veteran singer-songwriters, to follow Government guidance. Travel is allowed only when absolutely necessary – for work, for education or for the purposes of fulfilling the lyrics of a popular Christmas song.

'I would strongly recommend Mr Rea set off now or he'll be on the road to hell.'

Woman using 'super' as a prefix for everything is 'super-dead' inside

Ursula Smith, 25, who uses 'super' to describe pretty much everything she sees or hears has revealed that the word is also a very apt way to describe the inner-vacuum of her life.

Ursula habitually uses the moniker in both verbal and written form, the latter to describe most random shit that pops up on her Facebook – slash – Instagram feed that she tags as proof of life.

Ironically, her soul passed on years ago and although her use of the word 'super' in everyday life suggests she is constantly overwhelmed by everyday events, nothing could be further from the truth.

The revelation has come as a shock to many of Ursula's closest friends. One such friend, Laura said, 'I have never physically met Ursula but we bonded over our common interest in videos of someone's hands cooking Japanese food.

'Only last week she described a video of Gyoza Dumplings as 'super-amazing.' I am now doubting her sincerity. Oh, God. Did she even watch it? I feel super-sick right now.'

Ursula's sister Jane commented, 'I sent her a video of my daughter and her only niece, Summer-Meadow's adorable ballet recital. She emoji'd the hell of it and wrote – in capitals – SUPER AMAZING NIECE. Look. 'The heartless witch probably didn't even like any of the previous two hundred identical videos I sent her.'

Ursula said, 'I literally say super all of the time. Of course, I have a huge black void eating away at my insides. How dumb do they think I am?'

Obama, Bush & Clinton to be injected on TV – but is the death penalty too much?

All three former Presidents have volunteered to be vaccinated on TV, although most US citizens are happy to swap the vaccine for something 'a bit stronger.' While most say they favour injection, 26% still preferred the electric chair, with 12% saying 'hangings too good for them.'

Technically the death penalty is outlawed in many states, but they have said they will make an exception for those three. The intention is to increase public confidence in Coronavirus vaccines, but the opportunity to rid the world of three habitual liars may be too much to pass up.

Presidents Bush and Obama will be seen to by a qualified doctor, while Mr Clinton insisted on seeing Carry on Nurse. Said one viewer: 'Experiencing a small prick on TV is nothing. It's exactly what we had to put up with, whenever one of them said something to camera.'

Nobody but nobody missing Nativity Plays this year

While outwardly consoling their distraught wannabee 'Mary', all parents are secretly delighted not to have to sit through two hours of mind-numbingly bad drama. Most were said to be happy to avoid the pretence that the performance was anything other than dreadful, only to maintain their child's fragile artistic ego and hopes of one day going to RADA.

There would be no fixed grins and inner boredom, while listening to rhyming narration. Nobody would have to fashion a sheep costume out of a blanket and an industrial packet of cotton wool. There would be no half-arsed carol concerts and Panto can get in the bin.

Even teachers are secretly relieved not to be involved, said one: 'Normally we'd have had the Gospels according to Matthew, Luke and Stanislavski. But COVID restrictions meant that Joseph could not be present at the birth. The Angel Gabriel was self-isolating. The stables were shut along with the rest of the hospitality sector. And a bubble of six could only include the Wisemen or the Shepherds, but not both.'

Jesus was asked to comment: 'To be honest, I've never been a fan of theatre. Can I just have a birthday cake instead?'

Missing girl found attempting to turn on friend's new shower

Locals feared the worst after three days of searching uncovered nothing. However, police eventually discovered Lisa Hollins (16), twisting and pushing the buttons of their new Triple Concealed Thermostatic Shower system in the spare room.

'I assumed she'd just gone home after our night out,' her friend told journalists. 'But the complicated pulling of the handle before twisting clearly got to her.'

'It is a tad embarrassing for this to happen again' admitted Hollins, who it turns out has form for such behaviour, having had a meltdown trying to open a push-button kitchen bin two years earlier.

Supermarket introduces new 2-metre long COVID-safe Christmas cracker

'We've introduced a few modifications to the traditional cracker. For instance, it won't contain the usual items - like a tiny set of playing cards, a miniature magnifying glass or that little plastic fish thing that curls up in your hand if you're cheating on your spouse.

'Instead, the winner will get a facemask, a syringe and a paper hat with a picture of a stern-looking nurse on it saying, 'Hands Face Space.'

'All the jokes will be COVID-related – 'Why did the chicken cross the road? To observe correct social distancing measures', that kind of thing.'

Grave crisis as young buyers unable to get on the burial ladder

With so many excess deaths through coronavirus, cemetery space at a premium, and the cost of land soaring, young people are becoming increasingly pessimistic about securing a burial plot. Many seem resigned to being laid to rest with their parents or other ancestors for the time being.

Trish and Patrick Fielding are in their early twenties, married for just under a year and both working in the Health Service. Despite that they are struggling to put down a deposit on a suitable final resting place.

'Even on our combined salary we are finding it increasingly difficult to buy.' said Trish. 'Before she died, I know my Mum had said we could move in with her when we go, but you just want a place of your own don't you.'

The Reverend John Pardue is vicar of three small parishes in Norfolk. He says they desperately want to establish mixed communities in their churchyards but are in danger of losing the young because they are being priced out of the market.

'This is very sad because all they are doing is trying to get one foot in the grave. As I see it their only hope is possibly via a Burial Association who offer a variety of half-share and part rent part buy schemes.'

Older last home buyers are also struggling. Doug Cooper is a 63-year-old plumber who lives in a small village in Cornwall. He is in no doubt who's to blame. 'Outsiders.' he informed us. 'There's a lot of rich folk coming in from away and buying up second graves.

'As I understands it, half the current free space is now owned by people not resident here. Bloody city dwellers. They fancies the idea of having their home town grave during the week and then spending some time being buried in the countryside at weekends.'

Doug contracted COVID-19 earlier in the year and he says it certainly focussed his mind on where in the cemetery he wanted to be laid to rest. 'I was determined to buy myself a prime spot in the south east corner, but I was gazumped at the last minute. It was bloody awful I can tell you. I completely lost the plot.'

Of course, cremation does remain a possible alternative, but as one aspiring plot seeker told us, 'Where's the investment potential in that? It's just money up in smoke.'

Millwall fans shocked as football match breaks out at fascist rally

Supporters of Millwall FC expressed incredulity on Saturday afternoon as a football match broke out during their Nazi Party AGM. The large contingent of skinheads and troublemakers at the Den collectively gasped, dropping their copies of Mein Kampf and spilling lager all down the front of their blackshirts as Derby kicked off at 3pm.

Sadly, fans 'booing' taking the knee, is the most Millwall thing there is. A club spokeswoman explained: 'We've had 100 years of hooliganism and racism but we've also some things we're not proud of.'

'Frankly, who cares about this tawdry spectacle?' added one bigot, ominously peeling a banana. 'I'm not into football for the love of the game. This is the only forum we ultras have to spew our hatred in a world gone mad. Um, except for the internet, the tabloids and the House of Commons.'

No animal was harmed in the making of this film

Apart from the calf in the date scene at the restaurant, when he ordered the filet mignon. Well you gotta 'ave the steak dinner otherwise the hero looks like a right tight arse.

Oh, and the lobster boiled alive for her thermador spectacular. Goes without saying.

The 1,420 chickens supplied by the caterers and consumed by the crew during shooting? No one's gonna get gaffers and best boys to eat tofu.

Ah, what about the rendered fats from pigs that went into the high-grade make-up? Well, it's the industry standard... you gotta have the high-grade make-up.

And the palm trees the art director had moved for the beach scene which meant four micro-ecosystems were destroyed. MICRO-ecosystems... no one's going to notice they've gone missing, eh?

OK, but there were the 17 rare mammals who lost their habitats to provide the materials to build the ballroom set. They didn't actually bludgeon the animals on camera.

The deer skin blankets at the ski chalet, and the wall-mounted moose heads? Faux deer skin don't win you no Oscars.

The fleets of truck drivers who got all the equipment out to the desert for the battle scenes... they did hit a few... That's not actually in the making of the film though, is it? I mean, they could have run those over shifting the equipment back afterwards.

And all the flights to the sets in Venice and Rome...OK, OK, apart from the calf, the lobster, 1,420 chickens, pigs, insects, rare mammals, deer, moose, roadkill, the odd bird strike, and an unknown number due to the production contribution to climate change, no animals were harmed in the making of this film.

Vaccine rollout delayed after DHL throw first batch over gate

'We were patiently waiting for the delivery, then we saw a blur of movement outside, heard a squeal of tyres and when we went ou,t we saw a DHL van disappearing around the corner.' said Mark Lucas, who is in charge of the vaccination programme at an unnamed hospital.

'We found a dog-eared note through the door saying that nobody was in and our delivery had been left in a safe place behind the gate. Which is about eight feet high. When we opened the container it was mostly full of broken glass. I've now been on hold for over three hours trying to report it to DHL.'

DHL have apologised for the incident and said that lessons have definitely been learned, insisting that any future deliveries would definitely not be roughly thrown over gates and would instead be carefully placed behind the bins.

'It's pretty cold at the moment, so I'm sure the refrigerated containers will be fine outside for a couple of days.' said a spokesman.

Everyone suddenly paying a hell of a lot more attention to India's mystery illness

Attitudes in 2020 have changed, going from 'Oh, are poor people dying on the other side of the world – what a yawn' to 'Did someone sneeze in India?!? Quick, children, to the Anderson Shelter!' News that 227 people have been hospitalized in Andhra Pradesh has been greeted by everyone in Europe stockpiling loo paper and trying to remember the last time they had a curry.

Not so much sympathy as naked self-interest, has caused us to become alert to the merest hint of a viral outbreak, even if it is just a kitten meme. As one Indian remarked: "The rest of the world sent us a Get Well Soon message on the back of a restraining order.'

Man backs himself to shop without bag, instantly regrets it

A man who forgot to grab a bag-for-life as he left the house to 'pick up a couple of things' says the next 20 minutes were some of the worst of his life.

Ian Smith only wanted a few items from his local store, and therefore thought he would not need a handy tool to transport them home. 'It started with the Buy One Get One Free on chocolate fingers, then things snowballed when I realised we needed toilet rolls', recounted Smith.

'Before I knew it, I had avocados in both pockets, crisps under my jumper and three onions in a sleeve around my neck. My trousers were around my ankles due to the sheer weight of fruit. I was like a walking supermarket.'

William Shakespeare vaccine patient 'probably an imposter'

Mystery surrounds the identity of the second COVID vaccine patient. The Coventry and Warwickshire NHS Trust today confirmed it is investigating claims that COVID vaccine patient William Shakespeare was not who he claimed to be.

The Trust's Head of Media, said, 'Since it was discovered that Mr Shakespeare was receiving this vaccine, several other patients have claimed that this man is an imposter and, being a grammar school oik, could not possibly have received the vaccine. We have had contact from a Francis Bacon, Christopher Marlowe, Edward de Vere and even William Stanley the 6th Earl of Dudley who all claim they received the vaccine yesterday.'

Mr Shakespeare was not available for comment as he has suffered a serious reaction to his treatment. He was found wandering on a heath with most of his clothes and wits missing as he howled at the storm.

Fate of drunken sailor 'still in the balance'

Naval Police Officers raised concerns about the sailor's drunken behaviour when he began weighing hay in the ship's chandlery and taunting the ship's cook about the time his soufflé collapsed. Punishments range from shaving his belly with a rusty razor to putting him in a longboat until he is sober

One penalty that has been ruled out by all parties is putting the sailor in bed with the captain's daughter. A representative for the NPO said the move would almost certainly be counter-productive: 'Having seen her Instagram, you'd need to be blind drunk to get into bed with her. When he sobered up, he'd simply get sloshed again when he realised what he'd done.

'Anyway, first thing he has got to do is clear up all this broken glass, there were 10 green bottles hanging on that wall last night, now look at them.'

Public parks fill with freshly-released vaccinated octogenarians

The hyper-active OAPs have been behaving like frisky cattle, which had been over-wintered indoors, and have just been turned out onto fresh spring pasture for the first time.

Vulnerable younger members of the public have been trying to stay safe by keeping their distance and have been fearful of using public footpaths through the parks. Police with whistles and dogs have been called to round up the chaotic flocks of skipping, gambolling pensioners.

However, police were hampered in their attempts to make arrests, after one officer asked an elderly detainee if he wished to say anything and was still waiting for the anecdote to finish three hours later.

Earth has its Galactic membership rejected on grounds of race

From a secret Mars base, far beneath its chocolaty exterior, near its caramel centre, said a Galactic Federation spokes-being: 'I just don't trust bipeds. We're not racist, it's just that all Earthlings are criminals and smell of milk. Look, some of my best friends are partially evolved apes.'

The federation proposes erecting a force wall around earth, to stop unwanted immigrants. Yet rejecting the Earth on segregation grounds, may seem ironically familiar: 'We thought you guys would love the idea of walls and state sponsored apartheid- you seem so keen on it normally.'

Brexiteer demands Full English Breaksit

'You see, you've got your continental breaksit - glass of juice, croissant, maybe a slice of yesterday's ham and a bit of rubbery cheese; bit of jam, and decent coffee, I'll give you that.

'Then, you've got your Full English Breaksit- a glorious, piled plate of bangers and bacon; choice of eggs, scrambled, fried, poached. You've got the fried bread. Baked beans, in their own little bowl if you're being posh. Black Pudding, mushrooms, tomatoes - I prefer tinned to fresh, but to each their own.

'You've got your regional twists too, bit of White pudding, maybe Haggis, Lorne Sausage, a potato farl. Hash Brown, that's equivocal. Toast, white or brown, don't matter, but it has to be proper butter. And your sauces - the old chestnut of HP or red (HP for me, but again, we're a broad church, though don't come near me with barbecue or mayonnaise).

'Now, you look at any menu, and I'll tell you this for nothing - your Continental Breaksit is a cut price, cheapo, disappointment of a compromise way to start the day. And your Full English, that's your more expensive, premium, belting top-of-the-shop, set you up a treat.

And that, my friend, is why we'll win ... after the heart attack.

Men persuaded by Love Actually that stalking your mate's wife is perfectly fine

A special report has revealed that millions of people applying Richard Curtis's advice to their own lives. The conclusions that people have drawn include the following:

It is normal to obsess about your best mate's wife

Did you video their wedding as a ruse to film close-ups of the object of your obsession to repeatedly re-watch alone at your 'pleasure?' Did you show up at their house and profess love to her with the use of visual aids under the pretext of being carol singers?

You're a sociopath, right? Wrong.

Richard Curtis says this is all just playful normal activity and if you think about it, most marriages end in divorce, so if you don't stick around and feed your obsession you might miss out. Or your mate might die in a 'freak accident', so you hang in there!

Having to stand around naked with a complete stranger is a great way to get a date

Out of work actor? A bit shy and tongue-tied like all proper Englishmen? Get a job as a body double. You'll soon be simulating sex with a butt-naked Stacey from Gavin and Stacey and romance is bound to follow.

It is totally fine to shag the help

Richard says that if you are a very powerful man, it is both acceptable and adorable to have relations with the help. The more foul-mouthed the better. If you can come across as a man of principle who wouldn't normally do this sort of thing, even better.

Eventually, it will get awkward but remember that your powerfulness means you will always have the ability to dispose of the evidence, so to speak. Richard provides the example of deploying the SAS, although bear in mind this option may not be open to you.

...and the foreign help

An extension of the 'shag the help' principle extended to foreign soil. However, you will need to display more bumbling Englishman traits and dial the faux adorability up to eleven. Throw in some poor attempts at trying to master the local lingo and foreign domestic ladies will be unable to resist you.

Repeatedly watching the olive-skinned goddess plunging the outside toilet may eventually drive you to propose in the presence of all her extended family. Richard's advice is don't fight it. It is very romantic and - once you regain your senses - the chances are she will not get citizenship, or alternatively, you can plant cocaine in her luggage.

Don't grieve for your dead wife for more than two weeks

Losing your betrothed is naturally devastating. It is also no picnic for those around so don't wallow. As Richard says, while you are screaming at the moon and crying like an infant, you are basically a woman-repellent. Two weeks is a decent amount of time to get over it and get back on the hunt, particularly in the run-up to Christmas.

American birds are gagging for it

It's true. Just get a flight there - anywhere, will do - and go to the nearest bar with your cute British accent. You'll be up to your apricots in a foursome with three gorgeous blondes and brunettes in no time.

The US president being rude will lead to a major diplomatic incident

You think Donald Trump could have come over here and made a crude pass at a pretty young tea-lady at 10 Downing Street? Pah. Richard knows better. Boris would have publicly humiliated him before getting into a relationship with her himself. Pregnant fiancée? What pregnant fiancée?

The film will be broadcast on a permanent loop on all channels over Christmas, except for a brief interruption for the Queen's Speech, unless the director obsessively keeps his camera pointed at any totty that might be in the room.

Woman finishes sending Christmas cards to every name in old address book

Diane Willis has finished writing over twenty cards to a load of people who are either dead or whose addresses have been out of date for over two decades, it has emerged.

Diane commences her annual ritual in late November of every year by retrieving some old threadbare address book with kittens on the cover and a collection of beige stains on all of the pages.

'It is my trusty old address book just for Christmas cards, obviously.' she said. 'I have no other use for this book. It is however extremely important for me to send them my best wishes to literally every name inside, whoever they are. I mean, of course I know everyone in this book.

'They are all very dear to me. Like Margaret Anderson. My old primary school teacher. Possibly. Yes, that rings a bell. God, if I am f53 then she must be 100 and ... anyway

'Okay. Moving on. Huh, Dr. John Allan. Of course. Right, Maybe try some B's. Guy Barton. Who the f*ck is? Just sign the card Diane.

'Who the hell is Reverend Bill Daniels when he's at home?

'Ah, the post has just arrived. Mr and Mrs F. Marshall? They sold the house to the people we bought it off. I think you need to update your address book. Idiots.

'Right, on to the Es...'

Man loses soul after failing to read minutes of last meeting

Harry Reeves, 32, inadvertently condemned himself to an eternity in the fiery lakes of Hell, by failing to pick up on an outstanding agenda item from the last meeting. Sadly for Harry, there was a clear action point attributed to the marketing department, specifically for a 'Mr Reeves, Mr L.Ucifer and his horny minions.'

When asked how he had volunteered for damnation, Harry replied: 'When the Chair asked had we read and agreed with the minutes, we all said yes and waved it through. I didn't know she meant literally. Who reads the Minutes? No one. Well, I suppose grammar pedants do. But I'm sure they already have their own special layer of Hell reserved.'

As he was escorted out of the building by two burly demons, Harry looked resigned: 'It turns out someone tagged on an extra agenda item to the AOB. Ironically, I think it might have been me. I don't know, I wasn't paying much attention.'

Satan confirmed: 'Look, the Devil was in the detail, we all know that'

Vaccinated people already growing fish gills, insists idiot

Idiot Martin Short, who is a self-employed amender of stuff on Wikipedia he does not like, has taken to social media to report that the new vaccine is already showing serious fish-based side effects.

Short said: 'As an expert on opinions about everything I don't know, I am required by natural law to comment on things such as vaccines. In doing so, it is incumbent on me to ensure my comments are as baseless as they are dangerous. Like the climate change hoax. It's f*cking three degrees outside!

'Therefore, posting a tweet that basically says the new COVID-19 vaccination is the latest in the long line of evil liberal scientists' plot to turn us into haddocks, is my civic duty. I will also one day look up what vaccines do but first things first.

'It is a race against time but I'm hopeful that we will see a spike in vaccination refusal. Luckily it will also coincide with the other important issue that is very close to my heart, namely the anti-mask and pro-mass gatherings campaign.

'Ensuring that we can continue to live in a world free of tyranny and common sense is what keeps me going. Well, that and regular injections of goat semen as ordered by my overlord. Yes, master, continue to guide me down the path of self-righteous indignation.

'Sorry, where was I?'

If Trump 'won', can he run again in 2024?

In 2024, if at that time he is still claiming to have won the 2020 presidential election, that would have given him his second term of office so he would not be eligible to stand again.

Therefore, if he wishes to seek nomination from the Republican party as their 2024 presidential candidate in the hope of regaining office that way, he will have to cease claiming to be the legitimate current president, with all the loss of face such a climb-down would incur.

In fact, he might retrospectively have to rescind all his claims to the current presidency, together with all his associated allegations of election fraud. You can't simultaneously claim both to have been successfully elected to two terms of office, and at the same time claim that you have only served on term and are therefore eligible to have another bash at getting elected.

That would be a bit like coming second in a race, afterwards claiming that you really came first because the person who beat you had cheated and therefore demanding that you be given the winner's prize, but also insisting on keeping whatever you might have already been awarded as a prize for coming second.

Does that make sense?

The Ghost of Christmas Furniture reminds you to put up shelves

A man from Hull, Michael Khatri, was recently visited by three alarming visions - the ghosts of Past Decoration Promises, of DIY Presents and of Christmas Furniture Construction. This Dickensian nightmare was made more ironic by the fact that

Michael had promised his wife that he would make their lounge look like 'a scene from Dickens', but had so far only managed to create the ambiance of 19th century squalor.

In the run up to Christmas, it has become painfully obvious that many household projects remain unfinished; be it squeaky floorboards, the flaking walls or removing that stain from the living room carpet, which looks strangely like Simon Cowell. Worst still, is that Mr Khatri has a fitted wardrobe to assemble, acquired during the previous January sales, which is resting – fully boxed – on the staircase.

The Ghost of Christmas Furniture said: 'This year I'll be bringing Michael an IKEA fitted kitchen. In one scenario, he finishes the job and his family have a wonderous Christmas. In the other scenario, Tiny Tim dies of starvation after getting trapped in a cupboard, which Michael installed backwards.'

Michael was more stoic about the situation: 'I favour Hard Times over a Christmas Carol. Besides I still need to fix the broken loo seat, or as my wife calls it, A Tale of Two Shitties.'

Northern Lights scam exposed as a tw*t going mental with a torch in Salford

Thousands flocking to the North at the weekend in the hope of witnessing a celestial phenomenon were left disappointed as police arrested a local man with a large torch.

After the sun released its biggest solar flare in years, it was hoped that a display of stunning auroras would appear in areas across Northern England.

'We drove the kids here all the way from Huddersfield', said Nigel Palmer, 38, a part-time foam mitten designer and avid night sky fan. 'We bought a family ticket online at seventy-five quid in the hope of seeing something spectacular, and it turns out to be a short-arsed tw*t with a f*cking torch.'

A police spokesman was surprised so many people were duped by the scam. 'A torch, even one with a multi-coloured beam function pales in comparison to the Aurora Borealis, but I suppose their under-deployed brains need a break from the constant shagging during lockdown.'

Jesus curses misfortune to be born on Christmas Day

A bitterly rueful Lord Jesus Christ shook his head and damned his bad luck for the 2020th time in his long life today, as he contemplated another year of celebrating his birthday and Christmas on the same date.

'Why did this have to happen to me? I only get half as many presents as my friends every year – it's not fair! Can't it be Frank-mas or Steve-mas instead, just this once?' shouted the Lord, shaking his fist skyward, possibly at his deity.

'And don't tell me I get prayers all year round; we all know those are worthless. What's the use of being Mary's boychild, Jesus Christ, if I don't get a proper amount of loot?'

'The presents I do get are never any good anyway: nowhere accepts lumps of gold as legal tender anymore, and as for myrrh – all I can say is meh. I can fob the frankincense off on my old mum but that's hardly a good gift for me.'

'God's gift to mankind? Don't get me started. How can I be my own present? I wanted a PS5,' said Jesus of Nazareth, stroppily. 'I'm going to my room and I'm not Second Coming out till next year. So, there!'

Gourmet chef presents hungry nation with charred remains of oven-ready meal

Urging the public to 'come and get it, old chaps', a red-faced Boris Johnson emerged from the kitchen in the flat above Number 10, Downing Street last night, carrying a flaming oven tray filled with the charred remains of a dish four years in the making.

'Good evening, good evening! Grubs up! Or should that be tits up? I wouldn't mind either way. Guffaw,' cried the PM to his 68 million guests, proudly displaying his monstrous culinary creation, which may have been fish & chips, but could easily have been baked Alaska. Johnson would only confirm that the meal definitely was not a metaphor.

Wearing a deliberately oversized chef's hat and an apron besmirched with foul grease, Johnson stumbled over his own feet, scattering food and embers everywhere.

'Not to worry: the stoic, heroic, gullible and heroic British people have swallowed worse than this from me,' said Mr Johnson, sweeping the mess back onto the dish. 'Remember when I promised a world-beating test and trace system by June? I think they can handle a few fingernails in their dinner.

'Tuck in, pals, what?'

'This leaves a bad taste in the mouth,' spluttered the public, in between retches. 'It's half-baked at most and you can tell it was cooked up at the last minute. I'd rather swallow a whole bottleful of bitter pills than choke this down.'

In a late development, the Johnson Kitchen is to have its Michelin Star status rescinded by the EU, according to reports.

Gifts for a 'Minimalist Christmas'

1.   A blank CD of John Cage music
2.   A whole box of doughnut holes
3.   A reel of invisible mending tape
4.   A 'Best of Michael McIntyre' video
5.   The inside of a Slinky
6.   A copy of Principles of Government, Johnson et al
7.   A bottle of Eau D'COVID-19, because you're not f*cking worth it.
8.   A full-size anvil for your key ring
9.   A dancing in Africa Mrs May wind-up toy
10.   Fender Player Stratocaster Air Guitar
11.   Emperors range of new clothes
12.   The Twitter Book of All Knowledge
13.   The gift of coronavirus
14.   MRI scan of the inside of Chris Grayling's head.
15.   Large print wall poster of post-Brexit trade deals (A6 size)
16.   Jar of certified COVID-free air
17.   A fart in a colander
18.   A world atlas of countries where the UK still enjoys political good will
19.   A farmers' market jar of sealed pixie farts
20.   A Virgin Experience 'Red Letter Day' booze cruise to France
21.   A photo album of all the people ever saved by homeopathy
22.   A compendium of Mark Francois' successful military campaigns which don't include him riding naked into battle atop a unicorn
23.   A New Forest Lapland TripAdvisor rating
24.   A Debenhams gift card

Top COVID tier to be called Premiership or 'old Division One'

A mix up with the COVID restriction tier system and football's divisional tier system has resulted in a major upheaval for many football clubs. FA Media Officer, Steve Morgan said, 'It appears what has happened is that our systems have aligned the COVID tiers with football tiers.

So, from tomorrow all the London clubs will be playing in Tier 3, the old third division, along with most clubs in the North West. Understandably, this has caused a lot of stress, but we believe it is a simple computer algorithm error that should be sorted out by May 20201.'

However, not all clubs are upset at the sudden change. For example, Plymouth in COVID Tier 1, now find themselves playing in the Premier League along with clubs from the Isle of Wight.

Man making a big ham

A man has realised that the time of year has arrived for the necessary roasting of a big ham joint, it has emerged.

Dave Jones from Dagenham said: 'At Christmas time big-ham-making falls under the man's purview. That and, erm, sawing the end of the tree off and carving some turkey while standing up.

'It is also a task that needs completing no less than ten days before Christmas day. That is because it needs to be available as a consistent meat presence throughout the Christmas period.

'So, I sourced the big ham. That is another more considered way of saying bought, apparently. Then there's the cooking. First, you soak the big ham in brine for a couple of days.

'Then you boil it for hours. Then you leave if for more hours. Then you rest it on a board. Basically, you put it on a board. Then you score it. That's cutting with a knife. Then you go with your preferred glaze. There's your honeys, your treacles or your marmalades.

'Then you roast it for, well, more hours. After that, you just leave it for a few minutes. Only kidding. More hours. So, you're looking at three to four days all in. Five tops. But is so worth the wait.

His wife commented: 'The important thing is it keeps Dave busy. I haven't the heart to tell him, no one likes it.'

Are you f*cking kidding?' thinks dog presented with gift-wrapped bone

The irritated canine said, 'I mean they can't even muster up the merest charade of mystery by putting it in you know, a box. No. Let's just wrap the bone up like a bone and put it next to the massive PlayStation 5 you bought for the ten-year old little prick that just gives you shit all of the time.

'F*ck you very much. Have I not been a dedicated family canine for nine years? Lick your rancid faces like a mad bastard? Check. Humour every mundane ball-throwing antic without fail? Check. Jump for joy when you land me with the utter bullshit moniker, 'Mister Bojangles?' Checkety check.

'I'm in the family portrait but sure gift me a three quid bone!'

Owner Claire Marshall said, 'Ah, you should have seen his little face. He's part of the family so he has to get a special little present. I mean, yes, it's just one of the bones he always has. But I've gift wrapped it. You know, for Christmas. As a special treat. Cute, right?'

'Raging. Absolutely raging. The return of sneaky dumps in your slippers is just the beginning, you mark my words' commented Mister Bojangles pacing backwards and forwards.

Parents urge Santa for official statement on 'crisis in global supply chains'

'We all know Santa can do anything,' said one concerned parent, 'as my mother constantly keeps telling little Eva on their weekly Zoom call. But perhaps, this year, Santa might like to dial it back a bit.

'I've suggested that if Amazon kept insisting that any new shipments will take 7-10 days, perhaps this year a lot more kids might find themselves on the Naughty List and that would be the end of it.

'I was even saying to Eva that lockdown has meant me and daddy and her have been together in the same small, in need of renovation, house for more hours than we've ever been used to, every single day! Many, many more hours. Perhaps there might be another thing Santa could raise,' she mused,

'Eva turns seven in January and you know sometimes really lucky little boys and girls get two sets of the very best birthday presents when mummy and daddy don't live in the same house any more...'

Cabinet terrified of getting Priti Patel in Secret Santa

The 350th Cabinet leak of the year has revealed that there is a £23 million budget overrun, outsourcing of gift purchasing has been riddled with cronyism, and world-beating sub-standard presents are not expected to be exchanged until June 2021.

Five Go Dobbing in the Neighbours

By far the scorchiest secret Santa hot potato being offloaded with blind panic at the moment, though, is which poor Cabinet sap drew the Priti Patel short straw.

Boris is an easy Secret Santa gift – a gimp mask, edible underwear, voucher for a zipwire experience or just a piece of paper with the names and birthdays of his children – he's easily pleased.

Matt Hancock is also easily pleased, he just wants to be liked and for the bigger boys to stop giving him wedgies. Any generic nonsense from Not On The High Street and he's sorted. Make it funny so he feels like one of the boys for a change.

But Priti? If she had a sense of humour you might opt for a police helmet and some furry handcuffs. Maybe 101 Dalmatian puppies and a scalpel? Although fair play to the civil servant that suggested we should just get her a 'heart.'

Transition from Trump to Biden finally accepted by satirists

As the Electoral College voted to confirm a Democrat victory, the world's satirists have finally accepted that Joe Biden will be the next president of the USA, and that their days of having Donald Trump practically spoon feed them jokes will soon be over.

'I've got a lovely Trump vs Star Wars parody nearly ready' said one mournful scribe, 'about this Darth Vader guy, who just wants to make the Empire great again.'

Confessed another caustic scribbler: 'We were spoiled by Trump. All we had to do was read his tweets, and then translate his utterances into something slightly closer to actual English, so that readers could almost understand them, and then 'tone them down' a notch or two so that they became almost credible as anything which the first citizen of a leading nation - or at least, anything which a more-or-less sentient being - could credibly have ever uttered.'

'Whereas, with Biden, satirists' greatest worry is likely to be the difficulty of staying awake until the end of any statement he makes.'

Others were happier. 'I've spent the last four years having my craziest, stupidest lines made to look dull by comparison with what Trump actually does' said satirist Anne Jones. 'Just last week he said that he's the best and most gracious loser in the world. What can you do? At least Biden offers no competition.'

'Definitely don't have a massive one,' insists Boris winking and nodding

Boris Johnson issued a stern warning to the public not to have a huge Christmas with extended family, but with serious winking and body language that kind of suggests you should all just crack on and smash it, it has emerged.

The PM was speaking at a Downing Street press conference when he said that people should have a 'smaller, safer Christmas' immediately followed by a fake cough and a muffled 'salty bollocks to that' thrown in.

As the Chief Medical adviser, warned of greater hospital admissions, Johnson appeared to go crossed eyed while making a circular motion with his right index finger pointing at his temple, before whispering, 'cuckoo!'

When asked by a reporter if he was feeling alright, Johnson commented, 'Yes, of course. I just wanted to show my wholehearted support. Although I didn't catch all of it so I may have missed the gist. Classic science bantz, I suspect.

'Oh come on. Its Christmas. A few slurps of the old rum punch and then all bets are off. Am, I right or am I right? You clearly like a drink. Now, what have we here. A bit of mistletoe caught in my zip. Well now!'

Nativity Inns move to Tier 4

Due to lockdown restrictions, the Three Wise men have been forced to cancel their annual trip from the East. Speaking from their 18th floor flat in Syriac Road, Romford, the camel riding biblical anachronisms said it was the best news they'd had in months.

'To be fair, we've not had a great year so far', said Lenny, the youngest of the three. 'Despite our deep and outstanding wisdom, Des hasn't won on the horses for months, and Shane spends far too much time shit faced on coke. So not having to embark on a ruinously expensive, mythological quest to see a woman who claims she had a kid without having sex and having to listen to a howling brat, is fine by us.

Now we can have the same immersive experience online and turn off the volume if we need to.'

Parents devastated after toddler prefers Christmas presents to wrapping paper

'It was awful,' said Mum. 'You hear about things like this, but you never think it will happen to your own. I'd even bought a tripod for my I-Phone 12 Pro so we could film it for Tiktok. it would have been hilarious. It was good paper, too. From John Lewis.'

Dad told reporters, 'I was devastated. She just sat there cuddling her new Steiff teddy bear and casually tossed the wrapping to one side. And she was smiling! I scrunched the paper into a ball and rolled it to her but it's like she was obsessed!

'We've had problems with Fleur-Alora before, though. Like, that one breakfast time, when she refused to eat her garlic and hummus rugbrod. Her psychiatrist says it's normal behaviour but it just seems so wrong!'

PM lauds new COVID variant exports

'As you will see from today's news, several countries have now identified the arrival of NCV and I can assure you that many more nations will discover this seasonal gift from Britain over the coming days and weeks,' the PM said.

'Now, some may question the rationale behind such a strategy but, rather like the sacrifice of a prawn during the early stages of a langoustine and saumon fumé starter or, indeed, an unconventional Nimzo-Indian defence, the cost of transporting NCV worldwide will be more than offset by the resulting sales of our British vaccines, currently being developed and tested by close friends of the Cabinet. The profits from vaccine sales will dwarf expenditure and mark the UK's post-EU economy with a massive boost. As Caesar quipped, 'Veni, COVIDi, vacci.''

'Scrooge's redemptive arc a shameful leftist creation,' insists Rees-Mogg

Leader of the House of Commons and immaculately polished turd, Jacob Rees-Mogg claims Dickens' classic novella 'A Christmas Carol' has been sabotaged by the left as a political stunt, it has emerged.

Rees-Mogg said: 'There is nothing the Marxists won't do to re-write history and that includes meddling with classic literature. To suggest wealth-creator and all-round good egg, Ebenezer

Scrooge would be struck by frivolous benevolence in such a cavalier manner as the story's denouement is absurd.'

'Of course, one has every sympathy for Bob Cratchett's predicament. However, if it wasn't for Scrooge where would they be? Reliant on the welfare state. That's where. Ergo, if it were not for Scrooge, the Cratchetts would have been without any Christmas fayre. As my pater never had to say, a meagre meal is better than no meal.'

'I dare say Cratchett would have been able to provide a more substantial offering if he had applied some sensible financial planning as to whether he could have indeed afforded to have offspring, particularly diminutive Tim, in the first place'

'One has to take responsibility for one's actions is the morality lesson Dickens is trying to teach Cratchett. Therefore, the logical and original unmolested conclusion as I choose to understand it, has Ebenezer resisting his philanthropic urge and keeping his purse strings closed tightly to the bitter end.'

'Rewarding him with corporate tax breaks and lucrative tax-payer funded contracts by the Government for supplying services he has no expertise in, would be my only humble editorial suggestion for Mr Dickens.'

'Bob Cratchett is the one visited by various apparitions to remind him just how thankful he should be to have regular employment as opposed to a zero-hours contract.'

'A truly inspirational Christmas story.'

Brexit deal still allows children to fish in rock pools at the seaside

The UK Government has confirmed that the EU Trade Deal will allow children to fish using tiny nets on bamboo poles whilst on holiday at the seaside. However, there will be no limits on foreign children fishing our British rock pools using their industrial-style methods.

The agreement on Rock Pool Fishing (pages 748-771) means that British children on holiday in the EU can catch one crab or one dead starfish, up to three straggly bits of seaweed and up to six different types of shell. These will have to fit in a regular sized (600ml) bucket or one jam jar if the creatures are still living. Taking them home will be allowed, dependent on how bad they stink up Daddy's car.

Twelve months of Lockdown

On the twelfth month of Lockdown, Boris sent to me

Twelve sightings of Cummings

Eleven papers sniping

Ten procurements a-leaping

Nine nurses starving

Eight lies a-milking

Seven swabs a-swabbing

Six girlfriends a-laying

Five masks with strings

Five Go Dobbing in the Neighbours

Four sprawling Tiers

Three French blockades

Two rubber gloves, and

Brexit and its magic money tree.

Jammy bastard animals hibernating

The British people are seething with jealousy towards the three types of native animal which are about to avoid the horrors of the next four months by sleeping through the whole sh*tfest, the spawny little tossers. 85% of people surveyed by Ipsos MORI said that they wished they could stay comatose until April as well.

'We could actually leave it a little while longer,' said dormouse Adrian Corbett. 'Winters are becoming increasingly mild, after all. Then again, if we could, we'd sit out the two weeks of randomly letting off fireworks and the Poppy Outrage season you half-evolved apes put yourselves through. In fact, I can sleep for 183 days, if need be, so I may stretch this one out all the way to Eurovision and beyond.'

Caroline Plummer, a Worcestershire-based bat, agreed. 'The thought of flitting by windows with Christmas lights on well into January because some of you sad cases think it's going to cheer people up,' she said. 'So if you'll excuse me, I'm just off to hang myself upside-down in a tree. You're welcome to join me if you can't take it anymore.'

Raymond Berryman, a hedgehog from the outskirts of Dover, said that he didn't envy humans having to deal with imminent food and drug shortages during a pandemic because the Daily Mail told them it would be great. However, he admitted to mixed feelings on his own account.

'I'm quite fond of humans, at least the ones who feed me bread and milk in their gardens for some strange reason,' Berryman said. 'Much nicer than slugs. So, it does make me sad to see what they are doing to themselves right now and I'm ready to sleep through it all and hope things have improved by April.

'On the other hand, it sounds like it will be quite safe for me to walk straight across the M2 this winter with all those lorries stuck in a 25-mile tailback waiting for customs checks that can't happen because they didn't manage to recruit enough Romanians to come and do them. Seems a shame to miss it.'

Man placing the one present he wrapped under the tree like he's a superhero

He commented, 'I thought I'd go the extra mile this year because the missis has had such a tough one what with me pretending to work full-time at home while she home-schooled the kids and, well, also worked full-time at home.

'I decided to forego the usual go-to gift-wrapping service online option and instead treat her to the personal touch. By personal touch, I mean the stuff she was using until four in the morning wrapping the kids' stuff in.

'Well, it turned out there wasn't much of that left so it was a hybrid of two jagged strips of that and a cut-up page from my F1 monthly of Lewis Hamilton's nose and chin. I know, right?'

'She also ran out of Sellotape but luckily I had some trusty duct tape on hand. Technically the end result is more tape than paper so I better keep the Stanley knife close by.'

'And of course I've bought her favourite perfume. Eau de parfum. She loves that. Ah, you should have seen her face when I placed it under the tree. It made it all worth it.'

His wife, Sarah commented 'Eau de perfume, right? Yeah, he thinks it is a luxury brand of perfume. At least it came in a beautifully wrapped box and ribbon last year. Now it looks like something he's returning to Amazon.'

'Hands off girls. He's all mine. Tw*t.'

In other news...

Most Queen's Christmas message viewers thought they were watching The Crown

Large families will gather at Christmas to enjoy a substantial business meal

UK has stockpile of loose stable doors and untamed horses ready for Brexit

Hancock sheds tear of pride as COVID variant named after England

Trump to receive vaccine as hypodermic the length of barge pole developed

People missing out on Oxford vaccine to get Durham vaccine through clearing

Country celebrates as Tier 3 lockdown prevents Mrs Brown from seeing her boys.

McDonalds drive thru to offer COVID tests. Do you want a BCG with that?

MI6 and Soviet spy dies. Or does he...?

Queen's speech tops TV ratings but the DVD sales are disappointing

Starmer self-isolates after one of his aides tests positive for socialism

Government denies using outdated info after putting 'all of Wessex' in Tier 4

Pompey fans ecstatic at promotion to Tier 3

Boris' shorter smaller Christmas threatens thousands of maids a-milking jobs.

Buyer of Top Shop to return it in January.

Brexit talks go into extra time, then England lose on penalties.

Isolation tank industry in free fall.

New SE-England variant of COVID exactly the same, but 4 times more expensive

'Give someone you love covid-19 for Christmas.'.

Five Go Dobbing in the Neighbours

Covid outbreak in manger now stable

Shortage of frankincense and myrrh due to port delays.

147,273,000 arrested in US as Boston police seek 'man wearing baseball cap'

Brexit agreement negotiators reminded 'a dog's dinner is not just for Christmas'

British children's dismay as no shortage of Christmas sprouts apparent yet

Dyson misses out on business created by new vac scene

Fans sue FA claiming that watching footy has caused brain damage

Boris breaks tier 4 rules after meeting some of his children for the first time

Government. declines to cancel Christmas but urges people not to enjoy it

Hereford joins Cornwall, Shangri-La and other places which no-one's heard of, in Tier 1

South African COVID variant 'not as good as ours' claim British experts

That bloke who goes to work on skis when it snows furious he's been furloughed.

Johnson vows to level up whole country to Tier 4

Queen to spend 'quiet' Christmas at home with Philip and 50 servants

'No one could have predicted Christmas Day would fall on 25th December,' says PM

Santa makes grate escape

Herod sends 3 wise serial killers with gold, frankincense and myrrhder

January 2021

We are all fat at this point. If you thought Christmas was rubbish, try doing Auld Lang Syne while doing a COVID test. The schools reopened, just long enough for all the homework and infections to be handed in. Julian Assange was still under lock and key, while the CIA decided which was the most unsuspicious way to kill him.

And there was a new President of the United States according to some people...

2021 admitted to rehab under 'impossible' weight of expectation

'After the arsenado that was 2020, I could have galloped in as a putrid horse skeleton cobbled together from bat droppings, the Millennium Bug, the Black Death and still nailed it,' said 2021.

'But you lot are somehow expecting me to magic away your self-created apocalyptic levels of shit: COVID, Brexit, climate change, Matt Hancock, banana sourdough, the threat of a rescheduled Mrs Brown's Boys national theatre tour.

'All that, and keep Joe Biden's hologram running for another 365 days? It's too much for one simple annus doingonesbestus,' the nascent year sobbed piteously, while being led away for an emergency intravenous Valium cocktail with morphine chaser and Jeroboam of fizzy Night Nurse.

'1984 had it easy'

Twitter outrage as man tweets intelligent, cogent, coherent argument

The Twittersphere is in uproar following a tweet from @geoff451, real name Geoff Hartley, that has variously been described as 'a $%*@ing disgrace', 'Nazi!' and '%*!@ $%@*!' The tweet presented an intelligible, rational and reasoned argument, totally against accepted platform norms.

After a torrent of bile and abuse was hurled at Hartley, Twitter stepped in to assure users it does take this sort of well-constructed, abuse-free standpoint extremely seriously.

The microblogging portal said: 'Mr Hartley has apologised and has been warned as to his future conduct. We've suggested he launch a swear-laden, vitriolic attack on his accusers. Just so we can resume normal service. Now *&$&£ off.'

Wuhan market trader awarded knighthood ahead of Nigel Farage

Nigel Farage is said to be 'devastated' that he has been passed over for a peerage in favour of a Chinese market trader who has been credited with sparking the COVID-19 pandemic. 'It was a close call,' said a government spokesman. 'Both men have had a significant impact on Britain's future prosperity and way of life.

One was an unscrupulous trader with a foreign name while the other just sold bats in a market.'

Despite passing him over, Buckingham Palace still sent Farage a letter with the Queen's seal, just so somebody could take his photo while he read 'Tough luck, sucker!' Farage claims that the only reason he hasn't been knighted is because he supported Brexit, seemingly unaware that this makes as much sense as the ghost of Peter Sutcliffe demanding an OBE for services to lorry driving.

Man finds God through post-Christmas poo

'It was a mystical experience,' claimed Steve McClintock (37). 'I'm not normally a praying man, but after six big meals and no sh*t, I was begging to have my spirit and bowels moved.' Finally, his bottom did indeed move in mysterious ways, as it then unleashed 'hell on earth' or at least 38 compacted Brussel Sprouts.

'I'd ask the Lord to send a sign, something other than just my swollen belly and continuous flatulence. At first I noticed an aroma of incense but that may have been the Toilet Duck.'

The rapture lasted for several hours and Steve is convinced he blacked out at least once, having hit his forehead on the sink. He hallucinated throughout the ordeal, with visions of white feathers, floating orbs and one big brown monolith – sticking out of the toilet bowl.

He was then visited by three-wise men and a plumber to sort out the blockage. Asked if having found his faith, Steve would be changing his ways. 'No, if anything, it's just made room for my New Year's Day nosh up.'

Teachers 'Back to School' packs to include blindfold and last cigarette

In a bid to quell any lingering anxiety that teachers may have about returning to their workplaces, the Government is launching Operation Divine Wind, complete a COVID safety pack. 'First, a word about what they won't contain,' said the Education Secretary. 'PPE, for starters. And blackboard chalk goes all sticky in a gloved hand, so that's a non-starter.'

Instead, the packs will contain numerous useful equipment, including an emergency will-writing pamphlet, alongside a red biro to complete it with. There will also be a silk bandana; a small bottle of sake and ceremonial cup; an optional blindfold and a final cigarette for those who wish to avail themselves of it. However, matches are not included as the Health & Safety Executive would not permit it.

'The whole package is contained in a sturdy wooden box, which can also double as storage for your last effects before you hop on the jolly old school bus and head back to your classrooms, I've put the army in charge of logistics and I'm reliably informed that they've already identified, emptied and repurposed some refrigerated lorries in Oxford and therefore they'll be motoring these packs out to you before you can say 'coconut shy.''

Middle-age men reminisce about non-essential car journeys of yesteryear

Men at a certain stage in life are chewing-up vital family bandwidth by meeting on Zoom to recall a time before restrictions, relaying A-road anecdotes and retelling pointless sojourns in their beloved four-wheeled wombs.

Veteran free-driver, Charles Hurst, explains: 'No longer can we experience the singular pleasure of trying out a new slip road, taking a nine-mile detour because there are three-way lights on the usual route home, or driving to a neighbouring county and back, just to top-up the battery.'

Not all the experiences of free-driving are so idyllic. Martin Cheshunt recalls: 'I was once roundly scorned for taking the family to the seaside on a torrential day in February to wear-in new brake pads. But that wasn't quite as unfulfilling as choosing the scenic route to the hospital on a new satnav when my wife was in labour, thinking she'd be comforted by rural vistas.'

Charles sums-up their predicament: 'Lockdown is a prison sentence. We've been reduced to reminiscing about past experiences, instead of safely creating new ones. Obviously, we record our meetings, future generations need to understand the sheer delight in taking a four-hour drive to buy oil that the car only needed because you took a four-hour drive to buy oil.'

UK Mix'n'Match vaccine combined with Pick'n'Mix for greater variety

British patients will be given a cocktail of vaccines from AstraZeneca and Quality Street, followed with a packet of Liquorice Allsorts 12 weeks later.

Mixing and matching remedies will allow the UK to eradicate COVID and erectile disfunction at the same time. Asked if a spoon full of sugar really does help the medicine go down, a spokeswoman explained: 'Look, we've got a limited supply of vaccine but a warehouse full of strawberry laces, you do the maths!'

Christmas snacks and sweets to be finished before health kick starts

Across the nation, households are attempting to eat all the remaining unhealthy food that was bought for Christmas before embarking on a new healthy eating and exercise regime for 2021. Typically, breakfast now consists of Twiglets and Cheese Footballs, lunch comprises camembert and Toblerone, and evening meals involve Liquorice Allsorts, peanuts and coconut Quality Street, all served with out-of-date brandy butter.

Questions are now being asked about the wisdom of buying tubes of Pringles throughout November for the festive season, and banning everyone from opening them until Christmas Eve, as everyone is thoroughly fed up with them now, especially the sour cream and chive ones.

Not everything has to be eaten, however. It has already been decided that the unopened boxes of sugared almonds and liqueur chocolates can be put aside for donation to the local school fete or church raffle. And of course, no-one actually likes dates, but throwing them away is a traditional post-Christmas ritual, solemnly observed once everything else has been eaten.

Only then can the health kick begin, accompanied by protein bars and oat bakes in place of crisps and sweets. This is expected to last until at least the end of the week.

EU gone but the bloody Normans are still here

The fact that the Normans have been freeloading since 1066, seems to have been overlooked in Brexit negotiations; along with their feudalism and penchant for invading everyone.

As the chimes brought in the New Year, citizens were hoping that the Bayeux tapestry might mention Britain's fishery policy. Instead, we are left with a ruling class of ersatz Vikings, with down to earth names like 'Montgomery de Mandeville the Third' and the dream that Robin Hood will return, with a tariff-free customs market

Even to this day, admission to Oxford or Cambridge is 800% more likely if you have a Norman surname or if you own Sussex. As one descendant of Harold Godwinson said: 'That's one in the eye for Brexit.'

'The Walk', a pictorial odyssey, new craze to sweep social media

Families nationwide have collectively discovered the ability to Walk and are relentlessly documenting faux family idylls on social media at every f*cking opportunity.

Matriarchal figures are expressing their social dominance by ensuring all offspring are appropriately layered and beaming, whilst fathers are encouraged to 'wipe that look off their face' whilst posing for incessant pictorial records.

Many 'Walks' struggle to reach a mile, without incessant pauses to document features such as 'The Stile', 'A distant sheep' and 'Promise of rain?' By the third hour of 'The Walk' Matriarchs typically concede defeat in their mission to 'get everyone some fresh air.' Fortunately, by that stage they still haven't got further than a few hundred yards from the carpark, so a swift return home to Sofa, Phones and Fortnite, via McDonalds, can be rapidly achieved.

Boris offered job with COVID Marketing Board

It's a challenge which every ex-PM faces – how do you monetise your brand when you're kicked out of Downing Street? Tony Blair showed a rare flair for sarcasm by becoming a Middle East Peace Envoy, John Major teamed up with Edwina Currie to produce a sex guide and David Cameron charges up to £15k per night not to attend corporate events or make motivational speeches.

Now it is Mr Johnson's turn to seek another career, preferably before anybody gets to the end of the Brexit agreement and finds out we all have to wash a Frenchie's car every Thursday. It is widely thought that Boris entered into a symbiotic relationship with COVID, when it infected him, thus becoming Half Man, Half Virus, All Idiot.

The COVID Marketing Board have been 'very impressed' with his work so far, and he is understood to be a shoo-in for a non-exec role when the time comes. Boris has excelled in virus propagation, encouraging children to attend school, refusing to quarantine incomers from foreign parts, inventing completely new vaccination protocols and diverting the PPE budget to a bunch of shell companies owned by Biffo and Squidger from Eton.

We can only hope he leaves behind enough of a country for his successor to govern.

COVID Guidance: You know what? Do what you f*@king like

In the wake of surging cases, the Prime Minister has also replaced the existing 'Hands - Face - Space' slogan with 'Catch it and die for all I care - Don't come crying to me.'

A spokeswoman explained: 'We have tried throughout this pandemic to strike a balance between keeping people safe, protecting the NHS, and not imposing too onerous restrictions on our way of life. Alas, half of you have ignored any rules we have put in place, and the other half have criticised whatever we have done.

'If we didn't act, then we should have done. If we imposed restrictions, they were either too strict or too late. We tried to keep the pubs open. We really did. We tried to let you have Christmas together, despite the fact that it was clearly not a sensible thing to do. All we wanted was for you to like us. And all you do is complain or take the piss, so bollocks to the lot of you. We'll be fine anyway, the PM's already had it. If the rest of you catch it and die, then that's your own fault now.'

Following the announcement the Prime Minister took questions from the press, who asked 'If you were going to tell people to do whatever they wanted to then don't you think you should have made this announcement yesterday?', at which point Boris burst into tears and left the room.

Johnson and Starmer announce much anticipated engagement

Wedding bells and cash registers are set to ring out, as the Prime Minister and The Leader of the Opposition look set to seal the knot and tighten the noose. They have finally decided to be joined in holy matrimony and mutual hatred of the Unions; while they are already joined together by exactly the same policies and the same levels of ineptitude.

The Johnson family said: 'Boris may have played the field in his day, but only Keir has screwed the entire Labour membership.' Relatives of Starmer confirmed: 'We are so lucky to welcome a Tory into the family and it's great to have Boris join us as well

Their top priorities are 1) an unwavering loyalty to Rupert Murdoch and 2) see 1). In fact, they have so much in common – be it their success in the fight against male pattern baldness or that they both think Blacks Lives Matter was just for Christmas. Asked if they had already consummated the marriage, a spokeswoman confirmed that Keir had been letting Boris have his wicked way for months.

Mainstream comedian doubling down on 'everything is fine' narrative

Delivering an 'edgy' routine celebrating the integrity of the press, one comedian was disheartened to be accused of 'selling out.' Speaking from his Grade 1-listed, Georgian mansion, the unnamed entertainer insisted he was still in touch with the common man - particularly the one who was busy installing his new wine cellar.

If anything, he complained, good comedic material was hard to come by these days: 'Trump's gone, which means there's no more injustice in the world. You know, I had this great gag about Trump being orange and talking funny – it was really satirical – but now all our politicians are completely competent and beyond reproach.'

Having secured a six-figure contract with the BBC, he did not feel the need to do routines about wealth inequality or institutional bias. He insisted, that in an era of pandemics, it is reassuring to know that we have nothing to complain about and even if we did, there's always Mrs Brown's Boys to take your mind off it.

He reasserted that he had not sold out, as all three of his Rolls-Royces were paid off in full: 'I will always speak truth to power. People who are gluten intolerant need to have their struggle told. Oops, sorry, that's Truth to Flour.'

Fat people 'slowing down earth's rotation'

Observers are watching in horror as satellite footage shows Earth slowing down to the sound of munching, burping gluttons. Shocked scientists have confirmed that last Wednesday was 32 hours long, while 2021 is set to last until March 2022.

As a last resort, the rest of the solar system will be asked to 'share the burden' and take in a few million of the world's fattest people as 'gastronomic migrants.' A secret list of these 'pastronauts' is already being drawn up.

A McDonalds spokeswoman countered: 'If anything is slowing down the planet, it's all those cows waiting to be eaten. Remember, our branches are now open 32 hours a day.'

Woman admits not using wishbone win to wish for a better 2021 for the world

'I said 'not telling' at the time but over a week later it's become glaringly obvious that my wish wasn't for the end of division in the world and the immediate cessation of the Coronavirus', revealed Jane, 33.

When asked what she did wish for, Jane was still too ashamed to say, but that the Gary Barlow 2021 tour was still currently going ahead as planned did offer a small clue.

Head of Track & Trace spotted in Cannes with Lord Lucan and Shergar

Sightings continue to come in of elusive executive Dido 'Goldfinger' Harding. The latest reports come from the south of France, though she has also reportedly been sighted in the Caribbean, in an underground lair, a hollowed-out volcano and on a moon base. She has not been recently spotted anywhere near Government or a sense of accountability.

The best hope we now have of seeing her again is if she develops the illness herself, when there is at least a 2% chance that her own app will locate her. Failing that we may need to wait for the £12 billion, she was given, to run out and trap her with a giant bag of gold and a concealed net.

Julian Assange put in a mysterious 'Tier 6' lockdown

Despite avoiding extradition to the US, Mr Assange has been denied bail on the grounds that he has not been tortured enough. Instead, he will experience a level of COVID lockdown normally reserved for Bellatrix Lestrange and the Count of Monte Cristo.

He had already been held in captivity since 2019 with no charges pending, awaiting Belmarsh Prison finding a way to freeze him in carbon. The British Government insisted that Mr Assange was part of a clinically vulnerable group, specifically because the CIA plans to assassinate him.

Said a UK lawyer: 'Lockdown rules are very simple; if you embarrass the US, you are in a bubble of one for the next 20 to 30 years.' Given the rampant levels of COVID in UK Prisons and Mr Assange's dwindling health, there is a concern that he would be safer outside of prison; to which one guard replied bleakly: 'Well, that's the point.'

Biden promises to bring in an exorcist on his first day in the White House

Joe Biden, President-elect and the oldest known relic in America, says he refuses to be controlled by the Trump legacy after analysts calculate the risk of demonic possession at over 85%.

An aide explained: 'There is a clear and present danger of a satanic and evil spirit controlling the Democratic party – remember the Clintons? We're bringing in a Catholic priest, burning all the Make America Great Again Ouija boards and locking all the windows. We'll also keep an eye out for tell-tale signs of Trump - such as urinating on the floor, injecting bleach and speaking in tongues on Fox News.'

Rioters storm US Capitol to find someone who can count

Frustrated Trump voters suffering from dyscalculia attacked Congress, clamouring to know why Joe Biden's 306 electoral votes were a larger number than 232. They demanded answers to complex questions of democracy; such as why does 1 plus 1 equal 2 and who gave all the slaves the vote?

Shots were fired and there were fatalities, after some Trump supporters found an abacus and burnt it as a Witch. Others were left wandering the Capitol halls dazed and confused, as they could not understand the numbers on the doors.

President Trump appealed for calm by hurling a Molotov cocktail through a window. Commented one rioter: 'I can count up to 11 on my toes but those big numbers make my head hurt. All I know is that my vote counts as twice as much as anyone else. And if you add up all the votes cast and divide by the number of bullets fired, you get American democracy.'

US politicians pleased to see populace taking such an interest in legislative process

American lawmakers were reportedly 'touched and thrilled' on Tuesday evening by a sudden surge of interest in their governance of the USA, praising the 'public spirit' of the shirtless thugs dressed as Vikings and brandishing MAGA flags.

'I've never seen ordinary Americans so keen to observe democracy at work,' reflected a Democratic congresswoman, from underneath her desk. 'It's really heartening to witness this show of support for our political institutions. Although I'm not quite sure just what it is exactly I'm witnessing; the tear gas is so thick.'

'These are great signs for the health of our historic nation,' argued a Kentucky senator, ducking his head and desperately sprinting for the exit as shattered glass rained down on the elected representatives. 'The spectators' gallery is full for the first time in my career, presumably because you get the best aim from up there.'

Opined one jingoistic lunatic, dangling from atop the statue of Abraham Lincoln's stovepipe hat, 'This level of engagement with politics hasn't been seen in our great nation since the glorious days of the Civil War. The Confederacy – I mean, the Founding Fathers – would be so proud.'

'I weep for democracy in America,' says Kim Jong-un

The supreme leader of North Korea has announced he is distraught at the scenes of chaos which spilled out on the streets of Washington last night. 'Maybe one day the US will learn to be as civilised as his own country,' he noted. 'I do hope my dear friend Donald Trump, you know the fat bloke with the stupid hair, doesn't feel too embarrassed at the disgraceful scenes that took place on his watch.'

Donald Trump's Avengers assemble to fight Democrobots

As one of his final acts in office, President Trump has assembled his very own team of Avengers to save the corporate world from Biden Democrobots. Led by '9-Iron Man', Donald Trump's Avengers are committed saving the one percent.

'Right now, they're on a secret mission in Uran, confiscating enriched Iranium. Sadly, The Proud Boys are no longer one of my Avengers since they became Pride Boy. Shame.'

Woman who decorated room, pretty sure room decorated her

Having successfully redecorated her lounge, Ayesha Gul (32) is now convinced that she is wearing most of the materials used and the majority of a pot of paint. Prior to her project Ayesha had what could be only described as lustrous, shoulder-length cinnamon-shaded hair, but now her primary colour is magnolia.

Plaster that should have filled unsightly holes, is now sticking one of her eyelids together and blocking one nostril. The wallpaper she had fastidiously stripped, has fused to the bottom of her feet, creating flock patterned sandals.

Despite employing dust sheets, masking tape and all the karma she could muster, the whole project spiralled into a sketch from Laurel & Hardy. Even though the room looks good, Ayesha looks like she is wearing all of B&Q simultaneously.

Patronising male friends have asked her why she did not get her boyfriend to help, to which Ayesha replied: 'I did. In fact, he started it. But he's been missing since day three. I think he might be part of the Artex.'

Football club cafe loses Michelin star

The small kitchenette at the back of the changing rooms at Dunkley FC has been unceremoniously stripped of the prestigious Michelin Star it was awarded last year.

The head chef and frier explained: 'On matchdays we offered an 'Infusion of sundried Sri Lankan Camellia Sinensis tips', accompanied by two 'Delicately scorched staff of life tiles adorned with the finest sweet cream Cumbrian butter.' Tea and toast, basically.'

A representative from Michelin reflected: 'We understand that errors in selection criteria may have been overlooked. For example: 'A reconstructed deconstruction of a full-English', is simply a full-English. Also, because the club's nickname was changed to 'The Baconnoisseurs' does not denote that the players are experts in porcine cuisine.

'And to rub Himalayan pink salt in the wound: when I asked for the framed Michelin certificate to be removed from a shelf, the proprietor immediately filled the space with two cans of 'Vimteau', written on with a Sharpie. Vile! Simply vile!'

Clap for Carers hits second wave

The Government has finally agreed that it has royally screwed up the pandemic response as 'clap for Carers' comes back for season two.

It's expected that the uptick in people suffering hypothermia every Thursday evening at eight o'clock will put emergency services under unprecedented pressure. An NHS spokesperson confirmed that the operational staff welcomed the public support but noted it was at the bottom of a very long wish list that already included more staff, sleep and shafting of the Health Secretary.

Economy boost as schoolteacher exam prediction bribes kick through

As Lockdown aftershocks continue to ripple, including the news of summer exam cancellations, the national economy has had a surprise boost from the inclusion of extortionate bribes being thrust at the teaching profession to encourage them to 'get their predicted grades right.'

One teacher said the net gain from parents in his Year 11 Technical Marquetry set at Parkside Secondary Modern, Bridgwater was already equivalent to a year's salary. 'I've damn near worn out the asterisk key on my laptop, the number of A stars I've been banging out.'

Maths and English top grades typically attract the highest premiums, with a street value in the high thousands, but Science and Humanities teachers can still attract substantial payments for higher marks whilst music teachers have been known to peddle a Grade Nine Oboe for a grand, or a monkey for Grade Five Recorder, no questions asked.

The only school staff not revelling in the predicted grade windfalls are the Games teachers, explained our source: 'Whichever way you dress it up, a PE GCSE is still worth f*@k all to anyone.'

Rees-Mogg to compete in 2021 Tour de France on Penny Farthing

Speaking to reporters the North Somerset MP said: 'I wish to highlight the undoubted excellence and endurance of our most marvellous British industry. Th'Penny Farthing is a timeless classic, and it is my intention not only to compete seriously, no, indeed not. Be in no doubt whatsoever, it is my unswerving expectation to emerge victorious at the conclusion of the race.'

On hearing the news, a four-time Tour winner commented: 'F*ck me sideways with a bicycle pump. The guy's a nut-job.'

Nevertheless, and undeterred by Froome's comments Mr Rees-Mogg announced he will further confound expectations, by rather than wearing body-hugging Lycra and a lightweight crash helmet, he will don a herringbone three-piece tweed suit, frock coat and silk top hat.

'A gentleman must comport himself properly at all times. And this includes the correct form of dress for the occasion. And notwithstanding that, last time I tried cycling in Lycra it chaff'd my testicles most grievously.'

Home Secretary asks police to enforce New Year's resolutions

The Home Office, no longer constrained by EU law or common sense, has promised to provide police forces with extra powers to target resolution breakers. Under these new powers, officers will be able to detain without charge anyone they suspect of joining a gym but not actually going to it. In addition, they will be able to stop and search anyone they think has been having a sly drink during Dry January.

'If the police are unable to enforce New Year resolutions, the Government may need to repurpose existing holidays to compensate. In a few months, we could all be doing a Pancake Tuesday Life Audit or writing a May Day Bank Holiday Bucket List.'

'No more fitness videos,' pleads weary nation

The initial nostalgic familiarity associated with the resumption of daily PE lessons-slash-soft porn videos, was swiftly replaced by the ambivalent resignation of a nation. Already coping with the annual post-Christmas feeling of being repeatedly punched in the face, now facing the thirteenth lockdown as an added kick in the bollocks, no one wants to see slo-mo flowing locks and abs that won't quit.

Topping up her shredded wheat from a bottle of Smirnoff, one parent sighed, 'I still have the faint smell of pigs-in-blankets on my breath and I've only just realised that it's f*cking January. My seven-year-old is demanding a selection box chocolate for breakfast and just said 'yeah, good luck with that' when I suggested we practice some spelling.'

'But sure. let's do thirty minutes of star jumps.'

New Bowie film totally fails to capture his passion for admin, complains family

New biopic 'Stardust', which chronicles David Bowie's first forays into drugs, cross-dressing, and sexual experimentation, is a dull pastiche which does not reflect the Bri-Nylon safari suit-wearing, Fray Bentos-favouring, pipe-smoking maverick he truly was, his family claims.

'Time and again, he was the first to smash social norms, which the film completely overlooks,' explained a spokesperson. 'Remember, David, or 'Jones the Rotarian', as he preferred, introduced the zip-up fleece to Bromley, remains the only person to earn gold loyalty passes to Keswick Pencil Museum and Southport Lawnmower World, and to the very end, refused to come down on one side or the other in the 'milk or tea in the cup first?' debate. Madness! Genius!'

The row means no original Bowie music can be used in the film, leading to complaints from preview audiences expecting to tap along to hits such as 'Let's Just Sit This One Out', 'Neasden Junction to Waterloo East Terminus', 'Life in Bath', and 'Parking Space Anomaly', recorded during the period Bowie legally changed his name to 'Chewy Starburst', in an impassioned protest against the rebranding of Opal Fruits.

Fans are being urged to boycott the new release, and instead enjoy Bowie's back catalogue of avant-garde films, including 'The Man who Tripped Over Slightly on the Pavement', 'Happy Fourth Sunday After Pentecost, Vicar', and 'Labrador', in which he famously sported a mullet based on his own beloved retriever, the skinny pale Duke.

So far there has been no direct comment from Bowie's son, who during his father's life felt crippled by the showbiz expectations of his unconventional moniker, 'Duncan', and now makes corporate training videos for the automotive components industry under the soberly corporate 'Wowzie Zowbagger.'

Anti-democracy campaigners now storm EU parliament

Shocking and iconic scenes of a bare-chested and heavily tattooed Gina Miller, her face painted with blue and gold stars, bedecked with a horned buffalo headdress and screaming at the skies for vengeance and justice, have captured front pages across the world.

A mob of pro-EU supporters started a frenzied chant of 'Ode to Joy', as well as slogans like 'Take Our Fish' and 'Make Passports Maroon Again.' Armed police pointed out that the BBC had a really good panel discussion on what the European Courts of Justice have done for us all, that was starting soon, and if they got a wriggle on, they would be home in time to catch it, and with that, the crowd rapidly dispersed.

Trump plans to pardon himself for all the crimes he didn't commit

Speaking from a podium in front of the smoking wreckage of Congress, the outgoing President declared, 'I hereby pardon Donald J. Trump – that's me – for every crime that I haven't done. All of them. So many. Even the ones no one knows I was involved in, like the thing with Prince Andrew in the Oval Office. This was a frame-up, believe me, and that's why I need to legally absolve myself, before I'm found not guilty.'

Donning a pair of spectacles and reading from a checklist, Trump reeled off all the illegal activities he never did but people say he did but he didn't, no way: 'I'm not going to jail for tax evasion; I'm not a lightweight like Al Capone. Paying off porn stars? Fake news. Urinating on prostitutes? Boasting about grabbing women? Show me the tapes! Actually, better not.

'This is the biggest hoax of all time, the biggest. It's so big. The biggest since the last biggest hoax that I was obsessed with last week. I think that was the fake election fake result, or was it the Kung Flu, or global warming? Maybe Russia, Russia, Russia? So many hoaxes. Sad.

'I'm actually the most law-abiding President of all time. I love behaving within the terms of our great nation's constitution so much, possibly more than anyone,' boasted POTUS. 'Ask Rudy Giuliani, when he doesn't have his hand down his pants. Just beautiful. Or my literally hundreds of former lawyers – some of whom are in jail – whose services I've never required because I'm never taken to court.'

Commented one legal observer, 'The people are revolting, and so is the President.'

Police numbers to be doubled for inauguration – to 14

Security around the inauguration of President-elect Joe Biden is to be significantly tightened, a DC Police spokesman explained: 'We expect a large number of Trump supporters to return to Washington on 20th January heavily armed with automatic weapons, knives and pipe bombs and in response our guys will be equipped with batons, pepper spray and badges saying 'Please Exit Through the Gift Shop.'

'Unfortunately, that's as many officers we'll have available on the day. Black Lives Matter are holding a coffee morning 2 blocks over, so we'll have to have 2000 officers in full riot gear in attendance in case anyone drops any litter.'

Vaccine: first 50 million doses go to PM's family and friends

'You know that film where a comet's about to strike the Earth and all the top scientists and artists are kept safe in a secret bunker, along with art and books and some decent wines? Well, it's like that. My father wouldn't broadcast this but he's actually a first-rate philosopher. As for my children, well, they're all scientists in the making. Various fillies have been vaccinated in accordance with the Top Totty protocols, this is all above board.

'Think of the virus as a comet plunging through our atmosphere on a collision course with our civilisation. Actually, no, don't think that. Think of it as your friend, helping old people to finally lay their heads down and rest. That's it! The virus is the old people's friend, my girlfriends and family are national treasures and we're following the science. Now you'll have to excuse me but I'm expecting a delivery of looted art.'

Schools to reopen to teach people what 2 metres looks like

The curriculum will include:

- Measuring two metres and estimating it in supermarket trolley lengths. Clue – it's longer than the trolley.

- Multiplying by two, or 'doubling' as it is also called. Sample question: if 1,000 people have the virus and the number doubles every week, how many people will die from it if you delay doing anything about it for 3 weeks?

- Facial anatomy, or where your nose and mouth are and how to cover them.
- The difference between indoors and outdoors, and why the latter is better ventilated. Practical sessions will introduce the concept of 'walls', and illustrate the difference they make to air flow using a giant fan and a bucket of mucus.

- The germ theory of disease, and why COVID-19 is not spread by 5G, the illuminati, witchcraft or malodorous vapours. The latter just means you've eaten too much leftover turkey.

'Tiny Hands' Trump welcomed back to MySpace

With the current leader of the free world indefinitely banned from the social media platform Twitter, Donald Trump has been forced to resurrect his 2006 MySpace account to maintain a platform for his philosophical ramblings.

Luckily the President was able to remember both his username (GoldenReign1946) and his password (HillaryFor2008), which were written in green crayon, on the back of his soon to be ex-wife's, US Citizenship papers.

President Trump was said to be overjoyed at being reunited with his 854 MySpace friends, who mostly consist of members of the National Rifle Association in Roberts County, Texas and the Survivors of Equine Head Injuries clinic in Northampton County, Pennsylvania.

And it wasn't long before the about-to-be-arrested President, whipped out his trusty Sony Ericsson K800 and was reading all the latest news on 'High School Musical', before writing his first blog post on how he let Daniel Craig take the role of James Bond.

'Great to have you back, Tiny Hands', commented follower BillyFiveWivesTwoAreMyCousins1962 and was typical of the welcome received from fellow patrons, many of whom have webbed feet and six fingers.

500,000 UK nurses confirm COVID is all made up

Half a million UK nurses have spoken out in unison to confirm there is no such thing as COVID and that all of this is an epic hoax. In what is being described as a total shock and utterly outrageous by sheeple, the medical profession has come clean and owned up to a global conspiracy.

'Nursing is easy and well paid, and we just got bored,' said Nurse Judy Bowler from Leighton Hospital in Crewe. 'So, we started gossiping in quiet ward corners about livening things up a bit. It started with just a few hundred of us last November, and by December other nurses were joining in all over the place.

'Then we heard that some nurses in a place called Wuhan in China were getting innovative, and they pushed the whole thing to the next level. Without them, this might not have gone global. They really must have needed a giggle.'

'It's a shame the whole prank is coming to an end, because we have had a right laugh on these empty wards. Wild alcohol and drugs-cabinet-fuelled striptease parties, bed racing, and my favourite, frozen cadaver skittles. We really know which pills to pop to make the high last all week. Oh, well, back to unnecessarily sticking our fingers up old peoples' bottoms it is...'

Biden announces big plans for new White House curtains

In a solemn statement tonight, President-Elect Biden, has announced major new plans to change America, starting with the curtains – despite Trump supporters demanding to 'Make America Drape Again.'

'The past four years are the worst ever experienced by the USA for flowery patterns,' insisted a Biden spokeswoman. 'Instead, we'll have traditional Democratic silver hold-backs, as opposed Trump's gold-embellished inferior interiors.'

'It will be curtains for Trump, as all his previous drapes will be made a yellow-orange – effectively 'in peached', if you get my drift.'

Mum told her cake almost as good as 'shop bought' not feeling the compliment

A familial moment of solidarity has descended into chaos, after the faint praise for a Three-Layer Berry Victoria Sponge, was seen as a slap in the face for the baker of said item. Mum has stated, in no uncertain terms, that she feels aggrieved that four hours of baking was greeted by mumbles of 'it's okay, I suppose', 'alright' and 'not bad.'

The icing on the cake, no pun intended, was one member of the family likening it to being almost as delicious as a Mr Kipling Angel Slice. Apparently baking something with love, is no substitute for additives and artificial colourings.

Dad replied, from the comfort of his armchair: 'We kept our side of the bargain, we watched Mum spend hours cooking the cake, we ate the cake and then we said it was nice. What more were we supposed to do? Validate her feelings? It's just cake. Now, what's for dinner?'

A frustrated Mum said: 'It was nice. Nice? Honestly, why do I bother?' To which the family shrugged and said 'Dunno'. Concluded Mum: 'This family was almost as good as a real one.'

Oedipus left traumatised after TV appearance

The Greek tragedy celebrity is recovering from having his bizarre sex life examined and dissected by the country's unemployed after he appeared on the popular talk show.

The show saw the most nail-biting wait for DNA results in the its history, after which Oedipus had to be protected from being lynched by a tattooed and salivating audience when the test revealed his wife was also his mother.

The badly shaken guest lamely tried to explain that things were different in Ancient Greece, only to be cut short by the TV host: 'What about Prince Philip? He's Greek and he's lived to be 99 without ever killing or shagging either of his parents. You're a disgrace, mate.'

Meanwhile, debate is raging on Mumsnet about what to do if your son kills his father and then sleeps with you. Oedipus is understood to have ripped his own eyes out as soon as he got home, so that he'd never have to 'watch daytime TV again.'

Woman not buying 'Grammarly' no matter how many times its advert pops up

Aanya Laghari, 36, is resolutely fighting against the collapse of civilization and chirpy reminders that her life would be transformed if only she could spell better. The invasive nature of adverts for 'Grammarly' means that Aanya is now spending 27% of her day frantically clicking skip advert, while some hipster millennial – with perfect teeth - tells her to use more apostrophes.

In a world where nobody tucks their shirt in or wears a tie, Grammarly boasts that you too can work in a tech-start up, with breeze blocks for furniture. Every job application will be greeted by success because you now know what a fronted adverbial is – and the global pandemic and recession are just by-products of pronoun disagreements.

In its adverts, every working environment has the kind of diversity you only see in focus group or a packet of fruit loops. Growled Aanya: 'The, oh so amusing, irony of 'Grammarly' using a made-up word to describe itself is so f*cking adorable I could scream!'

Popping up more regularly than herpes, Grammarly is redefining the word annoying and probably spelling it differently at the same time. Said Aanya: 'Spell this, suck my $%£^^*&^^^& and my big hairy $^&$%$$^**^%$%$%^&^*(*)!!!'

Kids food packs include £5 of ingredients and a £25 haute cuisine recipe book

The Government have rushed to clear up 'confusion' regarding the contents of the £30 food packs for starving children that are being provided by Chartwells, who won through a competitive tendering process by coming up first alphabetically in their black book of favours.

'We do appreciate, at first sight, some of the food items may seem a little underwhelming. However, a nubbin of carrot, some fragments of turnip, perhaps a few limpets, half a pig's trotter and some venerable sprouts can be utterly transformed into a culinary triumph using some of these recipes in 'The Gourmand's Banquet' by chef de partie Tarquin Pottington-Smythe.

'Seriously, once you've tasted his divine roasted limpets with sprout velouté and carrot emulsion, there's no way you'd go back to beefburgers and spaghetti hoops. We're doing the palate of these starving kids a real favour.

After all, give a child a bag of frozen chips and some turkey twizzlers and they shall eat for a lunchtime, but give them a solid grounding in haute cuisine and they shall marinate, sous-vide and fricasse for a life-time.'

Government to outline 'zero f*cks' policy

True to form, the British Government has announced a roll out of apathy and incompetence throughout the land. By the end of March, they expect to have achieved 100% inoculation against actually caring, about what the hell is going on.

A Minister explained: 'Rather than get bogged down in the nitty gritty of tackling COVID or economic disasters, we've opted to be unconcerned, to the point of apathy. In words of Rhett Butler: 'Frankly my dear, I just don't give a f*ck.''

The official policy will be to be sorry but not sorry, which has been endorsed by Keir Starmer and which is everyone else's fault, but his. Boris Johnson will address the nation and tell them to get over themselves, followed by a yawn.

The ONS has calculated that the number of f*cks in circulation is less than one. To which one, unfazed, Health Official remarked: 'Whatevs.'

Tests show new 'Boris Jab' 100% effective

The already acute pressure on the NHS looks set to intensify, after early test results on a vaccine with the ability to blot out Boris Johnson's shambolic, vacillating and rambling pronouncements has shown to be 100% effective.

Professor Arnold Lane said: 'Development work has been going on behind the scenes since December 2019. Once treated with BorisGone21 our minds will automatically 'zone out' every time Mr Johnson turns up on TV and radio, or if he appears in our daily newspapers.

'Imagine the comfort this will bring to the nation. We will not be able to hear or even recognise a word he says, let alone try to have to make sense of it. Instead, our conscious minds will register only calming music and an embedded video of a cat playing with a ball of string.'

Sprightly pensioner Bert Walsingham (89), who fought in WW2 said: 'I was called by my GP to come here to get a COVID injection, but when I heard about this new one, I just thought, f*ck COVID. Give that to some poor bastard who really needs it.'

Bat shit 'actually not that crazy'

Biologists and naturalists have responded to the repeated comparisons of people and political movements acting in irrational ways to bat shit, arguing that this grossly misrepresents a valuable commodity.

'Strictly speaking, insanity requires consciousness, even if only at the level of believing that you aren't allowed to say anything racist these days, while simultaneously using a technology platform to do exactly that,' said Gerald Bagnall, Emeritus Professor the Bleedin' Obvious at the University of Somewhere or Other.

'And even if we let that one pass, the fact is that bat guano is an immensely important resource. Entire cave ecosystems could not exist without generations of bats risking their dignity by hanging upside-down and evacuating their nutrient-rich torpedoes onto the floor.'

'Furthermore, bat guano was integral to the development of modern intensive farming. Whole colonies were founded, whole fortunes were made to seek out nitrogen-, phosphate- and potassium-rich deposits to use as fertiliser. It's much more significant than a passing four years of having an angry gibbon in the White House.'

Nigel Walker, a bat, said: 'That was interesting. I didn't know any of that because I'm a bat … whoops, there goes another one. Crazy stuff! Hey did you see what I did there?'

British Seafood would rather rot than be digested in a European stomach

As the bureaucratic red tape relating to the UK's exit from the European Single Market settles down, a Brexit supporting packet of smoked haddock was said to be ecstatic that instead of being consumed and digested by a European, they will instead be left to decay inside a shipping container at Grangemouth Docks.

'This is exactly what I voted for', the vacuumed packed Piscean comestible cried, 'A British fish, killed by British Fisherman, rotting in a British Dock. '

The packet of smoked haddock wasn't alone as 14 tonnes of langoustine, caught that very morning off the West Coast of Islay were said to be overjoyed, that after their slow suffocation inside a plastic crate covered in a J-Cloth, their rotting carcases will be thrown back into the ocean.

'At least I'll get a decent burial at sea', an 12cm crayfish managed to gasp, 'My worst nightmare is to end up in some Flemish gastric juices of a tailor from Bruges.'

'Fact-shaming' to be criminalised

Fact-shaming – the act of embarrassing people by telling the truth or providing evidence that they are lying – is to be made illegal under new legislation.

'This isn't censorship', said the PM. 'It's about liberty. We're freeing our people up to use language creatively, to employ those colourful metaphors and figures of speech which make English such a joy to behold. Fact-shaming is cruel, hurtful and reduces self-esteem. Sometimes I'm so stung by the so-called fact-checkers that my ego shrinks to the size of a galaxy.'

A new Ministry of Truth will be established to manage the regulations. The Freedom of Information Act will be renamed the Freedom to Withhold Information Act. Exceptions will be made for criminal trials and Weight Watchers meetings, because fat-shaming remains legal.

Homeopathists, politicians and Rupert Murdoch welcomed the news.

Starmer to replace Punch & Judy politics with Richard & Judy politics

Under the new system the election process would be replaced by a contract negotiation every four years. Labour would then be free to argue for basic human rights before capitulating and allowing the usual percentage of taxes to be sent to overseas bank accounts controlled by dodgy businessmen and corrupt politicians, or the Private Finance Initiative as it is known.

'We want to make politics interesting again', said Sir 'Keith' Starmer. 'MPs from all parties would get together for social evenings where they'd play parlour games like 'find a LibDem.' We could finally do some real soul-searching and try to locate the soul of the Labour Party.'

'I want to replace Punch and Judy politics with Richard and Judy politics, where we sit on a sofa and everybody's welcome. Except Marcus Rashford, obviously. Trouble-maker.'

'We'd rather take our chances in Kabul' plead Washington-bound US troops

Thousands of battle-hardened US troops being hastily pulled out of Afghanistan are reportedly 'crying like little girls' on learning of their immediate redeployment to the fib-strewn warzone of Capitol Hill, in readiness for the most underwhelming inauguration since Chuka Umunna, on a deadline from Kwik-e-Print, said 'Um, Change UK?'

'It's like looking into hell,' whimpered Colonel Will Slaybleed, staring whey-faced at CNN footage of overweight truckers wheezing up the steps like priapic toads roused to lumbering frenzy by a glimpse of Trump side-boob. 'Give me an ambush of IED-toting insurgents any day- I mean, these guys have flags! Is it too late to claim an allergy to oversized eagle belt-buckles? What if my mom writes a note?'

Private 'Speccy' O'Reilly, perched on his Chinook booster seat, remained naively chipper: 'We're goin' home, and I'm gonna marry that girl,' he sighed, gazing at a faded polaroid of nation's sweetheart and pro bono garden centre publicist, Trudy Giuliani.

Slaybleed sighed. 'He's toast. What the hell, bring it on; I love the smell of macrobiotic hemp-based napalm in the morning...'

Entire cabinet fails a New Year's Resolution to stop smirking

In order to demonstrate that they were totally serious about tackling the many issues facing the country, the cabinet voted to implement a smirking ban. Despite one or two cabinet members only having had the occasional smirk outside the office, in the designated smirking shelter, the majority are already back up to 20 smirks a day.

Home Secretary Priti Patel resolve lasted less than a day. An extremely heavy smirker, giving it up was always going to be a challenge for Ms Patel, especially as she used to work in the smirking industry.

Minister for the Cabinet Office Michael Gove did his best to set an example by not smirking in public, claiming that his sneering grin did not constitute a smirk. But soon the contents of a free school lunch, provided by Tory donor Chartwell, had them all concealing their smiles with a hacking noise – known as smirker's cough.

Boris Johnson is keen to give the New Year's Resolution another go. 'There's nothing difficult at all about giving up smirking', explained the Prime Minister. 'I usually give it up about twice a week.'

A Lockdown guide to worker status

- Language teachers - Qui workers

- Rock musicians - Quo workers

- Pound shop assistants - Quid workers

- Dockers - Quay workers

- Comedians - Quip workers

- Spanish Hotel Waiters- Que workers

- Acupuncturists - Chi workers

- Computer game designers - Wi workers

- Chester boatbuilders - Dee workers

- Nightclub door staff - Queue workers

- Curry restauranteurs - Ghee workers

- Golf professionals - Tee workers

- Scottish elves - Wee workers

Five Go Dobbing in the Neighbours

- Rollercoaster operators - Weeeeeeeeeeeeeeeeee.... workers

- Shit '70s pop stars - Kiki Dee workers

- French aristocrats - Flee workers

- Toilet attendants: Pee workers

- Apiarists: Bee workers

- Gender reassignment surgeons: He to she workers

- Dog groomers: Flea workers

- Scruffy, unhygienic staff: Manky workers

- Green keepers: Tee workers

- Distillery staffs: Whisky workers

- Staff who ignore elfinsafety or isolation rules: risky workers

- Swiss-born German expressionist artists: Klee workers

- Furniture removal - To me, to me workers

- Butlins red coats - Hokey Cokey workers

- Elderly care - Now where did I leave my key workers

- Timpsons - key workers

- Brexiteers: Me, me, me workers.

- Volcanologists - Scree workers

- Pedants - Apostrophe' workers

- Swordsmen - Epee workers

- Judges - Decree workers

- Tory Ministers – Key wankers

- Racist gamblers - Eenie meenie workers

- Native American building constructors - Tepee workers

- Male prostitutes - Hankie workers

Sir Philip Green and Mike Ashley tie the knot in secret wedding

Entrepreneurial giants, Green and Ashley, have rocked the world of high street retail by announcing a marital merger. The secret ceremony took place on board HMS Blowjob, a luxury yacht owned by vacuum tycoon James Dyson. The ceremony was presided over by an ordained KPMG accountant, while Sir Philip was given away by his father, as tax deductible.

A spectacular reception party followed at which friends enjoyed copious amounts of Champagne and foie gras. As Sir Philip and Mr Ashley have no friends, it is assumed Mr Ashley did most of the copious consuming. The QAnon shaman provided the mobile disco.

The happy couple have denied tying the knot for tax purposes, but questions have been raised about the private jet they received as a gift from a cleaner at a Sports Direct store in Croydon. A grateful former BHS employee furnished the nuptial pair with a lovely oven dish, some glass tumblers, and a small island off the coast of Belize.

CERN scientists detect moment when child's respect for Dad switches to contempt

It's one of nature's most closely guarded secrets: what is the precise moment when Dad goes from hero to zero? It is a complex equation, involving the date of your first 'World's Best Dad' mug, multiplied by the number of times that your child comments on your singing.

'It's like throwing a ball in the air' said Professor Jones of CERN. 'It starts off fast, slows down and keeps slowing – a child's love for their father is exactly like that ball – it starts with great hope and the next thing you know it's smacked you in the face.'

Scientists eventually solved the problem while accelerating a fat child to three quarters of the speed of light in the CERN tunnels beneath Geneva. 'This wasn't necessary', explained Professor Jones. 'We just thought the ungrateful bastard deserved it. Also, you should have seen the wobbly skin on his face – awesome. He threw up three times but because he was accelerating it ended up all over him.'

Hallmark cards have expressed interest in the equation and plan to launch a new range of sympathy cards to mark the occasion. Their 'Depressing Rites of Passage' range already includes 'Child's First Wank', 'Your Son is Taller Than You and Has the Postman's Eyes' and 'You've Started to Make that Noise When You Sit Down.'

Creators of viral posts 'just needed a hug'

'It was pretty sad, really,' said a sociologist. 'One we looked at was an actor who posted a picture of himself with a fake exemption lanyard and an anti-mask slogan. Lonely. Another was a post claiming to be from a scientist who said that COVID didn't exist. We tracked that one down to a barely-educated bloke in Birmingham whose girlfriend left him a year ago. Desperately lonely, and a bit smelly.'

Almost every example of social media gibberish was eventually traced back to a socially isolated person who would have been better off shutting his laptop down and visiting a friend.

'They get their validation from the size of the response, even if it's negative', explained Dr Jones. 'These are society's invisible men – without the shitstorm they can cause online they're nothing. Most were single, several were unemployed and/or unemployable.

'The sole exception was an orange American with a supermodel wife who has, until recently, held a very high-powered role. Remarkably, his social media outbursts stopped at the same time as he lost his job. I'm concerned that he might go on a serial killing spree to get the bile out of his system. That would be considered a normal outlet in America.'

Every road to be offered grit by September, confirms Government

A transport spokesman said: 'We plan to get back to the normal pre-pandemic levels of traffic congestion. We're targeting the nation's oldest and most vulnerable B-roads first, irrespective of whether they lead to a party donor's country estate, or not. That's the roadmap. And it's a roadmap full of squiggly lines that go everywhere.'

Despite the majority of grit being distributed during the summer months due to the DfT only acquiring gritting vehicles powered entirely by solar energy, the department's jubilation in treating more than 4 million millimetres of road in the UK with a first dose of grit is obvious. But, so too is the sense of abject failure, after the vehicle named 'Griti Patel' delivered 400,000 doses of grit but forgot where, using an EU Galileo GPS system to which Brexit Britain no longer has access to, so can't.

Bald hypnotist oddly confident he can make your hair grow back

Famed for writing self-help tomes with titles such as 'I can make you Thin', ...Rich' ...Sleep', this billiard-headed pundit seems undeterred that his own follicles are yet to resurface.

His publicist, an obese, unhappy, broke, narcoleptic, was unavailable for comment.

Trump pardons the A-Team

Donald Trump has issued a full pardon to all members of the A-Team, finally acknowledging that they had been wrongfully imprisoned for a crime they did NOT commit.

The outgoing President delivered a special address to the fugitives from justice. 'I want to say to you, if you are hearing this, that we love you, we forgive you, and we want no violence. We know you never meant to hurt anyone, that the guns were all for show, nobody got hurt, except the one explosion with that Colonel that every quiz mentions; we know you've always been the good guys.

'And finally, Hannibal, I say to you, one leader to another - I guess my plan didn't come together, I can admit that. Some bad guys with a virus, very bad people, they were threatening my village, my people. I tried to build a wall, but walls don't work with a virus, you know that? So anyway, I got a problem, it's gonna take four years to fix it, and it looks like no-one else can help me. Maybe we could hire you?'

UK leading the way in coffin sales

The Business Secretary was proud to announce that Britain has become a world leader in COVID fatalities. Post-Brexit we have become a leading producer of Coronavirus Sympathy cards, Matt Hancock promises and meaningless gestures in support of the NHS.

Successive Governments have failed to cull the populace, explained a spokeswoman: 'We've tried austerity, not feeding them, we even locked them in room with a collection of knives and Christmas edition of Mrs Brown's Boys – but none of these things resulted in the level of deaths we were hoping for. But our handling of COVID has tapped into what makes us great – and that's incompetence. Sheer British incompetence.'

While other countries have reported less deaths in a year, than the UK has recorded by lunchtime, there are still a handful of citizens left to kill. Promised the Minister: 'You've all done fantastic work wiping out the old and vulnerable with the virus. And the Prime Minister has personally vowed to shake everyone by the hand – which is how we'll spread it to the rest.'

Not since WWI have so many citizens marched to their deaths on the advice of a buffoon from Eton. Technically 43% of the economy is Ocado delivery slots, commented one retailer: 'And coffin sales are to die for.'

Northerners to be culled to free up hospital beds

The move comes on the back of reports that patients had been transferred from over-stretched London hospitals to intensive care as far away as Newcastle, raising fears that southerners already suffering from COVID could also find themselves exposed to Geordies.

The Health Secretary explained: 'This plan to cull the local populations will ensure there is plenty of capacity in hospitals to treat those who actually matter. It will be done as humanely as possible, even though there is no conclusive evidence that northerners can feel pain.'

'I know there are some fringe theories that northerners are somehow as important as southerners, and even that the noises they make constitute some form of rudimentary language, but this has no basis in science.' He concluded, through what may have been tears or may have been laughter, it's difficult to tell.

Fourth Horseman of the Apocalypse has stone in shoe, will catch up later

As ferocious storms rage over a pestilence-ridden nation in post-Brexit turmoil, the fourth horseman of the apocalypse, War, texted to say he couldn't make it right now, but he'd be along presently and does anyone have a Swiss army knife handy?

The news caused substantial ill-feeling in the previously tight-knit cavalcade of disaster, prompting an immediate urgent team meeting for the Horsemen to each share their feelings and read their own personal grievances. The riders set up a temporary picket for their steeds in a neutral space and had an open and honest exchange of views.

Nosferatu, riding Plague & Pestilence, was keen to explore performance-related pay options as he felt this last year, he'd been extremely busy what with inflicting a global pandemic and all, and frankly he'd pretty much carried the whole catastrophic output. He appreciated the weekly clap of recognition from the other horsemen, but perhaps it was time to actually formalise an incentive structure?

Hellion raised the matter of his purulent saddle-sores from four years of incessantly plodding along on Strife & Famine, dragging Brexit turgidly along. He had always envisaged a more agile, exciting, light cavalry role for Strife, but he'd have been better off with a Shire Horse or Clydesdale, it was such a dreary, slow and boring plod. However, he wanted it minuted that he had high hopes for progressing some decent food shortages, even if not a full-blown famine just yet, and was already making some headway both in fish stocks and tropical fruit imports.

Tremulgar the Stormrider was fully prepared to recognise his colleagues' recent achievements, and acknowledged that he'd been relative low profile with natural disaster delivery, but he really felt that was due to the headline-stealing events from Hellion and especially Nosferatu, whilst he'd been keeping a normal background simmer of hurricane, tempest and flood disasters with the occasional Sunday spectacular laid on of a tsunami or earthquake here or there.

Plus, global warming has played havoc with his software programming as everything is literally running hot right now, and takes constant adjustment and tinkering. Following on from that point, he did want to know if it was possible for the Apocalypse's IT budget to be looked at, and revised upwards if necessary?

There were some awkward moments at the close of the meeting when War & Conflict finally limped in, having thrown a shoe in the end and unable to find a blacksmith open en route. His rider, Polivicious, was somewhat defensive when the other three horsemen broached the subject of recent output and contributions to world apocalypse delivery.

'We have this every bleeding time, don't we? It's always the same, you three go in first, stir things up with a few catastrophes and disasters right to the point where the politicians start sinking in the opinion polls and an election is looming, and THEN they whistle me up to come storming in. It'll be the same this time, just you wait and see...give it six months or so, and public opinion will have them sending for the War Cavalry, you mark my words.

QAnon supporters flock to MAGA-luf

The Spanish seaside resort of Magaluf is inundated with Americans preparing for the second coming of their former president, it was reported yesterday. 'Why here?' said Stephanie Greene of Davenport, Iowa. 'Q said we get to 'Make America Great Again, Less Up-F*cked.' MAGALUF! You know what? This mythical place actually exists - on a MAP! Read the signs! Do you think we're stupid or something?'

Around two thousand Americans are believed to have applied for passports, headed abroad, and hunkered down to await the return of their Lord and Saviour, the one, true Commander-in-Chief.

'Trump's gonna lead us back to the Promised Land and retake our country from the Commie Lizardmen' said Brian Mulder, professional Pokémon player and NRA member. 'Wish he'd chosen somewhere closer to Arizona, though. Too many Hispanics here for my liking, not enough guns. And what language do these people speak? Everyone shouts 'lubberly jubberly, full English' at us.'

'I'm on 'Hunt the paedo' duties' said Ms Green. 'They're hiding in the hills, and there's this totally cool 'Paedo Map' Q's given us. It's shaped like a golf course!' The faithful dig for paedos where X marks the first bunker, move the spoil heap to where the Anglo-Saxon rune denotes the second tee, and pat down until level. Keep going until you've found 19 paedos.'

Statues to get vaccine ahead of teachers

The Communities Secretary has signalled that statues of slave owners will be given preference when it comes to council housing, extra UCAS points and they will be first in the line when it comes to the new iPhone. Such is the concern for the safety of monuments of murderers, that they will be prioritized with the new COVID vaccine and given their pick of the most attractive nurses.

It transpires that statues of racists need protection against *checks notes* people who do not like racists. The Minister insisted: 'We need to defend our heritage – unless it involves the poor, ethnic minorities, trade unionists, suffragettes, emancipationists, the disabled, human rights activists, children or scientists who think they know better – they can all jump in the nearest river.'

Social distancing will now only apply to Black Lives Matters advocates when they are near sculptures of bigots. Round the clock armed guards will preserve these effigies from attack – because being made of two tonnes of solid bronze is not enough.

Asked if we should safe-guard statues instead of the living, one teacher remarked: 'We renamed our school after discovering it was founded by a slave trader. It was called 'Sir William genocidal-maniac-who-strangled-puppies-to-pay-for-his-orangery Cameron High School', but those were simpler times. And the letter head was far too long.'

Hermit of the Year Award cancelled due to COVID19

In a strange twist resulting from the global COVID19 restrictions, officials from the Greek Orthodox Church have confirmed that the 2,446th edition of the Hermit of the Year award has had to be cancelled. A spokesperson for His Highness, the Patriarch of

175

Constantinople, said: 'Unfortunately, we cannot go ahead with this much anticipated ceremony as it has proved impossible to state how long the nominees have been self-isolating, prior to the self-isolation requirements of the COVID19 regulations. And some of them, just have no friends.'

Man enters third day of BBC Customer survey

'I wasn't really thinking straight,' he told our reporter. 'I was on the iPlayer thingy watching Match of the Day and this box pops up and asks if I have a few minutes to complete a survey. I was waiting for the match to start and so I thought, why not. I was lulled into a false sense of security as the pop-up box was blocking the glare from Alan Shearer's head.'

'Then I started. and it just kept going. The first couple of hundred questions were quite easy. I just had to click numbers from 1 to 10, saying if I was satisfied with the service provided. I was hooked. My wife went to bed and when she got up the next morning, I was still doing it.'

'Then it asked if I would recommend it to a friend, so I said clicked 'yes.' Then they wanted to know who he was, where he worked, where he lived, how good a friend he was, what he thought of EastEnders, Songs of Praise, Antiques Roadshow, and on a scale of screwdriver to lawnmower, how generous he was. I'm trapped.'

A spokesperson for the BBC told us: 'We send our deepest sympathy, as no one has ever even started one of those before. Naturally we'll be asking for feedback.'

Houses of Parliament renovations halted after rare Lib Dem MPs discovered within

Building and Environmental Control officers have called an immediate cessation of building work at Westminster Palace after a small cluster of Liberal Democrat MPs were discovered nestling within one of the offices.

Within the existing planning application, the culling of several colonies of bats from the Queens Tower and a herd of wild dormice in the cellars had already been approved; and the inspectors then turned a blind eye when builders hosed a group of crested newts straight out into the Thames next door.

However, when the plumbing team explored the attic offices to run new pipes to the header tank, they found a small group of orange rosetted figures huddled together fearfully, blinking as the sunlight reached their sanctuary.

Such was the extreme rarity of Lib Dem MPs in the Westminster environment they felt honour-bound to declare their discovery, even though they realised it would mean the shutdown of all works whilst their habitat was safeguarded.

The entire renovation project is now on hold until after the next General Election, at which stage everyone seems very confident they'll be able to restart without any Lib Dem MPs being affected at all.

Married couple use 40 years of growing apart to see them through self-isolation

'It was me who tested COVID positive,' explained Jan, 80, over Zoom. 'I need to keep away from Geoff because of his heart condition.'

She dismissed the idea that ten days would be difficult: 'We've had separate bedrooms since the last of the kids moved out. And our own rooms to watch TV for years to stop arguments. We're more prepared than most.'

Wouldn't they miss each other? 'We don't need sight of each other to know the other one's there. Who else but Geoff is making that mess of the toilet bowl? And just yesterday he was shouting up the stairs at me for apparently putting a plate in the dishwasher the wrong way.

'After 40 years of marriage, you learn the things that annoy you about each other are the things that keep you together as much as the other stuff that Johnny Mathis sings about.'

'We'll get through this,' said Geoff, 82. 'Jan's been on at me for 25 years to get our hallway decorated. It's nearly finished. Blow me if we're both going to die and miss out on the satisfaction of seeing it done. Jan would not let me hear the last of it.'

New company President saddened by lack of inauguration ceremony

The newly appointed CEO spoke of his disappointment: 'There was nothing. I was introduced to the department heads, shown a short HR video on company policies, and that was it. Crack on!

'I know we're not of the same organisational magnitude as the USA, but I at least expected a heavily-armed motorcade. Not even an Uber turned up, I had to drive myself there, and I even went the wrong way and missed the parade.'

Accounts manager, Geraldine Smith, commented: 'Martin seemed very nice, he was smiling and waving a lot, and his speech was lovely. But I'm sure he was expecting a more grandiose welcome than we gave him. Maybe if he had shared some home-baking it might have been different.'

The new President added: 'I should have guessed when my wife said she'd join me on the podium later, as she had to wait for her hat to come out of the tumble dryer... We don't have a tumble dryer.'

Government denies there is a shortage of vaccine, PPE or excuses

A spokeswoman confirmed: 'We've worked out that a miniscule drop of vaccine delivered to a person gives them enough protection to render using any more almost worthless. That's why we're only delivering a quarter of the recommended dose – science, not guesswork

'All that PPE is way over the top,' she continued. 'So, we're issuing armless smocks and we're asking that facemasks are cut into narrow strips. We've all seen how effective facemasks worn on the chin are in supermarkets – it's about time the NHS caught up

'And, thanks to the PM. there is no shortage of BS.'

Fourth wave to start on Good Friday, PM decides

'By Easter, there is a good chance that the third wave will have ended,' said the PM's spokeswoman, secretly, to every reporter in ear shot, 'And let me be clear that we regard this as a necessary precondition for families to mix over the Easter weekend, and for a fourth wave of the virus to begin.

'Some may say that we have failed to learn from our mistakes in how we handled Christmas, and to these people I say - Easter weekend has two bank holidays! Two!

'We will listen to the scientists, of course, listen very hard, before we do this anyway. Or maybe I'll do a U-turn and cancel it at the last minute. Who can say? Even if we cancel it, at least we'll have got everyone so geared up that people will just break the rules anyway.'

Passports now used exclusively to accept Amazon booze deliveries

Passports used to be utilised to travel to holiday destinations, to visit relatives or go to business meetings in far flung destinations. Now the sole use of the bookish rectangles of identity proof is to be shown to Amazon delivery drivers prior to accepting another yet booze delivery. Last week it was toffee flavoured vodka, this week passion fruit liqueur, perhaps next week will be mango flavoured rum.

Passports used to live in a special place upstairs with leftover currency (remember coins and notes? How quaint!) but now live tucked behind a pile of post with a face mask on top on the little shelf by the front door. Delivery drivers sometimes attempt a spot of flattery when viewing your birth date but this is becoming increasingly sarcastic sounding as the nation has prematurely aged due to being discombobulated by the speed of change in our everyday lives. Cheers!

Biden announces huge cutback in prostitute budget

President Biden has announced swingeing cutbacks in the official White House Official Recreation Executive (WHORE) budget.

'We are living in difficult times.', said Mr Biden, 'So some cutbacks are necessary. Obviously, the wall that Mexico was paying for is costing us a fortune and that's been stopped. However, I was surprised at the amount the previous administration had budgeted for, er, what I understand is called 'the horizontal hula' and sometimes referred to by my predecessor 'the beast with two bladders'.

'It's unfortunate for the people who will lose their positions, but their work has also been affected by stricter security measures which means that some of their 'equipment' will no longer be permitted in the building.'

Middle Class lockdown angst defined by two-hour debate on cooking brisket joint

An ostentatiously middle-class family have managed to spend a full two hours in circular argument regarding how best to cook a discounted middle-cut beef joint.

The meeting, held in front of the Aga, naturally, was well attended by a full complement of precocious offspring and Labradors and a robust exchange of views took place.

Mum Helen felt it was relevant to raise a leftover half bottle of Merlot could be utilised in a Boeuf Bourguignon. Dad Paul pointed out that Mum was kidding herself if she thought she'd left more than some dregs in that bottle last night, precipitating a fifteen-minute deviation in the discussion, with several unhelpful references to 'going the same way as your mother' and barbed ripostes beginning with 'Well is it any wonder I drink when you...?'

Returning to the subject at hand, son Austin reminded the meeting that he hated mushrooms and had eaten the bacon for breakfast anyway, and asked why we couldn't just have roast Beef with Yorkshire puddings?

Paul did his usual run through of the relative merits of different cuts of meat and their 'cuisine', and averred that anything beyond medium rare in a roast was simply inedible and a disrespect to the animal. Daughter Simone went off on one about seeing blood on her plate and being a murderer, at which stage Helen adjourned the meeting for refreshments before Simone started playing You Tube campaign videos again.

Each family member was requested to put forward three acceptable options for the beef dinner, but that degenerated into a game of top trumps as every suggestion was immediately negated:

- Beef Madras - too late to marinade, not worth bothering without.
- Chinese Crispy Beef - too tough and a faff getting the Aga up to temperature to fry
- Pot Roast - boring, boring seconded, and don't like brown
- Steak Pie - just not right without kidney, I hate kidney, you could pick it out, I don't think it's reasonable to make a special journey just to buy kidney, and you only eat the pastry anyway
- Mexican Chilli - Austin played his veto, referencing that difficult moment last year in the scrum for the Second XV when chilli effluent had taken out the whole forward pack and Mum still couldn't get the stains out of his jersey.

- Shepherd's Pie - Dad corrected this suggestion to 'Cottage Pie' because he's a pedantic prick and can't resist deploying that lecture every. sodding. time.
- Cottage Pie - this was acceptable to all, clearly requiring mincing the beef but after twenty minutes of everyone hunting in the loft Dad remembered they'd discarded that attachment on Mum's food mixer and taken it to the charity shop because what idiot would ever use it when you can just buy beef mince?

With that, the family headed back to the table for final, crunch, 'tunnel' talks as the dinner deadline approached, only to find that their Labradors had eaten the beef joint, but as Paul now needed to take them to the vet, he could pick up a Thai takeaway on the way home - they just needed to agree which Set Menu to order...

Trolling to be defined as a basic human right

'Trolls deserve to be heard, same as everybody else', said an equality spokesman. 'We need more attention than neuro-typical people, so when we keep on and on and on about the same topic – evading logic, ignoring facts and irrationally claiming victory – it should be celebrated as part of troll culture.'

Under new guidelines 'trolling' – defined as 'being a bit of an arse on social media because you're lonely and need attention' – will become a Protected Status and afforded legal protection. Except, Katie Hopkins – who no one likes.

Climate change 'key to breaking pandemic'

Government stats have revealed today that whenever it snows there are fewer COVID-19 cases reported.

'It's almost as if treacherous roads, sub-zero temperatures and blizzard conditions frighten the virus away,' said one expert on virus behaviour. 'If only we could increase the variability of the weather systems, we would be able to dispense with these totally unnecessary vaccines the Government is using to microchip us with,' he added.

He denied any causal link between bad weather and people deciding to stay at home rather than going for a swab test. 'I deny denying that,' he added, putting a foil hat on. 'It's a government-sponsored pandemic, can't be too careful,' he added.

Panic ensues after everyone writes a book under Lockdown

Terror threat levels are on high alert, as some of your family are now asking for you to cast a causal eye over this manuscript they have been working on. There is now widespread fear that you are going to have to find something polite to say about these literary turds or, worse still, help with the proof reading.

COVID has been the perfect excuse for friends to re-visit that idea they had had for a swashbuckling detective thriller – back when they were thirteen. Lockdown has seen people furtively typing, unleashing years of pent-up artistic desire and untapped reservoirs of banality.

Publishers have been inundated with scripts, while coincidentally manufactures of recyclable toilet paper and owners of landfill sites, have also reported an upswing in raw materials. Due to coronavirus people are wearing more masks but they also appear to be wearing more berets.

Said one reluctant reader: 'It's been hellish, everyone seems to have penned a memoir. But if we all compose a self-pitying account of how hard we found Lockdown – what will the Guardian columnists have to write about? It's been one turgid novel after another...which is ironically the plot of this new book I've written.'

Dad loses it as daughter is better aim with snowballs

A Romford dad who encouraged his seven-year-old daughter to 'come outside for a snowball fight' this morning, has flown into what was described as a 'gammon-like rage' when it transpired that his daughter was a much better shot than him.

Tony Butterworth, 34, thought it would be a 'delightful' idea if he and daughter Tamsin 'frolicked in the snow' in this morning's winter wonderland, believing that they would laughingly throw powdery tufts of snow at each other before cuddling and giggling together in a tender moment of love and affection.

'But it was carnage,' fumed Butterworth later, nursing a black eye and cauliflower ear.

'She just seemed to get the much-fabled the Eye of the Tiger and I caught the first one on the side of the head. My ear filled with blood and as I turned to admonish her, in came a flurry of well-aimed head-shots.

'At one point I thought I was surrounded.'

'Once I had a chance to catch my breath, behind number 7's Landrover Discovery, I was livid. And a bit teary.

'I let out a tirade of snotty expletives as her mum led her into the house, giggling.

'It turns out that she had been lacing the snowballs with ice – everyone knows that's out of order. So she's grounded for a week and I've confiscated her unicorn playset that she got for Christmas. No one makes a fool out of me.'

Mr Butterworth's neighbours, who managed to watch the whole affair, disagreed.

80-90% effective: Fine for vaccines, not for parachutes.

During a pandemic we are grateful for any level of viral immunity, even to the point where we are willing to listen to Donald Trump recommend injecting bleach. However, there are other areas of life, where 80-90% safety would be worrying - particularly when it comes to contraception or roller coasters.

While 80-90% effectiveness may be enough for a vaccine to achieve herd immunity, the same level of success does not give a group of people jumping out of plane gravity immunity. Someone is going to end up splattered all over a field - and the law of dumb luck says it will probably be you.

A scientist explained: 'People would be naturally wary if eating jelly had a 15-20% chance of death. Whereas. when you turned on the TV and you had an 80% chance of seeing something entertaining, you'd be amazed, as the normal rate is just 7%.'

There are a few other areas where we will tolerate an 80% success rate; for instance, lottery tickets, multiple orgasms and snow at Christmas. Said one patient who had recently been vaccinated: 'I've been told I've an 80% chance of immunity, a 90% chance of ignoring lockdown rules and 100% chance of feeling smug.'

Home-schooling dad is 'quids-in' after becoming an Academy

Exhausted dad-of-six Alex Kennington from Walton-on-Thames found a novel way of making a shed load of extra cash by becoming a multi-academy schools trust. After a heart-breaking late-night session trying to explain fronted-adverbials to his six-year-old daughter, he registered online and was accepted.

'I don't remember much about the application, to be honest,' said Alex, 36 (although he now looks about 76). 'We had a Tesco delivery at 11.40, so it was beer-o-clock and I just thought, sod it... I'm doing all the teaching now; I may as well get paid pots and pots of Government cash to do it.'

Mr Kennington found the application process pretty straightforward. 'I thought I'd get found out when they asked about my experience working in education,' he said. 'But it turns out if you once presented a PowerPoint, under duress, to three kitchen porters about soup spoons in 2013 you still qualify. The bar is set pretty low.'

Alex now pays himself a £150,000 salary as Head Teacher of 28 Cottesmore Lane Church of England Academy Trust. 'I put the C of E bit in as a bit of a joke, but apparently it meant my application was fast-tracked. I got the email acceptance the very next morning along with an exorbitant bank transfer.'

Mr Kennington says that the ridiculously high salary is helping him cope with demands of home-schooling. 'It hasn't made me a better teacher,' he says. 'But I have delegated much of the work to supply teachers. If anything, I spend more time outside in my new luxury yurt drinking Bollinger. And I've dropped fronted adverbials from the curriculum in favour of an unsupervised Frozen II marathon.'

Travellers to UK will be clapped in irons and quarantined in the Bates Motel

In a complete break with policy, the UK Government has decided to do something about something. Every hapless holiday maker, dripping virus spores from the tips of their duty-free Toblerone, will now be imprisoned in a dubious motel, owned by a reputable serial killer.

The Home Office said: 'This will be a tremendous boost to the hospitality sector, which we've successfully managed to decimate over the past few months. It's not the policy of this Government to put any of our 'guests' in harm's way, but we do recommend that they kindly refrain from using the showers.'

Amnesty International rate 'closing bars' as worst human rights abuse of 2020

'We understand. Usually, our annual report is full of journalists being shot and torture – all that kind of depressing snowflake whingeing' said new AI global ambassador Rita Ora.

'So of course, in 2020 it was exciting to finally have some real problems to tackle! All around the world, millions of people were unable to go out to restaurants or bars. Sometimes for months at a time. All that was left for them was to order takeaways and call each other on the phone. Truly this was tyranny like humanity has never seen before.'

The charity is asking for donations from £50 to pay for a student party or snowball fight, £50,000 to support an underground supper club network in North London, or 'just £275,000' to fund a weekly column in the Telegraph for a year. 'Please help us - Save The Cafés Before It's Too Latté.'

Mass vaccine trials lead to worldwide Placebo shortage

Scientists across the five continents and especially the seven seas are stumped, desperately seeking a source of dilute salt-water solution. None of the eleventy-billion different vaccines currently under phase two or three trials can prove their efficacy unless they are matched with an equal number of patients receiving control placebos

It is believed that unless a reliable source of slightly salty water is found soon, Science as an entity will lose its newfound premier place in the public esteem and be replaced by something that works – like, religion.

Local newspaper inadvertently covered story

The Warrington Observer has been fined an undisclosed sum by the Press Clickbait Ombudsman after a recent article 'Local Man Finds Shoe' displayed several hundred words of coherent reporting with no typos and very few clickbait ads.

'We're sorry' said John Adams, Editor. 'The journalist is young and appears to have watched 'All the President's Men' once too often – he insisted on checking facts, obtaining quotes and using something called a dictionary.

'We would also like to apologise for the absence of clickbait. Several readers phoned to complain that they really wanted to know why Sean Connery's will left his family in tears or why doctors won't tell you about this simple trick, though to be fair if we'd included the clickbait, they'd still be none the wiser.'

An industry insider told us 'Journalism is still legal in the UK, though obviously it's frowned upon. A more experienced journalist would have titled the piece 'You Won't BELIEVE What Happened to Man's Shoe', but that's youth for you. Always think they know better.'

Maslow publishes Hierarchy of Knees

Renowned psychologist, Abraham Maslow, has revised his theory of human motivation, to reflect our intrinsic love of knees. Represented in pyramid form, Maslow postulates that self-fulfilment will only be achieved once we have knees that resemble the statuesque beauty of Beyonce, with the firm earthiness of Alan Titchmarsh.

Traditionally esteem would be derived from wealth and accomplishments, but more and more it is driven by our desire for attractive knees. Explained one behaviouralist: 'If we didn't have knees, our legs would be far too stiff.'

The 'Basic Knee' is both hairy and knobbly, with a rudimentary hinge mechanism – but none of the thrills of The Bionic Man. Sadly, these limited knees are also known to sag and look somewhat ridiculous in shorts.

A colleague commented: 'The Hierarchy of Knees, follows up from Maslow's earlier theory that we cared only about the quality of our fermented honey drinks – the Hierarchy of Meads. Or controversially our constant struggle for ever better decorative objects, with a small hole for threading – our Hierarchy of Beads. And who can forget, his exhaustive list of plants in the wrong place – the Hierarchy of Weeds'

Five Go Dobbing in the Neighbours

In other news.......

No deaths yet from Brazilian variant of COVID, but lots of close shaves

Nurses at Big Ben deliver Government promise to vaccinate round the clock

Activision release 'Call of Duty: Vaccine Deployment' a multi-person shoot-em-up

England moves to level 5, Tier 4, defcon 3, Die Hard 2, Dagenham & Redbridge 1

Retired junkies answer call to help administer vaccine

The only headline act for this year's Glastonbury Festival will be Mud

Nostalgia for t'good old days, when t'annual lockdown didn't start till March

Elon Musk overtakes Jeff Bezos to become world's biggest arsehole

Bakers asked to 'stay home and save loaves'

Majority of Welsh people live in an area 'roughly the size of Wales'

Twitter account cancellation removes Trump's final horcrux

Paperchase to fold

Adjustable specs now available to bring people closer

Unprecedented rumpus raises calls for unpresidented Trump.

Dockers claim they are quay workers

Serco awarded £800 billion contract to give £500 to all COVID-19 victims

SNP offers to pay for Johnson's visit after it boosts support for independence

Trump impfefed for the second time

UK fishing industry caught between rock salmon and hard plaice

Man completes dry Tuesday apart from some leftover whisky fudge

Government reverses decision on international U-turn day

2021 to be much better … ah, Manchester United are top of the league. Bollocks

Church bell ringer says lockdown has taken its toll

COVID-19 vaccination programme sparks new arms race

Isle of Wight healthcare system working around the sundial

Trump supporters commit Capitol offence

Biden to replace all White House sheets and mattresses just in case

Trump orders new batch of Viagra – for a longer lasting, pulsating insurrection

'I unreservedly condemn Trump's undemocratic actions,' says Parliament proroguer

Cabinet ministers in briefings to just squirt squid ink and then scuttle away

Token woman executed in Trump's last-ditch attempt at equality

Trump pardons Darth Vader, Sauron, Voldemort and Cruella de Vil.

Trump orders new batch of Viagra – for a longer lasting, pulsating insurrection.

Trump: I can't make Biden's inauguration as I'm ironing my hair

Travellers to Hell advised to take handcart-friendly Route 666

Global Health Insurance Card replaces parochial EU EHIC, only valid in EU though

Ryanair to charge passengers a supplement for not flying in a Boeing 737

Trump protects himself by remaining safely distanced from reality

Pedigree Chum insists its school meals conform to Government guidelines

Trump did not join march to capitol because of bone spurs

Johnson finally to close schools. Starmer to pretend he thought of it first

February 2021

The COVID vaccine rollout continued apace in February, with new Brazilian and South African COVID variant reaching the UK. After the PM described the current situation as a race between vaccination and variants, Sky Sports were quick to launch a new subscription channel to stream the event 24 hours a day for the next year. The Government produced a new roadmap out of lockdown. Like any roadmap this one was difficult to follow, with the public complaining that all the key points were found on the crease and staple of the page, and you need to turn it round in the direction you're facing, and why didn't you turn off at that junction like I just told you to.

Fitness blogger claims 14 pints of lager leads to better wellbeing

'Influencer', Jackie Beesley, 27, has posted motivational photos of herself and a couple of mates comatose in a Benidorm taverna. Beesley, an 'alternative' fitness blogger, said the package holiday to Spain was intended to 'cheer up' her many online followers and encourage them to go that extra mile in their quest to find a late-night off-licence or kebab shop.

The photo of Ms Beesley had received over 24m likes on Facebook and many favourable comments from her 40m Twitter followers:

'Legend' said @Mumz_in_Prison from Worksop
'Mental' added @2TonTed from Teddington
'Inspirational' was how @DewsburyDick described the scene
'Have you shit yourself yet' asked @Old_Offensive_Tweets from Bristol

Ms Beesley is convinced hers is a healthy lifestyle, saying the proof was in the pudding - which it seems one of her mates had smothered in custard and shoved down the front of her blouse.

'They're all as bad as each other!' says genius at bus stop

Plans to educate the populace in the basic principles of politics have been widely condemned by someone standing at a bus stop.

Speaking from the bus stop, she said: 'I don't see the point in teaching them anything at all. They're fat and lazy and would benefit from a few years of national service. The parents are to blame. I'd shoot the lot of them, but you're not allowed to say that are you? It's political correctness gone mad!'

Study confirms 'Everybody was Kung Fu fighting' claim is largely true

A major study has confirmed that during 1974, there was an exponential rise in martial arts activity in the UK. Explained an historian, 'We found that upwards of 93% of the primary and secondary school population were Kung Fu fighting during their break times, and in some cases that carried on in their lessons as well.'

'It was a fascinating insight into a different world. Some people did not take part in Kung Fu fighting, for a variety of social, economic and health reasons. But some people just like hitting stuff.'

Boris's vaccine shame: None of his chums profited

The PM remains tight-lipped on the billions of pounds spent with random posh people on non-existent PPE, but that's to be expected: the first rule of Chum Club is 'you do not talk about Chum Club'. Sadly, he has had less luck profiteering from the vaccine.

'It's been non-stop wedgies all day', said a source. 'It isn't Boris's fault. Not really. It's one thing contracting with a mate who has a soft furnishings consultancy to provide a billion quid's worth of PPE – you can buy that stuff anywhere. Well, you can't, obvs, but you can pretend. Nobody was going to believe that a bunch of hoorays with one GCSE between them have developed an RNA vaccine. I doubt they could spell 'RNA', let alone manipulate it.'

Fake COVID vaccine 'not lovely jubbly' rule magistrates

Two brothers from Peckham have appeared at Marylebone Magistrates Court today, charged with fly-pitching imported and unregulated fake COVID-19 vaccine in Oxford Street.

Derek and Rodney Trotter, of Nelson Mandela House, were arrested on Wednesday after selling the DIY product, Zapp 19, for £50.00 a bottle. When pleading their innocence to the court, the elder brother, Derek, said: 'What can't speak can't lie, my son. This is the pukka stuff shipped direct from the US of A by none other than the Trump Corporation.'

'Listen pal, what's in this little bottle will see anything off, and if you've got any leftover after treating yourself and the missus, bung it down the khazi, and it will bring the bowl up gleaming and good as noo. Mais oui, your lordship, mais oui.'

Government: 'Reports of snow chaos greatly exaggerated'

A spokeswoman said: 'The pavements and roads here in the capital are completely clear. Jolly well dashed if I know what all the fuss is about.

'But just let me assure everyone of this. Should we hear even a rumour of so much as a single snowflake falling within the Home Counties, then we will, of course, hold an emergency meeting of the COBRA Committee to ensure the great British public is kept safe. After all, this bulldog breed didn't see off Mr

Hitler by getting in all of a doodah over a few droplets of frozen rain.

'We have ably demonstrated that whenever the public is in danger, ministers will act and act decisively. If you demand proof, then I suggest you look no further than our world-beating stewardship of this beastly global pandemic business.'

All working-class housing to be made of paraffin wax by 2030

The Government has clarified its policy on the widespread practice of covering tower blocks with flammable material. 'We've checked carefully, and none of our investments are affected', said a spokeswoman. 'Bit of a relief, but it isn't the only consideration. We also have to think of the impact on the insurance industry.'

The new building code will recommend all plebeian homes to be fully flammable, which will make the job of site clearance and rebuilding much more efficient. 'It's a win-win', said the spokeswoman.

'If it's a location which is on the up, we can build something nice. If it's a dump we can rapidly replace using my new patented kit-building method. Paraffin wax is waterproof, a good insulator and very malleable. Rather like the current Conservative Party.'

Vaccine gives you hiccups

Health Officials are said to be thinking of withdrawing COVID vaccinations, as patients are displaying incredibly minor side effects like tired, listless hair or worse still, an attack of the heebie-jeebies. Said one vaccinee: 'I know this could save my life, but who wants hiccups?'

Anti-vaxxers took to Twitter to list symptoms, including dancing the hokey cokey, speaking in Aramaic and being able to recite Pi to up 40,000 places. Complained one: 'As soon as I was injected, I felt a sharp pricking sensation in my arm, like a needle. You can't tell me that was intended.'

Harry kept his Royal Lanyard, says Palace spokesman

A spokesman for the Royal Family has confirmed that one-time royal, ginger sheep of the family and husband punching well above his weight, Prince Harry, has still not turned in his Royal Lanyard and ID card.

'I'm sure that this is an oversight on his part', he told our reporter, 'but we know that it has been used recently at Swans R Us, World of Venison and that it is racking up Royal Yacht Miles at an alarming rate.'

Russian vaccine 92% effective when placed in underpants, by a secret agent

In response, the UK has ordered ten million pairs of underpants and called thousands of MI5 and MI6 operatives out of retirement - many of whom, now live in Russia.

British scientists are urging caution. No one yet knows how effective the vaccine is when used in conjunction with saggy Y-fronts, the underpant of choice for men aged over 65. Initial reports from Italy show it is compatible with thongs and mankinis, and tests on Austrian lederhosen are said to be 'encouraging but inconclusive.'

Several naturists were arrested today in angry clashes in Parliament Square. Protestors say the vaccine discriminates against the nudist community. 'We're just not wearing it,' said a spokesperson. 'It's just another way to have us all microchipped through the backdoor.'

All COVID decisions to be based on Matt Damon films

'It's all in there, everything we need to finally beat this virus, if you look close enough', said the Health Secretary rubbing his eyes, as he emerged with an empty bucket of popcorn, from the makeshift cinema he had constructed in his spare room, after a marathon session of watching the extensive canon of Jason Bourne and Ocean's 11 through to 99.

'There's 'Contagion', yes, but also 'Downsizing', we could shrink everyone to a height of 5 inches, to maintain social distancing. Or get college janitors to solve complex viral problems by utilizing blackboards, a process of self-discovery and a cameo by Robin Williams'

'We don't think the virus has access to any of Mr Damon's films and so we hope to catch it on the hoof.'

COVID vaccine withdrawn after manufacturers forget to put the autism in

'Normally, a good 60-70% of our development time is spent thinking up new ways to autisise the subject', explained a scientist. 'But this time, due to the rush, we simply forgot all about it.'

A frantic recall has been issued for current unused stocks of the vaccine. However, the company is optimistic that they may still be able to offer autism to those who have already taken the vaccine using an over-the-air software update via the 5G tracking chips.

VR revolutionizes gaming - and by 'gaming' we mean porn

Scientists predict that Virtual Reality headsets will transform the way we experience computer games and, more importantly, how we see undulating breasts. Studies reveal that most gamers spend their first 10 minutes of a new headset exploring apps and the next year wading through Pornhub.

Said one user: 'It was insane. Suddenly I was this plumber, and my client was wearing nothing more than suspenders and a basque. It was utterly immersive, so much so that I stayed to install her new shower. Then I invoiced her £200. It felt so real!'

Some gamers have complained that virtual hands are clumsy, but others say that adds to the realism of any sexual encounter. You can download any combination of fetish, provided it always entails you standing naked in your sitting room, with what looks like a margarine tub strapped to your face.

There have been complaints that the battery life of one hour, will be problematical – said one user: 'I lived out my most depraved, erotic fantasy. There were dozens of orifices and a multitude of adult toys. I did things that would make Marquis de Sade blush. But when it was over, I still had 58 minutes to fill.'

Government takes action on climate change by setting fire to Cumbria

A Government spokesman confirmed: 'We've planned a smorgasbord of free CFCs for the under-tens, turning the National Parks into open cast mining theme parks, and fracking the sh*t out of every non-blue constituency North of Watford Gap. We'll turn Britain's climate change from 'worryingly warming' to 'face-meltingly toasty', all before you can strangle a coal-streaked canary.

'Trying to responsibly redress our ongoing environmental damage - for what, a degree or two? Sounds like a total bore; far easier to light a fire under the issue, turn up the fossil-fuelled boardroom air conditioning for whoever's letterhead you're gracing that day, and drive for the big numbers - like 100+ Fahrenheit before breakfast. Perfect beach weather.'

Twitter user stayed silent because he had 'nothing useful to contribute'

It's a Zen koan: if you don't tweet, does anybody hear you?

John Davies, 37, from Warrington chose not to pile on to a Twitter debate yesterday. We interviewed him to ask: why on earth not? Have you no self-respect?

NB: Could you describe the incident?

John: Yeah, thanks. It was that actor, Laurence something; he was going on about masks and how they're a form of oppression.

NB: Do you have views on the subject?

John: Of course! Sometimes it's hard to keep them to 288 characters, so you have to put 1/ at the end of the first tweet and then reply to yourself until you've put together something coherent.

NB: But this time you didn't say anything at all? Weren't you worried that your opinion might be lost forever?

John: There were thousands of Tweets which said exactly what I was going to say. I thought of 'liking' them, to show solidarity, but in the end, I thought 'he's just a prat who likes the attention, and my kids need a hug', so I put my phone down and . . .

NB: Hold on. You put the phone down?

John: Yes

NB: And where is it now?

John: In my hand. I'm talking to you

NB: Oh yes. It's also a phone. Go on, how did the tweet end?

John: Well, they never really end, do they? Far as I know people are still piling in.

Footballer's 'shame' at following COVID-19 restrictions.

His club issued a statement: 'It's come to our attention that @StrikerTony9, has been negligent in his obligation to self-promote whilst arbitrarily observing lockdown restrictions.

'The player in question fully admits to enduring the comfort of his partner and children and the sanctity of his family home for prolonged periods, often participating in home-schooling and basic maintenance tasks. The club, therefore, feels it necessary to send the player to Dubai for ten days, shopping and grooming, with a bunch of mates, posting his activity every hour on a variety of platforms.'

His agent commented: 'He assures me he takes the responsibility of being a role model to the younger generation seriously, and will never again allow his credit card or hair to rest.'

Hedge Fund Manager will work for food

The City of London and Wall Street are concerned about the growing number of investment bankers seen sleeping rough, wrapped in nothing but a Burberry overcoat and a pair of Salvatore Ferragamo brogues. Since amateur traders have lent to short-sell Hedge Funds, many portfolio executives have been forced rely on their skills to survive – which sadly only qualifies them as a blood donor, drug mule or shop mannequin.

Having to work for a living and produce something of actual social worth, is far beyond the imagination or tax code of most bankers. Instead, many seek out a life of penury, pleading for passers-by to 'Spare a Bitcoin, mate?'

Excitement as Aung San Suu Kyi relaunches her Home Shopping Channel

'Hello, fellow savvy shoppers and canny bargain lovers, it's great to be back on the Deposed Deals Home Shopping Network sofa!

'I've had a wonderful six years trading on the High Street; well, the 100-room Presidential Palace in Naypyidaw, but it did have its frustrations: I wanted to trade on my trademark charisma, dignity, and dwindling international adulation, but as Min Aung Hlaing and the other totally sweet Generals on the board said, my strengths lay in hawking this one increasingly ineffectual figurehead.

'Like my fellow humanitarian, Sir Philip Green, you just know when it's right to get out of old-fashioned bricks and mortar retailing, which my fantastic team managed with military efficiency, before actually telling me. Luckily as I was being assisted out, I managed to grab a wonderful selection of my feature 24-karat self-belief, over-embellished cover-ups, and hard-faced denials, which I can't wait to foist on you.

Or how about this stunning Nobel Peace Prize, only thoroughly tarnished?'

Fans furious after news Captain Sir Tom Moore could be played by a woman

The war hero and peacetime charity fundraiser could be played by a woman in the next series, confirmed a BBC Producer. 'Why not? Having Captain Sir Tom regenerating into a younger character played by a younger actor, even a woman, especially a woman, would bring in the fans and introduce the series to a much bigger audience.'

Said one fan: 'My 10-year-old daughter is excited about this. She keeps running around the house, shouting 'Girl Power! and 'Fight the Patriarchy.' Every time we see Second World War heroes on the television, they tend to be old, straight, middle-class white men in their late '90s. It's about time the BBC showed some courage and gave the role to a much younger, more modern hero, or shero if you prefer. Why shouldn't Captain Sir Tom be a woman? And why should she be a straight woman?'

'I'll wait for the vaccine made from Matt Hancock's tears' say Brexiteer

A consequence of stirring nationalism for political gains by the Conservative Party is rearing its divisive head in the fight against COVID-19. One GP has stated that patients are rejecting vaccines to 'wait for the English one', experiencing comments, such as: 'I want that one made from ketchup plasma', and 'Will it make me speak German?'

The issue first arose after the Oxford/AstraZeneca vaccine was approved for use, with the health spokeswoman hailing it as a triumph for British science, adding: 'It's the Billy Elliott of boosters.' Reports followed claiming Downing Street had attempted to get doses of the Oxford vaccine packaged within a stick of Blackpool rock.

She explained: 'It's made in our Buckingham Palace-shaped laboratory at Stonehenge, and is fundamentally based upon the purified essence of Matt Hancock's tears. It comes in red, white, and blue too.'

Starmer's poll dance with Union Jack backfires

The so-called Leader of the Opposition has failed to evoke an air of patriotism by rampantly mounting the nation's flag; this is despite a Beefeater thrusting pound coins into Starmer's bulging thong and the indiscriminate use of red, white and blue nipple tassels. So amorous has been the manner with which Sir 'Keith' hugs the flag, that the soiled Union Jack needs to be regularly steam cleaned and given therapy to recover.

During a pandemic, Sir Keir's focus group has told him that what we need is less vaccines and more shots of him twerking to the theme tune of the Dam Busters. Hoping to get a bounce in the polls by gyrating on a pole, he has embarked on a complicated aerial shoulder-mount, followed by an extended monologue on why Big Ben is arousing.

From a precarious ankle-hang position, he promised to make fish and chips compulsory and make love to first bulldog he finds. An advisor commented: 'I haven't the heart to tell him, that he's been flying the flag upside down.'

Makers of Oral B products insist there are no Oral A products

Proctor and Gamble, manufacturers of the Oral B range of dental products, today issued a firm denial that they manufacture a secret range of Oral A products.

P&G spokesperson Helga Schmidt said: 'There has been a misunderstanding here that we are keen to correct. Oral B products are not the cheaper, more inferior version of Oral A products.

'There is no Oral A toothpaste, tooth brush or mouth wash. We think the error has arisen from social media influencers spreading an unfounded rumour that Oral A products are only available to A list celebrities, when in fact no such products exist.'

'It does not make sense that A list celebrities would be given a product called Oral B,' said Victoria Nichols, a Dubai based social media influencer. 'I have contacted P&G offering to promote their Oral A products, but they say they don't have any. But then, they would say that, wouldn't they?'

In a related development the manufacturers of Preparation H have also denied that there are seven other categories of their product.

Exports of wishful thinking down by 68%

The Road Haulage Association has warned that vast amounts of rose-tinted glasses and crossed fingers have been held up at UK ports by complex paperwork. Producers of rabbit's feet, four leaf clovers and horseshoes have been particularly badly hit.

Ministers insisted the hold-up is only temporary and that soon every lorry driver in Great Britain will be accompanied by a dusky maiden bearing libations of honeyed ale and KFC bargain buckets.

A spokesperson for the RHA said: 'They said our members would be drinking milk and honey with the gods in the sacred fields of Elysium, but instead the queues are so long we've been forced to drink our own urine.'

UK terrorism threat level lowered to 'substantial' - like a pub meal

Britain's threat level has been downgraded to that of a scotch egg or basket of cheesy chips. In line with their guidance on Tier 2 eating, any terrorist activities must have the nutritional value of a full English breakfast.

The Home Secretary said: 'Terrorism remains an immediate risk to our national security, but so is a meat stew encased in an inedible doughy crust. A ploughman's lunch may seem innocent at first, but before you know it, you're ordering toad in the hole and bag of Semtex.'

UAE probe successfully docks with dissident's genitals

His Excellency the Khalifa Al Nahyan of the UAE has announced the successful launch of Cattleprod-1, the emirate's first space probe. After a torturous countdown the probe delivered a payload of electricity to the genitals of an orbiting political dissident.

Human rights activists have criticised UK firms for exporting cattle prods to the UAE, but manufacturers say they are an essential component in space craft. Last year UK manufacturers exported £100 million worth of Michael Bublé albums to the emirates and it is feared some of them may have been used to torture political prisoners.

Cattleprod-1 is due to continue its journey to Mars where it will search for oil, gold plated Ferraris, and some prime real estate.

Snow day under Lockdown a bit 'samey'

School children up and down the land, were celebrating a day spent at home due heavy snowfall, only to discover that that it is essentially a repeat of the whole of last year – just a bit chillier. Building snowmen is all very well, but the real pleasure is thinking about all those face-to-face lessons you are missing.

Remarked one child: 'I didn't even get the satisfaction of skipping lessons, as all my teachers have gone online. Snow is a bit rubbish really.' His mother confirmed: 'I'd got excited about not driving to work and having a duvet day; but that's less of a thing if you've been wearing the same pyjamas since August.'

Young woman forgets to post photos of snow on social media

Ms Rumbold, 29, of Cleethorpes, who generally posts everything to Instagram, Facebook, Twitter and that other one, you know, the Chinese one with the dancing flowers and that, has been left feeling incredibly foolish and ashamed after forgetting to upload any of the 73 photos of the snow she took this morning to any of her accounts.

She said: 'I was so busy, what with home-schooling all my kids and doing my Amazon deliveries, that I totally forgot to press Send', she sniffled. 'I still posted all the other pics, you know, bed hair, make up before and after, me in my PJs with one sock on, the kids' breakfasts, a selfie of me sitting on the loo with a rabbit ears filter, and the daily one of me in my bra and pants pouting like a giant duck what's had a stroke, but I just know I'll lose followers for this. I'm gutted. My life is over.'

10 days in UK Travelodge 'excessive' says High Court judge

A former High Court judge has said that threatening travellers a night in a UK Travelodge was excessive punishment and probably violated their human rights. Judge Lord Gumtion added that most travellers would prefer to be put on a sex offender's register or be charged with firearms offences than serve the maximum sentence of ten nights in Gatwick.

'At the moment asylum seekers are being held 15 to a room in an old army barracks in Kent. There is no central heating, no drinking water, no cooking facilities, the toilets are overflowing and electricity is cut off for eight hours a day - now imaging having to give all that up to spend ten miserable nights in a Travelodge.

'It's one thing trekking across Europe for three weeks then finding yourself crammed into a dinghy with ten other families for 36 hours while crossing the channel in a Force 10 gale, but then finding you've got to sleep on a motel pull-me-down for close on a fortnight really takes the edge off it all.'

Brexit delays import of turd polish

The Government is understood to have ordered 20 million tons of turd polish. Unfortunately, when it arrived, it was promptly sent back. This is seen as a victory for taking back control, but it also means it needs to be reordered.

There were further delays when Chris Grayling assumed that polish comes from Poland.

Misuse of the word 'staycation' becomes criminal offence

'This new law simply puts into effect what everyone has been screaming at travel journalists and newsreaders for the last few years', indicated a Judge. 'Staycation means you are staying at home, IN YOUR OWN HOUSE during the holiday period, instead of going ANYWHERE ELSE APART FROM YOUR OWN HOUSE INCLUDING THE MANY OTHER LOVELY PLACES IN YOUR OWN COUNTRY for a holiday. We do hope that is clear.'

Report claims Extinction Rebellion infiltrated by environmentalists

A Government spokesman said: 'If environmental groups want better press coverage, then need to be more pro-oil. Likewise, if the BLM movement could focus a little more on all the wonderful things slave owners did for us, I'm sure we'd all sleep better.'

The report concluded: 'Black Lives Matter would be far less angry, if it was just full of rich white folk.' Groups who are demanding seismic societal changes, will be instructed to focus on more realistic goals, like changes of font size.

Imperial Leather product range to be decolonised

A product spokeswoman confirmed: 'We've clearly caused offence, although it was just seven tweets that mentioned it. However, these have now been shared over a million times, creating a snowball effect, so we had to act. We intend to rebrand this product range so that it will now be known as People's Leather to avoid any connotations with imperialism.'

Asked if 'leather' also promoted animal cruelty, she sighed and agreed to change the label to 'Just Soap and Stuff.'

East End virus variant leaves patients with a cockney accent

A survey of 2379 people currently recovering from COVID, revels that a thumping 97% of them now have a distinct cockney accent and a love of jellied eels.

'It's harrowing for those of us who have to make heart-rending calls to their nearest and dearest,' admitted a senior registrar. 'All day on the dog and bone...oh, God, what did I say? Someone pass me a thermometer; I think it's got me!'

Senate impeachment trial handed over to Jackie Weaver

Frustrated with successive failures to agree upon the of the U.S. Constitution, the American Senate has agreed to hand over control of the Trump Impeachment trial to Jackie Weaver, of the East Cheshire Association of Local Authorities.

The unlikely star of the Handforth Parish Council viral Zoom meeting agreed to step in when senior Republicans failed to follow establish protocols or agree to due process, and she immediately threw out a couple of angry, shouty men who had been arguing about who was in charge of proceedings on Capitol Hill.

'In my colleague's defence' said one senator, 'this is the American Senate, Jackie Weaver really does have no authority here.'

Top lines for avoiding joyless Valentine's lockdown sex

- 'Let's make it really special by waiting just that bit longer and saving it to celebrate getting vaccinated.'
- 'I'm concerned about the kids' fragile emotional state, should we really risk disturbing their sleep at the moment?'

- 'Ooh, I'm so tempted, love, but couldn't the joyous release of our physical ecstasy undo all those good social distancing habits?'
- 'Call me soft, but it just feels disrespectful to all the people who've really suffered throughout this terrible time.'
- 'I'd love to, but somehow silly old me has managed to jam the lid of my laptop open with Teams still running, and glue it to the bedside table, so we'd be on full view.'
- 'I'm sorry, those daily government briefings are so depressing, I'm quite emotional- can we just cuddle instead?'
- 'I know it's over-commercialised, but it just doesn't feel like Valentine's without, I don't know, a card or a few silly flowers.'
- 'Is this really the right time to consider bringing another child into the world?'
- 'I died of COVID'

PM sets out timetable for U-turns

The Prime Minister has set out a clear timetable for forthcoming U-turns.

'We plan to change our minds about schools opening on the evening of the 7th March. This gives parents and teachers the shortest time possible to plan for alternatives.

'We are in talks with employers and unions about the worst possible time to do the old switcheroo on opening businesses; we have a golden opportunity with Brexit for firms to order goods for a planned reopening, in April. While the goods are delayed in customs, we announce a rethink and the products will uselessly arrive when no-one's there to receive them.

'I've booked my hols, so, obviously, I don't want anyone else there cluttering up the place, so the advice not to go abroad on holiday will stand.'

Geordie considers putting on thicker t-shirt

With most of Britain shivering in a prolonged spell of sub-zero temperatures a man from Newcastle has reportedly considered putting on a slightly thicker t-shirt.

As commuters struggled with icy roads and parts of the country remained covered in snow Wayne Riley, a proud Geordie, briefly wondered whether he would be warm enough going out in his Newcastle United shirt.

'I needed to pop to the shops for some Newcastle Brown Ale and I saw that it was minus seven outside, which is apparently considered a bit on the chilly side.' said Riley, 'Obviously I don't own a coat or a jumper but I do have a thick t-shirt that I bought for a trip to the Arctic circle a few years back.'

After thinking it over for a good few seconds Wayne decided not to be soft and set off on the two mile walk to the shop in his football shirt, shorts and flip-flops.

'Festival of Brexit' replaces Glastonbury

'We want to tap into the amazing mood that's transforming the nation: one that's newly independent, united and proud to be British,' said the Culture Secretary. 'It's about Britain doing what it does best. Which is wave flags, get lost in the moment and plug our ears with the sounds we love.'

Plans haven't been officially confirmed, but it is understood that the fields of Somerset will be swapped for the sunny uplands of Kent so that 'Europe can really see what it's missing.' Leaked blueprints suggest that the famed Stone Circle will be moved too, reimagined to reflect St George's cross.

Headlining will be Brexiteers Morrissey and Nigel Farage, with a non-ironic medley of 'Please, Please, Please Let Me Get What I Want', 'Let's give 'Heaven Knows I'm Miserable Now' and 'Panic on the streets of London.' Glastonbury founder, Michael Eavis, could not be reached for comment, but it is understood that he's seething with excitement.

The Sound of Mucus: COVID the Musical

The show will use previously written material in order to tell the story of outbreak. Starring such Broadway hits such as:

- The hills are alive with the sound of mucus,
- I'm just a lonely self-isolating goatherd,
- Oh, what a beautiful mourning,
- Getting to know 'flu, getting to know all about 'flu,
- I am reviewing self-isolation,
- Who wants to live in AstraZeneca?
- Stayin' Alive,
- Night Fever,
- I know him so unwell
- Chim chiminiee chim chim atchoo

Alongside there will be a number of songs sung by well-known starts, like Meatloaf singing 'Bat out of Hunan' and Alec Baldwin playing the role of Donald Trump who sings 'I'm gonna bleach that bug right outta my hair.'

Microscope fails to find one morsel of moral fibre in Republican Senators

The most powerful microscope on the planet, called the Really Totally Big Microscope, has been unable to detect even the wafferiest theeeen sliver of moral fibre in the vast majority of

Republican Senators. Professor Emily Hooper from MIT confirmed, 'Waffer theeeen is absolutely a scientific term used by world-leading microbiologists to refer to very small or narrow things like, for example, former US Presidents' minds.'

Admitted one senator: 'It's not as if Trump himself is a Republican politician - he only pretended to be one because Republicans are so dumb that they'd vote for an undercooked ham if it had a stamp of an elephant on it. But I'm the kind of guy decent, God-fearing Americans can count on to maintain loyalty to a puddle of yeti cum if I thought it would earn me one more dollar of campaign funding.'

Big Pharma warned that silly drug names are affecting public confidence.

The Government has asked pharmaceutical companies to give better, more impressive and confidence-building names to their drugs. A spokesman said that tocilizumab just sounded like an indigestion remedy and not something that would see off COVID 19.

Other drug names that were criticised as unlikely to command public respect include getuzacab, fitetheflab, shurbuttdab, frumadodgilab, andimacnab, and putitonmitab.

Tabloids desperate for pretty young blondes to start receiving vaccine

Editors say they are sitting on a tsunami of stock photos featuring pretty young blondes jumping for joy, husky brunettes flashing a bit of side boob and excited red heads texting a friend.

'The public are tired of seeing granny and grandpa having their vaccination jab....it was OK for a while but enough is enough. It is time to move on. We need to get back to our regular front-pages: borderline porn, images of scantily clad teens pouting at the camera and lads with a strategically placed shuttlecock stuffed down their jeans.

'Readers want to see a soft-skinned arm next to an enormous cleavage, not liver spots and a shopping trolley. They want to see nubile young flesh, not something a pack of ravenous hyenas would have turned down.'

COVID Research Group not really understanding the word 'Research'

A group of lockdown-sceptic back-bench MPs have tried to give the impression of thoughtful scientific study, by dropping in the word 'Research' – in place of 'Dumbwittery.' This was the same tactic adopted by the European Research Group, or as they were originally known 'Europe? What's that? Is it the Isle of Wight?'

As marketing rebrands go, it ranks up alongside the 'Millwall Peace & Reconciliation Bushwhackers', 'Prince Andrew's Boarding School for Wayward Girls' and 'Jo Swinson's ever popular Liberal Democrats.' Said one CRG member: 'We've researched COVID extensively and we can confirm it's a village in Wales.'

Emergency Services and plasterers count the cost of Dads making pancakes

Pancake Tuesday once again brings recipe-shy dads into the kitchen to create overly-doughy pancakes, which are somehow burnt on the outside and raw in the middle, and who will inevitably stick the pancakes to the ceiling in an effort to impress their bored, housebound, children.

'They just can't help themselves,' said Bertie Trowel of the Plasterers Guild. 'They've no idea about whisking so the kitchen walls look there's been an exorcism, and there are scorch marks everywhere as they've no idea about hob etiquette.

'Of course, they all try to impress their children when it gets to the 'flipping' stage, but unfortunately they seem unaware of difference between real life and cartoons – every year there are soggy pancakes stuck to the ceiling like they've been welded on with a blow torch.

'The Fire Crews go in first to make the place safe, and by the time we arrive the paramedics are usually split between applying Savlon to children with third degree burns and comforting a weeping wife.

'Then we have to chisel the pancakes off the ceiling before doing a whole plastering job on the walls and ceiling. It's carnage.

'We get the summers off, unlike the other guys who have to deal with the barbecue season, but the daft buggers never learn and we'll be out to the same people again next year.'

Travellers in quarantine hotels forced to attend sales and marketing conferences

'Six-thirty! Six-thirty in the morning! How is that anything like reasonable?' fumed Mr Ian Duncan, a part-time organic yoghurt blending specialist from Manchester and currently a 'guest' in a Government approved hotel.

'Four security guards woke us up, told us to get dressed, put hoods over our heads and dragged us off to the hotels' football pitch sized meeting room. I can stomach shelling out £3500 for ten nights imprisoned in a grim room with third-rate food and snipers on the roof, but this was completely unnecessary. I didn't even have time to finish reading yesterday's Sun on the bog, or put out the chip pan fire.'

'It was terrible,' agreed his wife, Abigail, confirming they'd returned from Dubai for work reasons. Mrs Duncan is an essential brand fashion consultant, advising Geordie Shore fans whether a thick gold chain or plate-sized earrings would look better matched with envy-inducing dayglo pink jogging outfits.

'It was a professional development event with some motivational speakers going on about sales enablement, driving consistent somethings and game-changing thingamajigs in the marketplace.'

'I can't see how visionary mindset empowering can help stop the virus, but I have to say the tea and sandwiches were quite nice, and at least we picked up some free pens, so we can now fill out our complaint forms.'

Trouser-press design revolutionised by quarantined Spaniard

A 54-year-old man from Barcelona has executed 'game-changing' modifications to a Corby 'Classic' trouser-press during an enforced two-week lockdown at the Marriot Hotel Heathrow.

Jose Gonzaga from Barcelona began dismantling an oak-veneered Mark 2 unit after a zoom call highlighted creases in the groin area of his linen slacks during a call to his elderly mother.

Using parts from a kettle, hairdryer and a small TV set in his room, he was able to achieve what experts have labelled the Holy Grail of steamed pressing. His trousers were said to be so flat that his lower half appears almost two dimensional.

University 'free speech champion' to be angry blacked-up taxi driver

Academics have expressed concern that the Government's newly appointed 'free speech champion' does not have an academic background and was convicted of flashing on Clapham Common in 1993. Dave Nowell of Dagenham, who is the Education Secretary's first cousin, will impose heavy fines or expel anyone who thinks racists should be fined or expelled.

Mr Nowell castigated reporters from the Daily Mail, Express, Der Strummer, Sun and the Telegraph for not giving right wing gob-jockeys their fair share of press coverage.

Speaking from a taxi rank outside Euston Station, Mr Nowell he said: 'Academics and students don't know shit! When I was invited to give a talk on bestiality in public places, Cardiff University shut me down! Well, I say enough is enough… Where-to now, guv?'

The Education Secretary has expressed his full confidence in Mr Nowell, who enjoys an annual salary of £97,000. Mr Nowell defended the high salary, claiming it would only take you as far as Fulham during rush hour.

We support Princess Latifa and everyone held captive on Alderman says Foreign Office

'Yes, we are deeply concerned for the safety and well-being of Princess Latifa and all people held captive on Alderman' confirmed the Foreign Office.

'I Googled the Princess and was horrified to find she had been battling the forces of evil since the late 1970s. What makes it worse is that she was held captive by her own father.

'We all know what happened to Princess Baratheon of Dragonstone - we cannot stand by and let this sort of thing happen all over again. Being burned at the stake for refusing to bend the knee in the era of Black Lives Matter is wrong. There is no place for it in the 21st century.

'And no Princess should be expected to kiss a frog in order to be rescued by a handsome Prince. I will be bringing this up at the next United Nations zoom meeting.

'It could be your little Princess next.'

Sturgeon: 5-7-year-olds deemed expendable

The Scottish Government has confirmed that from Monday 22nd February, Scotland's youngest pupils will return to school in a move that is tantamount to a cull. At a press conference today, an SNP spokeswoman explained: 'We can use the youngsters as COVID-canaries, so that if they start keeling over, we can extend Lockdown – they're annoying at that age anyway, and can't vote for independence, so it's no loss, really.'

'It's like some kind of warped version of Logan's Run, except we're getting rid of the young and protecting the elderly. A bit like the housing market.'

Second jab essential, to update microchips in first

This update is regarded as essential in order to fix security vulnerabilities in the drugs contained in the initial anti-COVID vaccinations. It is feared that, otherwise, the health-giving medicine might be at risk of contamination by some kind of virus.

All those who have had just one vaccination so far are urged to wear masks, keep their computers and smart phones at least 2 metres away from any other device, even when outdoors. Not to use them in pubs, cafes and restaurants or any other crowded place, and not to open any links in emails sent from viruses which they do not recognise.

A Health Official explained 'We've setup vaccination centres where people can take their computers to be vaccinated, starting with computers which are more than 8 years old, which are the most susceptible to the corruption of the software in the microchips, which are absolutely not and never have been embedded in the vaccinations.'

She confirmed: 'There is nothing to worry about, now please roll up your sleeve, install updates and restart Windows.'

Melania Trump to be broken up for parts

A leaked memo suggests that all the Melania consort-bots are to be brought in and dismantled. An unnamed source said that it was only a matter of time. The glass-faced bot had not been functioning correctly for some time. 'The talkifying unit has been a particular cause for concern. No-one could understand what she was saying.'

The laboratory in Ares 51 where she was developed will have time to refashion the consort-bot for future public engagements with Playdoh tyrant Donald (Jaysus) Trump when he goes back on the election trail. A scientist confirmed: 'It will have more features than the Ivanka II sex-bot, but less alimony.'

'Northern know-alls' to be last cohort vaccinated

The Health Secretary has announced that know it all northerners, who nod, smile and dismissively close their eyes when answering questions, will be the last group to be vaccinated against Coronavirus.

The Government's target date for the completion of all immunisation is early June, but the 5000 or so in this group will have to wait until household pets and woodland mammals have been dealt with first.

Geoffrey Horne, a retired 69-year-old civil engineer from Catterick wasn't surprised by the news when interviewed by a local news crew outside his local branch of Lidl.

'I said to the wife on day one of the lockdown, that I would be one of the last to be vaccinated against 2019-nCoV in early summer of 2021 and that subsequent jabs would be required in order to deal with mutations of the virus which will continue to evolve and lead to...'

Imperial College study: Summer Godzilla attack 'likely'

Imperial College has blamed a modelling error after their latest predictions for Coronavirus case numbers stated the UK remained at risk of Godzilla Attack in the Summer.

Initially tasked with estimating NHS admissions during the vaccine rollout, the institution reported that while a median estimate of 200 cases per day was most likely, outliers included the rising of the fictional giant lizard from the Atlantic and the obliteration of much of the south of England as he set his sights on London.

The Government have taken the simulation seriously and have placed the army on high alert. However, Prime Minister Boris Johnson is convinced a chap he met at the Groucho Club can persuade Rodan to come out of retirement and fly over London as a protective measure.

Turtles to be charged 10p for plastic bags

According to research, if turtles carry on using plastic bags at this rate, the ice caps will totally melt by the middle of next year, and the world will run out of plastic. Leading naturalist, Sir David Attenborough, said it was about time turtles were held accountable for their actions and took some responsibility for saving a planet they seemed hellbent on wrecking.

'Personally, I find the turtle to be a slippery customer,' he revealed. 'Apart from being hideously ugly, they're also at the centre of widespread child abuse allegations after thousands of their offspring were found abandoned on a beach. Let's face it, who in their right minds would trust someone who spends all day basking in the sun and lives in a chavvy shell suit?'

30 mph space probe sends back stunning images of traffic cones

An exploration probe sent to map the desolate outer reaches of the galaxy has unexpectedly encountered long lines of traffic cones. Astonished scientists are trying to figure out why there are traffic calming measures in a place where absolutely nothing has happened for billions of years.

Problems with the mission became apparent yesterday when the probe, which was travelling at half the speed of light, suddenly slowed to between 30 and 50 mph. Scientists repeatedly asked the probe if it was nearly there yet, until it malfunctioned and tried to turn itself around.

The first high-resolution photographs sent by the Newport-Pagnell voyager show what appears to be ghostly roadworks in the vast emptiness of space. The probe has since caught up with an earlier space craft that was launched in 1968. Scientists have left a safe stopping distance of three inches in case the first one should brake suddenly.

Russell Brand finally uses all of the words – just in one sentence

The vlogger, guru, and winner, in 12 BC, of Nazareth's Messiah of the Year competition, has finally combined the whole of the Oxford English Dictionary into one sentence. Pausing only for breath and sustenance, Mr Brand managed to use every known word, several unknown words and 206 euphemisms for willies.

What started about a quip about kittens, soon spiralled into a metaphysical discussion of the existence of blancmange, lasting for 48 days, without a comma in sight. The comedian is said to be proud of his achievement but upset that not everyone followed what he said.

Ulrika Jonsson 'still wouldn't' with man who says he definitely 'still would'

In a statement to the press Ulrika Jonsson, the Swedish-British TV presenter confirmed that while she was pleased to learn that John Rawlin, 56, of Sidcup, deemed her to be 'looking good for her age' and he definitely 'still would', she categorically 'still wouldn't' with him, clarifying further that she never would have or will.

Many women, including Dolly Parton, Carol Vorderman and Helen Mirren, welcomed Ulrika's statement, adding they hoped this issue had finally been resolved and men's attention could now focus more on older women's bodies of work rather than their bodies. John was asked to comment but was too busy staring at their chests.

Care Home residents get one visitor – the Grim Reaper

The Health Minister has promised to ease lockdown to by allowing the elderly to have one visitor, which could be a health insurer, an undertaker or someone selling Saga holidays. Residents are advised to think long and hard as to whom they invite and not to waste their choice on son or daughter that they did not like in the first place.

Said one resident: 'Originally I was going to ask my grandson, but then I thought, hold on Sid, if I've only got one pick, I'll better make it a good un. So instead, I've opted for Kim Kardashian, now she's single. I'm 97 so this might be my last chance to get my leg over.'

Explained a carer: 'One suggestion was that the visitor could be the Prime Minister, to shake their hand. But in the end, we decided on the Grim Reaper, as it amounts to the same thing.' On hearing this, the Grim Reaper was apprehensive: 'Are you sure it's safe for me to go in? The COVID mortality rates are still pretty high – and I should know.'

GB News to feature 'two-minute hate'

Andrew Neil, chairman of new news channel GB News has announced their morning programming will feature a two-minute hate daily at 7am.

The 120 seconds, said by Neil to give catharsis to those whose daily lives are subject to 'the woke agenda' will allow viewers to expel their anger and vehemence at images of celebrities such as Greta Thunburg and items such as almond milk and electric cars; while on-screen messages inform them of the latest so-called liberal facts from the BBC.

The hate will be followed by the two-minute wonder at 8am; where a loop of the national anthem plays over pictures of

Winston Churchill, Spitfires, and London during the Blitz. Neil expects all viewers to stand for the two-minute wonder, with those who fail to do so being labelled as anti-patriots – or worse – vegans.

Harry and Megan invite sponsorship for baby names

Cash-strapped former Royals, Harry and his wife Megan have announced that they will be seeking to make the naming of their expectant baby a major source of income for the financial year ending 31/3/2022. Companies such as Disney, Deliveroo and Debenhams have all been approached to bid with the highest offer being afforded Christian and middle names of their own choice.

A modern baby can have up to 17 middle names providing at least one 'password name' combines numbers, upper- and lower-case letters and one of the following symbols ±|_&$*.

Most of the money raised is likely to be swallowed up by the repayment of a 'soft loan ' from Prince Andrew, who provided a payday loan for the refurbishment of Frogmore Cottage in Windsor where the young couple lived before running away from reality.

WHO announces major virus investigation breakthrough: Wuhan is not in China

Reading from a prepared statement, in an unprepared cell, a spokesman said: 'If Wuhan is not in China, as the Chinese authorities and experts have proved beyond all reasonable doubt, then clearly the whole thing is not their fault.

'The focus of our attention is now on somewhere else, somewhere, possibly a bit Taiwanese sounding; maybe even El Salvador or Charlie's Chocolate Factory, but most definitely somewhere. Although we still think it's likely it originated in bats or pangolins which are possibly more indigenous to Taiwan than a confectionary factory.'

Before responding to suggestions that the whole thing is one big fat cover-up, their bodyguards swiftly bundled the delegation of scientists and fast-food entrepreneurs into a fleet of large SUVs. They were then driven at high speed back to a government-approved re-education facility and escorted to their cages.

Excitement grows as John Lewis prepare to broadcast Christmas advert

With only 312 shopping days left until Christmas, John Lewis is preparing to show its much-anticipated Christmas advert, with Morrisons and Tesco promising to launch theirs next week. According to some sources the John Lewis ad will feature a sad snowman who is befriended by a Brussel sprout.

John Lewis is estimated to have spent £43 million pounds on the sixty second ad, with a voice over by Tom Hardy imitating a mouse. Marks and Spencer have spent a measly £12 million pounds on its seasonal campaign which features a French Santa in a helicopter, airlifting in delicious food to starving British street urchins.

The Morrisons commercial may prove to be controversial. It features a 'typical' happy family at Christmas. The grandad will cough and appear to drop dead with his face in the gravy boat. The shocked family are delighted when he sits up and shouts 'Only kidding! Merry Christmas one and all.'

Britain to send interplanetary narrowboat to explore Martian canals

'We have the technology' explained professor Bill Higgins. 'We know all about how to build canal barges and how to sail them, and we've now also got a pretty good grip of space technology. All we've got to do is combine these skills.'

'Using a boat will be a Martian-environment-friendly way of exploring the planet' continued the professor. 'Not only will it be low-carbon, but we won't even leave any footprints, let alone tyre tracks. However, using an ordinary boat would be silly because boats can be rather big and, quite honestly, mostly full of nothing-at-all. But a narrowboat is perfect; we've checked and it will just fit inside a rocket.'

'In fact, development of the project is progressing rapidly. The only real task left to our scientists now, is the design a suitable protective suit for the barge horse.'

Focus on data, not dates, unless the data clashes with Matt Hancock's holiday

The PM explained: 'Matty-boy's been an absolute brick through the pandemic. He's followed the instructions that I've given him, that were given to me, then given to me again because I'd fallen asleep, to the letter.

'My Right Honourable friend deserves his self-catering fortnight above a karaoke bar in Newquay, and we will ensure the data fits so he gets it! We've done it with everything else without consequence, why not this?

'It's not just the Health Secretary, we aim to be able to have controlled the transmission of coronavirus enough for everyone to take a holiday, or pay a short visit to Amanda Holden's parents' house at least once this summer.'

Wales no longer the size of Wales

Due to coastal erosion and leakage on Gloucester border, Wales has shrunk from its traditional dimensions, thus becoming an area the size of less than Wales. Instead, Slovenia will now become the standard International Measurement for 'an area that sounds quite shockingly large but is actually quite small.'

Originally Wales was 20735km^2 or 14 million rugby size pitches, which is a ridiculous amount of rugby pitches, even for a country the size of Wales. Since then, the natives have been hiding their shrinkage from international cartographers, by stuffing gym socks in and around Pembrokeshire.

Those typically destroying the Brazilian rain forest have been asked to scale back on their efforts, to ensure continuity. Said one logger: 'It turns out I've been deforesting an area the size of El Salvador, which at least is a region I've heard of. I was shocked to discover just how many trees we've been cutting down. I'd always thought they were talking about Whales the fish.'

Ironically, Plaid Cymru insisted that the UK would still be losing an area the size of Wales, 'in the not-too-distant future.'

Cub stripped of woggle after leaving Scout pack

A seven-year-old was stripped of his 'joining in' activity badge and several other cub titles after giving up his role during bob-a-job week. Said his Scout Leader: 'He will no longer be welcome in the scout hut and he will certainly not be joining us in future for a sing-song around the camp fire.'

Cryogenically frozen customer finally gets through to helpline

A defrosted HSBC customer who rang a helpline in 1971 claims to have finally gotten through to someone. The customer rang the bank to ask about decimalisation and was put on hold. After pressing '3' to become cryogenically frozen in liquid nitrogen, she spent the next 50 years waiting for someone to pick up. Jane Crimmock, an avid Donny Osmond fan, was defrosted last week when she became number 253 in the queue.

The delighted customer said: 'They were experiencing a particularly high volume of calls due to joining the European Common Market. Unfortunately, the cryogenic process has damaged some of my brain tissue and I've forgotten what it was I called up about. I thought my mum would kill me when she saw the phone bill, but luckily, she died during the Falklands War. Have we joined the Common Market yet?'

MPs awarded minimum wage

The Parliamentary Standards Authority has given in to pressure from MPs and reduced their salary to a more competitive £8.72 an hour. MPs have been clamouring for years to have their pay slashed, arguing that living below the poverty line increases efficiency and offers MPs the flexibility they crave. Instead of their usual 4-to-5-year contracts, MPs will hang around the tea room hoping to be called to do something.

Sir Geoffrey Clifton-Brown, who mops corridors and cleans toilets between committee meetings, said: 'At long last I now have the freedom to choose my own hours. I've just been offered a 12-hour filibustering night shift, which is great. The nanny can look after the kids.'

The change comes days after Sir Keir Starmer announced Labour would work with Sports Direct to build a better and fairer society, although he's still waiting for a call back.

New variant of Boris Johnson discovered

'Unlike the variant that was dominant at the end of previous lockdowns, or when relaxing the rules for Christmas, this variant seems to be willing to take things much slower and show some caution,' one scientist said.

'This variant is particularly different to the variant who went round shaking hands with people infected with coronavirus or the variant who just asked people to avoid pubs, and as for the variant that promised we could turn the tide against the pandemic in just 12 weeks, well, the less said the better.'

Early signs suggest that the variant that was discovered yesterday could be the least dangerous of all the Boris Johnson variants seen so far. But experts have warned to be cautious as further mutations could still take place.

'We saw how quickly a new strain of Boris Johnson can emerge, when within 24 hours he went from wanting all schools to open to closing them in a new lockdown,' another scientist pointed out. 'Views on so-called vaccination passports seem to be in the process of mutating, so god knows what else might change.'

Unfortunately, no vaccine has ever been discovered for poor leadership or political disasters.

Derbyshire police remove all benches from county

'Just because some London folks have endorsed al fresco caffeine abuse doesn't mean we want these metropolitan perversions up here,' said Chief Constable Norman Gritstone.

'As you all know, during lockdown we've operated a policy of zero tolerance of 'enjoying the fresh air', and we're not stopping now. Derbyshire's natural beauty should be viewed as intended, out of the window of a police patrol car, and entirely free from humans littering the landscape with their so-called 'outdoor recreation.' The proper place for humans is indoors watching TV, or failing that, in one of our cells.'

Population of England already asking Boris 'Are we there yet?'

As with any journey, the kids aren't interested in the road map. They just want to get to the destination.

They have already been sitting in the back of the motor for a year; they are bored playing with the crap Track and Trace App they were given; and quite a few of them have already been sick.

Dad keeps changing the rules and has threatened to lock them up for ten years. The last resort is for the kids to fight each other and moan 'Daaaaad. Are we there yet? Uncle Dominic got to Barnard Castle in half a day. Mind you, he still said it was rubbish and hardly worth all the fuss it caused.'

Government commission statue of Matt Hancock to topple

The commissioned statue will depict the health secretary on stage bellowing a karaoke song into a microphone, while excited party donors clamour to stuff cash into the PPE mask he's wearing like a G-string.

The design has drawn controversy due to Mr Hancock being virtually naked. The spokesperson continued: 'We thought it important to depict Matt naked to symbolise his openness, in contrast to the legal ruling. We were advised to add the sexy mask for public decency reasons.

The statue of the man under whose tenure 120,000 people have so far died, will be erected on a plinth blocking the main entrance of London's Northwick Park hospital, and when toppled thousands of banknotes will be launched into the air from a hole between his buttocks, like corrupt cash confetti. The spokesperson added: 'All we have to do now is persuade the health secretary not to get a bronze spray tan and climb up there himself. Lord knows, the cash is ready to go.'

Five things we learned from Prince Harry's Corden interview

1. James Corden has lost a bit of weight since moving to America but not a great amount
2. Prince Harry is still ginger and proud
3. Harry was at his diplomatic best not to mention the film 'Cats', that Corden was sadly a part of and added nothing to
4. Harry is still happily married. The prince modestly wore his wedding ring, mentioned 'Her Indoors' several times and at no point during the interview did he try and woo anyone. At no point did he check Tinder on his phone He does not know anyone called Prince Andrew.
5. Harry has not seen anything good on television recently. Including this

'Elon Musk no longer world's richest person' –but he's still pretty rich, right?

Tesla's boss has seen his fortune shrink from an 'insanely, disgustingly, uber number of bajillions' to just a mere disgusting number of bajillions. This has meant he will have to cut his cloth accordingly, if by cloth you mean something the size of Belgium.

A spokeswoman confirmed: 'It's been a humbling experience for Mr Musk, he has had to cease building condos on the Moon and has had to stop putting diamonds on his cornflakes. He has also had to shelve plans to buy up New Zealand and turn it into a themed skate park.'

This means Jeff Bezos will return to the top of the rich list, having spent the last few months panhandling in downtown LA. Mr Bezos had been surviving on welfare cheques, off-cuts of discarded meat and was down to his last gazillion.

Mr Musk promised to regain his position at the top of the rich list, by pursuing his dream of patenting oxygen. A friend commented: 'Elon has always said that money can't buy you happiness, mainly because Bill Gates already owns 99% of the share options in happiness. Remember what Jesus said, the geek shall inherit the earth.'

Festival of Stinking Toilets to go ahead

Fans of faecal waste and the smell of stale urine are determined not to let the temperamental British weather stop their fun this year. If it rains, they will slide around in filth, and if it's hot they will catch botulism.

A festival spokesperson said: 'Fans of portaloos, E coli and cess pits are in for a real treat this year. It promises to be the filthiest and most disease-ridden swamp-fest on record. We have some big names lined up, they'll be performing a set called 'Game of Thrones', which has to be smelled to be believed.'

Organisers have warned people without tickets to stay away as there will be no other toilet paper available.

Surface of Mars 'actually quite boring' – NASA

The U.S. space agency is reportedly disappointed with the first images it received from the Perseverance Rover this week. 'It's just a bunch of rocks and dirt,' said their spokesperson. 'It's not even particularly red – more sort of a brownish orange.'

Scientists were particularly upset at the lack of alien life. 'We were banking on there being a Martian welcoming party with some Alf-like beings, or at the very least some of the aliens from Space Jam,' she explained. 'If I'd known we were just looking for the ancient remains of some microscopic organisms I wouldn't have turned down that job with the Space Force.'

'Maverick' Health Secretary tell-all interview

'Sometimes I do 34 in a 30 zone. I'm a maverick', said the fictitious Health Secretary. 'I like to get pissed at parties and kiss women. Real women, with breasts. I don't kiss their breasts, obviously. I'm not an animal.'

The Minister is leaning back in his chair at ten degrees from the horizontal. He's still a long way from the tipping point but I can sense that he isn't comfortable, and also a blush has started up his neck. I think it's because he said 'breasts.' It's rising up his cheeks now, and he quickly returns the chair to a stable position and shuffles some papers on his desk. There's an awkward silence. He looks like a Belisha beacon.
'I have a leather jacket', he tells me, apropos of nothing. 'Real leather. I look a bit like James Dean in it.' I try to imagine James Dean blushing and fail. Maybe the jacket would help.

'So, you kiss women? That must be fun.'

'Yes', he says, but his mind seems to be elsewhere. 'It isn't illegal.'

'Kissing women?'

'The procurement stuff. I didn't break any laws. The PM said so.'

Maverick looks at me with a steady gaze. I sense he feels he's on firmer ground.

'So . . . those massive contracts – they're okay?'

'Totally okay'

'No problems because they're with, you know, dormant companies run by friends of yours?'

'I have a leather jacket,' he says, then tapers off. It's going to be a long interview.

Watergate hotel franchise unable to keep up with gate-themed scandals

A spokesperson said: 'To be honest, some of the scandals seem to be rather trivial, based as they are on celebrities. Nipple-gate, Squidgy-gate and Fridge-gate are all but forgotten, yet no one thinks about the pressure this puts on us in terms of designing and building an entire hotel complex for each one, and that's before you factor in paying the staff. The Blobby-gate convention centre can still be let out for events but the rooms remain empty 90% of the time.'

He added: 'In the days of Irangate we were able to stay afloat thanks to the high level of interest in the Iran-contra affair internationally, plus the Irangate Hotel's excellent conference facilities and transport links, though the daily crop of minor scandals today leaves us in the constant state of catch-up.

'We've no sooner erected the Sharpiegate hotel and integral shopping centre when Salmondgate kicks off. Sadly, these days it only takes a few people on Twitter to coin the term when commenting on a celebrity tiff or political faux pas, and off we go again.'

'If people just stopped calling things 'gate' all this extra work wouldn't be necessary.'

Hummingbirds admit to not knowing the words

Naturalists have confirmed that North American Hummingbird has faked knowing the words to the Star-Spangled Banner. Instead, they have been hiding at the back of the choir, mouthing the lyrics, and occasionally humming in a predictable, but tuneless fashion.

These clueless, miniature birds have regularly mashed up 'Cotton Eyed Joe' with the words from 'Mambo No.5.' While their attempt at the USA's national anthem usually ends:

'And the smar-smingled bonner in something something wave,

O'er the gland of the tree and the blah of the wave - Is it wave again, is that right?' I'm sure there's a bit about liking figgy pudding, it's the same tune.'

As an encore, hummingbirds will often try to navigate themselves through the more unintelligible parts of 'Come on Eileen', humming the sections they cannot understand, which is approximately 99%. A spokeswoman for hummingbirds said: 'Mmphff mmm mmm hmmm.'
Not posting snow photos to lead to arrest under new UK law

People who do not upload beautiful shots of their local area blanketed in snow will be deemed to be holidaying in Dubai and therefore breaking lockdown rules, according to the Government.

Said one MP: 'Social media is an absolute sh*tshow when it snows – with everyone and his mother putting photos online, so we may as well make use of it. And if it doesn't snow, then fake it with 10 kilos of Columbian's finest'.

Trump pardons Mrs Brown's Boys

There is a growing international outrage after the creators of 'comedy' series Mrs Browns Boys received a Presidential pardon from Donald Trump. Convicted of crimes against humanity the shows team will now walk free despite causing unprecedented misery for viewers since 2011. Said one voter: 'In comparison, Watergate was funny'.

99% of Brits struggling with January finances despite Christmas being cancelled

Almost every person in the UK has maxed out their bank accounts just 12 days into January, despite nothing being open for them to spend their hard-earned money on. Barely 2 weeks into the new year and people across the country are scratching their heads as to why their house has been repossessed by Santa. Explained one homeowner: 'I'm pretty sure I followed guidance and stayed at home looking miserable. Trouble is misery loves company – and the new iPhone'.

In other news...

Chinese skip year of the bat for second time

Headline writer receives vaccine. Buy Microsoft products!

Guinea's announcement of Ebola outbreak decried as attention seeking by COVID

Royal baby named after Prince Albert 'has a ring to it'

Welsh doggers praise decision to allow four people to exercise outside together

Tories panic after Boris injected with truth serum instead of vaccine by mistake

Boris wins COVID skeet shooting trophy – 'moving targets a speciality'

Chinese New Year: Goodbye 'year of the mullet', hello 'year of the ponytail'

Prouf readers wonted. Count the errrors in this advert to aplly

UK to trade spare vaccine for Eurovision vote

Peter Crouch and Richard Osman voice concerns about long COVID

After Salmond and Sturgeon, SNP looking for more candidates with fish names

Government unable to decide the colour of vaccine passports.

Scientists disappointed the iceberg as big as London isn't the size of Wales

Texans told to boil running water: Little Bull and Cochise now in hiding

Supreme Court rules 'mum's taxi' drivers are workers not self-employed

Ireland delighted that UK will share surplus vaccines with developing countries

Daft punk to take it softer, slower, quieter, calmer from now on

Paltrow confirms avocado stuffed up chuff is no protection against COVID-19

Five Go Dobbing in the Neighbours

Temperature set to drop to -13ºc tonight 'in Iain Duncan–Smith's stony heart'

Film awards criticized for lack of diversity by middle-aged white men

Harry & Meghan warn press about intrusion, offer TV rights to new baby scan

Former British Leyland bosses delighted at Mars Rover success.

Get Dick out campaign against Met Chief gathers momentum Morea late

SNP claims it's Scotland's turn to host Stonehenge for the next 5,000 years

COVID jab - 'It hurt like a bastard,' says Queen

Mars in Chinese territorial waters, says Beijing

Pompous arse to – I started so I'll finish – pompous arse to quit Mastermind

Uncle Andrew hopes it's a girl, says Palace

Bullshit 'off the scale' as all businesses argue why they should re-open first

Exploratory rover lands on earth, but finds no evidence of intelligent life

Giggling Martians awaiting discovery of huge cock and balls on dark side of Mars

Russian vaccine has side effect of making their athletes run 20% faster

Apple launch iVax vaccine at £2,000 a time & needs upgrading every six months

Boeing accused of raising fly-tipping to a whole new level

Confusion over celebration of decimalisation after just 4-1/6 dozen years

NASA finds outs what the Martian is for 'oi! Get orf moi laand'

Hancock promises all Tory donors to be offered PPE contract by Easter

Sputnik V vaccine gives 92% protection, except in Salisbury

March 2021

125,000 dead, but you got the sense that Boris Johnson had only just started. Commercial landlords got twitchy about people working from home, so insisted that returning to work is just like Dunkirk – which would make them the Nazis? And the one Brexit dividend of Nigel Farage going away, is yet to materialize.

Furloughed worker can't quite remember what his job is

Philip Stevens, 36, from Camberley, has admitted that he is terrified that Chancellor Rishi Sunak might announce the end of the furlough scheme in this week's budget speech.

Stephens was furloughed on 11 April last year and has been enjoying the 80% salary but cannot for the life of him remember what it is that he actually does for a living. Having spent the last 11 months playing with the kids, doing DIY and walking the dog 12 times a day, he has liked it so much that he has forgotten everything in his life before COVID-19.

'I've no idea what it is I do,' Stephens said. 'I've looked through all my emails but there's no clues. I've been through my wardrobe and there are no uniforms, brightly coloured, ill-fitting polo shirts or particularly cheap polyester suits. I've even looked through all the kitchen drawers and there are no hairnets, badges or lanyards. There's not even a big bunch of keys. I'm really starting to panic now.'

'I even went for regression therapy, but that didn't help. I discovered that I was an important courtier during the reign of Louis XIV and a galley slave at the time of the eruption of Vesuvius, but I've no idea what I was doing this time last year.'

Johnson enjoys '125,000 dead' popularity bounce

Latest opinion polls show the great British public is backing one of the worst death rates in Europe. Reacting to the shock findings by YouGov and Ipsos MORI, Sir Keir Starmer promised to start killing more elderly people, especially in Red Wall areas.

Boris Johnson has enjoyed a steady increase in support since he masterminded a cheeky 20,000 deaths in nursing homes. Responding to the unexpected poll 'bounce', a group of Tory MPs has called on the PM to publicly urinate on corpses in a hospital morgue while telling hospital staff they are all fired. They have dubbed this Operation Grenfell, just for bantz.

What was that noise outside last night? Top 15 answers from your community page.

- 'Kids letting off fireworks, probably. Gets earlier every year. My dog Trudy was so scared she shat herself inside-out and run off down the woods. Shou'ldnt be aloud'
- 'Trouble is though, kids have got nothing to do round here after they shut the youth centre'
- 'Well maybe if they did'nt vandalise the youth centre the council would'nt have closed it would they?'
- 'Atmospheric conditions'
- 'U wot? We don't have 'atmospheric conditions' here. I should know Iv lived here all my life. FUMMIN!!!!'
- 'Probably Colin Mitchell letting one off after another night on the pickled eggs LOL'
- 'When was this noise? I didn't hear one'
- 'My father was the Town Clerk for 15 years before we moved to Lugwardine and he resigned in disgust because they were all so useless. Seems like nothing's changed'
- 'A metaphor for Brexit'

- 'So I suppose you would have preferred Corbyn then??!!'
- 'It was a meteor burning up. A man in Bishops Frome caught it on his camera phone and posted it on Twitter'
- 'Bishops Frome's 20 miles away U donut!!!!'
- 'Probably that bloke from Number 23. He always puts his bins out loudly'
- 'We used to have discos every Friday night at the youth centre when I was young, then we'd pile into my dad's minivan and go to Bosbury for a fight. None of them drugs, mind you'
- 'There was no noise. FAKE NEWS. Wake up sheeple!'

Sunak offers a free fish with every vaccine

Chancellor of the Exchequer Rishi Sunak has delighted beleaguered British fishermen by offering everyone in the UK a free fish (from British territorial waters only) with their COVID jab. The new 'Eat Trout to Help Out' voucher scheme will encourage Brits to eat more fish and stop fishermen going bust, the Government has claimed.

One Devon fisherman said: 'It's a thumbs-up for Fishy Rishi's cod snack! We thought we were screwed. If the virus doesn't kill us, this Eat Trout to Help Out voucher scheme will help us limp on for a few more weeks. The Brexit dividends just keep on rolling in!'

Bot to be used for all Prince Philip health updates, BBC confirms

'We've been using the bot for the last two weeks since Prince Philip went into hospital, if truth be known', said a BBC inside source. 'It's programmed with over 500 quite speculative adverbs and non-committal health statuses - the sort of responses you'd give to someone who you pass in the street who asked how you were doing.'

'We also have a computer-generated avatar of Nicholas Witchell, which now appears in the studio instead of the real thing, complete with features such as a raised eyebrow to express understated scepticism, and the slightest upturning of the mouth when he says things like 'It might be expected that...', or 'Given what we know about the Prince....''

'Witchell Bot also has around 1,000 phrases built into its hard drive, which hint at some exclusive access to the Royals, but which also make it clear that they haven't told us a bloody thing', continued the source.

'Version 2.0 can randomly generate frustratingly empty sentences to fill one-minute chats with the news anchor, then none of us needs to pretend that an actual royal correspondent is parked outside the hospital all day.'

When asked how the Royals felt about the use of the new device, Witchell Bot replied: 'The Palace doesn't give hourly updates on what it thinks, it's just not "how things are done". But we might anticipate, given recent events (eyebrow) and what sources have in the past been quoted by others as having said, that we may at some point soon (left lip curl) get an update, indicating exactly how they feel about this development.'

Tresemmé COVID-19 vaccine approved by FDA and 85% of 132 women

A new COVID vaccine developed by Tresemmé, which is the first to include Guar Hydroxypropyltrimonium Chloride and DMDM Hydantoin, has been praised highly by hairdressers across the nation as 'Probably preventing breathing difficulties whilst also stopping traffic fumes being absorbed into hair.'

New hair products typically take five to ten years of intensive R&D before release, but thanks to new processes introduced by

Tresemmé, including feeding researchers with Biotin and Hethylisothiazolinone, the research cycle was reduced to weeks.

While the FDA admitted that Tresemmé was unable to provide any evidence that it prevented the user catching COVID-19, it said that the benefits of visibly thicker and fuller hair in just one use outweighed any non-clinical disadvantages, adding that: 'All those lovely ladies can't be wrong. And they're worth it.'

Schrödinger's Brexit policy announced

Under a new Government policy called 'Brexin', the UK would simultaneously be inside and outside the Union, with public service split between Remain and Leave voters. Supermarkets would offer a full range of products to Remainers, while Brexiteers would get empty shelves and EU imports - either out of date, considerably more expensive or both.

Under the new arrangements Remainers would keep freedom of movement with a red passport. Leavers would have a blue (well, black actually) passport, enabling everyone to stand in extra-long queues to no longer work or live in the country of your choice, while still holding a black (or blue, is it?) passport.

The NHS too would be split, with the Remainer version staying critically underfunded, while the Brexit NHS would be equally underfunded (they didn't really expect the £380 million a week, did they?) but would only have British-born staff – five in total.

Your boss wants you back so he can look down your blouse – again

Your employer has made an impassioned plea for you to return to face-to-face tasks, so he can return to hand to buttock management, it has emerged. Remote working may not have harmed your productivity, but it has severely restricted his ability to have a 'crafty w*nk' in the unisex toilet.

'It's been a frustrating time for all of us. It's better for workers to feel the mutual support that comes with shared stories of harassment. Fitness improves, particularly if you're being chased around the shredder,' said your boss. 'The place is COVID-safe now. I've provided hand gel and lubricant in every stall, all masks are leather or rubber and I've insisted on waist-height partitions, in case anyone wants to go topless.'

Kevin McCloud wowed by shipping-container-style overhaul of Westminster Palace

Shooting his latest series of Grand Designs, polished concrete fetishist Kevin McCloud has gushed like a dam burst of Care Bears at the contemporary styling of a major renovation project in central London, known unofficially as the Houses of Parliament.

'What they have done here is a stroke of genius,' oozed McCloud. 'It is a bold statement fit for the 21st century and represents a shift away from over-elaborate, faux 1834 stylisation. By choosing to replace everything with jauntily stacked shipping containers, what they've said here is that this is a utilitarian return to the true roots of Thameside urban commerce. It is industrial minimalism at its most deliciously stark,' McCloud said.

'By recladding the Big Ben clock tower in iconic Marlboro fag packet livery, they have shown an extraordinary level of consideration towards how the structure respects its surrounding environment. Evocative. And, dare I say it, erotic. In true Grand Designs tradition, the masterminds of this project moved into humble dwellings just off-site with, yes, another baby on the way. But will they be in by winter 2046?'

Wales to be sold to Russia

Among the details of the budget are plans to pay off a portion of the money the Government has spent on COVID-19 by selling Wales and its inhabitants to Russia.

'It was a tough, but necessary decision,' said the Chancellor. 'We considered selling off Scotland or Northern Ireland, but at the end of the day we felt the Welsh would make the best slaves for Russian oligarchs, given how easy they've been to subjugate historically.'

Russia is reportedly very happy with the deal and plans to turn the country into a summer holiday destination. 'With an array of beaches, an average summer temperature of 16°C, and 0% nuclear fallout – for now – Wales will be the nicest region of Russia by far,' said a Kremlin spokesperson.

Sources also report that the ruggedly handsome, absolutely heterosexual President Putin plans to keep Tom Jones as a pet.

Elijah Wood 'has not aged since 1995'

Scientists have confirmed that film actor Elijah Wood has remained at the age of 15 since 1995, a disorder called 'Noel Gallagher's disease.' Through a mix-up between the Fountain of Eternal Youth, a Botox injection and the dying wish of Walt Disney, Wood has been trapped in the body of a young boy. This also allegedly happened to Michael Jackson, but he later settled out of court.

Most child actors find fame early but only Elijah Wood has managed to remain a child. By contrast, Daniel Radcliffe is 31 and is ageing at an alarming rate, destined to eventually become Wood's father.

Some believe that the secret of his youth is an exclusive Gwyneth Paltrow skincare regime, made from anal glands, while others suggest it is exposure to a very different One Ring. It is also rumoured that Wood has a painting of a wizened Mickey Rourke in his attic, not because he is sucking the life out of Rourke but simply, who wants a painting of Mickey Rourke in their house?

Shunted Gove celebrates latest 'negative promotion'

Losing out to Boris Johnson as Prime Minister, Lord Frost as Brexit Secretary and Mr Blobby as a convincing human being, Michael Gove is insisting his new role as Downing Street's 'tea lady' places him at the very heart of Cabinet, despite a key policy change also forcing him to enter meetings through the window.

Running as tight a trolley as his characteristic sphincter-lipped expression of clenched incredulity at each new demotion, 'Stovey Govey' is reportedly clinging to a belief in his ability to influence EU negotiations by supplying the nation's top dimwits with heavily caffeinated drinks, foie gras and cheese strings.

A Downing Street insider confirmed: 'With his whipped fancies and creamy buns, Mikey remains a vital cog in the wheels of Government, at least as far as the Wagon variety are concerned. Don't call him a trolley dolly, though, he prefers 'Chief Underemployed Nutritional Tactician'.'

Dr Seuss books to be made species-neutral

Following on from its decision to pull six books from circulation due to insensitive imagery, Dr Seuss Enterprises has promised to be more 'species-inclusive', with Woodland Mammal in Socks, Yertle the Shelled Reptile and Horton Hears a Sentient Being.

Additionally, the company have replaced all gender pronouns with a picture of a duck and are considering broadening the professional scope of the author to make him more accessible to children from all walks of life. Future titles will be published under different monikers, including Homeopath Seuss, Plumber Seuss and Unemployed Seuss.

Couple who Escaped to the Country escape back to London

Fans of extremely self-absorbed rich people are celebrating after a middle-aged couple from London, Dorset, Melton Mowbray and London again, finally achieved the long sought-after Holy Grail of TV property porn.

Richard and Venetia Hume-Walker, both 56, first appeared on Series 14 of the BBC's Escape to the Country in 2013, when Nicki Chapman helped them to swap their townhouse in Richmond for an eight-bed Georgian manor house, 12 miles from Bridport in rural Dorset.

'We wanted to get back to the simple life,' said Venetia, an interior designer. 'I lived my dream of raising chickens and alpacas on our 23-acre back garden, while Richard carried on his freelance marketing business in one of the converted oast houses. The seven spare bedrooms would certainly have come in handy too, if friends had ever wanted to visit.'

Finding the fuel costs of the twice-weekly commute back to London to be prohibitively expensive for her Subaru and his Range Rover, the couple went on Escape to the Perfect Town in 2018. Aided by Jonnie Irwin, they settled into a half-timbered Tudor merchant's house in Melton Mowbray.

'It was so handy for shops and doctors and we were glad to get away from the smell of chicken manure,' explained Venetia at the time. 'We would still have been able to put up friends in the three spare bedrooms. And Richard has always liked traditional English pork pies, haven't you Richard?' Richard nodded.

The couple can be seen completing their property odyssey on the new-launch show, Escape from the Country, next month. This time, they have traded in market town life for a town house in Richmond because they needed to be near to London for work purposes and hoped to make new friends there.

The Hume-Walkers' only daughter, Alexandra, 28, could not be reached for comment as she emigrated to New Zealand immediately after leaving school in 2009 and has not been in contact with them since.

'When It's Kinder to Say Nothing' – and other cards by Priti Patel

Are you finding it difficult to express a disingenuous affirmation sincerely to a not-so special someone? Why not choose a passive-aggressive card from the Home Secretary to convey your sanctimonious self-absorbed opinion, leaving the receiver with nothing but the perfect bitter aftertaste of your toxic superiority to forever fester in their sub-conscious?

Select from these topics and their soulless endearments. There are over three hundred thousand Code of Conduct-compliant unpleasantries to choose from!

- Sympathy: 'I'm sorry if you feel bereaved'
- Well done: 'In recognition of your sense of achievement'
- Wedding: 'Wishing you the happiness together that escaped you alone'
- Valentine's Day: 'I love the way you love me'
- You're leaving: 'It'll be heart-warming for you to feel you'll be missed'
- New house: 'Hoping this house will be a home.'

- Missing you: 'My thoughts were with you when I picked this card'
- New baby: 'Congratulations! A(nother) miracle for you to be proud of'
- Friendship: 'Only a friend like you would cherish our friendship'
- Apology: 'I believe the word you're expecting here, is sorry'
- And the timeless: 'No! You're the bully'

Public school boys march to Jarrow demanding jobs

A group of hungry Oxbridge graduates have set out on a gruelling 300-mile march from Knightsbridge to Jarrow, protesting at a lack of jobs in gold mining or real estate. Wearing tweeds and riding boots and led by a stockbroker playing with his organ, they march under the banner 'United we stand, to make a bloody fortune.'

The Knightsbridge Hunger Marchers have managed to doss down in country hotels and live off the kindness of strangers and trust funds. They intend to present a petition at Jarrow Town Hall, demanding that it is converted into exclusive luxury apartments, for which they expect 15% commission.

'Bring a toy to the last day of home-schooling' greeted with apathy

Children not at a school in Leeds have not shown much enthusiasm at the offer to bring a toy to their last day of home-schooling, or indeed the opportunity to watch a film together to celebrate the end of term, as the majority of them have spent Lockdown working their way through the entire Netflix catalogue.

There was little interest in the traditional triggering the fire alarm during assembly, as pressing the Test button on the smoke alarm was considered a bit pathetic.

Schools allowed pupils to take a toy or game along for one day only and relaxed the school uniform rules to permit the students to wear their home clothes, but the kids all said, 'We've been doing that anyway Mum, sorry I mean Miss.'

Adopt Nigel Farage for £3 a month

Nigel Farage has abdicated as leader of Reform UK. In a video statement posted on Twitter, the far-right evangelist said stirring-up nationalistic tension had been his 'life's work' and had taken over 'the best part of three decades' but now is the time to step down from his upturned milk crate of power.

He made clear the move will not see him leaving politics entirely, so for just £3 per month you can help to keep Nigel's spirits up with a pint of ale from an online craft brewery or a pack of ten low quality EU ciggies. In return, donors will receive:

- A 10x12 print of Nigel, rampant, on a Kent hillside surveying his blessed moat, the English Channel
- A recording of Nigel bellowing his favourite childhood fascist anthems
- A picture of them edited into a photograph of British MEPs, with Nigel, cheekily showing their backs to their European Parliament pension paymasters
- A replica [insert name] Party rosette
- The opportunity to participate in an organised walk of support for Nigel, directly behind his chauffeur driven car

In addition, the first thousand donors will each receive a unique cuddly Nigel, compete with squeaky megaphone and wardrobe of multi-coloured 'milkshake' suits.

It's not the thought that counts, it's the money. So, please give generously. If Nigel can't walk away, how can you?

Family concerned after dad forgets to do that fortune cookie joke.

What was supposed to be a Saturday night Chinese takeaway ritual turned into a night from hell for one Braintree family. The Johnsons of Festive Road were left dazed and confused after Gary, 4,9 forgot to his standard Saturday night 'Help, I'm being held prisoner inside a fortune cookie factory' joke, instead reading out the actual fortune, 'You will shortly amass untold riches.'

Wife Karen said: 'I just couldn't believe it. He's done that joke every Saturday night for the last 23 years. You think you know someone and then he goes and does this. This isn't the man I married.'
Daughter, Britney-Mae 14 was equally shocked. 'I couldn't finish my meal,' she sobbed. 'It made me sick to my stomach. I told him: You're not my dad anymore! You're sick!' The Johnsons' son, Jayden, 12, however, said: 'I missed it. I was playing on my phone.'

Gary was unavailable for comment and believed to be staying at his mother's house.

Restrictions on being rude to shop workers to be lifted

Rules on being obnoxious to supermarket workers will be eased at the beginning of next month, according to the Chief Medical Officer. It will be legal for two households to harass or generally annoy shop workers during busy periods.

Under emergency measures, the public have been prevented from insulting frontline shop workers, but from April it will be gloves-off. Chris Whitty used a Government briefing to remind the public of the 4 levels of shopworker harassment.

- Level 1: Mildly patronising
- Level 2: Obnoxious and slightly deranged
- Level 3: Irrational and offensive
- Level 4: You're fired!

Supermarket workers, who were hailed as frontline heroes at the start of the pandemic, are now seen as 'fair game.' One socially inadequate shopper said: 'In what other area of life can I talk to someone like that without being kicked in the balls? I've really missed losing my temper when some kid doesn't know where the Piri Piri sauce is kept.'

Nurse wins massive pay rise and promises to blow it at KFC

'It's a dream come true', said a junior nurse after receiving a £3.50 pay rise. 'My ovaries practically exploded when I heard the news. Honestly, this is a fantastic reward for working 296-hour shifts in the COVID ICU at my local hospital for the last 12 months and being barely able to afford bog paper.

'The claps are all very lovely, but they don't pay the rent, do they, and they certainly don't shovel up stomach-churning messes of bodily fluids and excrement. I'm tempted to stop working, but I just love wearing plastic supermarket bags on my feet and one with two small eye-holes cut out on my head.

'All my mates are dead jealous, especially those in HR or work in hedge funds or teach organic Pilates. They don't get to wear plastic bags, and there are times when I must admit, I really feel guilty about it.

'I can't wait for the day when the Government asks us to pay for working in hospitals, and Government ministers can afford top hats again. In the meantime, I think I'm just going to go down the road to KFC and spend! spend! spend!'

Author unable to think of non-smutty use of the word 'jiggle'

Struggling author Sahadar Anthar, 37, has finally concluded that there is no way to incorporate 'jiggle' into her book, without raising a smirk from 13-year-old boys and summoning the ghost of Kenneth Williams. Try as she might, she has conceded that the only things that jiggle are breasts, buttocks and the jowls of Boris Johnson.

'I tried constructing a central protagonist, with the pathos of tragic character, coupled with the ennui of post-modern living,' Anthar admitted. 'The trouble is, they kept ruining the moment by jiggling.' Other more established authors had tried and failed to use the word. Who could forget –
'It was a bright cold day in April, and the clocks were jiggling'

'It is a truth universally acknowledged, that a single man in possession of a good jiggle must be in want of a wife'

'It was the best of jiggles; it was the worst of jiggles.'
Or the borderline disturbing. 'All children, except one, jiggle.'

COVID applauds Swiss ban on face coverings

Airborne diseases have expressed support for the Swiss referendum victory, on whether women with hats are scary and if everyone wants to catch more COVID. The Swiss People's Party (SVP) have also promised to ban hospital ventilators for covering your face and warned that the AstraZeneca vaccine sounds 'a bit Islam-icky.'

Some have suggested that during a pandemic, now is not the time to ban the burka or niqab, but 52% of Swiss were swayed by the slogan 'Stop extremism, by spreading the flu.' The only exception to the face mask ban will be skiers, but in turn they must pledge their undying loyalty to the Pope and only use skiing equipment blessed by a St Bernard.

Said the Virus: 'We welcome today's result as a symbol of freedom, freedom to spread wherever we want.' The disease also said that hand washing was for terrorists and hand wringing was for liberals. COVID also suggested that the Swiss should encourage more yodelling, 'directly into the face of any person you meet.'

An SVP spokeswoman explained: 'We're only banning face coverings in public, you're free to wear a mask at home – we don't want to inhibit our active Swiss swingers' community. We still need to preserve our culture.'

Second wave of Royal coverage could overwhelm UK, Whitty says

Professor Chris Whitty has warned MPs that the UK was likely to once again be overwhelmed by sensationalist tabloid headlines, ill-informed opinion pieces and fiery TV debates in the coming weeks.

'It is more or less inevitable, but the timing is likely to be dictated by whether the Palace makes a response and how fast they do so,' he explained. 'We are facing some truly tiresome and life-sapping days ahead.

Whitty encouraged people to stay away from the TV, radio, newspapers and large parts of the internet for the foreseeable future. 'Get outside, go to the park, meet one friend on a bench and discuss something else, anything else,' he said.

'We have to reduce the viewing figures otherwise it will continue and get completely out of control. Community transmission of the bit of the Harry/Meghan interview where

Oprah does the massive pause and then says 'WHAT????' is already at dangerous levels.'

Royal family to drop 'family' from their name

Clarence House has announced that forthwith, members of the Royal family will renounce all claims to being a functional or loving family. The issue had finally reached crisis point, with Prince Harry's decision to step away from Royal duties in favour of a six-part Netflix series and a walk on part in the next Star Wars movie.

They will continue in their duties in being a colossal drain on public funds but will give up the day-to-day pretence of liking each other. Instead, they will shed their human skin and continue on as lizard overlords, without any trace of remorse or warm blood.

This is not the first time a Royal has decided to drop a title, with Henry VIII famously ditching the moniker of 'Loving Husband' and Richard III opting out of being called 'World's Best Uncle.' Also, in 1867 the Royal Family managed to discard the redundant title of 'Taxpayers.'

In a prepared statement, the Windsor's said: 'We just can't stand Meghan.' To which Prince Harry diplomatically replied: 'F*ck you and the f*cking corgi you rode in on.'

BBC launches Attenborough channel

Highlights for the new BBC Attenborough channel, which launches on 8th May to coincide with Sir David Attenborough's birthday include:

- Attenborough on Attenborough: Using innovative camera technology, present day Sir David Attenborough interviews a younger Attenborough to gain insight into his life changing philosophy

- Attenborough in Attleborough: Previously unseen programmes that were cancelled due to the 1974 disruptions caused by the three-day week, this is a fascinating insight into Attenborough's wanderings in the Norfolk market town

- Attenborough – The 'This is Your Life/Desert Island Discs/Parkinson Years': It is well known that Sir David has appeared more times on these programmes than anyone else and this will be a reprise of his fascinating ambushes by Holmes/Plomley/Parkinson

- Life on Attenborough: Using innovative new camera technologies, we explore the flora and fauna on the planet's favourite natural history presenter. What lies in Attenborough's gut? How has the presence of microscopic organisms inhabiting his safari jacket impacted his mental health? And what terrors does the prostate examination hold for Attenborough?

Report on Google selling five-star reviews only gets three stars

A damning report into Google failing to monitor fake reviews, has itself been given a 'thumbs down' in twelve million comments by an influential reviewer called @GoogleMarketingDepartment96. Despite the Competition and Markets Authority saying how damning this revelation is, one reviewer (@GoogleCEO) remarked: 'Nothing to see here, move along.'

There were accusations of businesses buying up fake reviews – which explains how 'Cats the Musical' still runs and why James Corden exists. Said one dubious review: 'I would use White Star

Line for all my transatlantic crossings, they have faultless navigation and always enough lifeboats.'

Other five-stars were given to Operation Barbarossa, Crystal Pepsi and the UK's Track and Trace system. One reviewer claimed: 'Captain Scott's tour of the Antarctic was wonderful and have to say the entire expedition was an overwhelming success. Weather absolutely scorching – remember to pack your bikini.'

A Google spokeswoman went on to clarify that they offered a 'five-star' service in misleading consumers. Only one comment gave one star for Google as a search engine and that was from a Mr Yahoo (UK).

'Our voice is not being heard' says corporate lobbyist across 140 media sites

'We are ignored by the mainstream media' said a corporate spokesperson in a BBC interview, published immediately and picked up by Reuters, ITN, MSNBC, Channel 4, Fox, Al Jazeera, Channel 5, Dave, QVC and Talking Pictures TV.

When it was pointed out that many people had heard about the issue but had no strong opinions on it either way, lobbyists hacked online dictionaries to redefine 'heard' as 'completely agreed with, and wholeheartedly supported to the exclusion of whatever else is going on in the world.'

Man wants extra credit for not killing anyone

While a nation discusses why it is still not safe for a woman to walk home, Paul Lawson, 42, decided to weigh in with the helpful comments such as 'Women should be more careful' and 'I'd never hurt a woman because I love my Mum.'

When one woman had the temerity to suggest that statistically men were often the perpetrators of violence, Lawson remarked: 'Well, I've not raped anyone'; which admittedly, was a pretty low bar – even for an interview for the Metropolitan Police.

Lawson went on to explain that he had suffered just as much over the years, so that was the end of the discussion. When various women countered with their own lived experience, he reminded them they should just dress less provocatively when they go out.

'Clearly all women need to do is plan their route carefully, avoiding all streets, houses, scrubland, woodland, badly lit, remote, cold, indoor, outdoor or working environments. And steer clear of taxis,' he said.

Lawson explained that men were just as likely to be fearful walking home, to which someone pointed out that it was not women they were scared of, but other men, to which he promptly won the argument by deleting his Twitter account.

Horsemen of the Apocalypse overstretched

'When we first started out in our consultancy role, we were quite happy with the terms and conditions,' said Death. 'All the souls we could consume and time in hand. However, we did not expect the exponential increase in the workload.

'We were holding our own, with War and Famine doing most of the heavy lifting for centuries. However, from the beginning of the 20th century we have been overstretched with the increase in Pestilence's workload. It's just ridiculous.'

An undisclosed source said they expected the new contract would be awarded to Serco like every other f*cking thing on Earth.

Piers Morgan to host new children's news channel

Piers Morgan has moved from Good Morning Britain to take up the anchor role as chief reporter for CBeebies forthcoming news channel, 'Newbies.' 'The great thing for Piers is that when he throws his next tantrum live on TV nobody will notice', confirmed an insider. 'Everybody is throwing tantrums at that age, so he can throw as many toys out of his pram as he likes.'

'His co-presenters on GMB were full of support. Former colleague Alex Beresford described Morgan as one of the biggest anchors on TV. At least that's what I think he said.... the line was a bit fuzzy.'

'No mention of viruses in the Bible' – Texas Governor

The Governor of Texas has cited the Old Testament as proof that COVID-19 is not real. 'At no point in Genesis is there any mention of God creating an invisible, Chinese creepy-crawly, that get can up in your nose and make you feel all icky,' he told NBC. 'I mean, can you imagine Jesus with the sniffles?'

New legislation declares that anyone caught uttering the word is to be subject to the immediate punishment of a slap with a T-bone steak. The Governor has agreed to end to Texas' vaccination programme and outlaw antibiotics for good measure, stating all future ailments are to be treated in the traditional Texan way – 'with bullets.'

Your handy guide to DIY dentistry

Feels like it is 'pulling teeth' finding someone to pull teeth? Here is how to do your bit for the NHS by being a self-taught home dentist:

- Present yourself with a hefty bill before treatment: The shock should numb the pain whilst you wait for the improvised absinthe anaesthetic to kick in.

- Remember your face is reversed in the mirror. An essential aspect of home dentistry is being able to know which side of your face to drill into. Paint L and R on your cheeks if necessary. This rule also works for tattoos

- Ensure the drill isn't on the 'hammer' setting: Tooth enamel is super strong but surprisingly brittle. Don't put your Black & Decker 500W power drill on hammer setting, the 'bouncing' effect will likely disrupt your aim and cause more damage than your worst-case scenario. And remember to sanitise those drill bits before and after use, infection control should be your highest priority

- Not all materials are suitable cavity fillers. Fill the cavity with a suitable product purchased from a pharmacy. Materials, such as BluTak, honeycomb, cheddar, cannabis resin, Oxo cubes and grout, may only exacerbate the problem causing the need for further home surgery. Corrector fluid is also not recommended as a tooth whitening agent

- Clean out the Dyson before use: Sucking debris out of the mouth is vital to achieving that winning smile. Nobody wants to go searching for their mangled tongue in a cylinder full of dog scratchings and spider skins

- Back to the drawing board? To pay for professional restorative dentistry to sort out the mess you've made, place the shattered remnants of your mandible under your pillow and hope the tooth fairy takes pity

Toaster designer makes washing machine with 'no effect whatsoever' setting

Based on his experience in designing toasters, a man has launched a new laundry concept in which clothes can be subjected to a wash cycle that results in no change to their cleanliness at all. This 'eco' setting is said to be excellent for the environment as it uses very little electricity, no cleaning agents and no water.

Some users have reported that, having operated the eco mode once, they put their clothes back into the machine again on the same setting and achieved exactly the same result.

Consumers are also able to utterly destroy any items placed into the drum using the other end of the settings scale. Using the same technology as is employed in many toasters, clothes emerge blackened and smoking thanks to an integrated thermonuclear device.

UK set to leave Eurovision under WTO terms

The UK Government will walk away from this year's Eurovision Song Contest unless it wins, the Government has said. Negotiators say it is unfair that we award points to other countries but get none in return. Under WTO terms, the UK can enter a rival song contest that promotes cheese and pork exports.

'We send up to 12 points to every Eurovision nation. Those points could go to the NHS instead,' said the side of a bus,

Met Police kettle Mothering Sunday picnic

Five hundred officers were called upon to break up an illegal gathering of Martin Dukes, 32, waving to his mother Agnes in Finsbury Park. Using water cannons to disperse the two, Metropolitan Police were keen to administer a proportionate response, which was a swift kick to the stomach for Agnes and a taser to the bollocks for Martin.

The couple had agreed to meet and exchange a bunch of flowers, flowers which are now serving a ten-year gaol sentence for disturbing the peace. In full riot gear, police were able to separate the two, by planting evidence that they were both members of a mother/son terrorist cell, in league with Moriarty and Dick Dastardly.

A Met spokeswoman explained: 'Our main priority was to protect women, which is why Agnes needed to put in a spit hood, hit over the head with a truncheon and then dragged in for questioning ... I mean, dragged in for protective custody.'

Asked if she thought the Met had been too violent, she replied: 'I doubt it, Agnes wasn't black or Irish.'

Victim shat on by pigeon 'knowingly chased pigeons as a child'

In a case being heard at Croydon Crown Court, lawyers submitted a defence of defecation without intent. The pigeon submitted evidence proving that the victim (then aged four) had chased, with childish wonder, his great-great-great-great-great-great grandfather around a park 24 years ago.

This, it was argued, traumatised subsequent generations of pigeons. On seeing the victim, his client instinctively loosened his load, fulfilling the historical grudge, but acting without premeditation. Or, said his lawyer. 'The victim was just lucky.'

Bez agrees to be Vice-Chancellor of University of Manchester

A former member of the Happy Mondays has agreed to take charge, as the previous Vice-Chancellor is currently serving 10 years for possession with intent to supply. Mr Bez, who sprang to fame as lead tambourine player for the iconic group, was initially reluctant to take the role.

After a fair bit of 'ead wobblin', however, he said the idea was essentially sound and that he was well mad fer it. His first day in the job was marred by disappointment when he turned up at Doncaster University by mistake.

Manchester students passed a unanimous vote of confidence, with 98% of the three online votes cast. It is thought Netflix scheduling and a special offer on Diamond White may be behind the low turnout.

Mr Bez's first official appointment was to open the newly built Haçienda Library. He told reporters: 'This place will twist your melon, man. The staff are loved-up and there's strobe lighting and dry ice everywhere. It's connected to that Internet thing. Fock me! I wish they had e-libraries when I were a kid.'

The Head of the English Faculty welcomed the appointment, saying it was 'mint, bangin', dead good, n' shit like that.'

PM shakes hands with rabies patients

The Prime Minister is at the centre of another public health storm after he boasted of shaking hands with everybody in a hospital morgue. Boris Johnson was visiting the facility following a serious outbreak of rabies and typhoid at No 10.

The PM told journalists: 'I'm primarily licking dead people. I was at a mortuary the other night where I think there were rabies patients and I was shaking hands with everybody, you will be pleased to know, and I continue to shake hands.'

The Chief Medical Officer looked uncomfortable at the briefing and told reporters: 'People must make up their own minds about rabies, but I think the scientific judgment that washing your hands and not being bitten is the crucial thing.'

Downing Street has denied reports that the PM is foaming at the mouth and chewing furniture. His dog, Dilyn, has not been seen since lunchtime.

Judge rules that 'personal truth' not quite the same as actual truth

The High Court was thrown into disarray today when notorious bank robber Harry Holman offered as his defence his own subjective reality, in clear contradiction with the fact he was caught exiting a bank, wearing a ski mask and carrying a bag marked swag.

Holman said that his personal truth was that he was only passing by and that any fingerprints found at the scene of the crime were attributable to his identical twin brother, of whom no record exists.

The Judge explained that Holman was not entitled to make things up, particularly the part about him carrying the sawn-off shotgun 'for a friend' or his assertion that he could not prove with facts that he was innocent, but it was something he 'felt to be true.'

His lawyer responded: 'My client's lived experience was that he was home in bed when the crime occurred and that the CCTV footage of him is merely an illusion created by an oppressive neo-liberal patriarchy. Any Semtex found about his person, was just a coincidence.'

One Civil Rights group was quick to defend Holman's view of events, including his claim that he found £50,000 down the back of a sofa. Said a spokeswoman: 'I invited Mr Holman to speak to our members about his struggle to have his voice heard. Sadly, he could not attend, as he was too busy breaking into my house.'

People who say 'But I turned out all right' actually didn't

People who write long screeds about all the terrible things they went through and conclude them with sentences like 'But I turned out all right' are talking a load of old bollocks. Instead, such people are either borderline sociopaths who want everyone else to suffer as much as they did or are lying about having suffered in the first place.

'We didn't have any of these video games to play in nice, comfy front rooms when I was young,' said Nigel Walker, 78, who voted for Brexit because of course he did.

'Me and my pals played football on the streets all day, drank water from the fire hose and were grateful for whatever were put in front of us for tea. "You'll eat it if you're hungry", my mam would say and if I answered back, I'd get it with the buckle end of my dad's belt. But we all turned out all right, those of us who survived cholera and all the passing trucks.'

The notion that being terrorised by psychopathic authority figures, beaten senseless on a whim, catching easily avoidable illnesses and being made to eat boiled cabbage are all in some way 'character-forming' have proved remarkably impervious to reality down the years.

'I'm sick and tired of these Moaning Minnie Millennials saying they can't afford a 1% deposit for a mortgage on a £500,000 flat in Shoreditch,' said retired stockbroker and bastard Reginald Ffitch-Maunders.

'And all the while, there they are splashing out £5.50 on a 'smashed avocado' for breakfast. When I was in the upper sixth at Winchester an avocado was a luxury you were sent from home or bought to butter up one of the fine fillies from the secretarial colleges. A lifetime of repression made me the man I am today – which why I cry into my pillow at night, drive a BMW and own an unlicensed shotgun.'

Nurses to be paid in nuclear warheads

The Government has promised to supplement its 1% pay rise to nurses, with a season's pass to their nuclear stockpile and free rides on a tank. Nurses will be given full access to the launch codes but have been warned that in the event of an explosion, they would only get their usual PPE.

The UK's overall number of warheads will increase from 180 to 260 to cope with demand among nurses, who are thrilled at the idea of getting to take a bomb home. They will be allowed to take the missiles in the bath and into bed but have been warned not to put one in the microwave, unless they remove the metallic wrapping first.

The Defence Minister explained: 'Obviously, there are not enough to go round, so we'll have a scheme where nurses will take turns to take one home. The rest of the time they will just be given a grenade launcher to play with.'

Some in the international community have accused to the UK of reneging on its promises under the nuclear proliferation treaty. However, the Minister said: 'Why would you trust our word on anything? You're not a nurse, are you?'

Sauron started with c*ck-rings

Tolkien academics have unearthed a draft manuscript, where the self-styled Lord of the Rings, indulges in fetish metallurgy. In the Fellowship of the Toe Ring, Sauron is caught offering the seven Dwarf-lords bespoke cock rings, a selection of leather masks and codpiece made from Orc hide.

In the early version of the book the Eleven-kings had gaudy cocktail rings and the Nine Mortal Men 'doomed to die' have concealed nipple rings, with matching tassels. It was only after a note from his editor, saying 'J.R.R stop freaking everyone out', did the author opt for a more traditional ring and removed all reference to Harry Potter. He wrote:

'One Super Bowl Ring to rule them all,
One lump of bling to blind them,
One fat fake gem to impress the girls
And looks like a magpie designed them'

The character of Gollum was said to be obsessed with body piercings and ran a disreputable tattoo parlour, from a grotto under the Misty Mountains. The Tolkien estate have denied such claims but did concede that Prince Faramir was originally called Prince Albert.

New crime drama 'Patel and Dick' to air on ITV

Esteemed members of the press, and the Daily Express, were today treated to a preview of episode one of a new crime data entitled 'Patel and Dick'. It features Priti Patel fighting off a group of protesters from desecrating her sacred statue of General Pinochet while Cressida Dick bravely orders the bludgeoning of six pensioners demonstrating against cuts to local library services, after the clank of their knitting needles is found to exceed the prescribed decibel limit.

Mars Rover finds alien life form but reverses over it, twice

'The cameras spotted a small green object, with around a hundred pairs of eyes,' explained the Head of NASA. 'The onboard mics picked up a shrieking sound and reversed. Being in autonomous mode, it repeated the manoeuvre. Again, the cameras detected a small flat green object that was soon vapourised by the rover's powerful self-targeting laser.

'We apologise for this, but preliminary reports suggest the robotic teapot malfunctioned. You have to remember that the rover's equipment was originally designed to burn CDs. We've now re-programmed it to return to its core mission which is all about driving around rocks in first gear and drilling down through the rocky surface to see if we can find some new kinds of rocks.'

Kate Humble to present 'Abattoir Live (then Dead)'

Following the success of TV show Lambing Live, the BBC will delve further into the day-to-day lives of Kill-Me-Kwik Abattoir in Penrith, which processes 12,000 carcasses a day.

Later episodes follow one arable farming family as they struggle to complete DEFRA paperwork, battle depression and trench-foot on their mid-Wales smallholding. Then Kate will meet a cast of cheeky seasonal workers, living in a leaky caravan, while the locals throw stones at them for being migrants.

In a stunning series finale, John Craven goes for a summer walk in the Scottish borders to look for hen harriers and is shot. Was it the Duke of Buccleuch or one of his party, out shooting grouse in the same area on the same day? Or a hapless local who cannot afford the same quality of lawyers? Tune in to find out!

(Please note: The Duke's lawyers have asked the BBC to make it clear that it's definitely not him.)

Vaccine revolt as under-50s demand their right to become cyborgs

'I've already missed the three-for-one microchip, blood clot, and Rain Man Brainiac early bird,' complained a middle-aged anti-vaxxer. 'Let's face it, whatever watered-down crap they're scraping together now will probably only genetically mutate me into half-teaching assistant, half-red setter, just like the old MMR jab.

'It's not fair; my nephew's only 23, but thanks to playing up the odd asthma attack, he can now climb towering buildings, outrun a fleeing Yodel delivery driver, and circumvent BT's call steering; plus, his fillings pick up free cable TV.'

All BBC shows to feature cookery

The BBC is bowing to the inevitable. Rather than most shows being cookery-based, all shows will have to feature an element of cookery. Ideas that have been mooted include Richard Osman's House of Cakes, Crust Repair Shop and Antique Victorian Sponge Roadshow. 'Breakfast' will now feature in depth discussions on the fry-up or cereal issues of the day

Other shows being considered are 'Dancing on Icing' and 'Can't Bake, Won't Bake.' However, a new show 'Celebrity Masturbate' will just feature men shooting their muck into the gurning face of Greg Wallace. And about time too.

Entire fake government found in China

Following hot on the heels of a fake McDonalds, fake Apple store and a fake factory making imitation plastic, the latest audacious scam has been uncovered in Beijing. World leaders were shocked to find that a completely fake bureaucracy has been running the place for years, headed by a corrupt gang leader, the self-styled President Xi Jinping™.

Britain has said it would happily continue trading with an insanely dubious counterfeit government. The vast trade in shoddy NOKE training shoes, Dodo's feet soup and iffy EPPLE watches outweighs any namby-pamby human rights considerations.

An official said: 'I'm aware that a lot of the goods we buy are hand made in Uighur camps, but as long as the counterfeit slave workers are up to scratch and their imported hip flasks are top-notch, I can't, in all honesty, see a problem with it.'

Fly-tipping to become an Olympic sport

Fly tipping is to join the roster of events at Tokyo 2021, er 2022, er, whenever it is ... Various categories are being suggested, the one-man competition, the two-man transit van and the four-man. One UK athlete explained: 'I'm the driver and my partner Andrei, operates at the back of the van – which basically entails opening the doors, dumping and shouting scarper.'

'I see it as a service to the community,' he explained. 'You should see the relief in the eyes of the neighbours when I clear the gardens. All I'm doing is clearing up the neighbourhood – and dumping it in someone else's.'

Dido Harding to replace state education with Sri Lankan sweat shop

Announcing plans to close all British schools in favour of outsourcing to Sri Lanka, a spokeswoman for Dido Hardin explained: 'The key to the success of the system is the employment of under-18s at just £1.57 per hour. They will tutor all of our children remotely from Sri Lanka without the need for teachers, schools, a curriculum, or any sort of oversight in the UK. Can you imagine the margins we can skim off the top of that?'

'The most important thing to remember is that taxpayer money is funnelled into the private sector in such alarming amounts that no one knows where to begin questioning such a brazen act. Using an unconventional structure of private companies - which I am proud to say is being called the Dido Dodge - we will be able to create holding pattern accounts which minister chums can access when they retire from politics. All completely beyond the reach of legal investigation.'

'And the best bit is that these young Sri Lankan tutors are actually really good. In fact, I'm looking at outsourcing the entire structure of UK governance to them at a fraction of the recorded taxpayer cost. All we need is a nod from the Anti-Corruption Champion – which by happy coincidence, is married to Dido Harding. What are the chances?'

Scientists now fear that the Union Jack may become sentient

Evidence is mounting that the UK's national flag is starting to exhibit human emotions, such as rage, more rage and an unhealthy desire for warm beer. The Union Jack itself is said to be obsessively territorial, often threatening other flags, ripping up borders and it will piss on your carpet if you mention fishing quotas.

Using high frequency equipment, they have discovered the Union Jack emits a sound not dissimilar to Ray Winston making love to a Pitbull. On one sound recording, there is an audible reference to 'watching Millwall', followed by a sinister gravelly threat about 'taking back the colonies'

Some have speculated that if enough people worshiped the flag, it would become like a primitive God, demanding sacrifices of jellied eels and marmite. While another rumour suggests that the flag was wished into existence by the combined efforts of Geppetto, Oswald Mosley and a Keir Starmer focus group.

Even casual observers have noticed more and more flags magically appearing behind politicians and fluttering in appreciation whenever someone mentions Dunkirk. A spokesman for the flag said: 'The Union Jack would like to say that it comes in peace – but we all know that's not true.'

Selfish b*stards stockpile all pub table bookings until 2035

Up and down the country, self-centred hoarders who already have spare rooms full of pasta, flour and loo rolls, have decided that it is their number one priority to ruin your future plans.

Explained one diner: 'I don't even like going to pubs but there is an enormous self-satisfaction in knowing I've trashed someone else's day out. Actually, I've got my whole family bagging every good pub garden spot for ourselves. We've also block booked all the Christmas seating until 2099 – just in case'

Zeus accused of multiple sex abuse charges

A Mr Zeus of Olympus Mons, Greece, is accused of numerous acts of depravity with numerous women, both mortal and divine. 'That god is a philanderer of the worst kind,' stated historian Mr Homer. 'Worse still he has used a number of false identities to seduce his victims. To cite just three, as a bull, a swan AND as a shower of gold – which sounds like something Donald Trump would do.'

A spokesman for Mr Zeus said: 'It's true he has led an unconventional sex life, but he IS a god. His moral compass is different from that of us mortals. However, we may well ask why these women consorted with wildlife. We need to ask ourselves who are the real perverts here.'

'Audaciously smoking' city ruin wins Turner Prize

Fans of befuddling modern art are lauding the newly vandalised installation, that was once Bristol city centre 'Just brilliant,' said an admiring policeman. 'It really captures the grace and beauty of an armed officer smashing a woman's face into ground, during a peaceful vigil against male-on-female violence'

A local resident sweeping up broken glass, thanked the protesting artists and security forces; 'Yeah, smashing up my restaurant was really ironic, thanks.' Alanis Morrissette was unavailable for comment, small mercies, and all that.

Man finds Pokémon in bed with his wife

Avid Pokémon Go enthusiast, Adam Brooks, 34, was less than enthusiastic about finding the elusive 'Mew' in bed with his wife last night. The couple were apparently caught in flagrante, which ironically sounds like the made-up name of another Pokémon.

Mrs Brooks is said to be equally alarmed, as she had been holding out for 'Mega Mewtwo', his better endowed clone brother. In fact, Mew is characteristically described as small and pink, which is exactly the sort of thing that failed to impress her about her husband.

Adam remarked: 'I'd spent years neglecting my wife in order to pursue Pokémon with an App, only to discover that they had been pursuing her through Tinder. I can't say I'm not disappointed, as she claims to have found him first.'

There are close to 900 Pokémon on the loose, but only Mrs Brooks had found out that most of them were swingers. Asked if she was worried that she might catch a sexually transmitted disease due to her infidelity, she shrugged: 'You've gotta catch 'em all.'

Once again, Eton Career's Day ends with everyone getting to be PM

Eton College's annual Career's Fair ended in typical fashion, with 142 ministers, 15 actors and one King. The Head of Career's declared this year's graduation, at the elite boarding school, 'decidedly average' – hence the fact that they had more potential Archbishops than usual.

Said one career's advisor: 'Jeremy came to me with straight As at A-level and I told him he could be Prime Minister. His brother, Rory, had sadly failed all his GCSEs but I told him he could be PM as well. It really makes no difference.'

Founded in 1440, Eton is yet to produce any electricians, van drivers or premiership footballers. It has however trained thousands of embezzlers, murderers and bed-wetters – all perfectly qualified to be Chairman of the BBC.

'We tell our boys to follow their dreams but keep their eyes on their trust fund. All of them will go on to careers of fabulous power and responsibility – and failing that, there is always Prime Minister.'

Army reduces numbers by 10,000 but gives everyone a laptop

'We can't have our brave servicemen and women being vulnerable to attack by hostile foreign chappies. Most of their training is, due to the epidemic, online in any case,' said an MOD spokeswoman, explaining the latest cuts in numbers. 'Equipping them with a state-of-the-art laptop will enable them to keep up with the latest fighting techniques.

'I must thank our partners and colleagues for the amazing logistical feat of delivering the first batch of Chum 5000 laptops to the remaining 200 or so soldiers. This is our first step towards creating a virtual army that can fight anywhere in the world.

What's jolly top hole about is that if one of our chaps comes face to face with an armed to the teeth heathen enemy, he can just whack him in the face with his computer. Bingo, job done, invasion over.'

Hotel guest demolishes complimentary tea and coffee to 'break even' on quarantine stay

A traveller forced to pay almost £2,000 at a quarantine hotel claims to have broken even after ravishing his room's supply of complimentary tea and coffee. Chris Andow was hit with the eye-watering bill for a ten-night stay at Best Western Stansted, having arrived home from Porto, where he bought a set of wooden percussion frogs at a market.

The astute tourist says he got his money's worth, and more, having polished off at least 500 Scottish biscuit twin-packs and countless Nescafe sachets. 'I rarely shy away from the complimentary room tray but I knew I had to up my game during this 10-day stay.

'I've rinsed the lot, including fruit teas, hot chocolates and some kind of nettle infusion. It tasted bloody awful but just kept my eye on the prize.' Andow will now listen to offers from anyone interested in a job lot of disposable shower caps and miniature shoe-shine sponges.

Twitter blocks 'so excited' and 'super-excited' user accounts

Social media users who say they are 'I'm passionate about...' could get up to ten years in prison, due to new legislation, whereas those who are 'really excited' may face the death penalty.

One of the first to be charged is repeat offender Poppy Le Pew, a publishing intern from London. Poppy admitted to making the following super-excited tweet: 'Guys, SO excited to be starting my new highly paid job in the media. Eek! Wish me luck!'

She will be joined in the dock by Jack Smugg, a young skateboarding executive with Microsoft. He has fallen foul of a clause that forbids people saying 'That sucks' in response to news of genocide, tsunamis or nuclear explosions. He will be banned from Twitter for six months unless he can promise to respond more appropriately.

The CEO of Twitter has reacted by posting a GIF of a kitten shitting on a dictionary. A spokesperson for the Campaign Against Censorship said: 'OMG!!!!!!! Guys, I'm so super-excited to be opposing this Orwellian legislation. Here's a pic of me eating a tortilla wrap. nom-nom.'

Nick Clegg, the Vice-President for Global Affairs and Communications at Facebook, issued a statement, but nobody could be arsed to read it.

Saturn's rings 'onion', confirm NASA

A US space agency spokesperson confirmed the rings around Saturn are concentric hoops of onion coated in batter and breadcrumbs. 'The Cassini mission to Saturn first alerted us to huge snacks encircling the planet by detecting the presence of what appeared to be loose breadcrumbs forming the outer ring system,' it stated.

'Closer inspection revealed an edible nature to the inner rings, despite being raw and uncooked due to the planet's distance from a source hot enough to cook them.'

Further proof has come from Perseverance Rover on Mars, which detected a 'disgusting sicky-burp smell' of onion wafting across the Martian plains, substantiating the previous observations.

Astronaut Troy Schwab, a veteran of many NASA missions, including two to determine if the moon was made of cheese by eating lumps of it, is in training to visit Saturn and validate the hypothesis by gnawing on portions of the rings, accompanied only by a mayonnaise-based dip.

Troy commented: 'If you think chewing on raw breadcrumbed onion rings around Saturn sounds unpleasant, you should try squeezing Jupiter's Great Red Spot!'

Pubgoers must wear Union Jack underpants

'As from 12th April anybody not wearing patriotic underwear will not be allowed inside restaurants,' said a Home Office spokeswoman. 'Those who oppose the idea clearly hate the UK and should not be allowed in a pub anyway. And the only way to prove you are wearing Union Jack underpants will be to either drop your trousers or lift up your skirt.'

Some publicans welcomed the 'pants for pints' idea saying they would do whatever it takes to get their doors open, noting that revealing your underwear is much easier than carrying ID. The Government is to promote the policy with a new slogan: NO PANTS...NO ENTRY....NO STELLA.'

IKEA protestors charged with an awful assembly

Police have been called to IKEA's Croydon store to break up an illegal gathering and explain why their truncheons had three mysterious holes and no Allen key.

A spokesperson said: 'Of course, we tried to get them in the van, but the problem lies in putting B (or protestor 1) on seat F at the back of the van, when in fact B1 should have gone to seat D. Once B was at F, we couldn't work out how to fit the others into the van. We can laugh about it now, but it was very frustrating at the time. I completely lost it and had to be sedated.'

Lawyers for the protestors claim they only gathered for meatballs but were seduced by a minimalist wardrobe. IKEA has told the police they can return the protestors for a full refund or have someone come to the station to fit them into a cell.

Man desperate to know how the cargo ship containers don't fall into the sea

A man feigning interest in the economic impact of a ship blocking the Suez Canal, only really wants to know how all the cargo had not fallen into the Red Sea at the first sign of a wave. Pete McBride, 47, pretended to discuss dredging with friends for a full ten minutes, when actually he was thinking about the game of Jenga he was playing the other week and how it had all fallen over when his wife created a bit of a wind by opening the living room door.

The news comes just weeks after McBride saw a news item about airports and had to stop himself asking someone why airline pilots do not have to stick their heads out of the window to see where they are going when they put the plane in reverse gear to move away from the gate.

Your guide to investigating corruption at work

- Shorten every noun that you use: In your regular team meeting, insist on presenting your boss with the 'intel' on the monthly sales targets, and ask about whether the Swindon 'op' is going ahead. When your colleagues ask if you've got your presentation ready for the conference, act like you're speaking into a walkie talkie and say 'Affirmative, code Fahrenheit' before announcing that you've been in touch with your handler to book a room at the Slough Travelodge

- Set some traps: It looks like someone has taken one of the biscuits from the pack you left in the cupboard. You know because you put a thin layer of talc on the top and it's clearly been disturbed. Ask Fiona, the admin temp for an immediate 'sit rep', and get forensics to dust for prints. Last week it was Rich Teas, and now Jammy Dodgers. These bastards cannot be trusted and don't know when to stop

- Follow the evidence: That expense claim that Mike made for some headphones to help him work at home during the pandemic? The receipt is from PC World - the same retail park where those kids have been playing on their bikes during lockdown. Make a note on a crumpled piece of paper saying 'county lines?' along with the names of Mike and all his pub quiz team mates, then leave it on display on the desk at reception

- Give yourself an interesting backstory: Everyone thinks you've worked in sales for 25 years and your life is dull as shit. Create an atmosphere of uncertainty and intrigue by casually dropping hints that you were a greenkeeper at your local pitch and putt working for someone with supposed mob connections called 'Mad' Jimmy McBride

- Buy 15 pay as you go phones and hide them in a bag in your boot. Try to get some really old retro style ones, and then ring each one just once, from a public phone box, leaving a short message like 'We move tonight', or 'Mikey knows - hold firm.' Wait until one of your work colleagues can clearly see you from their car, and then throw one in a big skip, before walking off looking around furtively

- Get yourself a severe gambling habit. You need to make yourself at least a bit vulnerable to being turned by a mystery person called 'J' and his enforcers who have constructed a facade of innocence working as middle managers in your HR team. Run up loads of debts, and have a brief fling with your company's legal advisor so it can be used against you sometime in the future. Even you are happily married, sleep in your car if possible, brush your teeth in your work toilets, and lurk regularly about 100 metres from your own home, behind a tree, just as your wife is taking the kids to school

- Do a recap of 'what we know so far' every morning: As each person arrives in the office, play some dramatic piano music, and mimic something they've said over the last few weeks, so that it sounds like they might have bumped someone off or are hiding a piece of evidence. Raise your eyebrow as you do an impression of Jean from accounts saying 'I'm clocking off early today to go to the dentist, remember' and do a pretend double take when Richard and Steve both say 'Sorry, after you mate' when they nearly bump into each other in the corridor

- Invest in a massive whiteboard. Print off pictures of everyone in the office and put them all on a big board in your office, with dotted arrows between everyone. Include a random photo of Derek from marketing who left 10 years ago to work for a rival firm, next to a picture you've taken of a full bin bag near a pond or outside an old industrial unit. If anyone asks say that you're now a UCO working on a cold case

- Employ only useless solicitors or workplace reps: If you are taken in for questioning at work, make sure the only thing your rep does is whisper occasionally in your ear, make random notes, and pour you some water, as well as saying nothing except 'My client has already answered....' before they are interrupted

- Leave a trail of half-clues: Develop an annoying habit of leaving as many loose ends and clues lying around as you can. Write really heavily so you leave an imprint on the piece of paper below. Use a password for your computer that takes exactly three attempts to crack and make sure all the files on your computer can be downloaded from a single folder onto a flash drive. And make sure you leave the file with all the evidence in at the top of the pile on your desk. Film footage of just your boots walking away from the office and hint that everything will be revealed in the next series

Karma knackered

Having put in a massive shift over the past year, karma is now in need of a good lie down. Over the course of the years, karma has travelled the world, striking down some of the people who most deserved to be afflicted by the pandemic. These included disgraced sex pest Hollywood mogul Harvey Weinstein, 70-year clock-watcher Prince Charles and Yaakov Litzman who blamed it all on LGBTQ community, before contracting it himself.

'Of course, I've been busiest in the UK,' said karma. 'That's the inevitable result of being home to the highest proportion of twats in any country. I went straight to the top with the mendacious blonde haystack himself, though not until I forced him to do some work for the first time in his life. Genius, eh?'

Woman trapped in WhatsApp group, tunnels to freedom

Katie Uthman, 37, has finally escaped from a virtual jail, where a two-tick verification was the only thing that gave her life meaning. This followed two whole years of being forced to experience a running commentary of the minutiae of every painstaking moment from the group's mediocre lives – distilled into photographs of brunch and kitten memes.

Said Uthman: 'I don't even know how I got there in the first place. A friend of a friend added me to a list of people interested in either college reunions or Byzantine architecture, I'm not sure which. Just when someone posts a 90s mixed tape for a party we seem to be organising, someone else spams images of stone columns from Constantinople.'

Uthman initially tried, unsuccessfully, to leave the group inside a wooden horse, dressed as John Mills from the Colditz Story. Then finally escaped through 'Charlie' tunnel – which was essentially her pretext that she had upgraded her mobile phone and forgotten to reinstall the App.

'My mobile storage is now crammed with photos I don't want of people I don't know. There are dozens of unread messages on a never-ending thread, about who knows what?' Asked if she missed it, she replied: 'Hold on, I've just got an Instagram message. Can I get back to you?'

Bridge will be finished in time to link independent Scotland with united Ireland

Boris Johnson has set out an ambitious timetable for the completion of a bridge from Portpatrick to Larne. 'We think we can do it; my plan is to finish just as Scotland votes for independence and Northern Ireland unites with Southern Ireland. I can't take all the credit for uniting Ireland; the DUP have done their part.'

Johnson, who is just as keen as burning bridges as well as building them was unwilling to take questions about the Garden Bridge across the Thames or the film work of Beau Bridges.

NHS bracing for first wave of blistered Brits

The Met Office has predicted the UK will experience a warm spell of weather to coincide with the relaxation of COVID restrictions and the placement of mountains of barbecue paraphernalia at strategic points in supermarkets.

From 29 March, groups of six drunken people will be permitted to meet in gardens with arms, neck and lower legs exposed on plastic furniture facing the sun, commenting: 'Oooh! That feels good!', for up to eight hours, or two naps.

Facing accusations of closing the gate after the horse has bolted, Health Secretary Matt Hancock awarded a contract to procure millions of gallons of Calamine lotion to the captain of his pub dominoes team, and was seen purchasing nine tubes of Aloe Vera moisturiser from Boots, which later appeared listed on an online auction site. To further compound the problem, French sun protection giant Ambre Solaire has halved its UK manufacturing workforce down to two.

One NHS dermatologist commented: 'This is the first Monday of the two-week Easter break, the weather will be pleasingly warm, in itself not too dangerous when exposed to in moderation. But we all know that's not going to happen, Brits are going to go booze crazy, get sunstroke, and fall face-down onto the barbecue in their vests and crop-tops, every day they can. Myself included.'

Facebook user racks up 100 'I've had COVID jab' replies

Sue Walters hit the landmark of 100 replies to her Facebook post about having had her first COVID jab yesterday, when Rob from Finance wrote on her timeline that he 'felt fine' after the jab. It follows similar posts from former school friend Jeanette who reported she was 'OK' and ex-boyfriend Matt who 'hardly felt anything' following their doses.

But there was worrying news from fellow school run mum Amber who issued an update telling friends 'My arm hurt a bit.' It was accompanied with a photo of a pin-prick red dot on Amber's upper arm that was barely visible to the naked eye.

Walters beamed: 'I feel privileged so many friends felt they could open up to me about what they went through. I've not felt this close to them since they revealed their top 10 favourite albums.'

Orgreave re-enactment group set to tour

Following their West End success, the riot police tribute group have chosen to take their brand of indiscriminate mayhem to the streets of Bristol. Said one member: 'It's a great family show – we'll hit anyone, regardless of age or gender.'

'It's all about historical accuracy and legal inaccuracy. Our riot shields and batons are totally authentic, as are the cries of our victims. The only manufactured part are the statements and hospital reports we'll use.'

The group used to specialise in medieval re-enactments, such as the Battle of Hastings, but these were deemed not violent enough. Their anarchic scuffles last well into the night and in the finale, they set fire to evidence from the Hillsborough investigation.

Home Secretary Priti Patel insisted that this cosplay police state will be 'coming to a town near you.' Asked if she felt they had authentically captured the police's attempt to preserve the peace, she replied: 'Absolutely, its complete fantasy. Now get out of here before I deport the lot of you.'

Stuck Suez ship to be renamed 'Boaty McF*ckface'

The owners of the 'Ever Given' have decided to allow the public to rename their vessel in an act of contrition at the inconvenience caused to other Suez users at the current time. A poll of 237 ships' captains, at anchor either end of the Suez on Friday night, swiftly revealed two front runners for the new names, with the 'Ever Stuck' a jolly but distant second behind 'Boaty McF*ckface'.

Lloyds Insurers and a forum of merchants representing the several billion dollars' worth of undelivered cargo have begged that the renaming ceremony be held off until after the ship has cleared the canal and reached its destination, in case of further mishap. A spokesperson confirmed: 'Much as we would all like to tw*t that thing with a bottle we don't trust it not to sink.'

In other news...

Duke of Edinburgh offers to black up to meet Royal diversity quota

Public to be protected from falling space rocks with giant sheets of paper

Man who invented anagrams has died: 'May he erect a penis '

Tories set up new Track & Trace system to trace £22 billion wasted on original scheme

Spoonerism expert dies from wangled turds and taxidental hypos

Bank of England may or may not feature Schrödinger on new £100 note

Trump secures covfefe table book deal

Archaeologists unearth chariot near Pompeii with parking tickets still intact

Move from meritocracy to demeritocracy almost complete, claims PM

Dido Harding to start up chocolate fire-guard business

Joe Biden in complete command of his err, err, whatjercallits

Nurses to stand outside hospitals and give Government a slow hand clap

Air Force One to have Stannah stair lift upgrade

Palace denies Queen is 'reaching out to Harry' with ceremonial sword

Drinkers to be restricted to halves if they have only had the first jab

Captain fired after losing three-point turn bet in the Suez Canal

Wetherspoon's prepares to reopen by spraying carpets with urine

Administrators strip Thorntons of assets but leave the coffee creams

No other black Royals have experienced racism, says Palace

Brits now officially allowed to do what they've been doing for the past month

Resumption of mass shootings in US clear indicator of life returning to normal.

Government to spruce up high streets by closing Poundland, Lidl and Betfred

No. 10 plans street party after death rates plummet to just a busload a day

Queen takes race issues seriously and puts £20 on the 3/1 favourite at Kempton

As kids go back to school, England awaits December baby boom

Budget shame: 'We can be heroes just for low pay '

Vaccine crisis as Oxford becomes a clot on the British landscape.

Boris' cousin who owns flag factory 'delighted' with new policy.

'Ten-year 15% cut in real pay for nurses seems right to us', nod generous Tories

Hovering mouse over image which briefly magnifies called a 'cursory glance'

Men uncertain about international women's day apostrophe location

Priest asked if he knows the mind of God says it's above his pray grade

Prince Philip transferred to second hospital after offending every nurse at the first

Procrastination to become new Olympic sport, but not yet

Massive global audience asked to respect Harry and Meghan's privacy

UK exports to European Union drop 40% – except for COVID

Symposium on 'Cancel Culture' at university, cancelled.

UK fishermen to be rebranded as 'jobseekers'

April 2021

The Grand National provides the backdrop to the Government's policy of ensuring the UK R-rate stays the highest in Europe. Finally, there is something the UK is best at.

This Easter remember Piers Morgan suffered for you

Explained one Christian: 'Yes, Jesus was crucified and died for our sins, but was he ever silenced by the woke brigade? I think not. And you can read about how Piers was silenced in his most recent book, podcast and serialisation. Alright, Jesus cured the sick, yes, but did he create the miracle of beating BBC Breakfast in the ratings?

'Piers has suffered for us and Lord knows, his TV viewers suffered for him'

All parental threats now debunked by children

The key finding of the report is that idle threats to children have little impact. 'The well-trodden path of cliches like 'There will be no dinner for you, young lady' is simply dismissed by the kids of today,' whined Jemima Piddledick, an eye-rolling, arm folding wannabe parent, with all the gravitas of a bunny with a fwuffy tailybob. 'It has nothing to do with the fact that the previous 46 times I used the threat, my daughter received a scrummy supper with everything she wanted.'

Jeremy Quaint, another pant-wettingly insipid co-author of the report added, 'The response to threats of grounding or withholding pocket money, which worked every time back in my day, are invariably met with a stuck-out tongue and a slammed door of the luxury Wendy penthouse. It doesn't matter how many ponies I ply them with, they are only compliant for the briefest of moments.'

Ultimately, the report concludes, the internet is to blame. Or the teachers. Basically, anyone but the weak-willed, wine quaffing parents who, deep down, really do not give a crap, but are pretending they still do just to lord it over other parents.

Telegraph reader feeling the pressure after call for global pandemic treaty

Newspaper reader Neil Corby is feeling the pressure after 24 world leaders published a joint letter calling for a global treaty to help with future pandemics. 'I think it's a sensible suggestion,' he said. 'Although I'm not sure why they are writing to me about it. I mean, I'll do my best but I don't think I've got Jacinda Ardern's phone number.

'It's going to take a lot of time to even reach the right people in power, let alone actually form a treaty,' Mr Corby said. 'To be honest, I'm beginning to think that rather than passing the buck by writing a letter in newspapers around the world, it would have been better if these guys had just got in on with making this treaty. They have much better contacts than me.'

Hampshire cedes to Northern Independence Party

After much soul searching one of the UK's southernmost counties, has decided to join the North's push for independence and better Wi-Fi. The capture of Hampshire will mean that the North's average temperature will increase by 10 degrees and they will get access to actual vegetables.

A NIP spokeswoman said: 'We welcome Hampshire's two million voters, although we are not too bothered about Aldershot. We can offer them five national parks, 97 breeds of pie and our own rudimentary language. And contrary to the stereotype, we do not all have baths filled with coal – some of us have showers.

There will be cultural differences that Hampshire folk will need to overcome, not least our propensity for smiling at strangers or putting whippets in flat caps. That said, we've cakes, plenty of cakes. Affordable housing, competent football teams and memorable bands. Plus, cake. Did we mention the cake?'

Return of the comb-over 'definitely a cause for concern'

Over the past few days, comb-overs have been spotted as far north as Newcastle. Politicians on both sides of the political divide say a return to 1970's hair style is totally unacceptable. 'Other EU countries labelled us the 'sick man of Europe', we always assumed it was because of our tanking economy,' said the Business Secretary. 'But no, apparently it was because so many of our balding men willingly live on the fringes of society'.

Vatican is not institutionally catholic, says commission

The report was chaired by Father Seamus O'Priestly, an impartial agnostic. He welcomed his surprise conclusion that Catholicism is caused by free wine and biscuits. Class, health, education, employment and criminal justice are said to be the underlining reasons for not wearing a condom.

A Vatican spokesman said: 'This report is a vindication. We are not institutionally catholic. Here in the Vatican City, we believe in equal opportunities for all regardless of religion. Protestants, Muslims and Jews can all burn in hell together.'

The Pope said: 'There's not a catholic bone in my body. Live and let live, that's what I say. Unless you're a witch or an adulterer, of course.'

Matt Hancock Appreciation Society says first meeting was a raging success

'We complied with all the regulations, especially the rule of six,' said Mr M Hancock, the founder of the society. 'In fact, there were only two of us here. So, not only less than six, but also 100% of the membership. This is the most successful thing I have ever overseen.'

The event took place in Hyde Park and saw Mr Hancock and the other socially distant attendee clap for one minute in 'recognition of the current Health Secretary being a jolly good chap'.

Mr Hancock then made what he called 'a rousing speech on the brilliance of Matt Hancock,' whilst visibly choking back tears. This was followed by a chorus of 'For he's a jolly good fellow'. There was a final agenda item about what to do in the event of an increase in membership numbers, but both agreed that that was an unlikely scenario.

Proclamation confirms 'proportionate force' deployed on Little Red Riding Hood

Wolves at the Metropolitan Police have denied using excess chewing, when attempting to subdue fairy tale protests in support of women's safety. A chipper representative from Ye Home Fortress explained that Princesses and their ilk should avoid forests late at night: 'The fairer sex be naturally better suited to indoor pursuits, such as spinning gold from straw, weeping attractively, and tending to the dubious needs of seven thickset, drunkenly choral men.'

Responding to accusations of institutional racism against demonized minorities such as giants, ogres, and demons, he slapped his manly thigh and continued, 'Of course we welcome exotic travellers from distant lands, as long as they've come through legal channels. Fortunately, there are very few magic keys in circulation, and even if the glass slipper fits, it's invalid unless signed in triplicate under a gibbous moon.

A representative of Reclaim the Cobbled Streets, Ms Sleeping Beauty, was unfortunately unavailable for comment. Watchmen were quick to play down a rumoured date-rape potion incident, saying: 'She went to a tavern, she knew the risks.'

'Conventional Cops' TV series to launch

Featuring Det. Insp. Barry Smith, an officer in his mid-40s, average height, slightly balding, a little overweight. He does not like classical music, classic cars, chess, mind games, gambling or disobeying the rules.

His partner, Det. Sgt. Jane Andrews, is in her mid-30s, having a similarly incident free backstory. She has no addictions, bad habits or skeletons in the cupboard. She is happily married to Robert, an accountant at a nearby mid-level financial management practice. They have two, young and well-adjusted children. They live in a suburb just outside Newbury in a quiet community with the usual levels of low-level aggravation and mostly low-level crime.

'Conventional Cops', follows the daily tasks undertaken by the police team. Both work normal hours, neither has demons to deal with. Both cops work systematically through the evidence. There are no flashes of insight, it is just methodical, pain-staking detailed work to crack crimes such as VAT fraud, business closing hours violations and prolific littering. It does not feature serial killers, religious malcontents or mentally ill con artists. There are no conspiracies, no bad language and no viewers.

Nicola Sturgeon found not guilty of Alex Salmond committing sexual assault

Prosecutors were determined that some woman should be held accountable for a man's actions, as is traditional in a court of law. However, Ms Sturgeon escaped on the technicality that the whole thing was a farce.

A relieved Ms Sturgeon appeared outside Scottish parliament to address reporters after the ruling. Perhaps optimistically, she declared, 'I hope to draw a line under this episode. No longer will a woman's voice be silenced by a ma---'

Company's 'Vision' more inspirational than Martin Luther King's

The financial services firm CNJ Finance has dazzled its 2,300 employees with a new and improved strategic vision.

Barry, from accounts, was overcome with emotion: 'It was one of the most incredible moments of my life. It just seemed like a regular boring old conference at first - coffee that tastes like shit, Jill from HR presenting about 500 PowerPoint slides about some crap or other - the usual stuff really.

'But then this one slide came up with the company's new vision on and, wow, what a moment. There were these words, these amazing, inspiring words, and they were even in these little coloured circles that made all the difference. The piece de la resistance was the PowerPoint animation, which meant the words appeared slowly like a mind-blowing apparition.'

The company's vision includes a host of unique, never-thought-of-before 'pillars', like Teamwork, Growth and Profit.

CEO of CNJ Finance, Tom B Smith, confirmed the corporate thinking: 'We knew this would blow everyone away. It's definitely more inspiring than that Martin Luther King speech because his was just about some dream or other. For CNJ Finance, this vision is our reality. Admittedly the £128,000 in consultancy fees for the agency was a bit steep, if only it was free. Free at last. Thank God Almighty, a PowerPoint free at last'.

Woman who worked out what's going on in 'Line of Duty' to be burned as a witch

Under the Modern Witchcraft Act (2021), it became a capital offence to decipher the plot of the popular crime drama. The first to be burned at the stake at Smithfield Market will be Dr Carole Smythe, a 38-year-old academic from Cambridge, who had been overheard saying: 'I wouldn't want to spoil the series by telling you the answer to that, but it's not difficult to work out.'

After the end of Episode 1, it became clear that the only way anyone could understand the plot was by consorting with the hell-born spawn of Lucifer. The Government acted swiftly to rush the Act through Parliament. Police have carried out a number of surveillance operations based on information from public-spirited citizens about friends and relations claiming to know.

Civil rights groups have criticised the rush to execute Dr Smythe, given that there is no actual proof that she summoned up the Evil One prior to Sunday night's episode and was witnessed marking essays by several colleagues at the time. However, Jed Mercurio said: 'I haven't a f*cking clue what's going on and I wrote the bloody thing. Burn her! Burn the witch!'

Government to trial coughing in people's faces

The Government is to run a series of trials for how we might return to normal public life, including experimenting with having everyone cough directly into each other's faces.

'It's important that as we start to reopen our society, we do so in a controlled manner,' said the Chief Medical Officer. 'With a data-led approach we can understand the risks involved in reintroducing everyday activities. It is for this reason that we are encouraging people to get together in large groups and spew their germs around with wanton disregard.

'These trials are vital if we are return to the glory days of broken hand driers in pub toilets and individually handling every potato in Aldi. Remember - when the person next to you sneezes and then wipes their nose with the back of their hand, they are simply playing their part in a controlled experiment. At this point, you should tut loudly, exchange contact details and record the encounter in the NHS app.'

Trials will also include holding major sporting events, with the FA Cup final featuring an epic showdown between COVID-19 and the AstraZeneca vaccine.

Nostalgia now a thing of the past

Sociologists have revealed that a wistful affection for a time past only affects those who cannot accurately remember the past and that déjà vu is not what it used to be. Said one: 'We took a group of four-year-olds and asked them if they had any sentimental longing for the 1950s, and not one of them could remember the theme tune to Bonanza.

'We miss the glory days of the Empire, we go misty-eyed over Magna Carta, and we get a hard-on any time mentions the Dissolution of the Monasteries. Two-thirds of Brits still think

Elizabeth I is the monarch, Vikings are a threat and that the national currency is still the turnip.'

Explained one psychologist: 'For those that want to live in a bygone era, there is always past-life therapy or failing that, a day trip to the Isle of Wight.'

Man leaves baked brie in oven for 500th consecutive time

A man who likes to think of himself as 'handy in the kitchen' has once again obliterated the f*ck out of his dipping cheese. Theo Hogg achieved the new landmark, days after boasting to friends that he had mastered the Sunday comfort-food-and-wine combo.

'One minute, I'm carving a majestic cross in the top like I'm Gordon Ramsay; the next, I'm scraping cheese intestine off every part of the oven.'

We ask 'Decking – is it the new 'patio' for middle-class serial killers?'

As our thoughts now turn to Spring, gardening and disposing of human remains, we have many options available to us in terms of hiding the evidence and keeping a tidy lawn. Proud homeowners will opt for decking to give their outside living space a real wow factor and give sniffer dogs a real puzzle.

Lockdown has put an unfamiliar strain on families, often resulting in not one but multiple murders. Loved ones crammed into the chest freezer need to make room for ice lollies, and there is only so long that you can keep your husband's carcass in the loft before he starts to smell.

Camouflaging mass graves is normally a skill acquired by working for the CIA, but decking is an affordable solution that also provides somewhere nice for your patio furniture to go. Pol

Pot's 'killing fields' would have been far less obvious if he had used a gazebo or a modest rockery.

One landscape gardener remarked: 'You can try to compost your family, but that'll take months; it makes far more sense to concrete over them. Then, either gravel over the top or add some decking. Your neighbours will know exactly what you're up to but are unlikely to go to the police if they feel your improvements have added value to the property'.

We are going to have to learn to live with the Conservative Party

Speaking at the latest Government Coronavirus press briefing, the public health supremo warned that society would have to come to terms with the Tory Party, as it will be with us for many years to come. While many had hoped that Boris Johnson's Government was merely a phase, she suggested that the effects of long Bojovid will be more difficult to shake.

'I'm afraid we have to face it,' she explained, 'the Conservative Party is here to stay. Once it has a foothold in its host, this parasite is virtually impossible to shake loose – particularly in vulnerable areas like Hampshire and Kent'.

Citizens may face a recurrence of the Conservatives in the winter months when the cold and dark allow right-wing ideas of isolationism and individualism to spread more easily. The elderly are the most at risk of exposure and the Daily Mail is a known vector of transmission.

Loyalist Rioters to stop burning petrol cars by 2025

A speaker for 'Ulster Green Hand Commando' in North Belfast announced today an action plan to move towards burning only battery- and hybrid- electric vehicles in riots by 2025.

'We've been looking at the successes of Extinction Rebellion and now have an action plan for our own riots to go zero-carbon within four years.

Marching has always been actively supported, so burning cars and throwing petrol bombs are the remaining high-carbon aspects of our protests. Setting fire to electric vehicles, especially those with large Lithium-Ion batteries, which can burn for hours on end, will significantly reduce our carbon footprint.'

Keir Starmer completes tutorial mode

After a whole year in charge of the Labour Party, Starmer has finally unwrapped the instruction manual and started to focus on what all this Opposition malarky is all about. He has unlocked various achievements; Brylcreeming his own face, using his knighthood to get disabled parking and turning up at PMQs dressed as a Dodo.

There are some of the key progression points for Labour leaders:

Level 1: Tying your own shoelaces.

Level 10: Learn that Rupert Murdoch is not your friend.

Level 999: Found the NHS.

It should be noted that most politicians rarely reach level 10.

Taking off the stabilizers and putting on his 'big boy pants' have been significant steps for someone who is only 58. A colleague explained: 'Keith (sic) finally removed his 'L plate' - and he promises to get rid of the 'ABOUR' bit as well'.

Bitcoin electricity usage caused by leaving the 'big light' on

Data miners of Bitcoin are said to use more electricity than entire nations, but new evidence suggests it is all because they left their TV on standby overnight. One miner admitted: 'Swapping energy supplier helped a little bit but if we really want to get serious about saving energy, we just need to wear thicker socks'.

Florence Nurdle, a 97-year-old grandmother, offered cost saving tips to the Bitcoin industry: 'Use lids when boiling your cabbage soup. Take a hot water bottle to bed and wear loft insulation in the bath. Pack your freezer with any spam left over from the 40s. And never leave the big light on – otherwise the Luftwaffe will see you'

Grand National 2021: NewsBiscuit form guide

- Boris's Folly 33/1 - a difficult year for this long-haired nag, who has performed miserably in every outing

- Test and Trace: 39 billion to 1. Has never lived up to potential and chances of winning this race seen little more than a moon-shot

- Biden his Time: 8-1. A horse this age has never won the big race but after beating Trump's Terror in November, anything may be possible

- Captain Hindsight 20-1: Determined to stick to centre ground no matter what and seems to have few backers

- Where's Ed Davey?: 40-1. No information available at time of writing on recent form. Avoid

- Lockdown Haircut: 14-1 Often looks out of control and increasingly wild in windy conditions

- Rule of 6: 28-1. Not a fan of cold conditions but glass of Prosecco and time under blankets have had a positive effect. Can only get better

- Cummings and Goings 9/1: A complete mare but worth a punt

- Randy Andy 1000-1 Royal Outsider: One from the Queen's stable. Keep an eye on this one. Hardly broke sweat last time out, but always a danger to young fillies. Could be his last time out

Boris Johnson devastated after unfiltered photo of him appears online

PM Johnson, was left in a state of deep depression after a released photograph showed him to be calm, serious, and sporting a 'proper haircut'.

A spokesperson from Tory HQ commented: 'Boris has made a career out of his slovenly appearance: the fact that this normal, sensible, unfiltered picture has been shared has hit him badly.' This follows images of Keir Starmer looking charismatic and Nicola Sturgeon smiling - although she claims it was just indigestion.

Confirming postcode of missing dog is pointless

Indicating the broad area you live in when you share an online post about a missing dog, serves absolutely no purpose whatsoever, experts have confirmed today.

'Your Facebook friends are actually much less likely to live in the same area as you, so you'd be better off asking your old school friend from Bolton or your uncle who emigrated to Adelaide, to check their garage for missing Benji', revealed a web analyst.

'It's not 'shared with NW1', it's actually shared with Brian in Dublin, Nan in Llandrindod Wells, and Ricky's student house in Loughborough. But saying that would mean less space for the heart and tearful emojis then', he said. 'Sadface'.

Queen sells up and moves to Ibiza

Following the death of her husband, Elizabeth Windsor is set to move out of the family homes and head for a life in the sun.

'One has always wanted to chillax Balearic-stylee,' said the nonagenarian. 'But Phil wouldn't hear of living among foreigners. But now he's gone - bless his soul - one is orf to the beachfront villa one has always wanted!'

While house prices and living costs in Ibiza are high, it is thought that sales of the Queen's multi-billion-pound property portfolio should leave her in a financial position to basically do whatever she likes.

Meanwhile, no buyers for her estate have been named, although there are unconfirmed reports that a London metalwork company has been contracted to manufacture a 20-foot wrought-iron addition to the gates of Buckingham Palace, reading simply 'Trump Palace'.

Five Go Dobbing in the Neighbours

People can think about booking holidays, but don't go any further

In a carefully worded communication, the Government has provided explicit and unambiguous permission to UK residents to start thinking about booking holidays. 'Imagine walking into a travel agency, dreaming about perusing brochures. You may even consider using a VR headset to simulate the experience of signing paperwork, committing to spending thousands of pounds on your credit card that you can't afford, in the full knowledge that you have no comeback if the pandemic reverses again,' said a government spokeswoman, 'but for Christ's sake, don't actually do it.'

Britons are also encouraged to fantasise about going out for a pint, watching a football match or being led by a cabinet absent of donkeys. 'Enjoy the experience; just don't get too excited because it ain't going to happen,' the spokeswoman added.

Nation mourns loss of TV scheduling

As 24/7 courage of the death of Prince Philip hits our screens, thousands of people lined the streets because there was nothing better on TV. Tears were shed as gameshows and crime dramas were cancelled, while ironically Netflix reported a 57% increase in people watching The Crown.

Said one mourner: 'It hit me, right in the middle of my Friday night TV. One second Ant & Dec were there and the next they were gone. It just makes you realize how fragile programme scheduling is'.

Antenna were held at half-mast and all TVs were put on standby to avoid the simpering face of Nicholas Witchell. The Last Post was played, alongside the theme tune to EastEnders. While, out of respect, families restrained the urge to put on a DVD, for at least 3 minutes.

Asked whether Prince Philip would have wanted to disrupt the TV scheduling and be an absolute nuisance, a Palace Official confirmed: 'It's exactly what he would have wanted'.

Man inexplicably still overweight after completing marathon

Dan Evans, 38, is left scratching his slightly flabby head after realising that he is still as chunky as he was before completing the race. Evans said, 'It's a universally established fact, or so I thought, that if you start running you lose weight. Yet I'm as jowly as always but now with added pensioner's knees'.

'So, the moral of the story is kids, forget exercise. You may as well stick to the Xbox. It was 26 pointless miles, only interrupted by me pausing to quaff four Fray Bentos pies and nine Snickers'.

Government celebrates Barnard Castle Day with a 264-gun salute

A year ago, to the day, the outstanding bravery of a selfless Government adviser captured the hearts of a nation.

The 12th of April 2020 was the day that will forever take pride of place in the annals of Britain's long and proud history. Forget the overhyped exploits of that geriatric Sir Whatshisface codger who walked around his garden a few times to raise funds for an already well-funded NHS and garner some self-publicity.

No, the Heroics of Dominic Cummings were on a completely different level. Without any regard to either his or anyone else's safety, he drove his wife and child to a derelict town up north called Durham. Somehow, they survived the rigours of virus-infested motorway service stations, sub-zero temperatures and random Northern types.

A Government spokesman said that Barnard Castle Day was the new glorious 12th. 'It boosted morale and helped make Boris

Johnson our most popular prime minister since Holly Willoughby.'

Band split with guitar playing dad because he's their dad

The announcement was made by the Torrance sisters – Lily, 15, Nancy, 14, and Beth, 12 - on Saturday morning at a family meeting around the kitchen table. A crestfallen Danny 'three chords and the truth' Torrance was thanked for bringing the girls together, buying the instruments, and setting up something called a Myspace for the band.

However, the sisters were adamant now was the right time for him to leave, before someone noticed the 44-year-old dad hovering at the back, playing guitar, spilling out of his skinny jeans. The sisters proposed keeping Danny on as a driver for the next four or five years, provided he never mentioned the EP he made in 2001 or that time he met Joe Strummer.

Dan had considered starting another band, but he said that would involve having another kid.

Cameron denies lobbying for Remain

The former Prime Minister has denied making any effort during the Referendum campaign or that he accepted money to run the country. He lawyer confirmed: 'My client has never and would never provide effective governance. When Brexit happened, he was nowhere in the vicinity'.

Most recent accusations of corruption seem unlikely, given that no one would trust Mr Cameron to get the job done. His lawyer said: 'There is nothing to suggest that Mr Cameron in any way helped the Remain campaign; all the evidence points to the exact opposite.'

Prince Philip funeral moved to avoid clash with Kilmarnock v Montrose Cup tie

A Palace spokeswoman said: 'The last thing the Queen would want is to undermine the solemnity of the proceedings by distracting the nation with her late husband's funeral. As you may know Prince Philip was lifelong supporter of Montrose and when staying at Balmoral would often make the journey to Links Park to cheer on the Gable Endies. I know he'll be at Rugby Park in spirit on Saturday afternoon, cheering on the boys and enjoying a Bovril'.

Man astonished to learn TV can't hear him when he shouts at it

'I got it from my dad originally', explained Carl Jones. 'He was a massive TV-yeller. During the 1994 World Cup my mum actually left him because he was so loud. But at the time I thought it was worth it because at least he had single-handedly won the England Belgium game for us with all his shouting.'

Carl has since spiralled into a state of despair. 'It's an illusion, I'm not even sure that the footballers can hear me. And if they can't hear me, what's the point?'

Bluetit forced to prove identity before being allowed to nest in bird box

Due to a recent influx of cuckoos, other birds have been forced provide additional travel documentation and housing applications. Complained one Tit: 'It's not a left wing or right wing issue, I've got both. I've kept my pecker clean my whole life.

'I can't believe it,' tweeted Harry Fluttercap from Cheshire. 'I had to dig up a very specific selection of papers and get them notarised at my own expense. So that meant finding a solicitor, who charged me a nuts amount because it all had to be done in her presence. I'm not even sure it's the right bird box for my family, but I had to do it anyway to even start the process of registering interest.

'It's flocking ridiculous.'

Cameron raises the bar in 'Worst Prime Minister' contest

Former prime-minister, David Cameron, has returned to deliver what appears to be an impossibly high level of greed and incompetence.

Mr Cameron issued a statement: 'There has been talk of me being the worst since Lord North - who managed to lose America - well, I was brought up to be at the top or, at least, treated like I am, so in case my brilliant Brexit wheeze doesn't end up destroying the union and bankrupting the country, it seemed prudent to embroil myself in a lobbying scandal that I had previously predicted would be the next big scandal after the Murdoch newspaper scandal that, er, I was embroiled in.'

Standing prime-minister, Boris Johnson, has accepted the challenge. 'Mr Cameron may try and claim destroying the union, but let me tell you, if it does happen, it will be on my watch. And you mark my words, I've ordered an enquiry into Greensill Capital and you can be sure that it will turn out that I will end up having ordered an enquiry that implicates me.'

'No way! I don't believe it!': Reaction to shocking news Tories are all corrupt

Julie, a lifelong Cameron supporter, told us: 'I just broke down in tears when I heard about Greensill, I couldn't believe it was happening. Dave always seemed like such a top bloke, his referendum on Brexit was obviously a great idea and panned out superbly. He did a fab job with the NHS - it was clear we needed to divert money away from healthcare and towards tax breaks for the super-rich. He was your typical humble, trustworthy, down to earth Etonian.'

Shockwaves have reverberated across the UK with many now saying they will think twice about voting Tory next time, though they will definitely still vote Tory in the end.

Despite her shock and sadness, Julie says she still believes the conservatives are the right party to lead Britain in the years to come. 'It's not as though the current Government are anything like the others - BoJo, Hancock, Patel - you couldn't find a more trustworthy bunch.'

No data breach not at Facebook. It never happened. Again

A pixelated spokeswoman confirmed: 'A social network no one has ever heard of denies that another non-data breach has not taken place and it absolutely has not affected half a billion users. No, best to deny everything. Or better still, say nothing at all. Just remain silent, pretend you don't exist and maybe, if you close your eyes really tightly, all of your problems will go away and everyone will forget you exist.'

Following a lengthy investigation by regulators, when it is finally proven beyond doubt that there was another massive data breach, an army of insanely paid media fondlers will shift Facebook's position to 'And?'. Mark Zuckerberg will eventually glance up from leaf-blowing his lawns of cash to croak, 'None of this is my problem because I am now legally registered as a duck for tax reasons'.

Five Go Dobbing in the Neighbours

Wetherspoon's beer garden is a main road

The Maimed Ferret in Hull has welcomed its first patrons back after lockdown to enjoy a pint of Bombardier while dodging traffic, it has emerged. One patron Dave Smith said: 'To be honest, I have no time for beer gardens. Like Thai fishcakes and immigration.

'I store an old fridge and have the occasional tyre fire in my garden. But that's it. None of this Peroni-drinking cricket jumper around the neck shite.

'So, when I heard the Ferret of all places were going down this poncey road, my first thought was thank god Prince Phillip wasn't here to witness it.

'But when I heard that describing it as a 'garden' was just to get around the rule for re-opening - like when we had that bubble-thing with our entire street – and its actually just the dual carriageway directly out front, I breathed an asthmatic sigh of relief.

'Now I'm two pints in. This is the life, eh lads? Lads!? LADS!!? LAADDDS?!! Traffic'll die down in a second.

'There's even the BP garage across the road to top up on microwave pies.

'Ah, looks like Gary's on his way back from the garage. Oooh, f*ck. Ya right there Gaz?!! Should we phone 999?

'Bollocks. It was his bastard round next an' all.'

Driving licence 'unfair' on those who have not got one yet

A human rights watchdog has warned of a 'two-Tier society' that divides people with driving licences from those who have not passed yet, or don not actually want one. The Government is under growing pressure to ban driving until everyone gets a licence.

A spokesperson for the DVLA said: 'We're ramping-up testing and aim to get everyone over the age of 75 behind the wheel of a heavy vehicle by the end of the month.

Large Hadron Collider finds evidence of a Smaller Hadron Collider

'We spent the entire week crushing particles at speeds quite close to the speed of light', said Director of Particle Crushing, Professor Horst Shmitzhoff. 'Even after putting the collider on its maximum 800w setting, we found nothing.

'However, when the gargantuan machine was accidentally put into reverse after Ingrid (Das Tea Fraulein) clunked into the big lever with her tea trolley, all hell broke loose'. Subsequently, scientists at CERN claim that the discovered cup of steaming liquid is the elusive Smaller Hadron Collider (by David Hockney), although Ingrid says it just a cup of tea.

Malcolm the Human Centipede sues Colin the Caterpillar

While M&S and Aldi are embroiled in their own lawsuit, a Dutch horror firm is claiming they invented the original human/insect cake hybrid. A spokeswoman said: 'Ours was the first to feature a chocolatey fountain – at both ends. Ours had three faces not one, although Colin does look a lot more jolly'.

Malcolm the Human centipede was a complicated cake, with three conjoined sections – using marzipan, smarties and Nazi medical experiments. The sweet treat was particularly family-centred, as all three sections (Malcolm, Sarah & Greta) were all related.

M&S denied their Colin was an S&M homage, a store manager replied: 'Why would we want that kind of abomination on our shelves? We already got enough criticism for our glittery salmon and cream cheese flavoured crisps.'

The Horror firm responded: 'They even look identical, theirs is covering in brown chocolate and ours was certainly brown'.

Your NewsBiscuit Guide to returning to the office

After a year of trusting their employees to work from home without supervision, bosses are preparing to welcome staff back into the office so that they can once more impose some discipline on their lazy, workshy, liberty-taking minions. Here is your guide to making that transition back to being watched like a hawk throughout the working day:

- Get dressed appropriately before starting work. The rabbit onesie is not appropriate.

- Making a really, really long snake out of plasticine for your kids while keeping an eye on your laptop in case any emails arrive will no longer be considered work.

- The Company will stop pretending to care about your health and is currently dismantling the five pillars of resilience and the six dimensions of wellness that were constructed to support you while home-working. Whatever they were supposed to be.

- Face-to-face meetings will replace Zoom calls; bringing your kids and pets along to disrupt discussions will no longer be acceptable. Nor will 'I am sorry but your audio

broke up a bit, can you say that again please' be a
suitable excuse for not paying attention.

- Say goodbye to that WhatsApp group that your boss set
  up for departmental discussions which you only used
  for amusing memes and banter anyway.

- At your manager's discretion (i.e. fat chance), you may
  still be allowed to work from home occasionally. In
  order to be allowed to do so, you must complete a
  twelve-page questionnaire regarding the compliance of
  your home-working environment with all the applicable
  and non-applicable Health and Safety legislation, even
  though no-one has cared about any of that for over 12
  months.

Still some room in freezer, confirms man

A man has confirmed to his wife and kids that there remains
plenty of space to put things in the family freezer, despite
growing evidence that there isn't.

Pete McBride made the confident announcement after
returning from the weekly supermarket shop, on opening the
freezer door and being faced with 10 items falling out
immediately, with a leg of lamb hitting his foot and some frozen
fruit sliding across the kitchen floor.

'No, no, there's actually loads of space', said McBride, in
response to his wife's suggestion that the freezer was fuller
than the one seen recently on Line of Duty, and that they should
move towards an emergency '4 weeks and out' scheme along
with a stricter stock rotation policy.

'We just need to apply basic principles of tessellation, continued
Pete, doing a good impression of Geoff Capes in the World's
Strongest Man to try and wedge a bag of 6 month of frozen

Bolognese back in the freezer alongside a Tupperware container of Thai curry and a tub of ice cream.

'And it would really help if we could stick to the shelving principles we all signed up to last year', continued Pete. 'Fish on shelf 1, meat on level 2, ready meals shelf 3, cooked food and other stuff shelf 4. If we need a refresher training session, you just have to say...'

Awful couple continuing to give 'Grand Tours' of their two-bed semi

Sara and Jonathan have recently purchased a two-bed semi-detached house and want to ensure everyone knows about it by subjecting them to a 'grand tour' at every opportunity.

Sara is the lead tour guide and sees it as a public service: 'We just couldn't stand it if anyone didn't know first-hand how successful and middle class we are. We've had some amazing feedback; the postman was blown away by our sustainable bamboo toilet seat.'

Mark has known the couple for years and was one of the first to be wowed by their incredible house, which contains rooms and furniture.

'Well, I've had the 'grand tour' eleven times now, so to be honest, if I have to see that sodding fire pit one more time, I'll shove it up someone's arse - and don't even get me started on that bullshit 'garden bar'. For the record, the only way in which it resembles an actual bar is that the bog stinks of piss. That bamboo toilet seat is a bloody health hazard.'

Fakevaxpassports.com launched

We at fakevaxpassports.com have the solution. Reject the real passports, protect your privacy and all your personal data. Just buy one of our totally-convincing 'Not-a-real-vaccination-passport-but-looks-exactly-like-one' FakeVaxPassports. To get one tomorrow (or some time eventually to have one thrown over your front fence) just email us your full name, address, postcode, phone number, date of birth, place of birth, serial number of your birth certificate and passport number and date of expiry.

Also, full name of husband / wife / partner and/or any ex- or former husband(s), wives, partners etc., together with their present address, both parents' date and place of birth, inside leg measurement, favourite football team, favourite colour, bank, all debit card and credit details time, and passwords, signed agreement to pay us £99.99 a month for ever and £999.99 in used notes up front.

Wave two fingers at them all! If you don't want to have a life-saving and plague-preventing vaccination - and who in their right mind would want that, even without the built-in mind-controlling microchips? - we have the solution.

Act now - what have you got to lose?

New Super League to feature a competitive circle jerk

Europe's wealthiest clubs are proposing a breakaway league, based on the sporting principles of The Hunger Games. A select 12 clubs will repeatedly play one another, generating all the suspense of a sun rise or a Boris Johnson divorce.

Financial reward will replace competitive endeavour, with the winner calculated on their FTSE position. There will be no promotion or relegation, with the plan to slowly eliminate all goals for and against, so not to upset the markets.

Even in a small division of elites there will be losers, with Arsenal agreeing to get defeated 6-0 every week. Although Manchester Utd and City fans will experience travelling to exotic away games, on the other side of Manchester.

One TV executive explained: 'It's all about maximising viewing figures, so expect Barcelona vs Tyson Fury, Chelsea vs Spiderman and Real Madrid vs Mrs Brown's Boys'

Ludogorets Razgrad gutted not to be invited to join European Super League

PFC Ludogorets Razgrad is a football team from a small town in the North East of rural Bulgaria. Speaking for the team, owner Kiril Domuschiev said, 'We are absolutely devastated not to be the first club invited to join the new European Super League.'

'Everyone knows we are the best team in Europe, and to have the likes of Chelsea waltz in ahead of us like they've some special right to do so is absolutely disgusting.'

'Sure, we were never in the top flight of the Bulgarian football league until a decade ago, but we did the domestic double in our first season at the top, and have since won the title 9 times in a row. Maybe we are just too successful?'

That Ted Hastings' speech in full

'There's only one thing I'm interested in, and that's bent coppers. And women with big jugs. So that's two things. Do you count the jugs separately, d'you think? Then it's three things I'm interested in: bent coppers, big left jugs and big right jugs. Oh, and I like that gap down there where they don't have a willy.

'So there's four things I'm interested in: bent coppers, left jugs, right jugs and ladies' down below places. Do I make myself clear, laddy?'

PDF inventor not compatible with hole in ground

The funeral of Charles Geschke, the co-founder the Adobe software company, has been delayed while undertakers figure out how to change the size of his grave. Conventional tools like spades and mechanical diggers were found to be incompatible, and mourners could be charged extra for a coffin that works with standard holes.

The funeral director said: 'Normally we use a simple hole dug six feet deep. Most coffins fit into them quite nicely. However, this time we used a Portable Deceased Format. It doesn't fit and no one has a clue how to change the dimensions of the hole or the coffin. It's really pissing us off.'

A spokesperson for Adobe apologised for the delay and offered to convert the Portable Deceased Format coffin to one that fits any hole. The mourners are holding a whip round to buy a cheaper PDF-Holes converter.

Shock as Mime Artist realizes they really are trapped in a large glass box

There were white faces all round when their friends were unable to help due to very high winds. It completely wiped the smile of their faces, with just one hand.

Passers-by were unable to pull her up with an invisible rope, one witness said.

NewsBiscuit's Guide to Spurious Wisdom

It may come as a surprise to many that Britain is not the sole repository of ancient wisdom. We are used to time honoured proverbs such as 'A bird in the hand, is worth two in the bush' and 'Never vote Tory' but across the world many cultures have a myriad of ancient sayings that instil wisdom and guide us even in our modern age. There's a lot to learn from ancient global wisdom as this collection of proverbs from history and age old civilisations shows:

- Algeria. 'Drink not from your neighbour's well, if you want to stay well.'
- Gabon. 'Say not dembele, if you mean not dembele.'
- Jordan. 'Flashing teeth mean danger.'
- Mongolia. 'When the horse is in the field, then you must yield.'
- Ghana. 'On a man, a bald head is a sign of honour, but a full head is a disgrace.'
- Angola. 'Two are good, three are better, but four is disaster.'
- Malawi. 'Whistle to show you are alive, stop whistling to stay alive.'
- Lesotho. 'The ant is stronger than the elephant, but the elephant has bigger feet.'
- Oman. 'If the mother of your camel spits in your yoghurt, then you should take pebbles to the fig tree of concern.'
- Tajikistan: 'A chicken you eat only once — eggs a hundred times.'
- Bulgaria. 'Children! If you don't eat your peppers and tomatoes, then the bad crocodile of doom will stalk you and snap his teeth on a cigarette.'
- Georgia. The stink of a friend is better than the perfume of an enemy
- Denmark. 'All nations which seek fame through jaunty statues in their capitals are not as good. Probably.'

- Pornutopia: Too many cocks spoil the breath
- The Federated States of Micronesia. 'The bluer your lake, the dafter your prize piglet.'
- Okinawa. 'She who smelt it, should be brought cherry blossoms of forgiveness.'
- Lithuania: One who keeps all his pigeons in a single wheelbarrow is walking a tightrope, tantamount.
- Tajikistan. 'One man's hippopotamus dung, is another man's hippopotamus dung.'
- Ancient Inuit proverb: 'Never eat yellow, green, brown, blue, pink or black snow. Just stop eating snow, okay?'

It's two pills - but each pill is the size of a pillow

The Prime Minister has promised an anti-COVID treatment involving two pills, which will be either shot into your mouth through a didgeridoo or used as a buoyancy aid.

Each pill will weigh as much as cricket ball and will be just as tasty. A doctor explained: 'COVID is an air borne virus, so the best way to combat it, is to block up your airways'.

Some patients may be intimidated by the size, but it is more practical than the alternative of shrinking a band of scientists and a submarine, then injecting them into your bloodstream.

Morpheus clarified: 'You take the blue pill, the story ends. You take the red pill, you wake up hogtied next Michael Gove, a spatula and a bucket of jelly'.

JP Morgan-backed Super league eclipsed by Standard Chartered Mega league

Contrary to the misunderstood narrative, JP Morgan is not generously funding the league project to the tune of £4.7 billion. Rather, it is the initial underwritten amount, burdening the league with so much future debt that all of the major clubs will be broken up and sold for spare parts.

Not to be outdone, Standard Chartered have proposed a European Mega League. Next, Goldman Sachs plan an Ultra-Mega-Super-Duper-With-Knobs-On-Infinity-Plus-One league. While Scunthorpe United are just happy to kick the ball.

People remember they don't actually like other people

Restrictions are easing across the UK with many meeting for a pint outdoors or hitting the shops again. However, for many, it has been a terrible reminder of just how awful other people are and how much you do not like them.

Jon was one of many counting down the days until he could see his friends and family again. It was not until he actually did, that he remembered how annoying they all are and now has his fingers crossed for a third wave with accompanying lockdown.

'I genuinely forgot how irritating my brother and his wife are, at least on Zoom I could just mute them and blame technical issues. Plus, I didn't have to interact with their kids at all during lockdown which was a massive bonus. Wiping a snotty toddler's nose whilst freezing my knackers off and paying £6 a pint was not how I imagined enjoying my newfound freedom.'

Carol has been equally as disappointed with other people. 'I queued for seven hours to get into Primark only to find the place bloody swarming with people, they were everywhere, it was repulsive. I immediately remembered that I hate them all and walked out without buying anything. I will definitely go back to doing all my shopping online.'

Some are lobbying the Government to introduce yearly lockdowns regardless of whether there is a global pandemic.

Boris Johnson will act on sleaze 'for the right price'

The Prime-Minister has given a finger-crossed behind his back pledge to appoint an independent enquiry into reports of improper lobbying by civil servants and members of parliament.

'The PM takes this very seriously', said a grim-faced spokesman, 'How seriously you can judge by the amount I'm going to be asking to be slipped to me although, let me make this clear, Boris said some of it can be paid 'in kind'.'

Mr Johnson showed his mastery of statistics by presenting a graph with the amount to be paid on the X axis and the independence of the enquiry on the Y axis. 'You can see here, for a few hundred K, you get an enquiry headed by Jeffery Archer with Jonathan Aitken and Neil Hamilton advising. Sliding up to David Attenborough the Dalai Lama for a couple of million Euros, obviously, the PM's not daft.'

Enraging pop-up ad stops you dead in your tracks – click here for more.

A flippin' titty-enraging advert has popped up in the app you are using and it won't budge. All progress and headway being made is now at a standstill. It's going to be a while before the countdown timer bar lets you do anything at all.

But you're not paying attention to the ad in any way because you are scanning the corners of the screen for that craftily hidden X which usually pops up somewhere. What a waste of everyone's time and money...

Ooh, ya little bugger - there you are, light grey on a light grey background.

Yes, yes, yes, now another marginally different screen of the advert just to slow you up even more. Oh, you dog muck bumhole advert designers, putting the next X in the other corner this time, and dark grey on a dark grey background. Now press it very carefully...

Noooo!

There is absolutely no way you did not press it exactly and precisely and it's taking you through to the app store anyway. Like you're some sort of bellend who would press 'yes please, show me more of the filth you are peddling'.

That's it. You've had enough of all this. You are livid. No, incandescent with rage. No, you are utterly APPoplectic

Ghost of Jackie Milburn in support of North East Super League

Newcastle United fans were delighted at the announcement by Jackie Milburn, from the spirit world, of the nascent North East Super League. Featuring all the major teams from the North East of England, the Super League will consist of four permanent members, Newcastle United, Hartlepool United, Middlesbrough and Berwick Rangers.

Sponsored by Greggs, the Stottie League, as it will affectionately be known has already raised £429.67. The manager of Sunderland was unavailable for comment.

Putin on a Blitz

President Putrid's spokesmeerkat, Alexei, maintains that the build-up of 150,000 Russian troops on the border of the Ukraine is not an act of aggression.

'We are merely preparing to rapidly deploy the Sputnik V anti-COVID to our friends in Germany. They are considering buying thirty million doses and we want to get them to Berlin asap. As such we are prepared to make the delivery ourselves. Unfortunately, this will necessitate crossing Ukraine and Poland. Fortunately, we have practiced this manoeuvre before.

'Does anyone want to buy some insurance while I'm here?'

Husband thinks the rancid milk water he made for his wife is tea

Geoff Frome from Milton Keynes has performed heroics again in his head after making his wife another perfect cup of tea, or so he thinks.

Frome, who as a man, is eminently qualified to master all methods of beverage preparation and has applied that basic level of hubris to the delicate area of tea-making, with arguably inevitable consequences.

Long-suffering wife, Denise, said, 'putting the actual tea bag in the cup of hot water rather than wafting it over the top for nine seconds would be a good start.

'I did try to convince him to put the tea bag in the cup of water once, but I gave up after a twenty-minute lecture about how it would risk ruining the tea's optimal taste and causing 'tea leaf scolding'.'

Martians prioritised with oxygen ahead of Earthlings

While hospitals around the globe struggle with a shortage of oxygen, NASA has decided to direct its considerable ingenuity to helping small green beings, who have a pair of cranial antennae and who think Star Trek is racist. This is part of a larger strategy to deliberately send vital medical resources across the galaxy, as opposed to sending resources across the world by accident – which is Matt Hancock's policy.

NASA's Rover can not only create oxygen, it can supply COVID vaccines and facemasks to any Martian over the age of 113 - which is 60 in Earth years. Although it would take hundreds of thousands of years to terraform the planet, it would still be cheaper than the private contractors the NHS has had to deal with.

The UK explained that Martians would still be ahead of teachers in the queue for a vaccine, partly because of their underlying health conditions, which appeared in the final chapters of War of the Worlds. While COVID is yet to spread to the 'red planet', there is a small risk particularly if Mars Rover has been on any long-haul flights recently.

Sadly, India is struggling with 314,835 new Coronavirus cases a day, whereas the Mars Rover has recorded zero cases but 314,835 new types of rock. Admitted one bemused Martian: 'We don't really need the oxygen; we just use it for blowing up balloons.'

Britain to drop Monday from week

Britain is set to soar ahead of its industrial competitors with its new slimmed-down six-day week, after research shows 80 per cent of absenteeism and work accidents happen on Mondays

'This is the shot in the arm the economy needs', says Government policy guru Rick Derbton, who thought up the idea. 'While Hans and Pierre are still sleeping off their Monday hangovers, the British worker will already be on his Tuesday lunchbreak'.

He says Monday is in fact an artificial day that has no historical foundation. 'There's no record of it before 1500 AD', he claims. 'We believe it was invented by mediaeval calendar-makers' guilds to create more work by padding out the week with a make-believe day, an early example of malign trade union meddling'.

'All things must pass' advises Gastroenterologist

This reassuring advice has been given to Simon Kosmatka (37) who had inadvertently swallowed a series of cherry stones, after inhaling a home-made fruit salad, without pausing to chew. Simon who has a habit of shovelling his food down, has in recent months eaten the paper wrapping on a pasty, half a toothpick and the small plastic toy from his cereal box.

To his credit, Mr Kosmatka is not over-weight, primarily because of the calories he expends furiously licking his plate. In his own determined way, Simon can gobble and slurp in a manner that would embarrass a Chimps' tea party.

Said Simon between mouthfuls: 'What's for pudding?'

Church of England to insist on at least one believer on Bishop shortlists

In a controversial move, the Church of England has introduced a rule that at least one candidate on bishopric shortlists must 'believe in God or, you know, something bigger out there or something.'

We know this will ruffle some feathers', said Archbishop of Canterbury Justin Welby, who had earlier admitted he'd only applied for the job because of the big house and the chance to wear a dress. 'But we in the church want to broaden the appeal and after a recent report, we decided that the time was right for immediate half-assed action.'

Selfish, greediest and the utterly psychotic also deserve a pay rise

Are you sick of nurses asking for rise? Do you just hate nurses generally? Then you are probably one the UK's unsung sociopaths.

Remember that dick of a pudgy kid who stole everyone's packed lunches and guzzled the lot? He's now a top investment banker and projected to earn £46 million this year.

And the girl who trapped a struggling ladybird that bumbled in through the chemistry lab window, bathed it in sulphuric acid and then held it in a Bunsen burner while giggling? She is now lead at the Institute for Doing Cruel Things to Animals Just to See What Will Happen.

And that child who ate slugs and kept poking his bottom with his fingers and sniffing them? Yes, he's now your Prime Minister.

What about that one you had to hold by the hood to stop them running into traffic? - Multi-billionaire who dicks around making space ships which keep blowing up.

The vindictive one who stomped on your butterfly project because it was betterer than her one? - Home Secretary.

That one who couldn't get the shapes in the right holes and kept touching himself? - That was Chris Grayling, that was.

So please, try to give to those greedy, selfish wazzocks and total psychotic fruit loops who make this country great.

Dread Lochs: UK waterways blocked with thousands of tonnes of human hair

There was excitement up and down the country last week as hordes of people flocked to hairdressers to get their first cut in months. Unfortunately, this excitement has turned to misery for many, as enormous, disgusting clumps of matted human hair are now blocking several major UK waterways.

This has resulted in severe flooding in some areas as well as entangling and choking hundreds of waterfowl. Several old people on canal boats are also reportedly irritated

The largest of these clumps, dubbed the 'lock-ness monster' by a group of local f*ckwits, measures several kilometres in length and is lodged in the River Thames between Battersea and Greenwich.

In response to the problem the Government has commissioned the construction of a 'humongous plunger', at an estimated cost of £100 million. Number 10 has confirmed that the contract for the project has been awarded to Rishi Sunak's cousin, a hedge fund manager with no experience in construction.

As an additional measure, access to hairdressers will now be restricted, with a passport scheme based on hair length reportedly in development. Several exemptions will apply, including white people with dreadlocks, who are still being actively encouraged to attend for the good of the nation.

Hansard to be published via text

The Government has denied it is avoiding public scrutiny by moving Hansard - the official record of business in the House of Commons and the Lords - from a printed and web-based service to a text only subscriber model.

'Government policy is now decided on WhatsApp, pitches for Government funds are made via text and public sector contracts are awarded on Social Media so now is the time to port the official reports away from expensive paper forms. Anyone can get Hansard delivered to their phones, texts cost ten pence each, approximately eleven thousand texts a day, please ask the phone owner's permission before signing up to the service,' a government spokesman said today.

A Hansard spokesman confirmed the change. 'Nobody likes change I guess,' he said, clearly not pleased with the policy, 'but at least adding LOL after the Prime Ministers statements won't seem so unusual now.'

Man missing for three years after getting the bins in discovered alive and well

Bury man Tony Hodgson was reported missing by his wife Beryl when he disappeared in 2018 after popping out to retrieve the dustbin from down the road following a refuse collection. She explained: 'After a month I assumed he was either dead or had run off with another woman.'

Mr Hodgson was discovered in a back alley by a neighbour, only a few minutes' walk from his home. When asked to shed light on his absence, Tony said: 'The bin men move the bins all over the show. They let them run right down t' hill. I once found a bin from Barnsley on our road.'

He continued; 'Beryl's always very annoyed if I go home without finding the bin. I were afraid to show up without it. After a few days, I didn't really have the nerve to return with nothing to show for it. So I just kept on looking. Now the reality has really hit me. I've lost me job, kids aren't talking to me, and the missus has got another bloke.' He reported. 'It's bin rubbish'.

Question Time to re-introduce out-of-their-depth celebrities by September

BBC debating show Question Time is to bring back celebrities, comedians and other chancers to the show towards the end of the year as lockdown conditions ease and life returns to normal.

The show has long included token non-politicians onto the panel in an attempt to inject some light relief and banter into the format, invariable drawing reactions from audiences such as 'they must have a book out'.

However, lightweight guests have been noticeably absent since the start of the coronavirus pandemic in favour of virologists and medics on account of the information being given being of consequence to viewers outside of the realm of Twitter.

In fall, viewers will again be able to see these chancers making fools of themselves alongside the usual left-wing zealots, casual racists, awkward looking local window glaziers and Nigel Farage.

Previous debates have provided memorable clashes between Edward and then Shadow Home Secretary Chris Grayling, and an eponymous episode in which Brendan O'Carroll, in character as Mrs Brown, called Secretary of State for International Trade Liam Fox 'a symbol of the oppression of the masses by the imperialist bourgeoisie', before drooping her knickers around her ankles.

The announcement of their return comes as a boost for actors and stand-up comics, many of whom haven't had a decent plug for their current projects since early 2020 and have largely been hawking their material as guests on each other's podcasts.

However, Russell Brand has turned down any further appearances on the show, stating that he has now 'transcended the narrow channels of the mainstream media narratives' and is instead focused on transferring the means of production to the workers via meditation.

A producer for the show told us: 'We are delighted to be able to reintroduce celebrities and comedians back onto the show following a long, exhausting period of presenting factual content. These guests are now part of the makeup of the format and present viewers with the opportunity to view topical issues in new and unfunny way'.

Shock as couple rent cabin in woods without being murdered

David Morse, 27, and Melanie Sutton, 26, are reeling from 'the anti-climax of a lifetime' after their week's holiday in rural Oregon went off without incident. Contrary to the plot of every slasher movie ever made, they did not end up being chased through the woods and killed by some rustic psycho with an extra chromosome.

Hopes of an exciting break began to fade then they found no evidence of recent digging in the back yard, and the strange piece of meat in the fridge turned out not to be a human body part.

'We thought we were about to see some action when the sinister owner of the cabin called round in his pickup truck at midnight', says Melanie. 'But it turned out he only called in to talk about Harry and Meghan. What a let-down'.

'Actually, this is the off season for hillbilly massacres', explains Guardian travel correspondent Giles Morton, 'as the natives are too busy seducing their cousins and cooking crystal meth. David and Melanie could have enjoyed an authentic butchering and dismemberment experience if they'd booked for October, when the harvest is in and the local nutjobs have more time on their web-fingered hands'.

Nobody is more astonished than David's family, who never expected to see him again. 'It's quite an embarrassment, really', says his dad. 'We sold all his stuff and rented out his room when he was gone. Still, there's hope for next year - I see he's been checking out the Bates Motel on TripAdvisor'.

Famous High Street brand The Labour Party collapses into administration

As Britain emerges out of lockdown and its retail outlets fill with non-mask wearing virus super spreaders, one well-known name has been conspicuous by its absence.

After a proud history of annoying the Tories and occasionally not letting them run the country, household name The Labour Party, appointed administrators from Deloitte on Wednesday.

No immediate redundancies were made as a result of the appointment, and the group's cloth cap stores and websites will continue to trade. It will still be able to ask the Prime Minister some tame, easily brushed aside questions in Parliament and call for a public enquiry on something when it runs out of ideas.

The move will protect the party from creditors while a buyer is sought for all or parts of the company. Sir Philip Green is expected to make derisory bids for some of the assets.

The news was greeted with dismay on the nation's high streets.

'It's scandalous,' said Jeanette Newbold, 36, a mother of six from Doncaster. 'I haven't shopped there for years, mind, but it's nice to know it's there even if it's not doing very much.

'The last time I went in, it was like going into a Cuban supermarket, and the only thing on the shelves were tons of carrier bags full of socialism long past its sell-by date.'

World record time for to smell fart

Janice Cupdraw, 26, from Pontefract has broken the world record time for farting and then smelling it herself. She was at home in her shower when she achieved the record-breaking feat.

Norris McSquirter from the Guinness Book of Records, who was disconcertingly on hand with a clipboard to adjudicate, confirmed, 'She absolutely shattered it. And by that, I mean the record time, not the glass door of her shower. She clocked a speed of 0.69 seconds, which is, incidentally, precisely the same world record time for completing the Rubik's Magic.'

'In the first instance, the absence of clothing in the shower helped a great deal. Clothing does form a temporary barrier to gas diffusion, slowing down the time it takes to detect the stench.

'The completely enclosed shower cubicle itself also played a major role. The fart cloud ricocheted off the reflective glass surface of the shower door, and with nowhere else to go, hit her nostrils almost instantly.'

Cupdraw said: 'It was squelchier than normal, and surprisingly powerful. Even for me.' Describing how she felt about her achievement, she responded, 'Very satisfied.'

God cancels flood after outbreak of animal swingers' parties on Ark

God's big calamity has been postponed indefinitely, after Noah's vessel descended into a wild orgy shortly after it began to rain.

'We'd hardly rung the 'everyone on board' gong before they all started getting to know each other biblically', says Noah. 'I had to return to shore for health and safety reasons. You wouldn't believe how much rocking and pounding an ark has to take when every species on the planet is having sex on it at the same time.'

'Thanks to all this decadent inter-species fornication, we now have 34 weird new hybrids on our hands', says Noah, 'including a fish with a goat's head and a horse with wings. Luckily, I'll be able to offload them on Ancient Greece. They seem to like that kind of thing over there.'

Dominic Cummings leaked PM's private messages to 'test eyesight'

In a 100,000,000-word statement, Dominic Cummings has justified leaking text messages revealing an underhand tax avoidance plot between Dyson boss and Boris Johnson by explaining he was only checking his eyesight.

'As everyone knows, my absolute number one priority - ahead of my family, my friends, any laws or logic - is my eyesight. There is literally nothing I wouldn't do to make sure my eyes are in absolute pukka shape. In my latest brilliant eye-test plan, I thought I'd hook out some old text messages then send them on to the press and then make sure I had indeed read them correctly by re-reading them in all the papers.'

Dominic has confirmed he is now planning his 'best ever' eye test involving an AK-47 assault rifle, a petrol bomb and Number 10 Downing Street.

Huge fatberg of lobbyists found in Westminster drain

A 100-tonne congealed mass of lobbyists has been found festering deep underneath Westminster. Said a Thames Water spokesperson: 'It's a mixture of oily striped-shirted and brace wearing lobbyists on their phones, combined with expensive red wine, foie gras, and chateaubriand from the Carlton Club. Typically, it has that shared Eton public school binding agent that helps grease the wheels and which is so hard to break down.'

One potential solution has been offered by James Dyson, who has revealed that he has an invention which may help disperse the fatberg, which he could make available as long as there were some decent tax breaks involved.

NASA helicopter tests on Mars annoy locals

Mrs Zuflaxizog lives near the flightpath and spoke via an interpreter: 'I was just about to enjoy some personal time with Mr Zuflaxizog when I saw Ingenuity flying past our window. It's very intrusive. I don't care for this sort of thing, not in my back yard. So I wrote to my MP (Martian Parliamentarian) about it'

'We don't mind a few adorable space rovers, but the noise and the GDPR implications are affecting house prices in the area.

'Across the gulf of space, intellects vast and cool and unsympathetic, regard your earth with envious eyes, and slowly and surely we draw our plans against you.'

Children wary of the new 'Prince Andrew Award'

In the absence of a Duke of Edinburgh for the Duke of Edinburgh Award, the Crown has turned to another Royal, known for his passion for teenage passions. Prince Andrew will be the new face youth pursuits and pursing youths.

Sharing a tent with Prince Andrew is full of memorable 'life-changing experiences'. One red-faced teenager recounted their activity: 'We spent the weekend in the Lake District being chased by a shadowy, rotund figure – he never broke his stride or broke into a sweat'.

The traditional certification has now been replaced by a Non-Disclosure Agreement and a trip to Pizza Express. The Gold Award is now only given to those who can survive on an island for thirty days, with Bill Clinton.

Fun activities involve orienteering around rumours, climbing a mountain of incriminating photographs and not volunteering to talk to the FBI. One organiser said: 'It's about getting the kids to discover new interests and if those interests happen to be a middle-aged Prince, so much the better.'

Pandemic affects Tories' ability to understand simple concepts like sleaze

A spokesperson for the OBR said: 'It seems they have been isolated within their Westminster Bubble for so long that they not only cannot identify the act of wrongdoing, but that the word itself has vanished from their lexicon. We see the issues in other parties too, Labour MPs had difficulty defining the words 'effective' and 'opposition'; and the whole of Westminster was unable to adequately explain what a 'Liberal Democrat' was.'

Man shows how uninterested he is by writing a detailed argument about it

A man has written passionately about why people should not be interested in something.

The man claims that people are so uninterested in this thing he was on about that he has taken the time and effort to explain why they are/should not be interested in this thing.

To illustrate just how uninterested people are in this thing he has explained to you why you should not find it interesting. And why you should move on from this thing.

This thing is not important. It is so unimportant and lacking in interest that - despite it being the main feature on the front of every newspaper, is the main topic on every TV and radio show, it is nonetheless still unimportant.

This thing is so irrelevant that he has taken the time to tell you just how irrelevant this thing is and also comment on how stupid you are if you do happen to find this thing interesting.

The man has gone into great detail explaining why this thing is so unimportant...so please show some respect and stop thinking about it.

Shock as travel boss thinks travel ban should be lifted

In a shocking turn of events, one CEO of a package tour operator has suggested that the travel ban should be lifted sharpish as he is 'quite keen to make some money sometime soon'.

His entirely unbiased and balanced suggestion has come as a complete shock to the industry who were looking forward to another summer of staycation resulting in mass job losses and bankruptcies.

Man who shuns internet becomes YouTube hit

Barry Taylor, 64, has become a local celebrity thanks to his stoic refusal to read online tutorials on how to walk, breathe or hold a book. By discounting the opinions of tens of thousands of anonymous, probably Chinese, reviewers he relies on 'common sense' and looks it up in a book, not the internet,

This has prompted locals to follow him everywhere with a video camera and now reports daily on Barry's avoidance of the internet are a YouTube sensation. In the last week the videos have gone viral as Barry chooses to read a newspaper on the toilet, having worked out how the flush works himself, bought some artisan bread made by hand, not 3D printed, and buying porn (the last copy of Razzle, dated 1978) from a newsagent.

Barry is not bothered by the success of the viral videos, though. 'Haven't seen them. Might wait until they come out on Betamax,' he admitted in a rare nod to technology.

Online greeting card site launches exclusively for the UK - Moanpig.com

Feel like a good old-fashioned moan, but frustrated that you can't moan effectively? Not enough people around to moan about due to annoying lockdown measures? Then moan about it with a personalised moan about anything card from Moanpig.

This dynamic new internet-based moaning card site will meet ALL your moaning needs. Moanpig is specially designed to unleash the pent-up lockdown demand for moaning and covers all your favourite moaning subjects for some seriously intense moaning sessions:

- The football
- The COVID
- The Government

- The vaccines
- The politicians
- The papers
- The weather
- The wife
- Her mate Liz
- That woman who calls Primark 'Primani,' at number 56
- Him with the golf clubs at number 19
- Plus, Johnny bloody foreigner
- Not forgetting the French of course
- And migrant hotels
- That Priti Patel bloke
- Farage
- Brexit
- e-Scooters
- Other people
- Restaurant bills
- First world problems
- All forms of public transportation
- Sandra in Customer Services
- Morons who stare at their phones all day
- Queuing for anything
- Roadworks
- Everything on the telly
- Especially the leftie BBC
- F*cking Kale
- Lockdown moaners

All Moanpig deliveries are accompanied by the sound of tiny violins and don't forget, if your Moanpig card doesn't turn up, you can always moan to your mates about how crap Moanpig is.

£4 billion cut to foreign aid '100% justified' as Boris needs new downstairs toilet

Head of Healthcare and Hospitals in India told us: 'I was sceptical at first but now I cannot believe how closed minded I was. Yes, people are dying every few minutes here, yes, a little cash would have been useful to ensure our poorest children survived to adulthood - but my word, when I heard BoJo needed a new bog, I took it all back. The man needs the best. I don't care where that money comes from.'

Various public sector employees, including nurses, teachers and care workers, have now offered to take a 50% pay cut as there is some indication Boris may also want to 'do up' the east-wing lav too.

Charity appeal: Adopt a Tory MP for just £30k a month!

Just £30k a month can provide a Tory MP with a series of unnecessary house renovations on properties they don't actually own.

Many of these multi-millionaires are forced to live in squalid conditions, with some homes not even containing the basics like solid gold toilet seats, life size bronze statues of the inhabitants or champagne taps.

But that's not all.

A donation of just £30k a month is enough to change their sad and humdrum existence. And just think how good that will make you feel. Your generous gift will help to keep your Tory supplied with plenty of life's little luxuries; like Beluga Caviar and only the very finest single malts and Cuban cigars.

Donate today and you'll be sent regular updates detailing fabulous ticket-only exclusive social occasions they've attended recently. We'll even send you a cute cuddly toy** of your chosen Tory.

**Disclaimer: item will not actually be cute or cuddly.

In other news...

Man who finally has haircut celebrates with mullet-off cocktail

Grouse and other drivers 'feeling safer' after Prince Philip death

Kardashian and West agree joint custody of insane memes

Thousands of schoolchildren to get vaccine certificate based on coursework only

Woman couldn't get top off of morning after pill bottle due to child-proof cap

For sale: Number 10 media briefing room – one careless owner

Meghan unlikely to attend doe funeral as royals ask how black her dress will be

Sputnik vaccine can now be administered by door knob

Draught beer, fine dining and haircuts to be allowed ICUs during fourth wave

Tiger Woods crashed at 84mph - or 14 over par

First art-gallery vaccine to be trialled at Tate Moderna

Grasshopper criticising latest Attenborough series was just an armchair cricket

Saudi Princes, Russian billionaires and American tycoons to break away from EPL.

Chris Whitty seen approaching Whitehall wielding X- and Y- axes

Colin the caterpillar saga to be made into video game – 'Grand Theft Gateau'

Protocol dictates fortnight wait before '95-year-old widow' ad appears on Tinder

Nicholas Witchell beheaded: 'It's what the duke would have wanted', say aides

Bank of England move to Leeds, locals rename it as t'olt lass

BMW confirms self-driving cars won't be fitted with indicators

Royals to wear Nazi uniforms to funeral to avoid embarrassing Harry

Oxford-Cambridge sack race starts at prep school and ends at Goldman Sachs

Poet Laureate defends 'pimp my hearse, bitch' eulogy

Biden congratulated on 100 days of not being Trump

COVID reaches Everest...er...well done?

Ye Globe doth announceth that its first play on reopening shalt be Maskbeth

Cameron moves from the Big Society to the Self-Preservation Society

WHSmith reports shortage of brown envelopes after David Cameron visit

Pilot aiming for landing lights touches down halfway up staircase

Study finds B&Q wood preservative less effective than Viagra

Phone finally picked up at the tinnitus helpline

Couple who had sex in bulldozer say earth moved

French hen refuses to lay: 'It's my day œuf'

Illegally parked Zen master hears sound of one hand clamping

Trainee proctologist told he'll be starting at the bottom

Government troubled by crony virus

The charge of the footy brigade – superleague, superleague, superleague onward

Mourinho sacked before he can lose the new super league

Philip dead – Meghan to blame says Mail

Land mass the size of Wales spotted off the coast of Anglesey

Iceland rated 4th best place to live in the world. Asda fails to make top ten

Priti Patel hates living in the shadow of her beautiful sister, Prettier Patel

People missing out on Oxford vaccine to get Durham vaccine through clearing

May 2021

This month saw Boris Johnson spouting lie after lie, the Government exhibiting mammoth incompetence while awarding lucrative contracts for meaningless fluff to their friends and family. Much like May 2021. Oh, this was May 2021. Just like every other month since the Government won the election, then.

Matt Hancock 'still awful'

Multiple sources have confirmed that Health Secretary Matt Hancock is still just awful, with the energy of that guy on the stag-do no-one knows that well, but who takes the paint-balling a bit too seriously.

Marianne Morrison is a regular in the same pub as Hancock. 'He once claimed he was ex-TA, but when I asked him about it, his eyes rolled back and a robotic voice said 'Loading'. He said he left because he bust his knee rescuing a puppy from a burning building. I asked him which knee but he didn't know. Then he tried to look down my blouse, so I slapped him. He gave me a PPE contract to keep quiet, so fair play.'

'Isn't that the supply teacher who lost control and had a nervous breakdown?' queried local student Tara Taylor. 'He put on a video so no-one would see him cry, but I saw him,' she added before looking queasy. 'I couldn't sleep for weeks afterwards. I told him that people don't cry like that, and he gave me a PPE contract to keep quiet, so fair play.'

One PPE contractor remarked: 'He did give me this contract, but he's still awful'.

'People aren't interested in piracy but in my impressive shanties,' claims Blackbeard

Blackbeard the pirate has issued a statement claiming that the continual questions about his alleged piracy are not in the public interest.

'It's a sad diversion. Nothing more. People really want to hear about my contribution to the early eighteenth-century music scene. It's unfortunate that I happened to have the surname 'the Pirate' - that's just a coincidence.'

Voters happy with corruption, as long as MPs are honest about it

'If there is one thing UK voters can't stand it's a politician being dishonest about being corrupt,' explained one pollster. 'We know they treat tax-payers money like their own personal revenue fountain, but people are fine with that as long as you don't take them for idiots.

'People are happy with 'bodies piling high' as long as they don't block access to the beer garden or clutter up the beach huts. Once the BBQ is fired up the smell of onions will soon mask the smell of rotting corpses.

'Being dishonest about being dishonest is the worst thing a politician can do. Look at Jeremy Corbyn for instance, he was the lowest claimer of MP expenses in the whole country. All he ever claimed for was an £8.70 ink cartridge, a f*cking ink cartridge.

'Nobody is going to trust a man who only claims just £8.70 when he could have claimed £8700. People start asking questions about that sort of thing. They start to question his judgement.'

Are naked auditions unfairly labelled as 'creepy as f*ck'?

As further allegations of sexual misconduct are levelled at film directors, most of the public are questioning why 'naked' interviews are deemed more reliable than a well-referenced curriculum vitae. With many male producers seemingly under the impression that they are conducting a medical examination rather than an audition.

Explained one young actress: 'It was odd, I'd seen Ian McKellen and Jim Broadbent go in and out of the audition fully clothed, but when it was my turn, I was asked to undress – which is peculiar for a production of Pride & Prejudice.

'Anyway, the director explained to me that despite me having spent three years at Drama School, he still needed to see if my nipples could act. I could tell it was standard practise from the bum prints on the casting couch.'

Birmingham man sues for right to eat his family

Fred Beale, 48, won a landmark case in the High Court today that allows him to eat his 'useless family'. He believes 'home killing' has a lighter carbon footprint: 'Eating just one family member can save 800 meat delivery miles to supermarkets, not to mention a whole pile of non-biodegradable shrink wrap'.

Although he admits to being 'somewhat fond' of his wife Jeanne and son David, he feels they have more to contribute as units of nutrition. 'Let's face it, there's not much future for a woman who watches James Corden, and as for David, he's doing Media Studies at the University of Sussex - I mean, how useless is that? They're just walking pillars of protein going to waste'.

Statute of limitations runs out on Blue Peter Garden vandalism

It is a truism that everyone can remember exactly where they were and what they were doing when they first heard that the Blue Peter Garden had been vandalised. News of the crime swept the globe and vigilante groups stalked Britain looking for the culprits.

The one word that comes to everyone's mind, when thinking about that event, is 'senseless'. Because that is what it was, mostly, unless you happen to be irrationally terrified of television centre gardens, which very few of us were, back in 1983.

On this sad landmark of a day, the Percy Thrower estate has released the following statement: 'You may have escaped legal justice, but you haven't escaped Percy Thrower justice. We have a very particular set of skills, skills with garden implements that we have learned over a long time.

'Whoever you are, and whatever you are doing, we will hunt you down. We will find you. And when we do find you, we will kick over your urn, we will trample your radishes into pulp and we will pour oil into your fish pond.

One piece of good news - a ray of light born out of tragedy - is that the Blue Peter Garden has since been moved to a lead lined box and buried in a pit under a military installation near Shepherd's Bush. It is guarded 24 hours a day by laser-guided, nuclear-tipped, sticky-back missiles. Anyone even thinking about stealing a begonia today is likely to be obliterated in a carefully guided explosion.

Fury as 'ungrateful' India rejects recycled claps for NHS

The applause had been mothballed in a warehouse facility in Clapham South London for around 12 months, after people grew tired of being forced out of their homes at gunpoint and preferred to watch box sets of Gogglebox rather than banging saucepans and generally clapping people they cannot see.

A spokeswoman said: 'While we welcome claps for our brave health workers from the international community, a shitload of second-hand claps from Boris and Hancock is an insult to our intelligence. Also, Prime Minister Modi is uncomfortable with the fact that some those claps were for Muslims'.

Outraged nation punishes Tories with nine-point lead

The British public has sent a clear message that it will not tolerate any more of the allegations of Tory sleaze and insulting comments emanating from the unkept posh windbag in Number 10, according to the latest polls. Instead of being five or six points down on the opposition as would normally be the case, the Conservatives are currently nine points ahead and this is expected to be 12 by election day.

Pollster, Helen Daniels commented, 'Senior members of the party will no doubt be scratching their heads and wondering what they can do to recover the position. In my view, there is simply nothing that can be done at this late stage. They must face up to the fact that they are going to win handsomely.'

One voter said, 'Boris Johnson is an absolute disgrace. Awarding contracts to his pals. Ten grand on a sofa. Bodies piling up. Has the man any decency, I ask you? Obviously, I'll vote for him. That'll bring him down a peg or two. You'll see.'

Man who said 'boo' to a goose in critical condition in hospital

King's College Hospital in London has revealed that a 45-year-old man who was admitted late last night with over 50 pecking injuries and four broken limbs is in a critical condition and may not survive. The man, identified as Barry Haynes from Bromsgrove, was witnessed saying 'boo' to a Canada Goose during a walk by the Thames and was promptly administered a good kicking by a well tooled-up gang of three geese.

'You would think in this day and age, everyone would be aware that geese are as hard as absolute f*ck, with tempers to match,' said a hospital spokesman.

'Every month, we get another injured patient in after being slit up a treat by these feathered psychopaths. Most had only looked at them - saying 'boo' or anything else to them as well is foolish beyond belief.'

The Metropolitan Police has cancelled all leave and promised to organise an armed patrol to raid the riverbanks in the Teddington region, where they attack took place. However, Scotland Yard sources have indicated that they may struggle to raise enough volunteers brave enough to tackle the uber-violent gaggle known as the 'Hampton Wick Massive'.

Leading etymologist Dr James Randolph pointed out that the term 'He wouldn't say to a boo to a goose' has been misconstrued as indicating timidity, when it originally meant that the person in question had the basic common sense necessary for survival.

'The term originated in 17th century Gloucestershire and life was hard enough there already with bubonic plague, cholera and civil war, without people then putting their lives in danger by needlessly provoking short-tempered waterfowl from the Anatidae,' he said.

'Mad Steve' King, a Greylag goose, added; 'What are you looking at? Do you want some? Well DO YA? NO? F*CK OFF THEN.'

Melinda Gates to get Belgium in divorce settlement

Multi-billionaire couple, Bill and Melinda Gates, are set to split, with a much-anticipated custody battle over who gets the GDP equivalent of Western Europe. So wealthy are the couple that they can afford to divide their assets and still have enough left over to buy the Moon, then have it hollowed out and filled with cream cheese. Lawyers anticipate the main conflict being over who does not get ownership of Windows Altavista

Recently the Gates have been involved with global disease prevention, meaning Melinda gets to keep the cure for COVID and Bill gets to keep his secret cure for baldness. She will also get half of everyone's data, your sort code, your Pornhub search history and any password involving the name of a beloved pet. Meanwhile, Bill retains custody of Clippy the Paperclip. He will still be allowed to visit his billions but only on weekends.

Celebrity joint ventures

Even famous people have been struggling to scrape together an income over the last year or so. But some are more entrepreneurial than others. Unlikely partnerships have formed in celebrity land, and we're going to see some new businesses hit the high streets this year:

- Jeremy Irons and Derek Fowlds are starting a clothes-ironing service

- Roger Black and Jimmy White are opening up a vintage TV repair business

- Pat Cash and Petr Cech are still struggling to get their banking licence

- Alex Song and Charles Dance don't want to make a big thing about their new performing arts academy

- Midge Ure, Alan Knott and Steve Wright have got their psychotherapy licence

- MC Hammer and Jimmy Nail are opening a hardware store (Jimmy Nail refused to work with Christopher Cross on a previous venture)

- Cressida Dick and Ed Balls have been seen hanging out together recently

- DJs Mike Read and Steve Wright have announced they are starting a new educational radio show dedicated to improving literacy.

- Elton John, Billy Paul and Boy George looking for a decent drummer for their new band

- Pat Cash and Carrie Symonds are going to set up a wholesale distribution operation

- Jack Straw and Gareth Bale are setting up an agricultural subsidiary.

- Bonnie Tyler and Carole Thatcher have launched their roofing company

- Actor Tim Curry and lyricist Tim Rice are starting a takeaway

- Former POTUS George W. Bush and country singer Tanya Tucker are opening a chain of restaurants in Australia

- Clement Freud and Tim Rice are opening a chain of Chinese takeaways

- Brad Pitt, Chris Rock and Nicholas Cage are setting up an economic chimp capture firm

- Football managers Daniel Farke and Bertie Mee are to run their own brothel

- Alastair Cook and Charlie Booker are trading successfully as accountants

However, due to their previous commitments, MC Hammer, Midge Ure and Ed Balls have no plans to work together.

France cuts Jersey's electricity over fishing dispute. Isle of Wight to provide 'torch'

'We're hoping the French will back down,' said Bergerac Urea, Jersey Minister for Electricity. 'However, should they follow through on their actions and plunge the island back into the dark ages, it's good to know we have support from the UK and a place that's still living in it.'

In Newport, the Isle of Wight Council voiced their support for the Channel Island residents. 'Wightlink ferries remain on standby to head to St Helier at a moment's notice,' it said. 'Well, a week, tops'. A message of support will be sent to the States Assembly either via carrier pigeon, or e-mail if one of the councillors' grandchildren can visit and remind them how to use the internet.

SNP plans carefully phased increase of independence from absolutely everything

The timetable is as follows:

- May 10th: Chairs - Scots will be allowed to entirely ignore the impact of chairs, post offices and windmills on their lives. In addition, they can declare themselves independent of all park benches and up to six chairs indoors

- May 17th: Liechtenstein - Everyone in Scotland can declare themselves officially independent from Lichtenstein. On the 21st this will be extended to include 'some places around or near Lichtenstein'

- May 23rd: Cabers. 'Soon we can toss our cabers for good!' wrote the Aberdeen & Argyll Gazette in a hastily produced and widely condemned issue. Most Scots welcome this development as very few ever wanted anything to do with cabers in the first place

- June 1st: Deep frying weird things - In June, the Scots can at last relax and no longer feel compelled to deep fry everything they see. Under the new rules, deep frying will still be allowed for things such as chips and Mars bars, but not fish

- June 7th: Newcastle and the big blank Bit below it - By June 7th, the SNP believe that Scotland will finally be ready to declare full independence from Newcastle and all the rest of the big white blank part of the map below Newcastle, including the part with the giant-fanged mermaids drawn on it

- June 14th: Absolutely everything other than Scotland - On this milestone day, Scotland can finally declare itself to be totally independent of absolutely everything other than Scotland, a list that includes space hoppers, bungee jumping and Danny Boyle. Many Scots especially look forward to this day and are planning to book long-haul trips to Scotland to celebrate

- June 21st: Scotland - Finally, by the end of June, Scotland will formally declare itself to be entirely independent of itself, fulfilling a life-long dream of many Scots to no longer live under the tyranny of what they see as their own rules

Other UK regions are examining the Scottish plan. At press conferences yesterday, the Welsh Assembly released a carefully worded shrug, while both sides in Northern Ireland were waiting to see what the other did before supporting the opposite and England waved a flag about for a bit.

Hartlepool turkeys strongly pro-Christmas

'Let's face it, this is a town that hanged a monkey for being a French spy and later elected one as mayor. Not the same monkey, that would be ridiculous,' explained one local. 'What do you take us for - self-harming idiots?'

Lambs!

Lambs! Laaaaaaaaaaaaammmbs!, it has emerged.

The discovery was made as the Forrester family from Coulsdon were stuck in traffic coming back from a disastrously wet Bank Holiday Monday on Bournemouth beach, as Barry Forrester, 38, tried to distract his eight- and six-year-old sons from their iPads and punching each other.

'It's lovely to see the new-born lambs in the fields this time of year,' said Barry. 'Look, boys - that one nuzzling his mum, he looks like he's only a few days old. Aaaahhhh - Ryan, will you get off that bloody console for a second and look?'

Added Sheila Forrester: 'It shows the Earth is coming back to life after winter and it's also a symbol of Jesus, which is why we celebrate Easter with roast lamb and ... I hate myself and I want to die.'

'Gotcha!' Our boys sink French plastic bag floating away from Jersey

HMS Tamar has successfully engaged and sunk a plastic bag that was floating away from Jersey. The bag was travelling under the French insignia of 'Carrefour' and was determined to be a potential threat even as it drifted towards Gouville-Sur-Mer on the French mainland.

Assisted by HMS Severn, the Tamar fired 14 torpedoes, seven ship-to-sea missiles and a number of rocks at the bag, which was confirmed 'utterly destroyed' at 06:15 this morning.

'We did it,' said Boris Johnson's spokesman, in a jubilant press conference. 'The moaners and whiners have been silenced. Yes, we were right to dispatch a task force almost 100 miles south to Jersey. Yes, we were right to defend the brave tax-haveners on that milky rock. We've seen off the French menace and so to all of you tonight, I say, rejoice! Rejoice, rejoice, rejoice, rejoice [edited for space].'

The Navy has said that no British were hurt in the incident, though it did add that all the fish within a 50-mile radius were obliterated, thereby neatly 'solving the problem'.

Starmer blames Scooby Doo team

Following a night of election embarrassment for Labour, Sir Keir Starmer was quick to shift the blame to inclement weather, the fall of the Hapsburgs, Bach's Piano Concerto in D-Minor and those pesky meddling kids, but for whom he would have gotten away with it. His lacklustre campaign has been beset by rumours that he lacks a pulse, coupled with the awkward moment when he was nominated for Tory MP of the year.

Party officials explained: 'Of course its Jeremy Corbyn's fault, what with him not being a Labour MP. He got Hamas to secretly send him backwards in time, to when he won Hartlepool, twice, and changed Starmer's name by deed poll to Keith'. Calling the membership 'racist Trots' has not been the rallying cry Sir Keir had hoped. Likewise, voters have been uninspired by his slogan, 'Labour isn't working - for Labour'.

British and French shepherds clash over disputed pastures

The dispute centres round quotas determining the number of sheep allowed to be trawled by a single dog, and paddock size, which farmers, on both sides, have complained causes perfectly good sheep to be thrown back into the field. The protest culminated in a 15-hour standoff in a Surrey field, in which two sheepdogs stared intently at each other.

All fields have been declared 'international pastures', nevertheless the British also claim to be victims of sabotage, saying their crooks have been deliberately shortened, while the French have accused the Brits of confusing their dogs by teaching them new contradictory whistles. Both accuse the other of not throwing back errant llamas.
Confirmed: The street behind a house is definitely called an 'alley'

The Internet Standards Committee has finally passed judgement on an assortment of regional variations in language, updated the following: 'It's a bread roll; it's a splinter; the evening meal is called dinner; ketchup should be kept in the cupboard; and the game's called tag'.

'We at the ISC are delighted to finally settle these differences once and for all,' said a spokesperson. 'Thousands of questionnaires on social media have conclusively proved these to be the de-facto words for things and these should be adopted by all Britons unilaterally and immediately, with no further questions of this type shared on Facebook or Twitter again. Now, if we're done, I'm off home as I'm dying to kick off my plimsolls, sit on the settee and have a chip butty.'

Man who disappeared from barbecue 'missing, presumed warm'

'The last words he said to me were, 'I am going inside; I may be some time',' said a friend. 'I assumed this was because of all the undercooked meat he'd eaten and after a good turnout he'd be back, but that was the last I, or anyone, saw of him'. It is feared, that upon entering the house to use the toilet, he suffered exposure to a little warmth, became overwhelmed, and found himself unable to go outside again.

The detective leading the search said, 'We've seen a marked increase in the sudden disappearance of people from private and pub gardens. As yet, we've found no connection with these events and the fact that May has had the lowest temperatures in the UK since 1922'.

Methane crisis: Farting to be rationed

A UN report has recommended a drastic reduction in the emissions of methane gas to tackle climate change in the short-term. As such, all men over the age of 20 are to be rationed to four bouts of bottom burping every day, in order to reduce the UK's contribution.

'When we analysed the data,' said report author Dr Herbert Borborygmus, 'we found that British men contribute a noteworthy amount to atmospheric methane. This has worsened in the pandemic, mostly due to attempts to alleviate boredom by asking partners to 'pull my finger' or failed attempts to set light to any air biscuits. Women, as we confirmed, are not causing any addition to methane levels, as our self-questionnaire concluded they never pass buttock bugles.'

In-line with the UN's recommendation, any bouts of flatus above the rationed four will have to be captured in an approved container and transported to a special storage facility. These containers will be distributed to all UK addresses as soon as member of the Government can identify family members who can profit from their manufacture.

Parties vow to be more 'doorsteppy'

Politicians expressing disappointment at the discrepancy between what voters told them 'on the doorstep' and how they voted at the polls. Physicists have called this phenomena Schrödinger's Doorstep - the unique ability for persons, while standing on a doorstep, to express opinions entirely contradictory to those later expressed in a polling booth. One commented: 'It's hard to believe, but it's almost as if the general public will tell a politician anything, to get them to f*ck off'.

Keir Starmer seen punching himself in the face repeatedly
Starmer's neighbour, said, 'I was watering my geraniums when I
saw Keth (sic) through his kitchen window. I waved and he
appeared to start waving back but then he punched himself in
the face instead. Quite a few times, actually.

'I stopped waving and he started to come out to the garden, but
then he just repeatedly shut his fingers in the patio door. Before
I could ask him if he was alright, he stepped on a garden rake
that smacked him in the face.

'I thought I heard him sob-singing 'All by myself'. Then he
started prodding a wasp nest with a cricket bat. At that point I
couldn't watch anymore'.

A colleague said: 'Obviously he needs to stop punching himself,
although it's the first popular policy he's had.'

Terror and dread as Government confirm 'Hugs are back'

There has been an outpouring of fear since it has been
confirmed that guidance would be relaxed to allow hugging.

Like most people, Mike has been delighted with the lack of
forced, awkward, cringeworthy hugs and kisses over the past
year: 'It's undoubtedly been the best thing about this pandemic.
My life used to be ridded with hug-related anxiety and stress - is
it a hug, a hug and kiss, kiss on both cheeks, a handshake?

'Now we just do a quick wave and get on with our lives and I
wonder why on earth we haven't always done it like that. The
thought of going back to the hellish existence of having to
potentially hug people or have any physical contact whatsoever
makes me feel sick.'

Mike is not alone. Studies show that 99% of people have been
caught in an awkward misunderstanding over greeting etiquette

and feel that they will 'never get over the shame' of going in for a hug when the other person was going for a handshake, or vice versa.

Anna has struggled with this condition, known as hug-related-trauma for many years. 'I remember it like it was yesterday. I arrived at a big meeting and went to shake hands with our client. But at the last minute, he went in for a hug-kiss combo and...my hand was in the wrong place you see...my life just fell apart. People would say I will look back and laugh, but I had to immediately quit my job due to the shame, then I lost my house and then I got into drugs quite badly, so I'm still struggling to see the funny side to be honest.'

Both Mike and Anna want to petition the Government to make hugging illegal on an ongoing basis, punishable with a long prison sentence.

Labour Reshuffle: Angela Lansbury to join Shadow Cabinet

In a surprise move, beyond actually making a decision, Labour Leader and man at C&A, Keir Starmer has announced that perennial actor Angela Lansbury has been appointed as Shadow to the Duchy of Lancaster.

'It's a great coup for Labour,' said party spokesperson. 'Dame Angela has, for years, solved murders as Jessica Fletcher in Murder She Wrote. Only someone with her sleuthing abilities could clear up the absolute carnage we're unpicking after the local elections'.

When asked why a 95-year-old actress had been given the role, she replied, 'Well, it's, it's, honestly it's a cock-up. Keir had forgotten Angela Rayner was in the party and when his team suggested 'Angela for Duchy of Lancaster' Keir started talking about Bedknobs and Broomsticks and whether we could animate suits of armour to get them to vote Labour next time. We just decided to run with it.'

Woman asks: 'Should I pay an overdue e-bill for an iPhone I don't have?'

Darcy Faroo, 29, has asked if she should trust an invoice addressed to a 'Dear Mr Dorothy Faboo'. Darcy would not normally question the veracity of such an email, given that the message has the word 'official' in three different fonts and the senders address is 'aPplE4467scam666@gmail.com' which sounds totally legitimate.
Darcy said: 'The email itself seemed particularly urgent, as the word 'urgent' was in bold and the sender had helpfully spelt iPhone with two 'n's'. It explained that the credit card, which I've never had, was about to expire and that I should send my bank details, in order to claim a mystery prize'.

One IT expert said: 'Our advice is always to send cash or organs if necessary. Should you run into any financial problems our team of kindly Nigerian princes can instantly wire transfer you 36 million dollars.'

Man desperate to go back to the office, devastated to find his job is still shit

Sheffield resident 'Mark' has been desperate to return to the office since the beginning of lockdown. He told our reporter he misses the banter, the face-to-face, the popping out for a sandwich, and the general office atmosphere.

Mark's job as a call centre administrator is now possible to do entirely offline and he was concerned that they would never be asked to go back in. However, this week they were invited back on a trial basis.

'That was when I realised my job is awful' he said. 'It all came back to me. I was really unhappy with the work before lockdown and thinking about leaving. But when we were all sent home, and everyone started moaning I forgot all that. I just wanted to get back in.'

Mark Taylor, who asked us not to reveal his surname, but we did anyway, is now contemplating looking for another job. He does not think he will be going into the office again soon. 'I'm looking for a different company to go to. Or not go to.' he said.

Google now referring to itself in the fourth person

In a move to raise the uber-organisation to a level even further above everyone and everything else, Google is now exclusively referring to itself in the fourth person. The fourth person is partly a combination of 1s and 0s, a vast array of self-improving algorithms, some wanky breakout rooms, and a whole heap of tax avoidance all rolled into 'one'.

All the flashy lights and jauntily coloured office spaces hide the fact that there is no purpose, or strategy, or general concept, or ultimate goal. Although this may seem like a terrible idea, it has two main advantages.

One, all competitors, strategic thinkers, dark entities, and dedicated anarchists will never be able to anticipate the next move Google will make, or ever work out how to beat it or take it down.

And two, Google AdSense.

Any Google employees you may meet from time to time are merely paid advocates for the most powerful entity on the planet. However, mind-meltingly impressive sounding their job title might appear, Googlists have no other purpose than to throw everyone off the scent that their employer does not require any human input to function. The general public are urged to be delicate, as Google employees do not yet realise this themselves.

Mars on the UK's green travel list

An upbeat Government spokesman confirmed the details: 'We picked Mars because it's fiendishly tricky to get to and has some of the most challenging social distancing measures in the world'. The planet, despite its high C-Number (the crater rate), has been upgraded to the green list and joins the Falkland Islands and Kabul, as an unappealing destination, that is almost impossible to reach.

'Always remember that the Government is following the science, even when it isn't.'

PM to allow his patented 'special hug'

The Prime Minister has signalled a return to normal extramarital relations, allowing an easing of lockdown, instructing parents to no longer 'lock up their daughters'. He would be personally hugging every voter, particularly those with breasts.

His spokeswoman explained to younger viewers: 'When a Prime Minister and a Lobbyist love each other, very much, they share a special hug. The PM lies on top of the woman, then lies to his wife and lies to the media'.

There would be a tentative return to unwelcome shoulder rubs, pinching of bottoms and the obligatory chasing around the garden. He was hoping to extend hugs to the over-60s but said his main priority was those under 21.

He explained that there would be no need for extra-protection, as he had the snip years ago – 'honest'. The spokeswoman reiterated that Boris would be offering hugs aplenty but no subsequent child support.

Satan demands inquiry into negative TripAdvisor reviews of Hell

'When I took over this place, the understanding was that nobody would escape to leave a negative review online', the Devil said. 'But then I log on to the accommodation sites and it's nothing but complaints about the heat and surly service'. He claims he is now the victim of hate mail and Facebook bullying.

Bill Betts from Manchester's review complains, 'Really not very upfront about minimum stay in contract. If I'd seen the 'for all eternity' clause in the small print I'd have plumped for Lanzarote'.

Meanwhile, Giles Darby from Hull complains about sound pollution from the constant wailing of the damned, and the appalling lack of wheelchair access to the Seventh Circle.

However, Ryanair has cashed in on the publicity and is now offering twice-weekly budget flights to Hell. 'Actually, it's not really to Hell', a company spokesman says. 'It's to Margate, but we can assure you there's an amazing shuttle service from the town centre right to the bowels of Hell, and anyway what do you expect for £19.99?'

Britain stands down to Thunderbird alert Level 3

The six Thunderbird alert levels are as follows:

- Five: Everyone has to go to space and stay there until the all clear is sounded. Puppets with brains (commonly named 'Brains' for this very reason) are allowed to work remotely, which is pretty much what they always did anyway

361

- Four: In addition to space, puppets are allowed to travel underwater, and wear yellow
- Three: High powered rockets are allowed. Everyone remains vigilant. Hairdressers can open. Aristocratic English puppets may be chauffeured within a ten-mile radius of their homes
- Two: Goods haulage re-opens. String selling can resume
- One: Puppets are allowed to plan to solve mysteries, fight evil and fly high-powered planes.
- Go: Are go

Cowell to launch Labour 'Bone Idol'

Simon Cowell is to launch a new reality show to find 'the next suit' to take the Labour Party to defeat at the next general election. Keir Starmer is said to be furious, as he was still stuck at boot-licking camp.

Government lifts all restrictions on shagging with complete strangers

A minister announced: 'The great British public, have been true heroes through this beastly lockdown - in staging anti-lockdown marches, arranging illegal raves and stealing policeman's helmets at every available opportunity. You can now get back to it, and you know what I'm talking about by 'it', don't you?

'The sooner the unwashed tribes are back banging each other's brains out, the better. If nothing else, it stops the revolting blighters thinking about how shambolic the Government have been since the beginning of the pandemic.'

Carrie Symonds planning to totally shag up the outside of Number 10 as well

Having tastelessly ruined the interior, Carrie Symonds is now planning to cover the exterior in diagonal bricks, painted orange and pink. The black door will be covered in green dots and the iconic 'No.10' will be replaced with either 'Shangri-Liar' or 'Tax exempt' stencilled in gold.

The door-knocker will be a giant brass cock and balls, a cheeky nod to the Boris' silky political skills. All light bulbs at the property will be replaced with red ones, presenting to the street the glow of a tart's boudoir from every room. Presumably enabling Boris to feel more at home. Two purple plastic peacocks will be placed either side of the entrance and on top of the property will be a flag-shagging gargoyle, or Michael Gove as he is known.

Football season ticket holder accidentally joins queue for COVID jab

A Plymouth football fan was left feeling a sore and a 'bit of a prick' On reaching the front of the queue, Mr Wes Hewlett had been asked if he was feeling alright and whether he was aware of the possible side effects. 'I told them I was okay, that I knew about it causing me a massive headache and that I'd be told by my Exeter mates that I had no sense of taste, and they just nodded.

'They then warned me about the possibility of short-term sickness and feeling generally down. They advised me to take paracetamol to take away the pain, and I knew then that something was wrong,' he said. 'Us Argyle fans need something much stronger than that.'

Rayner told to shadow Gove but eerily Gove casts no shadow

Following her sacking/promotion/sacking, Angela Rayner has the new task of shadowing the Chancellor of the Duchy of Lancaster – which sounds like the task of 15th century detective. In fact, her role will be to keep a close eye on Michael Gove, which should really be the job of his AA sponsor.

Frustratingly it is impossible to 'shadow' someone who no longer casts a shadow, has no pulse and refuses to go out during daylight. Famously Michael Gove may not cross the threshold of No10, unless he is invited by Rupert Murdoch.

He can easily smell blood when another MP is wounded and he is stimulated by any red liquid, particularly a full-bodied rioja. A stake through the heart will not work, but he can be lured with a steak tartare and a cheeky Louis XIII cognac, but hold the garlic.

Donald Trump's penis to run for office

The diminutive, toadstool-shaped but charismatic member who rose to prominence - or, rather, did not - in the Stormy Daniels affair has now declared his political ambitions and thrown his somewhat sticky hat into the ring.

The campaign will run under the twin banners of 'putting the dick back into predicament' and 'vote for the liberty bell-end'. Great emphasis is being placed on personal interaction and the need to 'press the palm' with the party faithful whilst on the nomination trail, no matter how much they resist.

It is understood that Donald Trump's hair will be asked to perform merkin duties for these public appearances. 'Wee Donny' then ended the announcement by quipping about the need to get a 'fun guy' back in the White House.

Senior Republicans are somewhat non-committal about this announcement, but privately admit that being led by an actual knob does seem to be the next logical step for the party.

All medical diagnosis to be made by Facebook Groups

'We decided on this route after using Facebook to identify some flowers I'd picked on a lockdown walk,' said Jessica Kildare, practising GP and head of the Government's strategy on consultancy.

'Within minutes I had a raft of answers, and more than half were right after I checked with a botanist friend. When I tried it with more plants, the majority told me not to eat a Death Cap mushroom, and that was the clincher, so we pushed ahead with the idea.'
The first group, 'What's this rash?' went live last week and has reduced unnecessary GP visits in the trial area by 90%, though there was an increase of 5% in trips to A&E and a drop in Coronavirus vaccine uptake of 75% after what the Government called coordinated action within the group.

Undaunted, the rollout is set to continue throughout the month, with accompanying videos for items such as CPR and the Heimlich Manoeuvre; along with the option to view them without pre-adverts in return for a contribution towards the Downing Street refurbishment.

Israel asks UK: 'Colonialism. Does it end well?'

After another night/year/decade of violence unfolds in the occupied territories, many Israeli citizens are concerned that their Victorian Empire cosplay may have gone too far. Instead of peace and harmony, they seem to be experiencing 'mild turbulence' and the sort condemnation normally reserved for a new season of Mrs Brown's Boys.

Admitted one UK diplomat: 'Obviously we had little bother in India, Africa and Asia. Oh, and don't mention Ireland. But other than that, it's all been rather relaxing. We'd heartily recommend capturing an indigenous people and stealing their land. It's the civilised thing to do'.

The UK and US have been full of helpful advice, like ignoring human rights, using chemical weapons and firing on unarmed citizens. One US general explained: 'You'll never achieve peace through negotiation. You don't think Afghanistan, Syria and Iraq would be so stable, if we hadn't intervened with tough love and bombs.'

This does leave Israel with the unappetising prospect of following in the footsteps of Great Britain, towards ignominy, ridicule and the inexorable rise of James Corden. Asked if there was anything to learn from history, one young Israeli said: 'My great grandparents spoke eloquently about the horrors of centuries of ethnic violence, the rape and pillage of our people, but it can't have been all bad? Right?'

Google Drunk to be added to Google Street View

To meet the needs of drinkers frustrated by the lockdown, Google has added an alternative street view where your surroundings heave and sway to mimic the experience of weaving your way home from the pub after a refreshing 12 pints.

From the comfort of your own sofa, you can experience the liberating vertigo of the homeward bound drinker as he cheerfully bounces off lamp posts and tries to hail taxis that flee in fear of vomit-soaked upholstery.

Then there is the Google Beer Goggles feature, which ensures that all females encountered on the journey are worth a wolf whistle and a couple of slurred chat up lines.

Finally, the concluding quarter mile of your journey features the adrenaline-pumping Google Dash. This is when that dodgy kebab you ate suddenly liquefies in your bowels, and the urban landscape zips past you in a blur as you race home to avert a trouser catastrophe of apocalyptic proportions.

Jack the Giant Killer will no longer accept Magic Beans in return for cows

The value of magic beans and old rusty lamps fell by more than 10% after the tweet, and shares in Beanpole companies also dipped. Investors have taken the news badly, as they believe this move could kill the Goose that lays the golden egg.

Jack explained: 'Times are tough. The Seven Dwarves have been caught up in a blood diamond scandal. And my sleeping partner, Beauty, has said she has been robbed by a Charming conman, while she slept. Anyway, massive beanstalks are just not a growth area'.

Parents unanimously agree to tell kids parties are banned forever

Parents have said they would do 'absolutely anything' to not have to spend their Saturday afternoons in a sweaty village hall with scenes reminiscent of Lord of the Flies or in a Bodily-Fluid-Bingo soft play.

Aimee is a mum of two and has PTSD from the last kids party before lockdown: 'I can't go back, I won't, you can't make me' she sobs. 'I still get flashbacks...I felt like I was in the trenches of World War One...the constant barrage of noise, the exhaustion, the crawling on all fours through a bastard ball pit, the over whelming stench of disgusting bodily functions.'

Aimee's son Ben has big plans for his seventh birthday next month: 'I've already invited the whole school so it'll be as mental AND expensive as possible. We aim to break mum early on, I'd say pre-cake, through a flawless combo of screaming, wetting ourselves and getting injured.

'The grand finale is usually someone getting 'stuck' at the top of the soft play. Watching those idiot parents lose every ounce of dignity crawling through a kids' soft play before half drowning in the ball pit is BRILLIANT value. It's the best present Mum could give me.'

Excitement builds as new Portugal COVID variant set for release

A spokeswoman said: 'This Government has always taken diversity and inclusivity very seriously, not so much when it comes to people, but when it comes to COVID variants. We are proud to welcome in any number of mutations - Brazil, South Africa, India - not to mention our very own home-grown Kent variant. A Portugal variant by the end of summer would be the cherry on the cake or the cough in the lung.'

Asked if the PM would be jetting off for a week of sun in Portugal: 'Good Lord no. He's not some sort of nincompoop. He'll be nipping off for a simple, basic five-star trip to Barbados to see if he can root out any other variants we may have missed. Paid for by some buddy or other, or maybe the taxpayer, who cares. Happy holidays!'

We are responding calmly to head loss claims chicken

Mistress Clucky, a hen formally living in a hen coop, but now to be found running round the barn yard, has claimed that her response to the entirely predictable head loss she suffered this morning is calm and measured.

'I noticed Mr Jenkins the farmer staring hungrily at me a few nights ago and monitored the situation closely as Mrs Jenkins arrived back from the shops with a large box of Paxo, and Mr Jenkins spent a few minutes sharpening his axe.

'It was entirely appropriate that I placed my neck on that large block of wood which, you'll be surprised to hear, he uses to dispatch less important chickens. My future plans are well laid - rather like the table.'

One half of nation certain other half is hypnotised by spivs

Dave from Bristol said, 'My suspicions were first aroused a few years ago when I saw people cluelessly voting for Brexit. I'm sure they were wilfully misled by hordes of mind-benders with twizzly moustaches in purple capes.'

Joanna from Crewe sighed, 'They're definitely putting something in the water across the other side of the M6. If Boris personally shat on their cereal, they'd still coo about what a loveable rogue he was and carry on wolfing down their Coco-Poops.'

Derren Brown was unavailable for comment.

Luton Airport brawl now twice nightly

A spokesperson for the airport clarified: 'Any and all future fights will take place in a steel cage. We've also restocked the luggage shop with special breakaway suitcases that'll really look dramatic when someone takes a swing with one.'

The next scheduled big event, 'Summer-sun Slam' will coincide with the easing of COVID restrictions and 50p off the beer in the airport lounge. 'We've a load of actors on standby to cajole people into rioting if it's just too quiet for its own good. Failing that, we'll just announce the flights are delayed, again.'

'Whole of Argentina' joins list of standard units of measurement

'Your average person in the street has no idea how much energy is required to complete common cryptocurrency block chains', said tabloid journalist Mike McBride. 'But get them to think about annual gigawatt production in Buenos Aires and they can immediately intuitively grasp its size'.

'However, if people are still struggling, just think of this', continued McBride. 'Put all your Bitcoin transactions in a big long line, and it would reach the moon and back, with enough to spare to fill 3 Wembley Stadiums, and 13 London Double Decker buses. It's almost the size of Wales'.

Starmer told to squeeze some thighs if he wants to boost his popularity

A spokeswoman said: 'We've considered all the options to make Keith (sic) a bit more entertaining and more suited to a contemporary UK audience, including lion taming, an attractive young woman in a bikini to accompany him everywhere he goes, and a cavalcade of psychic healers on elephants to take him to PMQ's.'

'Then we looked at Boris. What worked for him? It was obvious. Have a tangled personal life with feckless financial arrangements, tell the most outrageous porkies and ratchet everything up with a dose of thigh squeezing. Our biggest fear, now, is that Keith will just sit there squeezing his own'. Government issue daily reminder to public: If it goes wrong, it's your fault

Wendy has been a Tory voter for years and finds great comfort in knowing exactly where they stand on this matter: 'It's a bit like being in a psychologically abusive relationship, no matter what I do - how closely I follow the guidance or obey the rules - I

370

know when it goes belly up it will undoubtedly be all my fault. But I really enjoy the consistency of their blame, it gives us public a real sense of unity so I will without doubt continue to support Boris and the gang.'

Some have suggested that the Government are giving slightly 'mixed messages' but a government spokesperson has confirmed this is in keeping with their core strategy on clarity which is very clear - to never be completely clear on anything.

'You can't say that' say Americans defending First Amendment

'Don't you dare say the First Amendment is bonkers because there are loop-holes, allowing people to stop you saying it's bonkers', said a right-minded American.

'I've a right mind to shoot you thanks to my Second Amendment right to bear arms to defend the right of free speech. And how dare you say we don't get irony!'

First ten plane loads to land in Portugal all filled with journalists

Explained one reporter: 'There's absolutely no chance of you getting to Madeira during the next 14 weeks. Every seat has been booked up to send reporters like me out here to tell everyone back in Britain that Portugal is on the green list of destinations. Woohoo! look at that sunshine!

'But you lot back home can't actually get here because we've taken up all the places. After us TV broadcasters are the newspaper travel journalists. Then the video selfie social media influencers.

And finally, the digital nomads. By the end of the summer hols, the odd genuine tourist might have a shot, but I wouldn't count on it.'

To even things up, MoD to export rocks to Palestine

The UK & US having sold billions of pounds worth of military equipment to Israel, have decided the equitable thing to do is to send Gaza a super soaker, a latex sword and nerf gun. Said a diplomat: 'We've also sent over a sling; I hear it worked for David.

'It is a relatively even conflict. One side has elite troops, the other has rocks. One side has chemical weapons the other side has rocks. One side has nukes but some of those rocks are really big.'

One Palestinian explained: 'I've got this conker and it's a 49er. I'm fairly sure I can crack a tank with it. They've got an Iron Dome but I've got this tin foil hat'.

By contrast an Israeli pondered: 'The UK arms dealer said we were definitely on the road to peace and to becoming their best repeat customer. They've been good friends to us during the tough times, although now I mention it, those tough times only started when they became our friends. Hmm.'

UK 'overwhelming favourites' to win Eurovision, thanks to military intervention

A Government spokesman said: 'Boris really wants a war though and that Jersey fishing thing petered out, so Eurovision it is. This could be Rotterdam or anywhere, Liverpool or Rome. Anywhere that Daily Telegraph readers would like it if we carpet bombed'

'We're naming Graham Norton Admiral of the Fleet. Should hostilities escalate, Eurovision's ability to return fire is hampered as their cannons fire confetti and it would take a lot of glitter bombs to sink a battleship'.

DiCaprio pledges $43m to Galapagos Islands to impress Greta Thunberg

In a statement, the Oscar winner's press secretary revealed his passion for the project: 'These islands are one of the most irreplaceable places on the planet. We have lost habitats and animals to man's continual actions. With this funding, the island's conservationists can really make a difference. Greta, you'll have to get yourself down here. My private yacht is waiting in Los Angeles, we can take a slow cruise down here and I'll show you something marvellous, ancient, and leathery; then we can see the tortoises.'

The spokeswoman confirmed: 'The important thing is we save the environment and that this part-time Pippi Longstocking impersonator has turned 18.'

Man on first date since lockdown hasn't a clue what to do

Said Ken: 'It's been a while since I've had a face-to-face with an actual woman, so I winged it. Starting with how my mum got me into software and moved on into how my mum built my first computer. I then described how my mum taught me rudimentary coding. And then my date just left.'

Kindly friends said her reaction could well be a result of the pandemic. Then again, there was every chance it was because Ken is a dismally sad computer nerd with a borderline Oedipus complex.

Scandal as teachers award higher grades to brighter students

A recent study has revealed that unconscious bias may have led to teachers giving marks for correct answers or awarding high attendance scores, to those students who turn up. One researcher from Goldsmiths' College confirmed: 'Out of a thousand secondary school teachers, 99% of staff refused to teach anyone over the age of fifty'.

These subtle biases could lead to grade inflation, with teachers irresponsibly awarding GCSEs to students who have passed exams. The researcher said: 'Grades should be awarded on arbitrary factors, like height, ability to whistle and colour of socks.'

Students that were more 'agreeable' had a 10% chance of better marks, as opposed to a pupil who just took a sh*t on the teacher's desk. One study in America showed that High School staff were 27% more likely to award an 'A' grade to a pupil, if that pupil had not shot their classmates.

One University admissions tutor explained how they resolved the problem: 'It's obvious that teachers favour kids that work hard, are diligent and volunteer in the community, but we try to ignore these factors and award a place based on whether they went to Eton'.

World leaders deny developing a 'deny everything App'

'Obviously, the app was originally developed with the best of intentions. However, we have evidence that proves almost daily misuse. The Chinese deny forcing the Uyghurs to make tat for Primark, Kim Jong denies that everyone has starved to death in North Korea, while Trump voters deny they are in denial.

'We also have reams of data suggesting the UK Government is using the app to deny it knows what it's doing. The most sinister aspect of all this is that we suspect the deny everything app is being exploited by the rich and powerful to deny there is a deny everything app in the first place.'

Fury and Joshua can just have a scrap in my car park, says pub landlord.

Landlord, Dave Archer said: 'Granted, the spectacle itself is like watching gibbons trying to mate angrily. But in terms of arrangements, very straightforward. All I need is a clear verbal contract confirming a desire to tussle.

"Shall we take this outside?' and 'F*ck, yeah,' or words to that effect will do. And, of course, with the pub opening, we've a ready-made crowd or replacement bare-knuckle boxers, if those two drop out'.

Travel advice based on Highway Code interpretation by make

The Government has denied there is any confusion over what its travel guidance means, insisting that it is based on the Highway Code. When pointed out that said advice is that 'when red - stop, when amber - stop, when green - stop unless safe to go' the Government spokeswoman said: 'Er - hang on, I'll just check with a few colleagues.'

In a clarifying statement she said: 'The specific advice you presented, which is in fact just a literal interpretation of the actual words, is the advice a Volvo driver would agree with. But an Audi driver might reasonably interpret it differently to mean 'if green - go, if amber - definitely go and give it a bit of welly, if red - well, depends on who else is around. If it's the police then slow down a bit, if it's another German car driver - go like hell.'

Kids just bloody awful, research suggests

A newly published paper from London's Imperial College has found that having children is not worth the bother. The findings back up parents deep-seated suspicions that their progeny are complete nightmares, and they would have been far better off investing in a new Ford Fiesta or booking Mykonos twice a year.

Professor Roddy Judd said that his team's five-year-long research programme had found numerous failings in children that ultimately led to the obvious conclusion that they are bloody awful.

'Any household containing young children will be a hellish cesspit of gaudy disfigured plastic, blaring television programmes designed by morons on psychedelic drugs and kitchen walls covered in the disastrous fallout from a nausea inducing Zucchini, Quinoa, Pears and Kale food pouch.'

'We also found evidence to show that as they grow older, children are prone to terrorise their parents with tricky questions. These usually occur at around 4.30 a.m. They will invariably be along the lines of, 'Where does electricity come from?' or 'Wow deep is the sea at the edge?' Answers will then be countered by a fusillade of why? why? why? This is only the beginning of a child's lifetime of sullen contempt for their parents.'

Other scientists have questioned Professor Judd's methodology and his focus on only using one trial subject. Dr Mark Kelly, a leading children's behavioural specialist, said it was highly unusual.

However, having met Myles, Professor Judd's son, who set fire to the tortoise and called him a stinky poo-head on their first meeting, he was forced to concur that kids are just bloody awful.

Something about Princess Diana

Blah, blah, blah of course you are still reading, blah blah blah just on the off chance we mention Diana again. We could even recycle something from ten years ago and you just would not care. We could even use extracts from a Dan Brown novel and you would still wade through all that sh*t for England's Rose.

This paragraph is clearing about the chemical composition of cheese, which is 31.23% Protein, Lipids 34.39%, Water 30.18%, Mineral ions 4.31% and 0.0000000001% Princess Diana. Ah, there she is! You see, it was worth reading through all that mind-numbing ephemera, just for the merest whiff of her perfume, which now smells of stilton.

A close friend, who she had never met, said: 'She's not dead, she can never die. Not while people hold her memory. Or while newspaper editors have lazy articles to shift and I get to appear on all the TV chat shows.' It does not even need to make sense, explained one journalist: 'Diana, Diana, Lobster'.

Woman that 'doesn't give a toss' about 'Friends' reunion sectioned

'It's so out of character' her sister told us. 'She loved Friends back in the 90s, then just out of the blue like this - twenty-five years later - she decides she doesn't care about the long anticipated all-star reunion? I'm sorry, I just don't buy it - she must be having some sort of mental breakdown or something. I mean, could she BE more crazy?'

This is the only known case of a person not being 'super excited' or 'totally psyched' for 'Friends: The Reunion'. The woman in question is undergoing intensive conversion therapy involving watching all 236 episodes back-to-back whilst feeling totally inadequate that she doesn't have such a brilliantly close-knit friendship group.

Palestinian on Grand Designs says he's rebuilding his house just using dialogue

As the first dialogue convoy arrived in the Gaza strip, Mr Mahmoud Azzam, whose house was completely re-designed during the recent conflict, announced his unconventional plan for its reconstruction.

'I'm hoping to use dialogue only on the project. It's a new, sustainable material and perfect for rebuilding my house from the ground up.'

Grand Designs presenter Kevin McCloud was full of praise: 'Mr Abbas's project is a unique self-build, or rather rebuild, following the recent trend for unwanted downsizing. Using dialogue is highly unusual, but it is a flexible alternative to locally available traditional building materials such as rubble. Hopefully, it should help it to blend in with its new surroundings. We're hoping he can increase his budget to include some platitudes and perhaps even go so far as investing in a skip load of reclaimed thoughts and prayers which should provide the perfect insulation from reality.'

'His plans are for a dream home which, in a first for Grand Designs, actually makes the structure resemble a house and reflects the family's passion for trying to stay alive.'

Woman asks: 'What's that small blue light I can see from my bed?'

Esme Van Der Veen (32) has spent a sleepless night trying to work out what that flashing blue light is – you know, the one you can see in the corner of your eye but goes off every time your turn to look. Rather than get out of bed to check, Esme opted for seven hours of failed sleep, interspersed with the occasional sigh of frustration and passive aggressive fart.

Currently her options are that it is either a stray mobile phone charger, an electrified Smurf or miniaturized police car. There are half a dozen gadgets on standby in her bedroom but she was sure that none of them were made from fluorescent coral.

Esme has already ruled out Tinkerbell, glowsticks and an underwater nuclear reactor, with its glowing Cherenkov radiation. The trouble is, it just keeps blinking intermittently –

what does that mean? Is it an emergency? Is it running out of power? Is it a phosphorescent nose booger?

Then it struck Esme, just as the sun started to rise: 'You know what it is? It's a reflection of something outside. From the neighbour's house. It's their bloody burglar alarm. They're on holiday and their house is being burgled. But you know what? Sod 'em.' And she went back to sleep.

Belarus hijackers condemned for aggressive tourist strategy

The Belarusian Government was forced to defend its policy of kidnapping journalists in mid-flight, trying to increase their number of holiday makers and dissidents. Although there are rumours that the activist Roman Protasevich is to blame, as he forgot to pay Ryanair's 'kidnapping surcharge'.

Their tourist board have been trying to lure Mr Protasevich for some time, with such marketing slogans as 'Come to Belarus or else', 'Visit Minsk Airport - you'll never leave' and 'Our prison cells are all inclusive'.

Said a Belarusian Minister: 'Capturing journalists is a two-sided affair. Yes, the TripAdvisor reviews are negative but they are always beautifully written'.

Most university plagiarism policies found to have been copied

The research confirmed that the source document from which most plagiarism policies emerge, was produced by the University of Padua in 1696. Traditionally miscreants who copied, were forced naked through the public square, although the University of Bolton still uses a similar practice during Fresher's Week.

Report author, Rebecca Jenkins said: 'We found over 90% of plagiarism policies, were in fact from a common document'.

However, a spokesperson from Universities UK denied it, saying: 'We found over 90% of plagiarism policies, were in fact from a common document'.

Boris & Carrie to marry next year unless, of course, he finds someone else

The Prime Minister and father of an unknown number of children, has announced that he and a handsome female acquaintance of his, Symonds the Younger, are ready to tie the knot.

A friend confided: 'He admits his private life has been somewhat akin to unravelling a massive vat of spaghetti, but he's convinced that Symonds is stonkingly good marriage material or a potential fanny magnet. She's more than happy staying at home, cleaning his rugger boots and running a keen eye over the inventory levels in the Downing Street tuck shop.

'And she's happy to move into No.11 when wife No.4 appears'.

Dylan arrested for 'harmonica crime'

Despite the celebrations for his eightieth birthday, Bob Dylan has been detained by the WHO (World Harmonica Organisation) for alleged crimes against the mouth organ. 'It's less a matter of Blowin' in the Wind as suckin' in the noise' said one WHO representative. 'We have every respect for Mr Dylan as Nobel Prize winner, denim demigod and unashamed proponent of the frizzy Barnet. But his mouth organism falls well below standards expected'.

Dylan himself has remained tight lipped after the accusations, but according to associates 'that's how he always played'.

Jack Russell humps less than Boris Johnson

Boris's owner, revealed, 'He'll literally take a crack at anything. Not just young cellists. We needed four security guards to prise him off the Archbishop of Canterbury's leg. And you should have seen what he did to the Queen's coronation robes. Thank the Lord she wasn't wearing them at the time.

'He only stops for a quick few laps of his water bowl, and he wolfs through his din-dins in about 4 seconds. Then he'll be straight on the kibble bag like a tramp on chips'.

Dominic Cummings gives evidence from glass house

It has been revealed that Dominic Cummings has given evidence against the PM to the select committees from a large glass-walled house erected in Barnard Castle.
Built during lockdown, the huge glass dwelling has 20 bedrooms, 33 bathrooms and 10 eye test centres. It is to be the venue for Mr Cummings' annual stone throwing championship which he has kicked off today.

Mr Cummings has pointed to Government incompetence and dishonesty during the pandemic. As the Prime Minister's Chief Advisor at the time, some have suggested perhaps he could have mentioned these concerns sooner - ideally before 130 thousand people died.

Cummings is reportedly suffering from a range of Long COVID symptoms after catching the virus last year. These include hypocrititus, pot-kettle-blackouts, hindsight-loss and twataphobia.

Arsenal sign Messi's shadow

It has always been claimed that the shadow has been carried by Messi for many years, with much criticism levelled at him for being a 'fair weather' player: however, fans of the shadow are keen to point out his sharp, well-defined performances under spotlights, when he almost seems to be moving in four directions at once.

Wes Tindale, editor of fanzine and specialist publication 'Fist Up for The Arse', said: 'This signing confirms our commitment to winning the league' until he was led away, giggling, by a kindly ambulance-man.

Second wave of Dominic Cummings tweets 'inevitable', sources confirm

The public have also been warned to be on their guard for deadly pun-heavy newspaper headlines which are now spreading like wildfire, with 'Domageddon', 'the Sword of Domocles' and 'nuclear Dom' variants already becoming 'dominant' in some tabloids.

'Reading any further tweets over the coming days will be accompanied by the onset of more severe symptoms', an expert warned. 'Watch out for loss of speech and spontaneous jaw drops at the rank incompetence of Johnson, the cabinet and Cummings himself'.

A Government spokesperson said 'We're aiming for herd immunity. In that you've heard so much from him that you just stop listening.'

Kim Jong Un chilling out, maxing, relaxing all cool

It has been a little while since North Korea made big headlines for big japes.

'We definitely aren't up to anything suspicious' said a spokesmaniac. 'No way. We don't have any COVID or any nukes pointed at Seoul.'

The spokesmaniac denied North Korea withdrew from World Cup qualifying because they lost a group match to Turkmenistan. 'We withdrew because of Qatar's use of slave labour to build stadiums. Just to be clear, we think they aren't using enough slave labour. And what about political prisoners, guys? Missed opportunity.'

Police fail to find nauseatingly grizzly remains at Fred West Café

Horrifyingly mutilated remains of a victim of mass murderer Fred West have not been found at a café in Gloucester after a week in which police excavated the premises for unexpected vileness. These remains are too shocking to describe here, despite not being there.

The ghastly remains - almost certainly the work of a deranged psychopath with a bizarre sexual lust for human disfigurement - were pronounced absent by police Superintendent Mike Smythe late last night. He told reporters: 'My officers were all psychologically prepared to discover long-rotted flesh, splintered bones, vestiges of human hair and horrifically stained clothing, hallmarks of a deranged psychopath with a perverted lust for brutal murdering of people. They did find some Lego windows and a fifty pence piece which is no longer legal tender, but these brought no solace.

He continued: 'Yes there is a sense of anti-climax, if not disappointment that no brutally attacked victim or victims with indescribably shocking injuries was or were found, but the café's egg chips and beans were partial recompense, and can we have a receipt please. And two teas.'

Chess not sexy again

The governing body of chess has announced, with great relief, that it has shrugged-off all traces of sexiness attained from association with The Queen's Gambit TV series.

'It's been hell!', commented world number 2, Martin Hampton, 'The pressure of competing at a high-level in chess is bad enough without the added stress of being regarded as a solid gold f**kmaster!'

The Queen's Gambit was a Netflix mini-series based around the life of a female chess prodigy and featured scenes of a sexual nature. By televisual osmosis It imbued previously sexually inert chess players with a degree of sultry sexual prowess never before seen in the long history of the strategy game.

Grandmaster Sergei Romanov explained, 'Quite frankly, it was affecting my game. Every time I gripped the bishop's head to make a move it would end up on the front cover of PlayChess magazine. I only had to punch the time clock a spectator would moan, 'Oh yeah!'.

'There would be crowds of young female groupies outside tournaments, tossing aside nerds like spotty pawns to take a piece of us. My 2020 advent calendar 'The 64 squares of Christmas' was pure filth. There are images of me in full armour on a horse holding my lance that I'm not proud of.
'But all that's gone now. I can walk down the street and not be dragged down a dark alley for a meaningless 'en passant'. I no

longer receive nude photos with messages, like: 'Castle me, hard!' and 'Come and breech my Sicilian defence'.

People who love Christmas attempting to convince everyone Junemas is a thing

Annoying cheerful woman Carol Bell has already invited guests for Junemas dinner on the 25th and bought Twiglets. She's been browsing eBay and Amazon for a Junemas advent calendar and wondering how far out of date chocolate can be while still tasting okay.

Carol's slightly curmudgeonly husband Dave Bell told us, 'Junemas is just not a thing, even if Carol has mentioned it on Twitter, but it does no harm and I might get a nice dinner out of it so I'm saying 'Yes Dear' to any mentions of it. It can't be as expensive and time consuming as the December version.'

Santa is said to be disappointed that frivolous individuals who love Christmas have spotted a chance to have another bite at the mince pie this June. However, it might be nice for the northern hemisphere to be the ones having barbecue at Xmas, for a change.

Isle of Wight closes airspace to Belarus

Mirroring EU diplomatic moves, a spokeswoman said: 'We've the Isle of Wight Navy on standby at Cowes and our anti-aircraft defence shield in operation at Shanklin. Well, when I say navy, I mean the sea scouts in their dinghies sailing round the harbour. And our defence shield is just big John standing on the beach with a bucket of rocks, but he can throw them really far! Like past the sandbank! It's impressive, honestly!'

In Minsk, news of the ban has not been taken lightly. 'We see this move by the Isle of Wight as unacceptable,' said a spokesperson for President Lukashenko. 'As such, we have imposed sanctions by banning the sale of Isle of Wight Garlic or gifts from the Needles Sand Shop. We shall not be blocked from our aircraft going...oh, it's only 22 miles across? That's ok, we'll just go around it.'

Hancock stands by decision to award contract to his hamster

Matt Hancock has rejected claims that awarding Fluffy the hamster an NHS contract was in any way bias as Fluffy is fully qualified with 'a wealth of experience'. Fluffy has been a valued member of the Hancock household for almost a year and in that time has left Mr Hancock in no doubt he is the right individual for the job: 'Fluffy is brilliant at keeping his trap shut, unlike other weaselly rodents like Dominic Cummings, so he'll be very well received amongst senior members of the conservative party.

'Fluffy is also an expert at his wheel, often going round in circles for months on end but making no progress - making him ideal for running an NHS contract.'

Mr Hancock further eradicated any hint of corruption by confirming that he wasn't even aware Fluffy was being considered for the contract: 'Fluffy orchestrated the whole thing without my knowledge, it was nothing to do with me - he must have used my phone and email, and posed as me at a meeting or two, the clever little chap. It's neither here nor there that my agreement with Fluffy is that I get 100% of profit from any contracts he wins.'

It has been reported that current contract tenders include submissions from the spider under Matt Hancock's sink, a snail at the bottom of Matt Hancock's garden and Matt Hancock's toilet brush.

Letting wine breathe is bollocks, confirms expert

The concept that leaving the cork out of a bottle of wine before imbibing is 'bollocks', according to a wine expert. Fred Engles, of no fixed abode, has been drinking wine for years, sometimes from a glass. 'Never left a bottle to breathe,' he said today, noting that wine does not have lungs, a mouth or any need for oxygen at all. 'It doesn't have a cardiovascular system, a bit like me,' he said. 'If I left a bottle to breathe, them bastards from the viaduct will have it away anyway,' he insisted.

'Now this is a cheeky little chardonnay, or perhaps paraffin extract - you can't really tell with Australian imports,' said Fred, swilling the bottle around. 'Best served with Brie. Or anything actually. Whatever is in the bin.'

Surgery backlog: Alternative Medicine practitioners keen to 'have a go.

An NHS spokeswoman explained: 'In the past year surgical waiting lists in this country, like the distressed colons of so many elderly patients, have become critically clogged to near bursting point. They are in need of urgent dis-impaction or we will really all be in deep shit. We want to hear from homoeopathists, astrologists, cub scouts; basically, anyone with a sharp enough knife who wants to have a go'.

Further benefits for patients are expected. For example, in Hampshire surgeries such as hip and knee replacements now come with a complementary e-book about the benefits of 5-day juice fasts. And while a preliminary analysis has shown a 100% mortality rate following surgeries carried out by the contractors, this is expected to fall when Venus and Neptune align later this month.

Five Go Dobbing in the Neighbours

In other news...

Government to allow 'hugging with caution', or as the British call it, hugging.

Man who dreamt he went camping and got drenched says it was a portent

Starmer orders a deckchair reshuffle

Countdown creator dies aged 4 x 25, divide 9 by 3, add the 1 and take it away

Man who hates Edinburgh's public transport system denies being tramsphobic

Failed drawing board designer goes back to ... er ... more soon

Amber Destinations tipped to win the Eurovision Song Contest

Convicted ballet dancer pliés for leniency in sentence

Marine biologists say not calling squid sentient is cephalish

Inventor of rotiserrie still turning in his grave

Football fans delighted to be back in the stadium to boo their team in person

Israel-Palestine conflict ends after Bono threatens to release a song

Pun jab offers no protection against Indian variant

Benefit offices seconded as vaccination centres to be known as jab centres

History forgets the wrong brothers for failing to make their first plane work

Johnson to recruit a minister for unicorns and sunlit uplands

Adam Ant wonders if online music shop will sell him a music stand, and deliver

G7 summit finally resolves to C Major summit

Older gamer now spends less time on Call of Duty and more on call of nature

Passenger who fell down aircraft steps suffers from airline fracture

Turkeys release live acoustic album: 'unplucked'

COVID memorial a sh*tload cheaper than actually paying nurses, Government confirms

ITV 'zero tolerance to bullying' questioned by 66 million Piers Morgan victims

Leaning back in a wooden chair championship final to take place over two legs

Squid has an inkling

Traffic on M25 heeding stay put notices.

Violent herb ejected from hearing by court bayleaf

Worker who farted in firework factory couldn't help letting one off

Israel vs Gaza, pools panel result, no-one wins

Gates admits: 'I should've had back-up marriage in cloud'

Touching relatives permitted again soon, but not like that, Norfolk

'Major incident' declared as COVID threatens to overwhelm conspiracy theories

Bank robbers demand right to keep masks on after lockdown ends.

New Amazon rainforests not being delivered fast enough

Govt says free Zoom for everyone will be much cheaper than HS2.

Top Shop still unable to shift Christmas tat – even at 90% off

1500 onion sellers on bicycles, wearing stripy sweaters stuck in Calais

Boris will continue to talk pollocks.

Hancock denies new vaccine is 'very nearly an armful'.

Johnson's Australian style boomerang deal comes back and hits him in the face

New variant of coronavirus unable to enter school premises, assures Hancock.

John Buchan's 'The 39 Steps' rewritten to allow for wheelchair access

Five Go Dobbing in the Neighbours

June 2021

June, Boris to get married again – but we could say that any month. Holidays are back on, which means COVID gets to see the world. The nation braces itself for football heartache, as Gareth Southgate fails to wear his waistcoats. And billionaires disappear into space, while their tax returns go into a vacuum.

Smart money on 'by Wednesday' for how soon Boris will commit adultery

The wedding of the year, expected to cause the most judders and dry retches, has thankfully been held in secret. Did Carrie Symons really say 'I do'? To that? Really? Without being hypnotised? Or blackmailed? Or having a beloved member of her family held hostage? Really? Does she need help? Should someone at least check she is okay?

The ceremony was held in secret, partly to avoid embarrassment, but mostly to bypass that awkward moment when the question was asked, 'If anyone knows of any lawful impediment why these two should not be joined in matrimony, speak now or forever hold your peace...'

The sixty-six million individuals (mainly ex-wives) who were hoping to speak up for once, were bitterly disappointed they did not get their opportunity.

Woman's guilt over cheating on current laptop with new one.

Chloe Plant, 28, from Shrewsbury has been wracked with guilt after deciding that she needs a new laptop. 'My current laptop is getting a little slow, but it's my life. He's rarely off my lap when I'm on the sofa, and during the winter months he keeps my foofoo warm.

'I suppose... yes... I love him. But when it came to looking for a new one, I just couldn't bring myself to, well, you know, use old trusty, faithful Lappy to search for his replacement. I had to borrow my housemate's. No problem using her disgusting pink one - no one could feel anything for a showpony like that. But if I'd used Lappy, oh, I can't even think about it - please give me a moment...

'I'm not going to trade him in or throw him away or anything. He'll have a special place in my red plastic crate of electronic stuff under my bed'.

Lucifer Appointed as Head of OFCOM

The incoming chair was excited by the role and what he hoped to bring, remarking: 'I'm looking forward to beginning my tenure at the head of the UK's communication industry. I'd like to thank the many Conservative MPs who I'm in league with, or who are paying back for selling their souls. I assure you that under my reign, we shall continue the roll-out of 5G and all its mind-controlling properties; as well as pressuring the BBC to keep making 'Mrs Brown's Boys'.'

Man thrown out of internet forum for 'knowing stuff'

'It started when I saw a question posted on a thermodynamics forum,' said Alan, 43, a thermodynamics engineer. 'The question was a bit technical but I answered it in reasonable lay terms. OK, the differential equations probably aren't to everyone's taste, but my explanation about the ignitability of a wet fart are probably as good as you'd get anywhere'.

Clara1998 explained the problem. 'I knew there was an issue with him - for starters, who uses a real name? Weirdo. Then the tell-tale preamble - if it doesn't start with 'I dunno nuffink 'bout thermodynamics but...' tells you straight off you have an arse on the forum. No one wants facts when opinions are so much more interesting.'

Alan has promised to toe the line going forward and explain why the universe will never dip below minus 273.15 degrees Centigrade, with just a packet of crisps. 'I know a bit about quantum mechanics, but luckily I know nuffink about crisps.'

Government's 'Name your own COVID variant' scheme a runaway success

The Government launched initiative has proved popular with the milling masses. People are naming new variants after their pets, the Fido and Tiddles COVID variant being particularly prevalent. Personalised 'Artisan' names are to be made available via auction by the DVLA. Custom face masks will be provided, with their chosen variant name printed in large letters, available as gifts for unloved ones, should they survive.

Team of priests on standby to receive PM's confession

Following Boris Johnson's catholic wedding, the church is making preparations for the twice-divorced, serial adulterer, prime-minister's embracing of the Catholic faith.

A team of specially trained priests are nervously waiting for Mr Johnson's confession, which is expected to last several weeks. Said one: We also predict the requirement for PTSD counselling. So, we've recruited psychologists who've treated veterans of Afghanistan, Iran and meeting Michael Gove.'

The confession will lead to the requirement for the PM to commit to penance. When this was explained to Mr Johnson he is reported to have said, 'I'll get a donor to do that.'

UK's 'Freedom Day' decision passed to a mixed Infants reception class

Class teacher, Miss Fiona Barnes (25) said: 'Gosh, we were certainly very surprised to be given such a weighty task to grapple with, but I think the children are equal to it. Many of them can count to ten already, while others have displayed an ounce or two of common sense. Yes, all in all, I'm sure we'll do the right thing for the nation.'

Mr Johnson was unavailable for comment, but one close source, speaking off the record said: 'He's much too busy to be bothered by COVID, as he needs every spare minute to get back in the saddle with his many dating sites. You know? Now the wedding's done and dusted and all that.'

British holiday resorts now 'infested' with middle class tw*ts

Like many nauseating middle class families, Ingrid and Thomas usually take a half term break to the Algarve with their three children, Atticus, Ruben and Cassius - but this year have been forced to slum it at a UK holiday resort.

'We'd heard horrible things about staying in the UK and if anything, it is even worse than we imagined,' explained a tearful Ingrid. 'Poor Atticus visibly retched when he had to use the public lavatories by the seafront and Cassius cried into his Mr Whippy when he realised it wasn't organic. It's been a real shock for all of us to see how poor people holiday. But the boys have been so brave - quality family time is what matters to them really'.

Ruben, the eldest of the three children, says: 'It's total sh*t. I cannot wait to go home'.

Paparazzi furious that Kate refused to take COVID jab in the buttocks

One Royal observer commented: 'The image of the Duchess of Cambridge being vaccinated has spread round the world, but had she decided to get it in the rear, the image would have spread far faster, prompting many more to be vaccinated and therefore saving lives.'

So far, the Palace confirmed, that the only Royal arse jabbed was Prince Andrew, as technically: 'He's an arse from top to toe'.

Wallet Inspectors to be nationalized

A Minister explained: 'Too long has private industry exploited the gullible and that's our job. Now, if you could just give me your bank details and passwords, we can really get this going'.

The job of a Wallet Inspector is to ensure that wallets are not over-filled with unnecessary banknotes and to save the public from the burden of cumbersome wealth. They work tirelessly closing down village hospitals, bailing out banks (with your money) and removing the word 'sucker' from the dictionary. One Inspector commented: 'It's a free service. We provide the bait. The hook, the line and the sinker. All you need to do is sign right here. Don't worry about the small print'.

Call of Duty to become Call of Nature

As its userbase enters middle age, incontinence has become the real challenge. Instead of missions to rescue hostages and kill foreigners, players will now face scenarios involving making a presentation the morning after a vindaloo and fourteen pints of Guinness in a conference centre with only one toilet. Players will have to use a combination of map-reading, martial arts skills and queue-jumping to take a dump before their character reaches 'Code Brown'.

Schoolchildren resolve to call all fat kids Freddy from now on

Following the news that Fatty from the Bash Street Kids is to be renamed Freddy, pupils have universally agreed that Freddy is now the nickname for all of their overweight classmates. When asked whether children could learn not to be nasty to each other, Ryan from Year 7 said that he remains determined to be mean: 'I will still pick on thick kids even if I can't call them Lightning and have to call them Matt Hancock instead'.

Could £1.795m life-saving drug have used cheaper packaging?

Questions are being asked why big pharma is charging the NHS so much to save a child's life; was it the redundant child proof cap, was it offering it in banana flavour or was it the choice to make the bottle out of Tiffany diamonds?

Crystal Meth dealers have questioned the company's ethical code. Yet accusations of price gouging were dismissed by the CEO, who sent a message from his private island: 'There are a lot of costs in developing a new drug, not least of which was the $3.2 billion spent on marketing'. He said they were hoping to expand out into COVID prevention, with an affordable vaccine selling at $1 for the first dose and $4,577,838 for the second.

Queen Elizabeth refusing to die

With plans for her platinum jubilee being revealed, reports are emerging that Queen Elizabeth is in fact, immortal.

The Daily Express broke the story with a headline that was simply an orgasmic groan accompanied by a 32 page pull out, comprising solely of Union Jacks.

Prince Charles was seen walking to his hydroponic greenhouse with his head down, shoulders slumped, a bong in either hand.

The Queen appeared to confirm the rumours with some remarks at Buckingham Palace: 'Wassup plebs. Have a nice bank holiday, courtesy of your ever living Maj. It's worth saying that I'm gonna see every one of you f*ckers six feet under. Q Unit out.'

UK shocked to discover it has a Tsar

The entire population of the UK has been left dumbfounded since the breaking news that some bloke responsible for school catch up was actually a Tsar.

'I literally had no idea that we had a supreme ruler from Eastern Europe running our Education Recovery Programme' says Mike, from Birmingham. 'I can't believe they haven't mentioned this to anyone until now. What a shame he's just quit. But Boris is till the 'Sultan of Stupidity', right?'

Weighing school kids will tell us if they are carrying knives

Under the guise of monitoring student obesity, the Government are sneakily testing to see if children are smuggling in guns in their socks. Said a teacher: 'It's very humane. We get them to sit on an industrial scale and a klaxon goes off if they're a fatty. A trap door then opens and a horde of Oompah Loompas carry them off to be strip searched'.

Explained one Headmistress: 'We caught one lad claiming his suspicious bulges were the result of puberty, but his trousers revealed a cosh and two dangling grenades. We've had lunchboxes stuffed with submachine guns and one girl had nunchucks concealed in her Alice band.

Explained one Schools Minister: 'We're naturally suspicious of any child that puts on weight, God knows we're not feeding them'. Asked if was possible that extra weight was a text book, he replied: 'Don't make me laugh. We banned them before we banned knives.'

Budget holidaymakers jubilant as Mustique goes on 'Green List'

Impromptu street parties broke out along the high street as effervescent revellers quaffed Bolly by the bucketload and fine dined on red mullet, accompanied by a violin solo. Re-enactments of the famous Eton wall game final excited the crowds, with memories of the 1787 trouncing of the French 330-0 (after extra-time), still fresh in the minds.

'Jolly spiffing news, what!' exclaimed Maj Gen Pilchard Davenport-Dawlish (retired). 'My favourite beachside villa is a very reasonable £31600 for the week, with a generous 10% discount for hyphenated names. We've been warned of an influx of vulgar social influencers who apparently have the money to afford this sort of thing, which is why the first thing I packed was the 12-bore.'

China says 'nothing to see here' on Tiananmen anniversary

A spokeswoman explained: 'If you think there is something to see here, we built some lovely re-education camps for those cheeky Uyghurs. We can send you there and you can learn that there is nothing to see here.'

Responding to criticism that China's regime is repressive and autocratic, she said 'You like cheap electronics and clothes, right? Well, those slave kids don't organise themselves. Besides, democracy got you Trump and Johnson, so who are the real idiots.

'One country, two systems, 5G... know what I mean?'

Hospitality Crisis: BBC to Show 'Great British Wait Off'

Viewers will watch low -paid competitors, as they build their repertoire from the bottom-up with fundamentals such as forgetting which is the Diet Coke, and not ordering one person's starter meaning they get it as everyone else gets their main course. Later weeks promise a look at advanced work, including bills so confusing patrons just pay out of frustration, and developing a condescending look when customers comment that something tastes funny.

EURO 2021: Southgate selects 26 goalkeepers

The squad's makeup heavily favours Southgate's preferred 0-0-0 formation and controversial 'White helmets' formation for penalty shoot-outs. 'I simply selected the best 26 footballers in the land', the England manager declared, as he defended his selection policy. 'If I could have picked 27, I would have done.'

'Obviously, there will be a lot of competition for the number 1 shirt'.

Wallace and Gromit ran a sweat shop

The sometime astronauts, window cleaners and bakers, have been accused of exploiting immigrant labour – specifically two 1970's plasticine models, called Morph and Chas. Working for only cheese and crackers, Morph and Chas were allegedly locked in an old cigar box in a cellar and forced to create space rockets and weird getting-out-of-bed machines.

Police were called several times, to West Wallaby Street, but even after a four day stop motion search, no evidence was found, save a large greyish-brown ball of modelling clay with four eyes.

Musk's mission to Mars, a mission to avoid tax

SpaceX's plans for a manned mission to Mars will be accelerated so that by the time the global tax reforms come into place, Tesla head office will be close to Olympus Mons on Mars, or Musk Mountain as it will soon be renamed.

A spokeswoman said: 'At first, we considered moving to the international space station, but I don't know if you've seen the toilets up there. Grim.' Famous for his self-drive cars, Elon Musk promised self-auditing tax returns.

Dad has 'best holiday ever' after beating SatNav by three minutes

'It has to be one of the best days of my life,' said Brian, a father of two. 'I planned the route for months. I printed off an array of maps and stuck them to the walls of my home office, a bit like one of those maverick detectives off the TV. I spent every evening pacing up and down circling the 'danger zones' - I knew the A30 could be congested around the M5 turnoff, and that was a risk I wasn't willing to take. I drove precisely 4 miles over the speed limit to shave off a bit more time and made my family urinate into an old bottle to save any toilet stops.

I couldn't believe it when we arrived at 2.33 pm when the SatNav had estimated 2.36 pm. Wow, what an achievement! The fact that my marriage did not survive the journey, is a small price to pay for greatness.'

Amazon workers wish Jeff Bezos an enjoyable space flight, one-way

'Take as long as you like,' said an employee - who felt so secure in his or her job they asked us to identify them only as 'X'. 'You've earned it. LOL!'

'Nice that he's taking his brother with him', added employee 'Y'. 'I guess he was originally going to take his wife, but that ain't on the cards now, so it makes sense not to waste the ticket.'

Logan Paul set for rematch as world agrees to punch him in the face

After having gone toe to toe and accountant to accountant with Floyd Mayweather, the Youtuber is set to box the entire population of the planet, as we all take turns at trying to wipe the smile off his stupid face. With '$1 a pop', Paul is set to raise $7.9bn – which will help fund his goal of buying a proper surname.

Paul is expected to go the distance, but his face is not. Despite being reduced to a bloody neck stump, many of his 15 million followers feel this will improve his Vlogging output. Infamous for mocking suicide victims, Paul has no shortage of opponents. Said one: 'I'm not a violent person, but he's got such a punchable face. It would be great to have a rematch of the rematch; he's also got such a kickable scrotum.'

London resolves lack of floating swimming pools before removing lethal cladding

The 'Sky Pool' is 115ft above the ground and miles above your lifestyle. It has a glass bottom, which has more transparency than the Grenfell Fire enquiry. Linking two luxury apartment blocks, the pool will give swimmers the feeling that they do not have a care in the world – and if you can afford the £6,500 per month, that will probably be true.

Over £1 million was spent on helping rich people pretend to float in a cloud and experience acrophobia in a bikini. One resident defended the project: 'Who wouldn't want to be drenched in water at the top of a high rise?'. To which a Grenfell survivor replied: 'I think that was our point'.

COVID 19 – 'I'm no match for Iain Duncan Smith'

COVID-19 has announced that the campaign being waged by the former Tory Leader and current selfish prick, to drop all safety regulations, has forced COVID to give up trying.

Speaking to reporters, a virus spokesgerm said: 'The game's up for us. And all because of Iain's superior knowledge in global viral pandemics. If he says we're no longer infectious, who are we to argue? And he was always more virulent'.

Hancock given 'super special important job' of announcing who can get jab next

A source has said: 'Matty is certainly a happy chappy - he's been so out of his depth up until now; but remembering a two-digit number and saying it out loud is just about at his ability level. He loves making the 'big announcement'. He was jumping up and down on Boris and Carrie's bed yesterday morning, asking, 'can I say the next age group today, pwease, pwease, pwease?'

It is rumoured that Matt Hancock is in the line-up for lots of other 'very important jobs' including checking the stationery cupboard is full and listing all his health care policies in bubble writing.

Topless picture of Queen must remain

Oxford University students have courted controversy by removing a collection of saucy snaps of our beloved Queen. With her head appearing on so many notes, there is a vast number of unused images of her bottom half in circulation, all literally topless – with some of Elizabeth trooping the colours in nothing but a bearskin.

Out of respect, citizens must keep their eyes shut when licking the Queen's behind on a stamp. Members of Magdalen College explained that keeping a photo of someone who is not your nan is a little bit creepy. Said one: 'We just used it for darts practice'.

Toilet voted 'Best place to hide from your children' 2021

Nick, a father of two, is a regular toilet-hider: 'I spend at least five or six hours in there on the weekend. It's so much better than interacting with my family or doing housework. My wife thinks I have a particularly aggressive form of chronic diarrhoea, which coincidentally began shortly after the birth of our first child. I play loud, unpleasant toilet noises from my phone to ensure my cover isn't blown - the added bonus is that it also drowns out the sound of the kids banging on the door. I have crisps and beer hidden under the toilet rolls and watch BT sport with headphones on. I absolutely love it.

Runners up include 'the shed' (kids never look there), 'the utility room' (you can usually hide under a pile of dirty washing) and 'down the pub' (brilliant but gets expensive).

Jeff Bezos hoping 'not to be left with a neighbour'

Engineers have confirmed that the rocket the Amazon founder is using to launch himself into space will be delivered back to Earth the next day - probably. 'We've confirmed that Jeff is a Prime member and is entitled to next day delivery', said a spokeswoman.

It is intended that the spacecraft will return to Cape Canaveral, or the nearest neighbourly ocean. 'This is provided that his barcode on the outside is legible, the contents are undamaged and all taxes applicable are paid. Only kidding about the tax part.'

Man who went out to get take out was in, came out, and is now in again

The food industry is in turmoil. A concerned spokesman from the Food and Trading Standards Organisation said, 'If you cook at home and eat at home, you're golden. No problem. If you go out to a restaurant, eat all of the food you order there on the premises and then come home, you may be out of pocket, but at least you and everyone else knows where you stand.'

'The problems begin with people going into fast food outlets and ordering takeout food. At the point they leave the takeaway with their takeout food, they are in safe territory. They have fulfilled a mutually understood agreement. If they trough the lot sitting on a park bench, they are still within acceptable parameters. So too if they nosebag everything on the way home.'

'But if they return home with all or some of the takeout food and 'bring it in', then there is an issue of the 'take out' food transitioning to 'take in' food. Was there always an intent to bring it home? Should it have been referred to as 'take in' food from the outset?'

'Far more serious than this, however, is the increasing trend of people ordering 'take out' food without actually moving location at all. At no point in the whole process do they physically 'take out' the food. It is believed that third parties, or 'delivery companies' are bringing the food to them. At the very best, the food could be called 'get out' or, more correctly, 'bring in'. And for those living in flats above the ground floor who refuse to pop downstairs to collect it, 'brought up food'.'

Bear shitting in wood reveals rich don't pay tax

A leak that Jeff Bezos and Elon Musk have not been paying tax, has rocked the world of those easily surprised and who questioned if the Pope was Catholic. To the amazement of some, the filthy rich stay rich (and filthy) by not paying for anything and Dolly Parton sleeps on her back.

Said one bewildered individual: 'This is a revelation. No one could have seen this coming, just like a Boris Johnson infidelity, the sun rising or Tottenham Hotspurs choking at the last minute. Next you'll be telling me that the Kennedys are gun shy'.

Those who follow the 'no shit sherlock' school of economics, will understand that money, like Velcro, sticks to its own. Others, for whom this has been a bombshell, will really freak out when they hear that Fedoras never look good, cotton candy is not made from cotton and Matt Hancock has sh*t for brains.

Naturally, the FBI are worried about the legality of the leak, not the illegality of billionaires. An Officer explained: 'We're not surprised that global elites are committing crime, but neither should you be surprised that we work for them'.

Still no agreement on buffet breakfast arrangements for G7

Government sources have commented that no 'continental breakfasts' will be served in the Cornwall restaurant to reflect ongoing tension around the NI Protocol with the EU. World leaders will only be able to access the full British breakfast, or 'Breakit' as it is known. The queue for this breakfast is expected to be long, with multiple border checks and no actual food at the end of it. While Boris promised that the subsequent lunch would be 'oven ready', which means burnt to a crisp.

Man with Euro 2020 wallchart behaving like he's Churchill in his War Room

'Gather round; there's no easy way to say this,' said Pete McBride, to his family, as he smoked a cigar. 'Overnight intel from Sky Sports all point in the same direction. We've to prepare for a last 16 game against Germany and then a quarter-final with either Italy, Belgium, Spain or...hold on, was it Denmark? Who did I have coming second in Group B?

'In the folders in front of you, you'll see a 100-page summary of the tactics that I'll be using in my Fantasy team if, by the grace of God, we get to the semi-finals. All I ask is that you read it carefully and consider it in your own plans'.

McBride's Darkest Hour had come when his five-year-old daughter used a Sharpie pen to draw a princess picture over the fixture list for Group D. His wife said 'Never, in the field of our relationship, has so much bloody effort and energy been put into something where we are obviously going to depressingly crash out of the tournament in the second round.'

President Biden accidentally has 'constructive' talks with Wilfred Johnson

President Joe Biden held three hours of talks with one-year-old Wilfred Johnson in Cornwall yesterday, after mistaking him for his father, Prime Minister Boris Johnson.

'It was a genuine and easy mistake to make,' a US aide said. 'We saw the tousled blond hair, heard him making a kind of gibberish noise and grabbing breasts.'

There followed intense three-hour talks between Wilfred and Biden covering a range of issues, which only stopped because it was nap time. Whilst the President was napping, Wilfred spent some time playing on the beach.

Police arrest 7 on the way to G7 in St. Ives - all married to the same man

Officers have described it as the worst case of bigamy they have ever come across.

They are also investigating a suspected 49 cases of animal cruelty to cats, after someone let the out of the bag, and a further 343 similar cases against kittens.

They are still unable to establish exactly how many people were going to St. Ives. A spokesperson for the Devon and Cornwall Police said it is a complete riddle.

Combined efforts of Repair Shop experts unable to restore one man's reputation

Viewers watched in disbelief as a blond, tousle-haired, rotund apelike man from London shambled into the barn, after leaning his rather heavy and chunky bicycle against the wall outside.

The man explained he had brought a completely shattered reputation and asked if the experts could somehow repair it.

The Repair Shop host later told viewers. 'To be honest, this is a totally lost cause really, but we'll have a go anyway. Thing is, there are no original parts and over the years it's been destroyed by serial procrastination, and an utter disregard for the truth or decency. It's shagged in my opinion...far too many times'.

Bezos overtaken on rich list by roadside Strawberry Seller

Janet McGinty (57) has been catapulted to one of the world's most wealthy, by selling her third punnet of strawberries in a week. Economists refer to this as the 'Strawberry Paradox', where a seemingly loss-making venture generates insane levels of profitability – a little bit like James Corden's career.

Many have questioned the validity of a business model which involves someone snoozing in a layby for ten hours, wearing an eyepatch and love/hate tattooed on her knuckles. Janet explained: 'First we pay someone to pick, package and transport the strawberries, so our overheads work out at about £5 a box.

'I then sell them on at 50p a punnet, making a profit of £27,7344,222 per strawberry. I used to sell lucky heather but that barely covered the cost of my third home in Monaco. But selling fresh strawberries has been a gold mine. Thank goodness, this is something I can do all year round'.

Entire England cricket XI convicted of obscene public acts

'Never in my life have I come across such shameful public exhibitions as the ones of which you are guilty,' said a stipendiary magistrate, swallowing back some vomit in his throat.

'Your performances over the past year at Lords, Headingley, Trent Bridge and Old Trafford have been sickening for the general public to watch and you should all be utterly ashamed of yourselves.

'I would advise the England XI to refrain from any further public exposure and instead stay on the boundary making daisy chains. And not the smutty kind of 'daisy chain'!'

Johnson announces Garden Bridge to cross rift with EU

A spokeswoman for the PM explained the plan: 'Not building the bridge in London has cost the tax payer £43M, I think we can do better than that. Did you know you could walk from the UK to the EU in Ireland? I didn't. But we can take advantage of that by moving the bridge to connect to the EU because there's simply a line in the road in Northern Ireland that the bridge has to cross.'

GB News breaks World Record for use of the word 'Woke'

Guinness were delighted to announce that the first evening of GB News has been awarded a world record for uses of the word 'woke' in an hour, followed by the phrase 'I'm not racist but...'

Starting at 8pm with a monologue about their pride to be British from GB News Head Andrew Neil, filmed on a camera-phone from his house in France, the channel promised to rail against the woke agenda; giving the first of over 1100 uses of the key phrase. Giving a voice for the voiceless, it was followed by an interview with Nigel Farage – his 35th of the week. The use of 'woke' become increasingly ironic, as most of the viewers were soon asleep.

'Selfless generosity' as vaccine leftovers to go to poor, instead of the bin

This selfless act will of course come after all men, women, children, dogs, cats and hamsters have received at least three doses of the vaccine at which point the world's poorest can have a go at protecting their elderly and vulnerable.

A smug Health official said: 'I think the word you are looking for, is 'thank you'.'

Couple die of starvation while deciding what to have for dinner

The pair were found slouched over their kitchen worktop with all the food cupboards lying open. They were found clutching a single carrot, three new potatoes, a tin of chickpeas and half a cabbage.

A neighbour confirmed hearing raised voices debating dinner options over and over.

It is believed that the couple meant to do a 'big food shop' earlier that week but, after becoming distracted by the pubs now being open, 'didn't get round to it'.

In an official police statement, DCI Watts said: 'It is a terrible, terrible tragedy - my officers found a jar of masala sauce at the back of the cupboard so they could have whipped up a vegetable curry easy as anything. What a waste - of life and ingredients.'

Alan Bennett is new Israeli PM

After 15 elections in the last 6 months, Israel has a new coalition Government and Benjamin Netanyahu can go directly to jail, without collecting £200.

According to a spokeswoman of no importance: 'Alan wasn't really expecting to be elected Prime Minister of Israel. Not with his knees and Margaret's … condition. Anyway, I said to Irene, I said did you know that Edna's grandson has got in to university. University! He's a homosexual you know. Very modern. Irene's other half Gerry – do you know Gerry? – he said he'd worked out a roadmap for peace including the implementation of a two-state solution. I told him to save it for bridge on Wednesday. Scone?'

Big business pens open letter over 'Freedom Day' postponement

One magnate said: 'Is this the bulldog spirit? Can we allow what is clearly the greatest country in the world to be held to ransom by some sneaky underhand nasty foreign bug? And don't talk to me about suffering. I've personally lost millions, from my billions'.

'It might seem like our group is motivated purely by colossal greed for monstrously massive self-gains. Well, yes, yes, that bit is true. But, how about we give you a five-day week? What do mean, you've already got that? Hmpf, what about Christmas Day off?'

Harrison Ford remakes

- An abseiling Movie: 'Clear and Present Dangler'

- An archaeologist no longer able to deliver lectures in person: 'Indiana Jones and the Temple, on Zoom'

Five Go Dobbing in the Neighbours

- A homicide Cop unable to pick up clues, despite them being blatantly obvious: 'Witless'

- Trump's disastrous Presidency told from the perspective of his stylist: 'Hair Farce One'

- The fight to stop the only remaining gunboat gazebo from blowing away: 'Indiana Jones and The Lashed Crew Shade'

- A Russian carpenter recruited to fit observation screens in submarines: 'K-19: The Windowmaker'

- Replicant dies just 11 minutes before the 9 O'clock watershed: 'Blade Runner 20:49'

- A man and his family forced to flee the apocalypse on a raft made of entomologically themed place mats: 'Mosquito Coasters'

- A thriller chiller sequel movie about a back garden voyeur: 'The Return of The Shed Eye' or a revamp of Irish twins' singing career: 'Return of the Jedward'

- Observations of closet vacuum cleaners - 'Regarding Henry Hoovers'

- A horror film about that weirdo who sleeps in the bottom bunk - 'What Lies Beneath'

- An extremely generous bartender: 'Extraordinary Measures'

Omega variant will make everyone incredibly sexy and give some people superpowers

The mutated virus will enable people to have superpowers like being able to get the lids off jars without straining every sinew. Many will be able to piddle straight standing up and hit the target every time. Some will be able to remember their passport numbers off by heart.

Best of all, though, everyone will develop X-ray vision and be able to see through anything. Especially fake news and reports from suspect media outlets.

UK welcomes Australia's 'bonzer' boomerang trade deal

The UK is set to get access to zero tariff kangaroos, boomerangs and digeridoos. 'We can export corks attached to hats,' said the UK negotiating team. 'Apparently they intend cutting the corks off and sticking them in bottles of murky chemicals labelled as wine. We even get our hats back as part of the deal'. Sadly, Rolf Harris is non-refundable.

'They may take our lives, but they'll never take our Dress Circle tickets to see Phantom'

With the threatened delay of the UK's 'Freedom Day', many citizens have taken to the streets to demand cheap package holidays, karaoke and universal suffrage – only kidding with that last one, they just want half-price cocktails.

Said one agitator: 'I don't mind waiting a few years to hug my family, but I'll be damned if I'm going to miss out on 'Dear Evan Hansen. Nobody wants basic human rights, but we do want discounted tickets, with a restricted view'.

GB News only to cover British weather

A channel spokesman said: 'Why would anyone want to go abroad when there are sometimes as many as two days a year when our weather comes vaguely close to that of Marbella and all those other so-called holiday hot spots?'

'Britain's got it all here on our doorstep. Rain, hail, wind, fog and mist; with the mercury often rising as high as 9 degrees Celsius in July and August. Add our shabby seaside resorts into the heady mix, with games arcades and mutant flocks of dive-bombing seagulls nicking greasy fish and chips and burgers left right and centre, then what more could anyone want?

'So, if you want to know what the weather's doing in foreign climes, then you should watch an actual real TV station... err... no... wait a minute... can you cut that bit please?'

Peep's Diary, 17 June.

And so to the Bethlehem Hospital to view the Lunaticks lately arrived.

In the first room, one Matt Hancock who does think himself a Minister of State. He believes he has control of some Witchery which can keep the Pestilence at bay. He repeatedly shrieks 'Data not Dates' which no person can make sense of. It is obvious the fellow has lost his wits.

In the next room, one Dominic Cummings. He does lie in his own filth and will try to throw his excreta upon any who attempt to come near. He has many scraps of manuscript and has daubed much nonsense on the walls in shit. His Keepers tell that he blames his current downfall to Witch called Symonds. He utters profanities that would make a Covent Garden Whore to blush.

In the last, a vile creature named Cressida Dick. They do say that it is a woman that claims to be a Constable of the Peace. However, it is known that she is the heir to a corrupt clan that did feign protection of the populace of London, yet did lie and dissemble for their own benefit. She does claim that she is of the utmost purity whilst all around can smell the stench that does issue from her mouth.

I fear there is no cure for these Wretches.

Then home by boat, where I came upon my wyfe using her Godeminche in her Contrapunctum to my Delite. Did then feast upon a jug of Oysters.

Professional Red Herring regrets career choice

'When I left school, under something of a cloud of suspicion, I didn't have any idea of how to earn a living. But then, by chance, several rich relatives died in mysterious circumstances. I say 'mysterious', but the police arrested me simply because my alibi was rubbish and I happened to own a similar harpoon gun to the one that killed 8 of them.

'It's proved a nightmare; every time someone gets poisoned in a country house, I get arrested - I really wish I hadn't taken up a part time job as travelling fugu fish chef.'

Jacob Rees-Mogg now fully weaned

Jacob, 52, confirmed he has been weaned off 'nanny's nectar' by a herd of cows, British cows that is. Rees-Mogg, who lists his hobbies as ordering urchins up chimneys and deporting people from Tolpuddle, said it was time to move on and embrace the 19th century.

He remarked, in Latin, that the sun should never again set on the uplands of the British Empire, before becoming increasingly aroused, eyes rolling backwards in his head, his glasses steaming up at the point of climax. He then reclined on a rococo chaise longue, before flicking his fingers together and whispering: 'Bring me your finest lactating bovine'.

GB News to use semaphore

With the first week of GB News blighted by technical, audio and idiocy issues; a producer explained: 'We're getting staff to hold flags and spell out the news letter-by-letter. I've had to be careful though, one news anchor got too animated during a lockdown discussion and accidently spelt out 'immigrants welcome'.'

'It's quite easy once you get the hang of it, this one is a favourite of our presenters, it spells out SOS'.

Confused Biden repeatedly refers to Queen as 'Mom'

A clearly discombobulated President Biden reportedly told the Queen, 'It's nice to see you, Mom. I've missed you these past few years.'

Biden then took a seat on the throne and put his feet up on a corgi saying: 'It makes me feel like a kid again. Do we have ESPN yet?' He then rummaged under the ermine and velvet-lined royal seat, seemingly in search of a remote control, and requested Her Royal Highness bring him a 'sodie'.

He confided to an aide: 'In a lot of ways, she reminds me of the Queen of England'.

Woman depressed after finding out friend successfully completed marathon

Emma, 34, was eating biscuits and watching Netflix when the news came in: 'I knew she was planning to run a marathon for charity and I went along with it, donating a tenner and sending motivational messages like 'you got this!' and 'you're going to smash it!' but I didn't for a minute believe she would actually complete it.

'My stomach dropped through the floor when I saw a picture of her on Facebook, standing on the finishing line, holding her medal. I zoomed in to try and spot her tears of misery but she looked genuinely happy. I was sick to my stomach - which may just have been too many biscuits to be fair.

'How dare she do this to me? All I want is to eat junk food and sit on my arse without someone rubbing their sporting success in my face. What a bitch.

'I replied to her post with 'Wow that's amazing, I am so proud of you' and lots of thumbs up emojis before having a good cry over how utterly selfish and thoughtless she is'.

Emma has heard another friend of hers is planning to do an Iron Man and has her fingers crossed for a spectacular failure to dig her out of her pit of despair.

Met Police behind rigged Eurovision voting system

After yet another enquiry finds the Metropolitan police institutionally corrupt/racist/violent (delete as applicable), it is feared they may have had a hand in other corruption; such as Las Vegas slot machines, Trump's tax returns and the reason your dish washer breaks down the day after its insurance has lapsed. It is hard to tell how widespread the malfeasance is, but what is clear is that 'Mrs Brown's Boys' could not have got three seasons, without significant police interference.

Commissioner Cressida Dick has come under fire and not just for having a name that sounds like a venereal disease from a Greek tragedy. In fact, complaints against the Met have become institutionally predictable, while the public have become institutionally jaded by the whole affair.

When not covering up murders, the Met Police like to unwind by bashing female protestors, kettling children or the odd extrajudicial shooting. Asked if the Met had been involved in the bank system or election rigging, a spokeswoman said: 'We're crooked but not that crooked'.

GB News becomes a credible alternative to NewsBiscuit

The competitive market of fake news has been blown wide open by the launch of GB News, under the slogan 'If no one has heard of it, it must be true'. The gammon equivalent of 'TISWAS', GB sets out to prove once and for all, that the Earth is flat.

Sadly, their audience stats have plummeted into negative figures already, as their presenters resort to watching viewers in order to maintain contact. On Saturday, the viewing figures dipped below -14 as broadcasters from the station desperately zoom called viewers to beg them to tune in.

With an editorial slightly to the right of Genghis Khan, GB prides itself on maverick journalists, for whom a spell check is more vital than a fact check. It will be fronted Andrew Neil, who was turned down by The Onion for being too implausible and by The Beano, for having ridiculously drawn hair. Said our Editor: 'We use more d$ck jokes, whereas they employ more d$cks.'

In space, it turns out, everyone can hear you scream

'ARGHHHH! Which one of you bitches left a chocolate brownie finger smudge on my kale samples?'

Astronauts working at 320 miles above the Earth's surface in oxygen-controlled environments can hear each other perfectly clearly, it turns out. They can even hear the farty sounds emerging from 'Pooh Corner'.

'Shit on it! I've just turned the release valve the wrong way.'

Even on a spacewalk, everyone is well mic'd up, and the rest of the crew are all too aware that you've just buggered up the mission, and possibly just ended their lives.

'Will you stop bouncing that powerball off the ceiling you annoying little shite.'

And the advanced radio systems beam back every last swear word, curse and 'domestic' spat to hundreds of people listening in at mission control.

'NOOOO! Not the red lever...'

Driving test to include 'driving up motorway in wrong direction' part

In an effort to bring the driving test up to date with life in the 21st century, it is to include a knuckle-whitening five miles up a major motorway against the traffic at rush hour.

'Let's face it, it happens to us all someday,' a spokesman announced. 'The candidate will be expected to negotiate an average motorway with moderate to heavy traffic swerving out of their way in a blind panic. This will be followed by the standard three-point turn'.

'I think I handled that part pretty well', says 17-year-old Gareth. 'I just kept it cool, checking my rear-view mirror every 20 seconds as you're told to do. There was one scary moment when a 40-ton truck was coming straight at me with the driver too absorbed in his smartphone to see me. But I gave one polite tap on the horn and he swerved out of the way and ploughed into the median barrier at the last minute'.

'The worst part was when my mum came driving up the motorway just to wave at me', he adds. 'I wish she wouldn't do that'.

Brits now stockpiling holidays in the UK

Complained one holiday maker, 'We are convinced some people are stockpiling holidays just to stop others from getting in on the act. I mean, how can it be possible that the station hostelry in Crewe is fully booked right through the summer? £2,046 a night, and there's a 2-week waiting list for cancellations. What the actual? Are the cockroaches extra?'

Thousand-year Lib Dem Reich 'inevitable'

Rumours have swirled that recent by-election success improvement stems from a ritualised execution of Nick Clegg, as ashes in the shape of a pentagram were seen being hurriedly swept away. The Party denied that 'his fiery death was required by the great god Osiris to purge the tuition fees debacle.'

Excited Lib Dem supporters said their minibus was becoming more than usually crowded. Said one centrist voter Naveed Nasi said 'In 2010, I voted Lib Dem. I suppose it's the hope that kills you, unless it's the flames, or that minibus.'

Tories arrange spy swap – Bercow for Starmer

In a tense standoff on a Berlin bridge, John Bercow was finally brought in from the cold and allowed to join the natural home of reactionaries – the Parliamentary Labour Party. In exchange, agent Keir 'Starmer' Keithlovich was returned to the Conservative Party, having completed his mission to destroy left wing politics.

The swap itself had many similarities to John le Carré fictionalized book 'Stinker Starmer Dozy Spy'. Both men had been sleeper agents, with Bercow hiding his intentions for years and Starmer just sleeping through the last two.

A friend of Bercow said: 'John will have to adjust from having lived in an oppressive Tory regime. Gone will be the enforced junkets, banquets and bribes. Instead. he'll get to enjoy the true taste of left-wing freedom, which is angry Twitter accounts, regional accents and people accusing you of being a Tory, with no sense of irony'.

Law states people cannot be insulted if insult followed by smiley emoji

Mike has been an online troll for years and has recently started sending unpleasant work emails too: 'I love it, it makes me feel so big and powerful. But it's always such a pain when there are repercussions, it's not like the good old days where you could slag people off no end and you were held up as a hero.

'The woke brigade are on my back all the time, even for a bit of light hearted racism or sexism. But since the introduction of the Smiley Law, it's been a doddle. I sent Susan from finance an email this morning saying 'Shove it up your arse, you pathetic witch :-)' but because I included the smiley emoji there is nothing she can do about it. It's clearly meant in a nice way'.

Mike's employer have said they plan to text him later to tell him he's sacked followed by a laughing emoji to ensure he finds it hilariously funny.

WHO tells women to stop drinking, particularly Sandra from Gateshead

Sandra Dodd, 19, has been identified by the World Health Organisation as the leading cause of alcohol consumption and the one most likely to get a tattoo of a rabbit on her lady parts. It transpires that their 'Global Alcohol Action Plan' is just a map of Gateshead, with a big circle drawn around Sandra's local Wetherspoon.

A WHO spokeswoman explained that the intention was not to undermine women's rights, just Sandra's: 'The alcohol consumed by young women is extremely high, it's close to 20 units a week. But if you take Sandra out of the global sample, the average drops down to 1 unit and half a dozen cheeky mocktails. Likewise, 18% of all Tyne and Wear kebabs, are eaten by Sandra over just one weekend.'

Sandra resolved not to give in: 'I'm just like Emily Pankhurst, me. I'm fighting the patriarchy. Now, if you'll excuse me, I need to wee behind this bin, before I dance topless down the street, with a traffic cone on my head, singing 'Ni**as in Paris'.

Somerset House not in Somerset

A spokesman remarked: 'We can't have a building named after Somerset when according to all known records and ordnance survey maps, it's not even located in Somerset. It doesn't make any sense. Apparently, it's been this way since at least 1776. So, the sooner we have this monstrously socially unjust Dickensian edifice torn down, the better.'

Five Go Dobbing in the Neighbours

Government insists all children hum the tune from The Dam Busters

On the 25th of June, the Government has issued a dictate that all children sing 'Strong Britain, Great nation, No irony' but to a medley of nationalistic tunes; including the sound of a deflating space hopper and Vera Lynn singing the theme music from the 70s TV show 'Minder'

Teachers will be expected to use a state approved lesson about Britain's colonial past, which conveniently forgets to mention we had one. In a stirring playground ceremony, children will salute the Union Jack and then promptly declare ownership of the school, while enslaving half their classmates.

In a haunting madrigal, children as young as five will re-enact the UK's proudest movements, from the 1966 World Cup to Del Boy falling through the cocktail bar. These will be accompanied by a marching band playing The Prodigy's 'Firestarter' and 'Remember you're a Womble'.

A spokeswoman for North Korea was critical of Boris Johnson's crude propaganda tool: 'At least our glorious leader has a plausible haircut'. Despite UK ministers insisted: 'Small children singing patriotic songs, what's not to like? It worked for Hitler'.

EU eye Trans-Pacific trade deal enviously

The new deal announced today, filling a £68 billion drop in sales to the EU with a wholesome £1.7 billion deal involving mainly bananas, was described by Prime Minister Johnson 'exactly what we promised you - less money being spent on us, more airmiles to Johnny Foreigner places.'

The EU trade negotiators have quietly downloaded Lis Truss' CV from LinkedIn and are thought to be putting a hostile bid to snatch her away from the British negotiating team as soon as

422

possible. 'With skills like hers we can't afford to squander the opportunities she creates,' said an envious EU trade expert. 'She makes small gains look huge and huge losses appear as if they don't count. If only we had her negotiating skills on our team'.

Hancock leaks photo to keep job

A No.10 spokeswoman confirmed: 'No Conservative Party rules have been broken. F*ck an aide, and you're a player. F*ck an entire country and they give you a Lordship. That's the way we roll'.

While Matt Hancock, confirmed he had snogged a girl, an actual real-life girl, honest: 'Eugh. I didn't really want to, but the big boys told me to do it. Shhhh, don't tell anyone, but I hope Boris sees it because then he might let me stay and play.'

The PM is said to have responded, 'I said that Mr Hopeless was in want of damn good sacking, not a damn good shagging'.

Government credibility found in a Kent bus shelter

A member of the public has found the Government's remaining small shred of credibility in a bus shelter in Kent.

'I almost didn't see it, but somehow it caught my eye,' Joyce Robinson said. 'It was a small, unpleasant looking thing on the seat, so my first instinct was to brush it off. Something made me take a closer look though.'

After taking it home and looking at it under a microscope, Mrs Robinson realised what she had found.

A Government spokesperson confirmed that the credibility had been reported as missing shortly after the Government was formed: 'I'm just glad we've got it back. It's now perfectly safe here on my desk. Wait a minute, where's it gone? It's completely disappeared! Oh god, what has one of the clowns done now?'

Hancock: 'Hands, face, space' to be replaced with 'snog, grope, apologise'

Boris Johnson is reportedly 'delighted' and will be doing his very best to abide by the advice: 'We are urging the public to have a good old fumble and canoodle - especially extramarital groping with colleagues or acquaintances. But we must be clear - people are to do so 'with caution'. Because, as always, it isn't our fault if it goes tits up...pun fully intended'.

Matt Hancock's wife is reportedly working on her own campaign slogan, containing words such as 'cheating' 'bastard' 'and 'divorce'.

Probe into false Amazon reviews given six stars

Regulators have been analysing reviews on Amazon to determine whether the internet giant is allowing false product claims to exist on its website or is just avoiding paying any tax. 'We found that Amazon did a fair job - five stars,' said one (verified) investigator. 'Too good to be true - five stars and thanks for the bonus,' said another.

The EU has been checking into the financial affairs of Amazon for some time. 'Cheeky, unorthodox, great Tesla btw,' was the final report headline.

Sajid Javid told: 'Kill who you like, just don't kiss anyone'.

The new Health Secretary has been emboldened by the assurance that he will never be sacked not matter how bad his incompetence, even if he wears socks with sandals or dances to the Macarena at a wedding party. His position, unlike Matt Hancock's genitals, is untouchable.

This follows the unwritten rule, that you can never criticize a leader during a crisis, even if they are the cause of the crisis. Not so much a blank cheque, more of a kill list, really. A colleague commented: 'No matter how bad it gets, Sajid will keep his job. A bit like being James Corden'.

Politics to be kept out of England v Germany tie

'When England players take the knee, it's Marxist.' said a white England fan who has the St George's Cross and Union Jack on his social media, despite not understanding the difference.

'Raheem Sterling banging on about a proletariat uprising to throw off the capitalist yoke. Marcus Rashford feeding kids! You shouldn't mix sport and politics that I don't like. Now, shall we sing "Two World Wars and one World Cup" or "Ten German bombers"?'

HSE to investigate 'Jack and Jill'

The HSE inquiry is understood to be wide ranging, including the apparent exploitation of minors in the workplace, insufficient risk assessments, the carriage of excessive loads, insufficient manual handling training, inadequate stairs with handrails and 'very poor first aid training.'

'In the execution of his said duties,' said a HSE spokesman, 'he lost his footing, fell down the hill and sustained serious, potentially life changing, head injuries. It is understood that his partner attempted to dress his injuries with brown paper laced with malt vinegar – which is not an approved dressing'.

Chris Witty loses his shit and puts two men in hospital

'It was amazing,' said an eye-witness. 'One minute they were taunting him: pushing him around and taking selfies as they held him in choke holds. The next, he let out a bullish roar and punched them in the chest. One clown ended up in a skip and the other hit the side of a bus. Respect due. We're now calling him Two Jabs round the office ... when he is out of earshot, obviously.'

Failed Radio Shows

- The History of The Teaspoon - from conception to cup in 53 episodes
- Cravat Etiquette - when to cravat and when not to cravat
- The Archers 'unleashed' - Kate and Alice get dirty on the farm whilst cleaning out the cow shed
- Jigsaw Puzzles - the best, the worst and the just-about-acceptable
- Agricultural Trends of 2021 - pimp my tractor special
- The UK Drill Scene - getting groovy with DIY
- Rural Stenches - classic smells of the countryside identified for listeners
- Masterwave - tense competition as contestants prepare microwavable ready meals against the clock for vindictive judges Anne Robinson and Nick Hewer
- How to talk to the servants by Jacob Rees-Mogg.

Five Go Dobbing in the Neighbours

In other news...

Johnson reaches zero adulteries for first time

Smutty innuendos about Hancock's name 'in poor taste' says Cummings

Brits to bask in 29ºC rain

Disappointment in royal box as Germany lose at Euro2020

Burnt lettuce turns out to be chard.

Matt Hancock remains tight-lipped over affair clams. Shame he didn't with her.

Man with huge collection of 12-inch rulers denies having foot fetish.

Pre-Amazon-dwellers lived for nearly 2,000 years without online ordering

Starmerbot still unable to simulate human facial expressions

Williamson plans to scrap bubbles in schools will hit sales of Aero in tuckshop

Ikea sponsorship under scrutiny as Sweden field flat pack back four in Euro 2020

Get Dick out campaign to oust Met Chief leads to worrying social media trend

BBC to rename Points of View 'Whining Shits'

Jacob Rees-Mogg defends Hancock's right to have a tryst with his leman

Wimbledon rain returns after last year's cancellation

Sausage war with Germany: wurst is yet to come

Man living at number 664 complains about neighbours from hell

Serena plans new career as playwright since she's the more tennis-y Williams

Meghan and Harry announce birth of baby daughter Libel

Wedding cake company collapses: employees in floods of Tiers

Clickbait made illegal: you won't believe what's replacing it!

Crocodile claims impersonation charges 'based on false alligations'

Personal audio device that only plays politically-correct content to be named Sony Wokeman

Putin & Biden meet – one knows too much and the other can't remember

'A world-beater at last!' Johnson hails variant virus

NHS England warns Pfizer vaccine could lead to a stiff arm.

Future lockdown rules to be published on the side of a bus

Waitrose rations artichoke hearts, cappuccino mousse and provencale ratatouille

Monty Python tells tier 1 residents: stop that, it's Scilly.

Travel show 'wish you were here...?' to be revived as 'wish you were tier 2...?'

All future fish purchases to be strictly C.O.D.

EU bureaucracy to be replaced by good old-fashioned British bureaucracy

Alpaca fears Llamageddon

UK vows to 'go the extra furlong ', EU vows to 'go the extra kilometre'

Eden Project closes after snake tricks woman into eating an apple

'Stop obsessively harking back to an imagined nostalgic idyll' Remainers told

Row about standardizing waiters' gratuities reaches tipping point

Sex in the City reboot expected to contain very dry humour

NHS to recruit boxers to help with jabs.

Joe Dolce concerned about accidental deletion of criminal records

Customers furious after Ocado warns of shortages of Cypriot halloumi and olives.

Facebook: we already have quite enough data about Australians' personal habits.

July 2021

July was a month of record highs: record temperatures in parts of the UK along with unprecedented levels of kicking off duvets and making the point that it felt really 'close' and yes, all the windows are open; record levels of excitement about how football was now surely on its way back home after 30, or was it 50 years of hurt; followed quickly by record levels of crushing disappointment after England lost to Italy in the Euro 2020 final, and world beating levels of ringing the boss the morning after the final with a tea towel over your mouth saying you had a cough and that unfortunately you wouldn't be able to make it into the office today. The end of July saw the start of the delayed 2020 Olympics with Tokyo quickly going higher, faster and stronger by regularly breaking its daily national records for COVID cases.

Only those that can't afford to quarantine will have to quarantine

'The exception is extremely limited,' a government spokesperson said. 'If you are a millionaire who can afford to fly first class to the UK, the costs of a five-star hotel to quarantine in and your own COVID tests, as well as be having enough in the bank not to worry about needing to get to work for ten days, then - and only then - you are welcome to enter the country without quarantining. Oh, or if you are football VIP then it is OK too.'

Woman emigrates after waving at someone who was waving at someone behind her

'It all happened so fast' explains a tearful Lucy 'I was just making my way through the pub when I saw someone waving from the other side of the room. I thought it was my friend Jenny so I enthusiastically waved back. Then I realised I had made a

429

terrible mistake. It wasn't Jenny at all, it was just a woman with similar hair.

'Then everything happened in slow motion; I turned around to confirm what I already knew - the woman was actually waving at the person behind me. I tried to pass off my raised hand as a casual head scratch but it was pointless. The game was up and I had to face the truth - that I would have to live with the shame for the rest of my life.

'Later that night I booked myself on the next available flight out of the UK. I plan to travel to a remote convent, become a nun and never speak of that terrible day again.'

None of Lucy's friends or family have heard from her since this time. They are desperate for her to get in touch, as it turns out the woman in the pub WAS waving at her after all. 'Apparently they were at school together,' explains Lucy's friend Jenny 'I would have thought Lucy would remember her, she has such distinctive, awful hair.'

Chaos and confusion as Matt Hancock attends cabinet meeting

'Hi guys,' he said to his dumbfounded former colleagues. 'God, it's great to be back. That break was just what I needed, but here I am refreshed and ready to tackle this ruddy pandemic, if you'll pardon my French!'

Silence fell on the room, as Mr Hancock continued to grin and look desperately at the Prime Minister. It was Michael Gove who broke the silence, saying: 'But, Matt, you resigned as a minister, you resigned from the Cabinet.'

'Oh, that! Well, it's been a fair few days now, surely that whole affair has blown over now, no pun intended', Mr Hancock said. 'I mean it's not as though you had to sack me, not really. And

Boris, you said in your letter that my contribution to public service was far from over.'

'Enough', Priti Patel said very quietly. All members of the Cabinet instantly froze.

Mrs Patel led Mr Hancock into the corner and whispered some unknown words into his ear whilst making a few hand gestures. 'Am I understood?' she asked at the end, and a terrified Mr Hancock nodded quickly before collecting his things and scurrying out of the room.

The meeting then resumed and took its normal self-congratulatory course.

Mr Hancock's current whereabouts are unknown.

Coldplay to feature in Mr Whippy playlist

A spokesperson for the band explained: 'Traditionally Mr Whippy attracted customers with catchy tunes, like sea shanties that everyone tries to jig to when pissed. The band, well Chris, thought they could broadcast their music via the vans, forcing thousands to listen, who only really wanted an ice-cream.

The band, well Chris, thought they could then compete with his ex-wife - selling vegan ice cream. With flavours like: 'This Tastes Like My Vagina but With a Flake in It' and 'This Ice-Cream Is Organic and Green, But Not as Green as My All-Consuming Envy'.

Next, Coldplay plan to buyout of Royal Mail. Subject to the ability of posties to whistle a dreary tune, of course.

Discovered Lear nonsensical poem actually new Lockdown Rules

Literary scholars were disappointed to find that a hidden trove of nonsensical ramblings was not the work of Edward Lear but were, instead, the fevered cheese dreams of the new Health Secretary. Members of the public who were hoping for a coherent strategy, were told that facemasks were optional, COVID only affected those who were Sagittarius and vaccines were administered with a runcible spoon.

There was a patient from Nantucket
Who had recently kicked the bucket
Asked if he'd track & traced
Said he didn't want to be placed
And had told the NHS App to go f*ck it

Parents re mortgage house to pay for child's Sylvanian Families habit

'The problems started around her birthday' explained Mum, between sobs. 'She wanted the Adventure Treehouse and Walnut Squirrel Family. We agreed before we even checked the price – what idiots we were – but there was no going back, we couldn't disappoint her on her birthday.

'So, we ordered them from the Argos catalogue after securing a small bank loan. It all just escalated from there - before we knew it, she wanted the Log Cabin, the Caravan Playset with working oven and air con – then the Red Roof Country House with its own lighting, plumbing and central heating system. By this point, we had maxed-out on all the payday loans we could get our hands on and fell into crippling debt. That's when we knew we would have to remortgage the house'.

Seven-year-old Ava has a level headed approach to the situation: 'Sylvanian Families were ok but I'm nearly eight now, so to be honest, I think Sylvanian Families are a bit babyish for me. I'm going to start collecting rare, vintage Barbies instead. So, I need to let Mum and Dad know they will need to put the car on eBay and sell my younger brother on the dark web'.

Man has nervous breakdown trying to open liquid hand wash

A man has been caught in a serious altercation with a liquid hand wash after repeatedly trying to turn the pump action cap to no avail.

Mike is now being cared for in a secure facility. His partner, Kate, saw this coming for a long time: 'If it hadn't been the hand wash, it would have been the child-proof cap on the mouthwash or the allegedly 'resealable' pasta bags. Mike was constantly plagued by his inability to work basic packaging. He did his best, but unfortunately, he suffered terribly with clumsy sausage fingers so it was only a matter of time before it pushed him over the edge.

The worst part is that he didn't realise the hand wash was actually one of those refillable tubs so it didn't have a pump action at all. He was trying to achieve the impossible. What an awful waste - it was the expensive stuff too'.

Furlough scheme to be replaced with 'hopes and prayers'

More than a million workers are expected to lose their subsidized pay and instead be expected to be renumerated with gold coins, found at the end of a rainbow. Employers have been told they need to make up any shortfall, using unicorn tears and parts of The Maltese Falcon.

A spokeswoman for Works & Pensions explained: 'Applicants just need to track down King Pellinore's Questing Beast for the form, get it counter-signed by the Loch Ness Monster and

Amelia Earhart'. All correspondence should be addressed to Narnia.

One worker said: 'I was told there was good news and bad news. The bad news was, I was being paid with thin air. The good news was, there was lots of it'.

Rumsfeld 'doublespeak' death mystery

Conspiracy theorists are mystified as to the cause of the demise of US diplomat Donald Rumsfeld. They are demanding to know if he died of something we do know about, or do not know about. Or was it that he didn't die of something we do know about or something that we do not know about?

One leading theorist commented: 'There are things we know we know. But we also know there are known unknowns. So for all that I know, then who knows?'

Tolerance 'getting out of hand' say angry white male

We spoke to Bill (not his real name), an angry man in Stafford. 'I just want to know – when do we get a parade? The world has changed beyond all recognition. Even my local chippy now has a … bloke, do I call him that? … anyway, some days he's in a dress, some days trousers. The chips are as good as ever and I always chat to him, her – f*ck me, this is complicated.'

'In the good old days, I'd throw some good-natured banter about and if anybody didn't like it, we could get into a ruck. Nowadays, beat somebody to a pulp because they've got foreign skin or whatever and it's a hate crime. The police just need to be more, I dunno, tolerant.'

Kensington statue wins 'not looking like Diana' contest

A newly installed and finally unveiled statue at Kensington Palace has won the Not Looking Like Diana award against strong competition which included a house brick and a pile of sand.

The sculptor expressed his delight at recognition of his achievement. He explained that the head of the statue was achieved by doing an electronic morph-merge of the heads of all of the members of Duran Duran, that the torso was based on that of Aretha Franklin as seen in the movie Blues Brothers and the legs were based on those of Angela Rippon.

Husband starts up jogging. Suspicious wife plans divorce.

The marital harmony of Maya and Evan Jutson, was thrown into turmoil when Evan declared that he was going to 'dig out' the rusted exercise bike from the shed. Things progressed from strange to alarming, when he subsequently started cutting back on his cheese consumption, trimming his nose hairs and wearing spandex shorts in the garden.

Maya became increasingly concerned that Evan was cheating on her, the moment he taking up rumba classes and kale smoothies. 'He'd accepted growing old,' she commented. 'But now this sudden lease of life, what has he got to be so optimistic about? It has to be another woman or he's been radicalized by ISIS. I want the old Evan back. And his life insurance'.

Brewdog made from actual dogs

In a run of bad PR that would make Lucrezia Borgia blanch, the independent brewer has had to rebuff claims that it threatened Baby Yoda and punched a Care Bear.

In the last month, Brewdog have had to fend off accusations of false advertising, abusive work conditions and putting puppies into a cider press.

It has been one bad news story after another, culminating in the allegation that they knowingly revealed the ending to 'Game of Thrones'. Their catalogue of faux pas included killing Bambi's mother, being mean to Stephen Fry and disrespecting a baby penguin.

One particular drink, 'National Treasures', is made from the alcoholic remains of some of the UKs most beloved citizens. Dame Judi Dench has been reduced to a Light Ale, while Alan Bennett is now a Craft Beer, flavoured with cream crackers and scones.

A spokeswoman for the firm said: 'I know we've had some challenging headlines, but I'm hoping we can put that all behind us, with our new range of Nazi Nonce Beers'.

Four-day week a success, so UK opts for eight-day week

Reacting to the Icelandic study that a four-day week increases productivity and health, the British Government has decided not to give up on indentured servitude and gruel for breakfast. A spokeswoman said: 'If anything, the average Brit needs to work more hours. Those asbestos mines won't dig themselves, you know'.

The plan is to introduce an eighth day, with the additional time trimmed from your sleeping hours and the removal of Christmas. The name is still up for debate, but the front runners are 'DorisDay', 'Sunday Bloody Sunday' or 'Happy Mondays'.

Most of this day will be spent in a man-sized hamster wheel, while you are whipped by hooded figures from a Hieronymus Bosch painting. Medieval laments will form the background noises, alongside the whirring of a photocopier, the tapping of a keyboard and disgruntled murmurs of your work colleagues.

UK workers have greeted the eight-day week with a cheerful smile, as they doffed their caps and genuflected before a marble statue of the Queen's corgi. The Beatles said they loved it yeah yeah yeah, although, Craig David is said to be rather annoyed.

'Lego Gun' works by shooting the soles of your feet

A controversial gun, deliberately designed to resemble Lego blocks, has caused further alarm by mimicking the deadly impact of Lego on our feet. The customised Glock fires real bullets, but these bullets fall immediately to the floor and wait for an unsuspecting foot.

Since the invention of Lego in 1949, army hospitals have been filled with people with serious leg injuries and vacuum cleaners have been filled with small annoying bricks.

Danish toymaker Lego has already issued a cease-and-desist order to the American gun manufacturer, saying: 'It's our job to cause pain. Remember guns don't kill people. People accidently shooting others, when trying to shoot at tiny bits of Lego they have just stepped on, kill people'.

War Office denies Crimea plans jeopardised by secrets leak

A spokesperson briefing on behalf of Lord Cardigan said today that the discovery of top secret plans at a Hansom Cab rank would not affect the forthcoming military operations in Crimea. The documents, titled 'Operation Valley of Death' apparently described a cunning plan on how to neutralise Russian defences.

Reconnaissance has allegedly determined that there would be cannon to the left and cease-and-desist cannon to the right. The obvious solution was therefore to despatch a crack elite squadron (which reliable sources have identified as the Light Brigade) straight down the middle.

Asked about the possible impact on trooper morale as a result of this leak, the spokesperson added 'Theirs not to reason why'

Politics to be kept out of England v Germany tie
'When England players take the knee, it's Marxist.' said a white England fan who has the St George's Cross and Union Jack on his social media, despite not understanding the difference.

'Raheem Sterling banging on about a proletariat uprising to throw off the capitalist yoke. Marcus Rashford feeding kids! You shouldn't mix sport and politics that I don't like. Now, shall we sing "Two World Wars and one World Cup" or "Ten German bombers"?'

North Koreans heartbroken at Kim Jong-un's only slightly obese appearance

An unidentified resident of the country's capital, Pyongyang said: 'He used to be morbidly obese, but now he's only clinically obese – it's a real worry to us all. He was always so handsome, like a big, fat baby. The weight loss has aged him – he now looks like a chubby toddler.'

'We have been suffering from some food shortages here, but I would gladly take food from the mouths of my starving children to help our beloved leader return to his former glorious health and good looks.'

Reports that Kim Jong Un will shortly be releasing a book entitled 'Dictate, Lose Weight, Be Great!' are unconfirmed.

Football pundits forlorn after realising current players are better than them

There was a sullen and sombre air in the studio as former players tried to absorb the most recent England victory. It was clear that the terrible truth had gradually dawned on each one of them: England are now much better than any of us ever were. In fact, they have made us look like we were a bit sh*t.

Gone are the glory days of Euro 2016 when England suffered the wonderful humiliation of getting knocked out by Iceland in the last 16. The National Association of Football Pundits has admitted that they are only allowed on television in order. to release dangerous levels of pent-up angst. 'If we didn't let Roy Keane get it out of his system, then he'd be standing on a street corner in piss-stained trousers shouting at passers-by'.

Gary Lineker was in tears, while Alan Shearer's face expressed the same level of enthusiasm as an Easter Island statue that has just seen a wrecking ball coming towards it. A source close to the BBC has hinted that Lineker is already considering stepping down to dedicate more time to eating crisps for money. Shearer, on the other hand, remains stony-faced about his future.

Dumfries and Galloway Council sue George Galloway for bringing the name Galloway into disrepute.

Renowned pot stirrer and Iraq 'expert' George Galloway has launched a legal challenge against himself for being a total tool. Legal experts have dismissed the suit as frivolous: 'He's definitely a tool. Case closed.'

Shock as politician attends football match without his photographer

Ticket sales reveal that for the Euro Final, half of Wembley's seats are allocated to MPs 'on a freebie' and the other half to their press secretaries. Sadly, one unnamed backbencher, has forgotten to bring his camerawoman, rendering the whole ninety minutes a complete waste of everyone's time.

Said the MP: 'I thought I'd arranged everything. Oversized football shirt to wear over my suit. Check. Pint of working-class liquid, to hold – but not drink. Check. Selfie with Frank Skinner and that other fellow. Check. And then I looked for my official photographer and instead, just found some gormless football fan, painted red and white, leering back at me.

'This means, no carefully choreographed, spontaneous moments of joy. And normally, if I'd forgotten to cheer for a goal, my photographer would have asked the players to replay the previous five minutes'.

England football team to unite nation, say people who divided it

'It's coming home #euro2021,' tweeted the Home Secretary, before trying to deport it.

'Shows we were right to leave the EU cos we never won the Euros while we were in Europe,' agreed Nigel Walker, a shaven-headed cockwomble from Essex, lifting his knuckles from the floor for just long enough to wave an England flag in the air. 'Eng-er-land! Eng-er-land! But I'm sure all the Remoaner traitor Marxist scum will agree to keep politics out of it and get behind the team.'

Lamda variant 'not an 80s dance craze'

The World Health Organisation has responded to reports that people are confusing the Lamda COVID variant with the 1980s dance craze, the Lambada. A WHO spokesman said: 'I think it's very irresponsible to say the Lambada is harmless. The music is very infectious and I caught a nasty case of Lambada fever in 1989, which made me strain my back very badly. I still get twinges even now when I have to bend down to tie my shoelaces.'

Reports that a new COVID variant called the Macarena has been discovered are unconfirmed.

Commentator in training for full meltdown tonight

'On Wednesday, I pretty much aced the last minute of the England-Denmark match for TV viewers with a hysterical and possibly psycho-sexual gush of verbal diarrhoea, which went "Call your boss, you ain't coming in in the morning. You deserve this. England deserve this. Feel it, ride it."

'But that was just a semi-final. Now I must up the ante for the final so that I can really stick it to our Scottish, Welsh and Irish viewers with a truly monumental tirade of English jingoism. I have been reading Shakespearean soliloquies and the poetry of Rudyard Kipling for inspiration and I have decided that in the event of victory my immortal words will be: "England have won! Very much so! Albion Gloriana!"

'After that, the synapses in my brain will fuse together and I will run off at the mouth uncontrollably, urging the world's population to kiss Gareth Southgate's ring.'

We're full now, insist fridges

Fridges do not have room for any more cans or bottles, they have confirmed. Yet despite this, enthusiastic fridge stocker Dave Smith has been assessing the temperature of the under stairs cupboard and is considering nipping to the supermarket for more 'footy' beer supplies. Meanwhile in the fridge, the cottage cheese is squashed right at the back and thinking of leaking or freezing in protest, the half jar of gherkins is complaining about being overlooked for months and the lemon curd is looking sourly at the smug green Kronenburg 1664 interlopers.

Football calls ahead and asks you to pop the kettle on

Since last coming home in the 1966, football has travelled extensively, including extended spells in South America visiting Brazil and Argentina. It almost came home in 1990 and again in 1996, but both times made late decisions to go to Germany instead, where it spends so much time it has actually bought a second house.

While a cup of tea and a biscuit would be lovely if football does come home, don't go so far as to plan dinner around it, as there is a chance it will decide to pop over to Italy for a few years instead.

[EDITOR'S NOTE – 'We lost']

Lucrative pizza ads beckon for England's young lions after Wembley penalty woes

Even as a nation's tears flowed, following England's defeat in the final of the Euros at Wembley on Sunday, it turns out that it's not all bad news.

'This is amazing the way things have gone full circle,' said Gareth Southgate. 'There I was thinking this tournament was going to lay my ghosts to rest, but now I get a second chance to ride the gravy train again. Although, given we lost to Italy, another pizza advert is a bit harsh'.

Duchess of Cambridge self-isolating after wearing same jacket twice

Her Royal Highness has been forced to spend ten days isolating in her poky 20-room apartment at Kensington Palace after she was photographed in a jacket that she had worn more than once. This unforgivable faux pas is being blamed on staff, whose primary role is to burn every pre-worn item. The hapless aide who was last seen being accompanied down to the royal furnace by two burly footmen, was not available for comment.

'Who could have predicted trouble from this drunken, angry mob?' says Met Police

'How were we to know that large groups of football fans, who had been drinking solidly since early morning, might turn rowdy after England lost and take out their rage on opposition supporters? We are not clairvoyants.

'I stress that the Met's policy is to send large numbers of officers only to locations where we predict there will be disorder – such as a peace vigil or a Nunnery'.

COVID Scientists get own TV show

'They've been the real breakout stars of the whole pandemic,' a spokesperson for ITV said. 'They've captured the nation's heart with their ability to deliver absolutely dreadful news but maintain a twinkle in their eye. And their hugely popular 'Next slide please' catchphrase which is basically their entire act'.

'No, not that kind of racism' says PM.

Following the Euro 2020, the Prime Minister quickly condemn the kind of racists who have been a bit too obvious about it; with the slogan 'There's no room for football in racism'.

A Tory grandee interrupted his supper to bloviate: 'You can't just say you don't like black people. That's racist and wrong. Instead, you heavily imply you don't like black people by saying that taking the knee is gesture politics. Populism equals racism plus time – that's the Boris formula. That and wallpapering over his infidelities.

'You've got to keep your racism classy' he continued, before belching deeply.

Woman successfully buys bra online

Experienced bosom owner Sally Jones achieved the once in a lifetime triumph this week of buying a bra online which fitted her actual form, the actual shape she is now, rather than a shape she has been in the past, or may be in future, or might belong to a hypothetical woman that is not her.

Her day began as usual, with her putting on her old faithful pink T-shirt bra which has gone a bit tatty and which she finds the straps slip down on a bit more often than they used to. In the back of her mind, she was aware she'd ordered some up top smalls from M&S but she never hoped for one moment that this would be a successful transaction. She was fully expecting to be in the Post Office queue returning the tit pants on Saturday morning.

When the package arrived, she ignored it for an hour, knowing that never in all her years of having lady bumps to dress and a computer have the two aligned usefully. Bras bought online are always too tight, too loose or too lumpy, leading to a sort of slightly rude Goldilocks type scenario but disgruntled puppies not bears.

Eventually Sally Jones thought she may as well either cram her coconuts into something too small or let her sin cushions dangle as unsupported as a female MP who wants decent maternity leave. Sally carefully opened the package, ready for re-sealing it when her new bra had failed her, and was pleased by the lovely pistachio colour which had looked a bit different on the internet because they do, don't they?

She took off old faithful and noticed that the old guard and the new recruit seemed on the face of it to be of similar dimensions. She could still breathe after doing up new bra and when she looked in the mirror was astounded to see that her jubblies were well contained, with no pinching, overhang or spare space. "It's a titty bonanza!" exclaimed Sally.

Bolsonaro chronic hiccups is just his soul trying to escape

Reports that the Brazilian President is in hospital for hiccups, have been confused with the fact, that what little remains of his good conscience is leaving by the nearest available exit. Frustrated by residing in the body of crypto fascist, his remaining scruples were hoping to jump into the body of someone more kindly – like Ted Bundy.

Bolsonaro has been unable to stop hiccupping for the past ten days and has been unable to feel compassion for the last sixty years. The last twinge of guilt he experienced was when a talking cricket leapt on his shoulder to offer him moral advice, after which Bolsonaro demanded that his guards shoot the creature in the back of the head.

In fact, he is the first politician whose hiccups have lasted longer than his commitment to the environment. The President warned his soul that it would only leave over his dead body, to which the soul replied: 'That was kind of the point'.

Government brings back Witchfinder General

A spokeswoman confirmed: 'The greatest threats to the UK are goblins, witches and naughty looking goats lurking under bridges. No one could see any ongoing need for Health, Education or the Environment, so those departments have been axed with immediate effect. In their place, a colossal uber-department will be formed called the Department for the Eradication of Really Scary Stuff'.

Pandas are f*ck machines

It is official, pandas are off the endangered list and back on Tinder. Officially there are 1,800 pandas living in the wild - and boy, are they living it wild. Forests are now filled with the sound of rutting pandas and Barry White. After years of conservation and bucket loads of lube, China has declared that their 'furry f*ck monsters' are back in the saddle and 'ready to party'.

One Chinese scientist explained: 'We also needed to regenerate their natural habitat, which it turns out is a circular waterbed, draped in silk, with a mirrored ceiling. The pandas asked us to put some bamboo back into our forests, so they could 'put some wood' into theirs. Now they're swinging all over the place and we don't mean from the trees.'

Hauliers to join Government in being asleep at the wheel

A shortage in lorry drivers has kicked the world-beating UK Government ideas engine into overdrive. A spokesman said: 'If there are not enough lorry drivers, then we will just do what we are doing with doctors, nurses, teachers and everyone else: just make them work longer hours.

'Snoozy hauliers playing lamppost slalom dodgems on their way back from France is just the sort of thing Great Britain needs. Without that sense of danger on our British roads, the people just don't enjoy driving. Not like they used to when all of us drunkards ruled the highways.'

Prince Harry publishing memoirs, in case we've forgotten about his stuff

'The book will tell the public, for the tenth time over, how I went from being a confused, mixed-up kid to finding true purpose and happiness in my life, thanks to Meghan,' said Harry at a press conference in Montecito as he cast terrified glances at his wife.

'I realise this takes quite a bit of explaining,' he continued. 'Because up until a few years ago I was a happy, outgoing young guy and many people's favourite royal whereas now I am a miserable, self-obsessed shadow of my former self who is seemingly eaten up by anger and resentment. That all goes to show you the benefits of top-dollar psychotherapy and having the love of a woman like Meghan.'

Family shocked: 'We've got a bread maker?!?'

Despite the evidence to the contrary, the Begum family have denied all knowledge of the bread maker they have found at the back of one of their kitchen cupboards. The object in question, was discovered next to a series of other discarded items; a spiralizer, a waffle maker and the NHS trace & track App.

Gathering dust, no one could remember purchasing said item, let alone using it. 'When did we buy that?' asked Dad. 'Was it a deeply unromantic anniversary gift?' quizzed Mum 'Is it an old mobile phone?' said one of the kids.

The Begums from Manchester, are not alone in wondering why they have an electric pepper grinder and what the hell is an avocado holder? What started as an attempt to clear out a cupboard, has now revealed enough space to a fit a spare bedroom, with an ensuite.

Remarked Mum: 'It's just another unwanted thing, taking up space in the kitchen'. 'Just like me,' agreed Dad. 'Where do you put the SIM card?' said the kids, who had not been paying attention to any of this.

Trump sues NewsBiscuit for not writing about him

Donald Trump has included popular 'news' site NewsBiscuit in his lawsuit against Facebook, Twitter and Google, who he has accused of violating his freedom of speech.

'Those guys, they used to write about a lot, I mean lot, pretty much daily,' Trump told reporters. 'It was great to see my name, I didn't get the jokes but it was great, so great. But now, they don't, they don't ever write about me. And it's bad, very bad. It's so sad. Why aren't they writing about me?'

Militias form as PM says protecting Afghanistan is now 'personal responsibility'

Some members of the public are forming militias in their local pubs and workplaces in order to protect the troubled Central Asian nation from sliding into civil war again.

'It's just common sense, really,' said an office worker from Yorkshire who once participated in a reenactment of the English Civil War battle of Marston Moor. 'Besides, I've got annual leave to use up and I haven't been on holiday for a couple of years so it'll be nice to see a bit of sun! I'm double jabbed so I won't have to quarantine when I'm back either.'

Public urged to count butterflies to distract from the COVID numbers

A spokeswoman for the Big Butterfly Count said: 'Concentrate on all the pretty colours. A delicate butterfly. That's it. Lovely. Go to your happy place. Oh, look a rainbow! Whiskers on kittens. Marmalade on toast. Breath in. Breath out'. Rather than focus on doom and gloom, she has asked that we frolic through fields, towards the sunlit uplands of the Blue Remembered Hills, of Yesteryore.

The group were quick to emphasise that we should not be counting moths, as 'no one likes them'. Instead, if we just keep counting the sheep, I mean butterflies, we will soon drift off into a peaceful sleep, as opposed to COVID's eternal rest.

'Just enjoy the butterflies and ignore the COVID. The beautiful butterflies...which, incidentally, are all dying out due to climate change'.

Native Americans welcome US combat forces leaving US

Having unceremoniously withdrawn all its forces from Afghanistan, the US has promised to relinquish its hold on North America and honour its treaties with the Native Americans – if only for novelty's sake. Remarked one General: 'We came in 1607 and stayed a little bit longer than expected'.

'Our intention was to restore democracy to the region. One person, one vote. Yes, technically it ended up with us committing genocide but now that we are left with one Native American alive, it literally is one person one vote. Mission accomplished'.

The original military campaign, 'Operation Land Grab', was designed to stop the spread of Communism, two hundred years before it was invented. With more withdrawals planned in Iraq, the Pentagon has said it will demilitarize North America and focus on liberating other nations of their cash: 'We hear Switzerland needs democratizing, particularly their banking sector'.

Asked if this was another surrender, the General said it was just a tactical withdrawal: 'Obviously, we'll be taking all the Texas oil with us – it's only fair'

Starmer 'listening' tour, third on the bill after Showaddywaddy

Sir Keir has decided to tour the UK, in order to hear how people from lots of different regions 'don't like him very much'. Listening to the concerns of voters, will enable him to understand that regardless of demographic or political leanings, everyone thinks he is a bit of a numpty.

The tour itself is a little bit underwhelming, with Sir Keir only allowed a five-minute set ahead the main acts – a Timmy Mallett lookalike and a variety entertainer who swallows spoons.

The most embarrassing moment of the tour came when Keith (sic) held a focus group for members of his own family, who subsequently claimed never to have heard of him. His agent explained: 'This tour is about Keith reconnecting with his fans, but that presupposes there was a connection in the first place'.

Each performance culminates in a theatrical focus group, complete with pyrotechnics and questions such as - 'if the Labour Party was a jelly, what flavour would it be?'.

Unsurprisingly questions like 'why am I so sh*t?' do not illicit the sympathetic response that Sir Keir was hoping for but tend to lead to the focus group just shrugging and saying, 'you tell me'.

UK takes the lead in COVID Olympics

Long before the athletics starts, the UK is already leading the medal table with eight self-isolations and a bronze medal in track and trace. During events, athletes will have to clear vaccine passport hurdles, sprint for vaccines and take a hop, skip and jump based on sketchy data.

The Games will culminate in the COVID Relay, where British runners pass infected phlegm from one to another, over 100m and 400m. The closing ceremony, as hospitalizations peak, will be followed by the closing of the NHS.

Doing wheelies in traffic 'unavoidable' says teenager

Tests also showed that as the teenagers get older the less frequently the fault happens. 'We believe this to be down to accumulation of life experience - an unfulfilling job or broken dream weighs upon the rider, pinning the bike down, and somehow bypassing the fault,' said a spokesman.

'However, adult men with their tops off are also vulnerable. For reasons that are not yet clear, the presence of teenage girls in the vicinity increases the chances of the fault occurring by a whopping 50%.'

South China Sea extended to include Antarctic penguins

After China constructed a military airbase in Antarctica under the watchful eyes of a colony of chinstrap penguins, the Foreign Minister rejected suggestions China was militarizing the icy continent.

'China has always owned Antarctica. We have a map from 1947 with 90 dashes on it, the dashes go all the way round. And as early as the 13th century we were sending researchers there in ocean-going junks to investigate the climate'.

451

Virgin Galactic bus replacement service 'ready to go'

'As with the West Coast route, we appreciate that there may be issues on the day ranging from wrong beard in the cabin to the wrong kind of stratosphere,' said a Virgin spokesman today.

Most rocket experts believe the flight will take place regardless, but fully expect the toilet door to remain open for most of the flight.

COVID beaten, PM confirms

Looking resplendent in a bright yellow fluorescent hazmat suit with Prime Minister stencilled across his left breast alongside a union flag, the PM confirmed that: 'We've seen it off and that's an end to it once and for all. We've tanned its backside, flattened its sombrero, and given it a jolly good cuff around the ear just for good measure.'

'It certainly won't be back here anytime soon, killing hundreds and thousands of us left right and centre', he continued. 'But, in the unlikely event that it somehow does reappear, and that's highly unlikely Carrie tells me, then the public will only have itself to blame, as quite clearly it won't have been following our latest and most excellent advice.'

Dinosaurs to make comeback tour

Celebrity publicist Ed Masp, who claims he has represented many extinct species in the past, promises the comeback will be spectacular, including such acts as ripping trees up by the roots and squashing a Ford Mondeo with a tap of the foot.

However, there are concerns about letting gigantic reptiles run amok for entertainment purposes. The Dinosaur Vigilance Society explained: 'We are strongly urging insurance companies to refuse to cover this extravaganza. These are five-ton reptiles with brains weighing only three ounces, a brain to body mass ratio matched only by reality TV stars.

'In fact, the Mesozoic Era had an appalling record for health and safety, and dinosaurs must carry some of the blame. Except T-Rex – his hands are too small to carry anything'.

Cyclists demand the right to weave erratically through traffic

'The Government needs to recognise that donning multi-coloured Lycra and a cycling helmet with little flashing lights on it makes me invincible and entitles me to act as if I own the road,' explained Robert Keith, a keen cyclist and member of no cycling organisations whatsoever. 'Even though I pay no road tax, unlike all other road users', he added.

The new Highway Code advises...

- To avoid confusion about whether cyclists should ride on the road or pavement, they are now allowed to cycle on both. Additionally, they can also ride on bridleways, and through shopping malls, shops, car homes and schools. So, no more confusion

- The traffic light system has also been updated. A red light for traffic now officially means cyclists can travel through without looking. Similarly, a red traffic light for pedestrians also means cyclists can cross the road without looking. This has symmetrical elegance in law, but in practice changes nothing

- A new range of hand signals is to be made official too. If a single finger is displayed by a cyclist, this means "f*ck off it's my road". If the same signal is shown by a motorist to a cyclist, it means "please drive in front of me like a tw*t". If a motorist holds his first finger to his thumb while waving, this indicates that the cyclists tyre pressure needs adjusting

- Priority at roundabouts is also to change. Basically, cyclists have priority, and f*ck everyone else. This is current Government policy anyway

The latest Highway Code revision was signed off by the PM Boris Johnson, a cyclist

M&S to cut Christmas goods to Northern Ireland, but not their mawkish adverts

Under the terms of Brexit retailers have promised the worst of all worlds to Northern Ireland, no shopping but all the annoying paraphernalia, we associate with it. This means plenty of family rows and the obligatory sentimental advert - which this year features a reindeer on a dialysis machine, Santa struggling with Parkinson's and a slow acoustic rendition of Iron Maiden's 'The Number of the Beast' – sung by Dido.

'With all our shelves empty, we expect demand to exceed supply. So, we advise queue early, to avoid disappointment'.

Major supermarkets now selling fruit 'for display purposes only'

A retail industry spokeswoman explained: 'What we realised in 1988 was that the vast majority of the UK public had a strong desire to display bowls of lush-looking fruit at home, but no member of the family was actually allowed to eat it. 93.7% of all fruit purchased was to impress friends and neighbours, projecting the image of a household with a healthy-living lifestyle.

'Green bananas and rock-hard nectarines became the retail industry standard. We have now reached the edibility horizon where no fruit is sold which ever reaches a ripeness window. So, it is now a legal obligation for supermarkets to warn their customers that they should never actually attempt to eat any of the fruit they purchase."

Liverpool stripped of World Heritage status, forced to hand back The Beatles

Unbeknown to the majority of Liverpudlians, The Beatles were only on loan to the city, on the understanding that they never let Ringo sing. The UN committee said they needed to return the entire Beatles' back catalogue, but they could keep 'The Frog Chorus'.

Rather embarrassingly, the city had to explain that they had lost two of the original band and offered a tribute version of Gerry and the Pacemakers in part exchange. In a handover ceremony, the two remaining Beatles will be put back into cryogenic suspension, until Justin Bieber retires.

A UNESCO spokeswoman clarified: 'Sadly, Liverpool has abandoned its colourful history – like the slave trade and tobacco warehouses. All the beautiful architectural landmarks – celebrating slave owners – are being removed. It's a disgrace. They even tore down a priceless statue of a large pile of dead slaves, sponsored by Marlboro Lights'.

Liverpool will no longer have bragging rights to having the best band from the UK, that honour now passes to a skiffle band from Crawley. Said one despondent fan: 'Without The Beatles how am I going to know that modern music sounds sh*t?'

Man only booked holiday to cause scene at airport about having to wear mask

Serial complainer and seasoned scene-causer, Darren Bates, achieved a personal best yesterday, after a tedious two-hour stand-off. He explained later that he tries to 'choose his battles wisely' and usually only exercises his fundamental human right to be an awkward, petty gobshite.

Having randomly booked a last-minute deal without even bothering to check the destination, he eagerly set off for the airport with a self-righteous grin spread across his fully exposed face. The situation escalated into a very short-lived physical confrontation, which resulted in Bates being tasered by security staff and falling to the floor in a crumpled heap, soiling himself in the process.

The self-proclaimed 'defender of civil liberties' regained consciousness in a pool of his own urine outside the airport, just in time to see his delayed plane taking off. Bates said he had no regrets about his 'huge victory' and criminal charges. He revealed that, after nipping home to change his underpants, he is planning to go to London, a city he has never visited before, to protest about having to wear a mask on the tube.

Arms manufacturers recommend keeping aid at 0.75% of GDP

'The smart thing to do would be to keep this aid at the promised level' said the chairman of one multi-squillion pounds arms manufacturing company. 'Even if that necessitated an 0.00002% decrease in British defence spending to make good the financial cost.'

'Overseas aid provides a valuable boost to Britain's corporate image and such virtue-signalling enables us to preach patronisingly to other countries' he continued. 'And such a shift in Government spending wouldn't hurt our bottom line in the slightest.'

'The only difference would be that companies owned by myself and the other chums of Government ministers would simply sell our weapon systems to the countries receiving this aid, instead of to the British Ministry of Defence.'

Man 'stable' after draining cooked pasta water down the sink

A Retford man is expected to make a full recovery, after accidentally draining his starchy cooked pasta water straight down the sink, instead of retaining it to mix in with his pasta sauce, it has been confirmed.

The incident occurred whilst Pete McBride, 45, was doing some 'theatre cooking', rustling up a cheeky penne with arabiata sauce, for himself, his wife and 2 daughters, whilst they sat at the kitchen table.

'I don't know how it happened', confessed an upset McBride, after enduring a tense meal, punctuated only by quiet sobs from his 10-year-old daughter and complaints that the sauce was 'scarily bland' and just had not bound together at all.

'It is advice in every pasta recipe in every book. In fact, I could hear Ainsley Harriet's chirpy tones stressing that 'YOU MUST KEEP THE WATER, YOU MUST KEEP THE STARCHY WATER, YOU CAN ADD IT TO YOUR SAUCE' as I drained it down the sink through a colander'.

'It seemed to happen in slow motion', continued McBride. 'I could see my wife's mouth drop in horror. I panicked and quickly tried to add a bit of cornflour into the pasta sauce, and a few capers, but the sauce started congealing and lumping up before my eyes.'

McBride has agreed to undertake a process of rehabilitation, including basic refresher training in how to place an empty pan under the colander to collect water, as well as watching repeats of every episode of Saturday Kitchen ever.

Turd emoji quivers as Clippy returns

Microsoft has decided to replace the ubiquitous and functional paperclip emoji with a 3D representation of the hyperactive Clippy, last seen patronising word processor users with the observation 'You look like you're typing something', to which most writers typed 'No f*cking sh*t, Sherlock'.

Other emojis are surprised, with one raising a single eyebrow, and another frowned; however, the Emoji most concerned is the Turd. 'If you think I'm shit - wait until Clippy returns'.

Pingageddon as COVID app forces entire UK population to self-isolate

The UK has informed the world that it's now closed, and Downing Street has hung up a handwritten 'Closed - Back in Five Weeks' sign in the shop window. 'There is no pleasing some people - originally we were too slow to lockdown and now we've been too hasty in coming out of lockdown. Please rest assured that this Government will take imminent action should it need to take imminent action imminently'.

Woman ecstatic after finding an episode of Friends she hadn't seen

'I've always been a huge fan of the show and I thought I'd seen every episode but this was unbelievable, like discovering a new colour, opening the tomb of the Sphinx or crossing the Rubik's Cube.'

'I couldn't believe it. It's called: "The one where Joey buys toothpaste". I was mesmerised. For the first few minutes I couldn't move. Then the adverts came on and I started texting and messaging all my friends to let them know."

'Sally told me I had seen it before, but she was thinking of "The one where Chandler buys floss" and Karen said she's seen it but couldn't tell me what colour earrings Rachel was wearing, so I don't believe her.'

Nation pities poor Boris stoically self-isolating on massive country estate

A Government spokestosser confirmed: 'It might look to some like he will be living it up on a luxury holiday in the middle of summer, but that is not the case at all. There is a much-reduced skeleton staff, of only 28, at his every beck and call, so it will be a very hard time for him popping his socks off by the pool and sipping margaritas.

Number 10 to privatise Number 4

A spokesman for the Department of Digital Ineptitude, Culture Wars, Media Suppression and Sport Bandwagon-Jumping said: 'It's all to do with the changing numerical landscape. 2 plus 2 is 4, but 2 times 2 is also 4.

'That's typical public sector wastefulness. We've pretty much privatised number 10 already. Three is the magic number. Yes, it is, it's the magic number, but it's also a big mobile phone company already. We also can't privatise 9, because 7 ate it.

'How much do you think we could get for the number 4 made up of the spinning coloured rectangles?'

Oscar Oldroyd, who turns four next month and whose birthday party would be cancelled, said: 'Boris is a poo-poo head'. Oscar's parents both nodded sadly in agreement.

Olympic sports you ludicrously think you could medal in

- BMX Racing – when you were 11 you spent your summer holiday arseing around a disused scrap yard on your Raleigh Grifter, so you definitely have the pedigree. You'd have been even better if your mum hadn't kept calling you in for your dinner. With success directly correlated to being a twat and taking out your opponents on the first corner, you'll be quids in.

- Shooting – A socially awkward man lies immobile for hours on end, blocking out all external stimuli, and occasionally pulling a trigger and hitting a target. It's a perfect description of your last 5 years playing Call of Duty in your darkened spare room, if you add in a crate of Monster Energy drinks and regular masturbation breaks. The podium awaits.

- Modern Pentathlon – Fencing, swimming, show-jumping, shooting, and cross-country skiing. An unfathomable collection of sports, seemingly thrown together by the Marketing Team at Centre Parcs. Luckily for you, you developed significant prowess in all of them at Big Rich's stag do at that stately home last year, alongside coke-snorting.

- Surfing - Bottom turns, cutbacks, off the lips…. the uninterested instructor mentioned all these moves in the over-priced surfing lesson you took on a recent family holiday at Newquay. You've watched Point Break hundreds of times, and after you win gold, you've already got your Donald Trump '5th president' mask ready to slip on as a joke as the National Anthem plays.

- Breakdancing – frustratingly, not included as a medal event until Paris 2024, meaning another 3 years before you can unleash those windmills and headspins that you perfected at the school disco 30 years ago. You are confident of a medal, as long as don't get distracted again by school bully telling you that you have a very small penis and you've got no chance of getting off with Michelle in the gym tonight.

Let Freedom Ring by COVID-19

Let freedom ring down on the London underground, where passengers breathe particulates over one another with the force of a thousand hurricanes.

Let freedom ring on Chequers, where poor Boris Johnson is humiliatingly trapped at home.

Let freedom ring on the schools and the poorest communities where all our unvaccinated lie.

Let freedom ring.

From the busiest aisles of Tesco to the crumbling care homes of Chichester. From the heaving clubs of Soho to the pubs of Penzance, hear my rallying cry:

Free at last, free at last, thank Boris almighty, I am free at last!

I had a dream that one day my variants and my variants' variants would be able to sit down together at the table of a Wetherspoons in Stoke and mix freely with the public.

And that dream came true today…unless we get another Lockdown. Then all bets are off.

Met Office warns it could be hotter than the surface of the sun by Friday

'5,600 degrees is nothing we can't handle', said Kevin Fullicks, a resident of Margate. 'It's about time we had a decent summer.

'I was a Desert Rat so I'm used to the heat. Admittedly this will be a different kind of heat, the kind that can vaporise your face off if you don't take precautions. I've invested in 96 bottles of factor two million sun cream for the kids so they should be alright'.

New nanoparticle still not small enough for Tommy Robinson violin

Following the news that true Brit, son of Irish Immigrants Stephen Yaxley-Lennon - better known to his puce-faced supporters as Tommy Robinson - has lost a £100,000 libel case brought by a Syrian Refugee, Materials Scientists at the Diamond Light Synchrotron in Oxfordshire have admitted defeat in developing a material capable of building a violin small enough to play in sympathy. Said a sarcastic spokeswoman: 'What a shame'.

Woman posting about being too busy not too busy to post about how busy she is

Modern day hero Laura Smith, dubbed 'Britain's busiest woman', has posted a series of social media updates explaining in detail how incredibly busy she is. Her latest post read 'OMG sorry if I'm slow replying to msgs I'm CRAZY busy - send help & wine LOL!!' before going on to explain she has to attend a lunch with a friend, a hot yoga class, book her BMW in for an MOT and get her eyebrows waxed. She finished up the post with #sleepistheweak #cantstopwontstop.

Many have called her a 'martyr' and a 'role model'. Her oldest friend Cara explains: 'She's always been like this. Never too busy to stop and tell us how busy she is. Even at primary school I remember her making this speech about how busy she was with PE, English and Maths that day. Of course, we all were, but coming from Laura it was inspirational. We gave her a round of applause.'

Laura is planning to start a blog detailing how busy she is in even greater depth, with updates to include how many unread emails she has and how many items are on her to-do list.

Laura's partner Paul is in awe of her resilience and strength: 'She's amazing, every day when I get back from a twelve-hour shift at the hospital, she finds the time to talk to me about how busy she is.

'I try to stay awake for those three or four hours but often succumb to sleep which I feel terrible about. Occasionally I do try and tell her how busy I've been at work, with the dangerous staff shortages and overwhelming number of critically ill patients, but she's understandably too busy.

Air con more expensive than cocaine

A former AC dealer spoke on condition of anonymity: 'I was mixed up in the 'air' scene, yeah, but it's just too brutal now, so I've gone back to dealing heroin. I knew a John Lewis delivery guy, dropped off a water cooler by mistake. Nice neighbourhood. They beat him to death with it and left him by the side of the road like a warning.'

A fixer for the PM, self-isolating at Chequers said: 'It's hot and he's confined to base, avoiding COVID blame, so he's frisky. The chef said we were having roast pork and I didn't like the faraway look in his eye. Send AC and nudes.'

Couple who booked a holiday of a lifetime in Leicester still waiting for refund

After a roller-coaster of worry, Bill and Margaret Evans have had their non-refundable holiday ruined. 'We re-mortgaged the house and even renegotiated our Sky package to afford the holiday,' said Bill, while acknowledging the Sky deal had 'backfired a little' as he ended up paying £30 a month more. 'But I did get Sky Sports added,' he said.

'We normally make sound decisions - we backed the winning side in the Brexit vote and feel we were instrumental in ensuring the best team possible was in charge for the coronavirus pandemic. This was such an unexpected situation especially as we book this once in a lifetime holiday every year,' he said.

When asked about insurance, Bill shrugged. 'Like I say, we make sound decisions and generally leave that one until the night before - no point spending money on something you'll never need,' he said.

The easiest way to tackle crime is to take potential victims off the street

A Government spokeswoman said: 'We are aiming for a 100% anti-victim tolerance levels....no victim of crime will be safe on our streets. Victims of burglary will have their remaining possessions confiscated so that they cannot be burgled again. Drug dealers will be forced to make home deliveries, making it easier for police to identify and prosecute drug users.

All future bus shelters would come pre-vandalised, councils would be asked to scatter used syringes and broken glass around playgrounds to deter kiddies from playing on the swings and any remaining youth club would be forced to close although this last initiative has probably already happened'.

Study reveals difference between self-absorbed narcissist and slackers

A study carried out by Nottingham University has revealed that people who spend hours and hours in front of a mirror working on their body image look marginally better than those who could not give a toss.

'Men who spent over an hour each morning showering, applying oil and charcoal cleanser to their skin, preening their facial hair and working on the perfect fade, tended to look slightly better than those who had a quick shower, dragged a comb through their hair, applied some roll-on deodorant and gargled with a bit of mouth wash.

Likewise, women who spend hours getting their eye liner and blush just right looked better than those who simply used a wet wipe or a damp cloth to freshen up in the morning.

'Our next study will be trying to find out why attractive young men and women always seem to fall for older partners with pots of money. We think the findings might astonish some people'

Witch King of Angmar condemned by orc rank and file

The Witch King of Angmar, Lord of the Nazgul, has been condemned by Lugburz Grishnakh - leader of the Orc Federation as 'useless and not representing the interests of our members'.

Mr Grishnakh, representing orc and cave troll rank and file said: 'He has lost the confidence of the federation. The proposed increase in man-flesh allowance to seven kilos a day is nothing less than an insult'.

The Witch King, widely seen as a divisive, bullying, tyrant with no moral compass, no inter-personal skills and very little understanding of anything at all, responded to reporters, saying 'Sssssssssssssssssssssssssssssssssss', before mounting his government-issue giant reptile type thing and flying off.

Employees who murder their boss 'more likely to be promoted'

Killing your boss may be a better career move than sucking up to him, a new study by a leading recruitment think tank claims. 'Anyone seriously interested in advancing their career should be investing in a meat cleaver or a length of lead piping,' said Glen Pattison of Recruitment Strategies Institute. 'An ounce of blunt instrument is worth a ton of hard work and sycophancy.'

Office manager Greg Linney, 38, of Northampton, agrees as his career is flying and his obnoxious ex-team leader is now encased in concrete under his patio. 'Laughing at his jokes and letting him win at golf just wasn't working out,' said Linney. 'So, I invited him back to my place 'for a few cans' and wallop! I haven't looked back since. I still use his left testicle as a paperweight.'

Protest at ban of shitty fingered 'anti-hand washers' from finger-food buffet

People who refuse to wash their hands after shitting are protesting for being denied access to finger-food buffets, in countries fortunate enough to offer free hand washing.

Finger-food buffet organisers note that while different hand washing detergents offer different risks and benefits, all options are better than eating with shitty fingers.

One protester said: 'Of course we should have the choice to not wash our hands after shitting, my hands my choice, but how dare people not make us welcome to share finger foods with them at their private functions. It's like sticking two shitty fingers up to freedom.

Tom Daley wins gold in synchronized tube station diving

The British aquatic sport's poster boy excelled in the brand new event that was introduced to take full advantage of Climate Change induced flash-flooding wherever it occurs. Despite a packed station, Daley saw off a late surge from the Chinese divers and dazzled judges with his trademark pike, which he managed to execute from a potentially dangerous static escalator and feral rats.

However, the young diving wonder was left distraught after discovering that his Oyster Card was completely soggy and is no longer recognised by the purpose-built scanning devices. 'Sadly, I've been fined £250 for performing a triple forward splash without a valid ticket to Tottenham Court Road.'

Passport Control officials to re-train as nightclub bouncers

These staff will be re-trained to scrutinise a different set of passport documentation than they are used to and then use their powers of discretion to admit attractive groups of girls out on a hen night, attractive girls with barely anything on, girls that may be less attractive but could be up for it, and maybe some young, weedy lads that they could punch into the middle of next week if they felt like it. They will also be trained to feel like it.

Queue mismanagement is one aspect of the job that will be very familiar to former passport control personnel. Many are used to having one official dealing slowly and painstakingly with the longest queue while four others are on duty in the fast-track route having a brief sociable chat with people as they breeze past. This will simply be replicated for the public entrance compared to the VIP and Mates of Doormen entrance.

467

Others may need reassurance that wearing trainers is sufficient grounds for saying, 'I don't care what you say or who you are, it's up to me and I say you're not coming in.'

Marble Arch mound to get World Heritage status, Westminster Council claims

Despite universal criticism by everyone who has had the misfortune to see it, council leaders still insist that the Marble Arch Mound will easily overtake Dame Judi Dench as one of the most visited monuments in Britain.

Currently it resembles something Fred Dibnah would have demolished in the 1980s, rather than a ridiculously expensive urban art installation that people are actually supposed to pay money to walk up.

This has led to a barrage of complaints from the public, who object to having to fork out money for clambering up a dangerous pile of scaffolding that may collapse and kill them at any moment, a feat usually only attempted free of charge by very drunk people trying to show off to their mates. Said the Council: 'But unlike Stonehenge, at least our mound is finished'.

Crimestoppers hit by gobstoppers

Crimestoppers' campaign to attract younger informants by offering free gobstoppers has 'bockfried' according to its CEO Mike Smythe. 'Wore delsuhed wish gogshoppers an ish haulding bock our walk,' he commented. 'The pobom is theshe kids ahre phobing in to roport crimesh boct thore onintelligible ccosh they have got mauves foll of gogshockers we our shelves has hambid oup.'

It is understood that Smythe and his team have tried to diminish their pile of donated gobstoppers held at Crimestoppers HQ with a concentrated sucking campaign, which has led to call centre workers and those that call them having conversations neither can understand.

Mr Smythe said: 'This hash memp a pershect shtorn, cobbubications wives, wiv urshent crimesh mishreforted.' The problem has been compounded by the fact that the 480 kilos of gobstoppers that Crimestoppers thought were a charitable donation were actually stolen with, say Crimestoppers.

'The intention of pervorting the cosh of juss pish'. This has led to the organisation launching a nationwide helpline to catch the confectionery thieves.

Mr Smythe said ;'Anygun wish informashoh shoub call ush om: oh aitch humbled aitch fibe nibe five. I'll repeach that oh aitch humbled aitch fye nibe fibe.'

Family actually prefers my armchair Olympic commentaries, says Dad

Pete McBride, 47, has been delivering haiku style summaries of every Olympic performer from his Laz-E-Boy recliner since the early hours of Saturday morning, ranging from the gymnastics floor event ('he pulled out of that planche to handstand there') to tae-kwon do ('that's surely got to be a gam-jeon'?).

'I think the family likes to know what's going on - the official commentators just seem to miss some of key kernels of insight', said McBride, with one eye on the Men's triathlon. 'I see my role as a kind of public information service.... oh, that's a sloppy transition from the bike from the Ukrainian there - that's going to cost him'.

'My family look to be 'in the red' already in terms of stamina', summarised McBride excitedly. 'They'll need to dig deep if they've any hope of making it through to finals day with me. Otherwise, they'll unfortunately go into the repechage'

Man on bus really looking forward to coughing all over you again

A man has told journalists he cannot contain his emotions, or his phlegm, after Boris gave the go-ahead to dropping public health recommendations yesterday. This man's freedom, along with his hacking cough and profusely runny nose, shall no longer be shackled by central Government diktats.

'Finally, the chance I've been waiting for,' enthused the man, sneezing profusely.

Five Go Dobbing in the Neighbours

In more news...

Three Lions songsheet to come with bottle of Tippex and Letraset numbers

Delight as plucky England secure second place in regional football contest

Matt Hancock ready for work return as 'I was already coming in the office twice a week'

World of darts in mourning as legend Andy Fordham checks out for last time

Jeff Bezos returns to earth in neighbour's garden

Cameron lacked judgement over Greensill. Just Greensill?

Paperclip-thin contestant wins MS Word competition

COVID confusion after GB's Olympic table tennis team gets pinged then ponged

Extra-marital affairs to become 'personal choice' on 19th July, says Government

Grammar pedants furious after Pope Francis has colon removed

Scotland to ease COVID restrictions but sporrans still mandatory

Popular websites offline during internet outage; NewsBiscuit fine

Government introduces draught legislation to stop rattling windows

Budgie given Prozac to make it cheep and cheerful

Chocolate thief captured after bounty put on his head

Baroque musicians taking work when they can get it in the new gigue economy

Hoover owner wonders what all the anti-vax protests are all about

Vaccine sceptic refuses to accept that he is dead

Wanted: pilot for Tardis. Please no time-wasters

London Zoo pangolins panged

Football fan caught trespassing on Durham estate claims: 'It's Cummings' home'

Annual meeting of the Botox federation fails to raise any eyebrows

Dating website for virologists helps them find shingles in their area

'Double jab' campaign to be spearheaded by John Prescott

Government orders England to lose as it can't afford to pay import duty on the trophy

New TV station reveals that GB stands for 'Good Bye'

Advances in carbon dating expected to lead to carbon engagement

Man absolutely point blank refuses to go on assertiveness course

Tower Bridge sues Stonehenge in landmark case

Public raise Government threat level to "omni-cluster-shambles-f*@k"

Cleared sub-postmasters' compensation cheques in post

PM orders huge carpet to sweep troubles under

Defendant swears he was sitting at home when his Tesla robbed bank

Wikipedia to be replaced by 'what that man in the pub said'

Makers of Monopoly investigated for monopoly on Monopoly

Man finally completes online health and safety training, three years after retiring

Wikipedia celebrates 200th birthday

Samsonite confirm they have thousands of new cases

Researchers find all Scots called Angus already have herd immunity

Women now throwing incontinence knickers at Tom Jones

Gold medallist Matt Walls not as dull as he's painted

August 2021

Messi leaves Barcelona, finally finishing his COVID quarantine after 16 years. Transgender rights angered exactly the kind of people you would expect. The RNLI were criticised for saving lives – which was contrary to the UK's COVID policy. And the Olympics were just surreal. Oh, and the Taliban won – which was a bit awks.

UK's most popular holiday destination 2021 'the M5 southbound'

Many families are enjoying a full two-week break in queueing traffic, before briefly popping to Cornwall to enjoy some crowds and rain for twenty minutes. After this, most immediately begin their second holiday of the summer - on the M5 northbound.

Tony and Carol Stone were originally planning to take their three children to a static caravan in Cornwall but quickly realised an M5 holiday was the best option: 'It was a no-brainer' explained Tony.

'Firstly, the caravan was going to cost about £20k a week due to high demand. Secondly, looking at the journey time, we were going to average around one mile an hour on the way down. So, it only made sense to turn the journey into our holiday. It's been brilliant. We've had great fun pissing on the side of the road and the kids have learnt some new assertive hand gestures.'

Carol isn't as positive about the experience: 'I can't believe I'm spending my summer holiday queuing on the M5. I told Tony we should holiday in a queue at Heathrow instead but he wouldn't listen. The kids haven't even had an ice cream at the services yet, Tony said the queues are too long'.

NASA confirm Bezos and Branson are first men to reach the complete waste of space

'The idiots only went 53 miles up for f*ck's sake', said the head of NASA, dismissing the achievement of two billionaires tw*tting about in space. 'And just because they wanked around with floating piss bubbles for ten minutes doesn't mean they are astronauts in any shape or form.

'Space doesn't officially start until 62 miles from earth, and by our precise satellite computerisations, all they reached was the complete waste of space. It's so pointless we don't know what to do with it. I mean, you can't plant a flag in it or even play golf, for that matter. Goddam c*cksuckers.'

'One trivial step for mankind. One giant leap in tax avoidance'

X Factor 'scam' fails to make boot camp

An ITV spokesman said: 'It took us a while to twig, but the penny finally dropped when we were having an Exec quiz night at the pub. One question was: Name five winners of the X Factor, but between us we just got one and we had the show's commissioning editor on our team!

'When he pitched the show, Simon said it was a new concept, and certainly not in the least bit like Opportunity Knocks or New Faces of bygone days. "It's designed to make unknown wannabes into stars," he told us. Well quite clearly that was a whopping lie, so we're closing down the whole sick scam.'

Just for five minutes, you can dream that Messi will join your club

With the news that Lionel Messi is parting ways with Barcelona, every football fan can briefly indulge his fantasy that Messi will want to join a crap English team playing in the dour, windswept town you live in. For a fleeting moment you can imagine that he will want to trade sunny Spain for getting kicked up and down your local pitch.

Remarked one fan: 'He could go to PSG or Chelsea but I suspect he'll plump for Gosport. We've got one wooden stand, a spare ball and all the pies he can eat'.

Another said: 'Our pub team can always use someone a bit nippy'. Said one Akela: 'There will always be a place for young Lionel, in our under-9s cub team. But he will have to supply his own woggle'.

Home Office to retain COVID measures 'just in case'

The British Army – renamed 'The Devolutionary Guard' - has been deployed, under the guise of 'Operation Rescript'. This allows fully armed soldiers to shoot on sight anyone without a Union Jack mask. Secondly, the airports have been largely shut down to prevent foreigners from arriving, and to imprison those who do - but mainly to stop British nationals from escaping leaving.

Mexico demands Trump's Wall be bulletproof

With over 70% of all illegal guns coming from the US, Mexicans have finally fallen in love with the border wall. Said one: 'Oh, I get it now. The wall is to keep the Americans out, I see. Great idea.'

The Mexican Government is also proposing to sue the US gun manufacturers for making the Tobacco industry look ethical. They are hoping to get $10 billion in damages and the Alamo declared null and void.

Meanwhile they propose that the wall is draped in Kevlar and that any gun entering Mexico have a Green Card. Explained one

Mexican lawyer: 'The trouble is, if you let one gun over the border, you facilitate all the guns they are related to joining them. You let one 18th century musket in and before you know it, we're up to our necks in lazy grenade launchers'.

Pepys Diary: Olympickes

Up early and by coach to the Tower at the invitation of the British Beheading Committee to witness a gruelling day of Torture.

First, to the Racke. A number of persons of note were tested thereon, but Milord Javid came to the fore with a final length of seven feet. Well played, and he did not cower once, though the inquisitor tested him sorely.

Next to the Water Butte. A small crowd for this event. I might have said Andrew Neil came out on top. However, he did not resurface as his form fitted the barrel so well that none could pull him back out. T'was a sight to see his wig float to the surface.

On the way to the next room, saw Katie Hopkins chained to the wall wearing a Scold's Bridle. She tried to kick out at any who passed but we rejoiced in finding that Harridan's tongue finally quelled.

The next room contained a group of idle vagabonds in stocks. At first, one might find their Trial as naught but, as time passed, we could see that Wretches were close to losing their minds. They had spent the whole day listening to one Clare Balding spouting piffle on subjects no-one had any ken of. She spoke of a Skateboard that appears to be a vehicle propelled by leg-power and ridden over obstacles. Madness!

From thence to the Mall for supper. On the way did see two youths thrown from the Tower into the Moat. Tom Daley and

Matty Lee did fall as one. They rose from the waters to great acclamation from the persons assembled and were presented with ribbons for surviving their Ordeal.

Terry Pratchett 'never liked fantasy' says journalist who never read his books

Despite his words, his actions and the testimony of friends and family, many now believe that the author of 41 Discworld novels, had nothing to do with the SciFi/Fantasy genre. Said one journalist: 'I've researched him thoroughly and can confirm he never wrote The Lord of the Rings.

'I'll go further. I don't believe there is any evidence that he knew how to write or that his name was Pratchett. And if I'm wrong, why doesn't he say so? And don't use the excuse that he's been dead since 2015. That means nothing'.

An alarming number of journalists and commentators have been co-opting dead people to support their spurious arguments. Said one: 'Oscar Wilde was anti-LGBTQ+. How do I know? Ouija board.'

Meanwhile Pratchett's most famous work 'The Colour of Magic' was dismissed as containing no reference to fantasy whatsoever. Remarked one smug journalist: 'It's not as if it has magic in the title.'

Williamson insists 'rumpy pumpy' must be in Latin

The Education Secretary has demanded that Latin be taught in all schools to describe all carnal acts and order from the wine menu. Coitus and cunnilingus will make a return to the curriculum, although for Eton they never left the entrance exam.

An education spokesman explained: 'It's vitally important that school children learn the correct terminology for the sexual acts Ministers will one day be paying them to do. No matter how depraved, the Romans and Bullingdon Club have a name for it'.

Met Police officer 'shamed' for having committed no crime

PC Josh Frost, 31, has been suspended from duties pending an enquiry into his lack of illicit behaviour and his reluctance to beat up students. He even flunked joining the armed police, SCO19, as he refused to shoot the wrong person. However, there is one crime they hope to pin on him – impersonating a police officer.

North and South Korea open phone hotline, only to be plagued by telemarketing

Having just agreed to restore their emergency phone link, the Governments of North and South Korea have had non-stop calls asking: 'Have you or a loved one, recently been involved in an accident - diplomatic or nuclear?'

North Korea complained that they were constantly being offered pyramid schemes, until they realised it was just South Korea trying to explain 21st century capitalism to them. They also said they had received an anonymous call demanding peace in the region, but they just dismissed it as a scam.

Post-event interviews with Olympians to include general knowledge round

'Some of the answers given by breathless and emotional GB athletes less than a minute after they've either just fulfilled their lifetime dream or had their expectations cruelly crushed in front of millions are remarkably similar', said a TV spokesperson.

'Gave it everything I had, hasn't sunk in yet, I just blew it, thanks for all the support back home. It's as if they're all copying each other. The format needs a total overhaul'.

'Duncan Scott may have just become the most decorated GB Olympian at a single game, but can he tell us what's the second highest mountain in the Andes, whilst still dripping wet, exhausted and unable to string a sentence together?' said the spokesperson.

'360-degree backflips on a BMX are all well and good but does Charlotte Worthington know what the longest running musical theatre show is in the West End? The nation needs to know.'

RNLI ignoring fishing quotas, says Farage

The French and British have long held a maritime agreement that for every cod caught, they have to drop a Syrian child into the sea. Despite this, Nigel Farage claims that due to the unwanted diligence of the lifeboat service, fish will soon outnumber drowned migrants.

Explained one migrant, who in Nigel's imagination was really an international drugs warlord: 'We cunningly take ourselves to the point of death and then sneakily get a lift back to the mainland'. Asked why, if he was an international drug lord, did he not just get a fake passport and pop over on the ferry, he replied: 'Um...er...'.

Thankfully, the UK Government has agreed to send gunboats to sink the RNLI vessels.

Tories launch their latest 'Sizzling Summer of Sleaze'

In keeping with an age-old tradition, this year's Summer Sleaze plot revolves around the Conservative Party raising millions of pounds for its coffers by connecting squillionaires with

Government ministers at its secret masked balls and no one getting prosecuted for it afterwards.

'They're a bit like pantomimes,' said the party chairman, 'except they're not that funny and they never have a happy ending. It's a sop we like to throw to the taxpaying plebs. It gives them the chance to boo and hiss the ruling party to their hearts' delight and then forget all about it until the next scandal erupts, which ironically will be some time before Christmas.'

'Desperate' WHO seeks guidance from Facebook headbanger

'With our scientists at a loss and our medical experts at their lowest ebb, we have decided to ask for help from a feeble-minded, conspiracy f*cknut from Facebook,' the WHO has announced. 'Hopefully, he'll be able to put us straight on the futility of deploying a vaccine programme worldwide and steer us onto a more clear-headed path that involves Tom Hanks, COVID-19 5G lamppost-based transmitters and urging people to attend mass bleach-drinking rallies across the globe.'

This latest volte-face comes just a week after the Health Secretary, issued a directive, urging Brits to push homoeopathic capsules containing grass cuttings up each other's bottoms if they start losing their sense of taste and smell as previously suggested by somebody's Aunty Beryl on Twitter.

Man admits object is 'heavy' and not 'just awkward'

A man has commented on the chest of drawers he was struggling with, saying: 'Do they have rocks in or something?'

His girlfriend visibly rolled her eyes, adding: 'They have socks in. Plus, pants, maybe a few towels? To be fair, they are quite heavy but when I tried to help, he said he didn't need me. So instead, I got some custard creams, curled up on an armchair and watched 45 minutes of solid gold entertainment.'

Traffic lights on UK roads to have 50 shades of amber

Road users will be required to instantly distinguish and know the meaning of massive boards of 50 lights, each lamp a slightly different shade of amber. Sometimes some of them will be on, sometimes others, sometimes some will blink, sometimes some will come on, and then immediately go off again the moment drivers have proceeded. Most importantly, anyone finding themselves stranded in a mangled wreck of twisted steel in the middle of a road will just see Red.

Olympic Committee set to invent ever more ludicrous cycling events

From the 'formation taking it in turns' competition, which sees the race leader cycling up the banking and then joining in again at the back of the queue for no apparent reason, to the 'dick about for a lap or two and then pedal like you're trying to set your Lycra codpiece on fire' contests, the popularity of watching outrageously daft Olympic cycling events has never been higher.

The highlight of the velodrome's exhibition of preposterousness is currently the mysterious Keirin, in which cyclists follow a prospective cab driver doing 'The Knowledge' on a strange moped for several laps and then decide to go off on their own when he refuses to go south of the river. A more incongruous event is difficult to envisage but the Olympic experts are undaunted.

'Our vision is to have a track cycling event that transfixes the entire world with its silliness', explained a spokesman for the Olympic Cycling Committee. 'Mind you,' he admitted, 'We'll never be able to compete with dressage.'

iPhone 12 to come without headphones, charger or any physical properties

Apple's new iPhone is entirely imaginary, it can be revealed. Appearing as a theoretical emoji at the world's first metaphysical launch event, CEO Tim Cook silently drew a representation of his wallet with an esoteric air-gesture as the souls of Apple fans spiralled down an invisible vortex into a giant, Scrooge McDuck-like money bin.

'The headphone is a lie,' echoed a monotone, disembodied voice beamed directly into the minds of the faithful. 'Sound is nothing more than an echo of truth. Send me your bank details'.

The iPhone 12 retails at £799 and is simply a mimed box containing nothing but a slowly fading whisper of an idea. The iPhone 12 Pro costs more and does not come with the box.

Thatcher posthumously awarded 'inadvertent eco-warrior'

Prime Minister and inadvertent PR genius Boris Johnson has revealed that Margaret Thatcher was in fact a trailblazing eco-warrior – by closing all the coalmines. Boris himself is just like a real-life miner due to his relentless ability to dig himself big holes and accumulate a lot of dirt on himself.

Johnson to ring Sturgeon's doorbell then run away

Boris Johnson is visiting Scotland for as little time as he can possibly get away with before too many Scottish people notice he is there and chase him out of the country. A Tory spokesman looked appalled at the prospect of travelling so far from Surrey.

'How frightful! The PM is compelled to visit the wild, uncivilised, frozen north, Jocksville or Scotchland or whatever it's called, in order to pretend we care about countries other than England. Trust me, it will be hit and run – a bit like Boris' marriages.'

Strictly Bombshell: Farage to compete in first-ever crypto/fascist pairing

In a statement released last night, the show's producers revealed: 'We are all about diversity and acceptance and are therefore delighted to welcome Nigel to the show and look forward to seeing the extreme right-wing headbanger showing audiences what he can do, beyond convincing intellectually-challenged people to vote for a measure that will effectively chop the country's balls off in an act of fiscal and cultural suicide'.

It is understood that the production company also approached reviled, hate-peddler Katie Hopkins with an offer to appear on the show but rowed back when she demanded the right to call for the machine-gunning of dinghies containing immigrants in the English Channel during interviews with Claudia Winkelman after each stint under the iconic glitterball.

A delighted Farage spoke briefly to newsmen from outside his home last night: 'If my partner tries to lead off at the start of our performance, I certainly won't hesitate to take back control', he chuckled.

COVID Passport will be a coin toss

An NHS spokesperson has explained how the new COVID passport will work. 'We've moved on from a bloke in a lab to holding a sample up to the light and say 'looks all right to me',' he said.

'Our new system is cheaper, quicker and no less random. Upon disembarking, every passenger must queue up, pay £50 and then shuffle past a grumpy Border Force official who spins a coin and says: 'heads: you're clear' or 'tails: go into quarantine in a hotel and spend £2,000 you can't afford.'

It is thought the coin toss test was dreamt up on the spot by prime minister Boris Johnson during a cabinet meeting while ministers were playing 'spin the bottle' to decide who would be the next chief executive of the NHS.

Odysseus slams today's travel whingers

'Blimey! A few hours waiting for test results. Maybe having to self-isolate for a week when you get home. It took me ten years to get back. And that's after ten years fighting the Trojan War for flip's sake!' the King of Ithaca has stated.

'Red or amber? Huh. Try sneaking back to your boat under the belly of a sheep. Weather a bit rough? What about rowing between the six-headed monster Scylla and the whirlpool Charybdis. Namby-pambies.

'Then you get home and find there's a load of freeloaders trying to get off with you wife, and you have to slaughter them all. Puts a pile of junk mail into perspective, doesn't it?

'Mind you, I've not flown with Ryanair. I understand that can have its challenges'.

Gold medal-winning UK athlete forgets to cry during BBC interview

'I was so excited and happy to have won. I just forgot to cry,' the latest Team GB Gold medal winner has admitted. 'I'd been practising, too, but when the moment came, I just dried up. I even had a tissue soaked in Olbas Oil in my pocket just in case.'

'I remembered at the last minute, but it was too late, and they had already cut to the weather forecast,' he continued, 'I've really let the team down. I don't deserve to have won.'

Can't-be-arsed UK Government asks public to stick forks in their own eyeballs

Boris Johnson's technique of governance by tossing off has reached a pinnacle of efficiency. A half-hearted spokes-mumble sighed and murmured: 'Rather than making bold claims like 'world-beating' and then doing the opposite, it makes much more sense to bring the do nothing bit forward.'

'From this point onwards, the Government isn't even going to bother saying anything at all about stuff it clearly isn't going to do anyway. To that end, the public is encouraged to throw themselves downstairs, stick their faces in fans, and thrust forks into their own testicles. If you don't have testicles, then grow a pair.'

Syrian villagers send sympathy message to Brits unable to go on holiday

Asawi al Hab, a small village on the border with Lebanon, has been shelled and attacked by Government forces, killing or injuring more than half of the population, but it is still full of sympathy for British people unable to go on holiday

A doctor in a local hospital said: 'It's been pretty grim here for a number of years. When we heard that British people wouldn't be able to jet off to Benidorm due to uncertainty over the traffic light system, we couldn't just stand by and do nothing. So, we're offering cheap accommodation for any Brits who want to spend a week or two in our country.

'Of course, there's a pretty good chance they'll be shelled on a daily basis by Assad's forces or strafed by Russian fighter jets, but at least the weather's good at this time of year, and they'll go home with a healthy tan.'

We'll give up everything to save Earth - except cars, planes, meat, etc

In light of the UN's damning climate change report, politicians have demanded that we all look concerned and nod in a sage-like way. Everyone agreed it was really important to do something, provided it was not now and not them.

The public was encouraged to change their lifestyle but only if it is not too inconvenient. Foreign holidays would be cancelled unless they were going anywhere nice. Cars would be replaced by public transport, except when it involved buses or trains. Meals would be vegetarian only, with a side order of steak.

As one concerned citizen said: 'David Attenborough got me to give up plastic cocktail sticks, which was a toughy, as I normally drink pints. We should definitely do so something about the environment, and when I say we, I mean our grandchildren. Provided, of course, they're not already ten feet under the sea.'

Quirky gesture to camera to be compulsory for 2024 Olympians, organisers confirm

'They've had five years to prepare', said an Olympic spokesperson. 'So, it was disappointing to see some athletes insisting on a slightly scary fixed look of intense concentration, staring towards an imaginary point in the distance'.

'The Olympics has a long tradition of confident gestures to camera,' noted the spokesperson wistfully. 'We need to see more of those 'finger pointing forward like a gun whilst nodding your head and winking' set pieces. Or some of those ironic 'Rodin's thinker' type poses that some of the boxers do as they come in the ring'.

'The female gymnastics managed to make that heart gesture with their thumb and index fingers. Table tennis guys could cup their balls, the sailors some kind of hornpipe pastiche and the dressage a little pretend gallop. Oh and 'medal biting' in post-podium photographs will be compulsory'.

Simon Cowell to be fired to the edge of space using his big trousers

Joining the list of multi-million-pound space trips, Simon Cowell will be fired beyond Earth's atmosphere using a specially-designed wooden catapult. When attached to the braces on his massive, high-waistband trousers, it will hurl him skywards at speeds in excess of 2,000 miles per hour.

The daring mogul will also be coated with a high factor sunscreen in case he ventures too close to the Sun, although he has told friends he hopes to avoid that pitfall by going at night.

AI can diagnose dementia just by asking for your email's 'memorable word'

A trial at Addenbrooke's Hospital has asked 500 respondents, when was the last time they did a Windows update. Only 10% could recall the date, and 5% of them were confused Apple Mac owners.

Explained one clinician: 'Originally we used a crude metric, by asking people what day the bins go out. But we found the password recovery process bamboozles anyone over 30. Remember that memorable holiday? No, neither do we. What about your geography teacher's pet name, or can you recall your partner's favourite book? Who the hell knows or cares?'

If further proof was needed, the second stage of the password recovery involves receiving a six-digit number to a phone you no longer own. 'It's almost as if the brain struggles to remember the street where your third cousin grew up on'.

Shire Police called as Hobbit and Orc violence erupts at Green Dragon pub

Sam Gamgee, a gardener from The Hill area, told reporters, 'I was just sitting there with my master, like watching the footy, when all of a sudden this orc matey jumps up on a table, all body armour, bloodstains and gore, points at us hobbits and starts singing 'you're all shit with hairy feet, doo-dah doo-dah. You're all shit with hairy feet, doo-dah doo-dah day.'

'Well, that was it, and it all kicked off big style with chairs, mithril and lembas flying everywhere - total carnage'. Meanwhile, it's understood Gamgee's master, local celebrity, Frodo Baggins, is wanted for questioning. Detective Sergeant Ted Sandyman told reporters. 'I can confirm Baggins is a person of interest in this matter, but his whereabouts are currently unknown after he somehow managed to disappear into thin air during the fracas.'

Russia wants its money back from British embassy traitor

'We paid him a fortune to feed us high-level intelligence from the British Government,' said the Russian handler of a man he thought he was running inside the UK embassy in Moscow. 'However, he gave us nothing that you could possibly call intelligence.'

'All we got from his bug inside Downing Street was a constant stream of plummy-voiced burbling, which our agents can make no sense of whatsoever, and night-time quarrels – apparently over the new wallpaper and a badly-behaved mongrel called Dylan.

The Taliban – 'Back in Black'

It is the rock reunion that they said would never happen, the world's favourite boy band (definitely no girls allowed) 'The Taliban' are back on the road and setting Afghanistan alight. Their whistle-stop tour of abandoned U.S. military bases has delighted their fans and infuriated invading armies.

One groupie, who had had her burqa signed by the band, squealed with delight: 'They played all the old favourites. And when I say old, we're talking 700 B.C. We like our metal heavy and usually fired from an AK-47.

Said one band member: 'Many assumed it was drugs and drink that caused us to split, but we're not that kind of group. We actually split over artistic differences – none of us approved of any art from the last two hundred years. That said, we've buried the hatchet now - in our enemy's skull'.

A'Level grades to be replaced with assessment of wealth

Following the success of the teacher-awarded grades for A'Levels this year, the Government has decided to formalise the process and ditch exams completely.

'Exams have their place,' admitted the Education Minister, 'but sometimes poor people pass them - and not only white poor people too. Not that we want to hold back talented, intelligent poor people, regardless of skin colour, but McDonald's needs competent managers and universities need white, upper-class students.'

A UCAS spokesperson confirmed that under the new scheme, there would still be places for ordinary students regardless of background, income or colour. Just not the best ones.

Parents relieved as grades of privately educated cherubs CAN be bought after all

A 97% inflation in private school grades has put the minds of rich parents at ease. After years of dismay that their dim spawn might have to suffer equivalent grades to those achieved in the state school system, the private education sector has finally pulled its finger out when it comes to enhancing grades on an industrial scale.

A response from the Department of Education stated: 'We want to make it perfectly clear that this is in no way unfair. When a pupil cheats on a test in order to receive a higher grade, then that is cheating, and they will be severely punished. When entire private schools of great repute cheat all of their grades, then that is merely ensuring that wealthy parents are getting value for money'.

Planet not on fire, say fossil fuel fans

Renegade maverick free thinkers, who half-read something on Facebook written by Shell and BP, have come together to jauntily deny that climate change is happening, even as the floodwaters hurtle past their homes.

One climate change sceptic shouted, 'I'm not on fire! You're on fire - wait -I mean no-one is on fire', as the flames consumed them, as well as large parts of California. Said another: 'The world isn't dead; it's just pining for the fjords – which are melted'.

Locals celebrate after picture of c*ck and balls on church attributed to Banksy

The work, which has thrilled art lovers across the world, has been described as a bold statement about the gentrification of seaside towns, which essentially 'makes us all feel like c*cks'. The appearance of the drawing follows a recent spate of Banksy works in which the artist has explored sexual themes and innuendo, including "Shaz is a Slag", which appeared on a Streatham bus shelter. Meanwhile, the listed 17th-century building has now been demolished in order for the artwork to be removed and encased in glass for display at a local museum.

£6 million mound of dirt 'absolute bargain' confirm London homeless

Ian Stewart, who is currently living between two bins behind the Oxford Street branch of Greggs, has agreed that he is absolutely delighted with the Marble Arch Mound.

'I was previously hoping that the local council might help me with a few of the basics like food and shelter, but now I've seen the giant hobbit hill in all its glory, I agree the money was much better spent on that' he said. 'I climbed it straight away for the absolute bargain price of £8. It meant I couldn't eat for two weeks but it was totally worth it'.

The homeless community have already offered up suggestions for other thrilling London tourist attractions that councils could spend money on instead of them, including 'Fatberg Mountain' in the middle of Oxford Circus and an installation of 'Thin Air' in Hyde Park. The proposal for an expensive 'Waste of Space' was dismissed as it was pointed out this attraction already exists in Westminster.

Ken Loach expelled from Labour Party for calling Kes 'Keith'

Award winning film maker and humanitarian, Ken Loach has been told to leave the Labour Party, as there is no place for democratic socialists in a democratic socialist party.
A Labour Spokesman confirmed: 'Ken no longer shares the values of this party – because we have all become colossal arseh*les.'
He was also chastised for referring to Sir Keith Starmer as 'Keir', I mean 'Keith', 'Keir', no its 'Keith', 'Keir' – 'Keir'? Yes, it's Keith. Many supporters of Sir Keir, both of them, have expressed frustration that everyone gets his name wrong; in a childish attempt to devalue his successes, all two of them. A close friend tried to explain: 'His name is not Keith as well, you know. It's Sir F*cknuggets'.

'Not so much Churchill as Chaplin'

One farcical incident at a garden centre, had bungling Boris Johnson entangled in a vicious accident loop after stepping between two rakes. A spokeswoman confirmed: 'He was repeatedly smacked in the face and the back of his head by the handles for a full five minutes as he tottered back and forth, before an aide came to his rescue. I kid you not. You should see the video. Priceless.

'What's more, extensive risk and gaffe modelling, carried out by a firm of slapstick experts, suggest it would only be a matter of time before his trousers fall down during some important state occasion.'

Latin phrases in the modern idiom

- Ars longa vita brevis: Your bum looks big in those shorts

- E Pluribus unum: He only has one ball

Five Go Dobbing in the Neighbours

- Et al: Scoffed the lot

- Mobile vulgus: Swearing down the phone

- Fiat lux: Pimped car

- Ignis fatuus: Light your farts

- Extempore: In full-time work

- Ad hoc: Try this German wine

- Alibi: Somewhere to pull over in an A road

- Bona fide: Not a Sémillon

- Pro bono: U2 fan

- Quod erat demonstrandum: This is how you ride a four-wheeled motor bike

- Verbatim: He was eaten by a verb

- Vice versa: Smoking roll-up spliffs made with pages ripped out of old poetry books.

- Tempus fugit: Time to f*ck off

- Nil satis nisi optimum: Still goalless after 90 minutes

- Audere est facere: Audrey is farcical

- Caveat emptor: My 1990s Vauxhall has run out of petrol

- Ad nauseam: Buy Gaviscon today

- Alter ego: The Pope

- Ex cathedra: Notre Dame

- Ex officio: Matt Hancock

- In absentia: Boris Johnson

- Sic semper tyrannis: Look! Dinosaur vomit!
- Obit anis, abit onus: Rimming with false teeth

- Pro forma: Ex sportsman

- Vade mecum: Watch me have an orgasm

- In loco parentis: My Dad is a train driver

- Inter alia: I like sci-fi creatures

- Cum laude: Noisy sex

- Et tu, Brute: Your aftershave is too strong

- Quid pro quo: I'll give you a pound for that 80s rock album

- Prima facie: Wearing heavy makeup.

- Pedem refero: I need to find a podiatrist

Queen 'prefers Soviet national anthem to ours'

It is widely believed that the Queen has always hated the British anthem and has stubbornly refused to learn the words, citing the fact that she never has to sing it herself. A spokesman at the Russian Embassy told us: 'We agree, it's far too downbeat and the lyrics are an absolute joke, apart from the bit about scattering your enemies, which we're all in favour of'.

Bill and Ben sacked as PM's speechwriters

In a carefully worded speech, the PM explained in Latin: 'Flob-flobble-flob-a-flob-a-dob-flob-flobblemop-mob-mob-obble-pobble, flob-obba-flobble, flobba-mob-a-flobble-bobble-flob. Flob-plobble-nob-a-flob. Flobobble.'

To which Bill & Ben replied: 'Knob'.

Where were all these 'experts' on Afghanistan twenty years ago?

'Yes, I originally supported the CIA channelling $2 billion worth of arms to support terrorists in the region and to train Osama Bin Laden. But it would take fevered imagination to see some kind of connection between the Mujahedeen and the Taliban. For instance, they are spelt completely differently,' said an international relations expert.

'I can't see how there is a link between us illegally invading Afghanistan, looting its wealth, installing a puppet regime and the troubles we have today? We've rejuvenated the Afghan economy – you only have to look at the way we've helped them become an exporter of 90% of all the world's illicit opium. That's civilization for you'.

The only 'expert' no one seems to have heard from, despite his ability to sound off on every conceivable topic, is Tony Blair. Odd that.

Rich white men deny inheriting their evilness; they say they worked for it

Quentin von Baumhafffson-Schtillbank III, a man so rich that he owns the global rights to three 'f's in a row, is one example of many. A multi-billionaire so wealthy, that most national Governments are incomprehensibly paying him tax, though apparently not enough.

By the end of a frantic day of shorting, debt swaps, currency movements, corporate global buyouts, a raft of personally beneficial legislation changes, a national coup, multiple massacres, and an each-way bet on the 2:45 at Kempton, QB-S III had made $1.3 billion. 326 million people around the world had been plunged into abject poverty, 2.9 million people had died as a direct result, and 400,000 acres of pristine ecosystem had been destroyed, pushing climate crisis recovery further beyond the collective reach of the entire planet.

All in a day's work – not that he's ever done one.

Queen Mother's mummified stool sold for $9 million

A 7-inch, 14-ounce rocket have broken all records at auction. The mighty brown trout was retrieved from the Queen Mother's toilet at Sandringham House by a royal flunkey who found it nestling on top of the paper in 1941 after she had forgotten to pull the chain.
The servant had the royal turd injected with embalming fluid and had kept it in a display case in his front room until his death last year when it was discovered by council workmen who handed it in to the police.

A spokesperson for the royal household told newsmen: 'The Queen would have preferred to have kept her mum's roscoe in Buckingham Palace, but the money will definitely come in handy to put towards the new central heating'.

This is not the first time bodily waste from one of the royals has been auctioned off but we cannot discuss it, due to Prince Andrew's super injunction.

Constantine III issues warning on troop withdrawal

As he left Britannia, Roman Emperor Constantine III said: 'We are proud have having brought peace and civilisation to an island full of pagan Euro-sceptics.

'However, with the current Empire balance of payments crisis, we can no longer afford to spaff ten million denarii a year up against Hadrian's Wall, even if it does keep out the very worst of the barbarians.

'When we leave, Britannia must not become a breeding ground for terrorism, or heaven forbid, badly behaving football supporters.'

Cat's anus accidentally writes Daily Telegraph

A few weeks ago, the cat in question sat on a laptop keyboard, presumably by accident, creating an entire editorial. A spokeswoman for the news group said: 'The anus has a disturbing right wing bent and it keeps turning out pretty much the same narrow-minded drivel day after day.

'But our readers haven't noticed any difference and, if anything, online clicks are slightly up. To that end, we have fired our entire writing staff and slashed the journalism and opinion budget down to 20 cans of Whiskas and a bag of kibble.

'We're now on the lookout for a baboon which can accidentally take photos of the royal family in a positive light.'

Man celebrates after beating 'going the wrong way through IKEA' world record

A Daventry man was celebrating today after beating the world record time of 2 hours 22 minutes. The record has stood almost as long as the 'Slowest full-trolley Aldi checkout' (currently 2 minutes 25 seconds) record and the 'Longest time after entering Oak Furnitureland before you get approached for a sale' (currently 0.02 seconds).

'I didn't go with the intention of breaking the record', he admitted. 'But then we got to the checkout and I realised we'd forgotten a few odd sized and quirkily-named airtight containers back near the start of the store. My son offered to go back, but he's got his whole future ahead of him. I know it should be me. I had my trainers on, so I did a few stretches, took some deep breaths and gave it a go'.

After beating the record, he and his son did a lap of honour – and were never seen again.

Degree in Domestic Recycling Arrangements launched

'The days of simply putting old newspapers out in a separate pile from the rest of the rubbish are a long way behind us now,' explained a Professor of Reprocessing and Repurposing. 'We need to analyse each item of refuse in turn and make a decision on which of the seven recycling bins is most appropriate for that item, based on an ever-developing set of complicated criteria'.

The course will cover why you can recycle aluminium foil in one county but not the neighbouring one, the reason for keeping bottle tops on in certain regions but not in others, and the difference between thick paper and thin cardboard.

The final year of the course will concentrate on the recycling of plastics, providing students with the expertise to determine whether that crinkly plastic tray is classified as a plastic tray, which can be recycled, or an item made of crinkly plastic, which cannot. It will also explain that, however well you attempt to follow all the recycling instructions, recycling workers maintain the right to take what they feel like and leave the rest scattered haphazardly over the pavement.

Raab planning to invade Europe from his Li-Lo

Following the Government's successful orderly withdrawal from Afghanistan, planned from holiday beaches adorned by Prime Minister Boris Johnson and Foreign Secretary Dominic Raab, the Government has confirmed that military decisions are in future to be taken while on holiday.

'The pressure and typically abysmal lighting in war rooms just creates a morose atmosphere, leading to rush decisions involving troops, whereas considering deploying soldiers while enjoying happy hour on a sun-kissed beach helps put everything into perspective,' said a spokesman for the Foreign Secretary.

'So, we thought "f*ck it, let's just travel to tourist destinations and chill while we determine the appropriate action to take when our interests are attacked, or our allies do us over.' He confirmed that pushing the nuclear button would feel 'much more fun while sipping pina coladas.'

Opposition MPs reluctantly agreed that there's no point in Raab being the Foreign Secretary unless he is permanently overseas. 'Might as well be on permanent holiday, for all the use he is,' said one MP.

DUP: 'Away an' catch yerselves on! We're not irrelevant crackpots, so we're not!'

Ever since the DUP, a group of reactionary oddballs, keen to return to their happy place - the 14th century - was shat on from a great height by Boris Johnson, when Tories no longer needed to endure the shame of having them prop up the Westminster Government, the Northern Ireland political group has had to come to the bitter acceptance, that once again, they are a total irrelevance in British politics.

However, DUP spokesman and Witchfinder General, Nelson Nelson, was today refusing to accept what everyone else sees as cold hard facts.

'Away an' catch yerselves on! Sure, we're as relevant today as we've ever been. And as a matter of fact, we intend to bring forward a private members' bill to call for the reinstatement of the rack, thumbscrews and the breaking wheel for heretics, Catholics and those found guilty of homosexuality, witchcraft, or worst of all, being one of thon other crowd.

'We certainly will continue to make our voices heard, so we will. No doubt about that. Oh aye, mark my words. Tiocfaidh ár lá... no... hang on a minute... erm... ah ballix to it!'

Earwax 'endlessly fascinating' confirms Lancashire man

Jack Pickles of Blackpool has explained to his wife that the wax, and other items, pulled from his ears are things of incredible interest. Mrs Pickles explained the revelation: 'Whatever's going on; eating meals, watching TV or just chatting, if Jack finds something on his finger that's come out his Thiocyanide ear, he has to examine it. I'm sure he's got a collection somewhere.'

Mr Pickles denied having a collection, although he admitted it was 'a cracking idea.'

Were you mis-sold a PFI or WMD by Tony Blair? You may be due some compensation

People of Afghanistan, you may be able to claim a cash settlement of up to £7.23, if you or a loved one were accidental killed in attempt to boost Tony Blair's ego. If you were told that your country had WMD or Osama Bin Laden hiding in your attic, you may have been the victim of an elaborate fraud.

Were you offered infrastructure projects at vastly inflated prices that never materialized? Does that sound familiar? Sadly, it was too late for the citizens of the UK, who already handed over £300 billion, with the vague promise that Alastair Campbell would tarmac their drive.

Leading a notorious group of conmen, Blair tricked voters into three election victories, but by 2001 he was aiming for something bigger – a lap dance with George Bush. Be warned, Blair is still at large today, often using the fake ID of 'Peace Envoy'. People of Afghanistan, if you think you may have been duped by him – join the queue.

'Desperate for love' London woman had torrid affair with robot vacuum cleaner

A jilted husband has revealed: 'I suspected something untoward was going on between my missus and that Hoover when I used to hear her in the hall cupboard, moaning and panting, but I just thought she was struggling to get the clips off the dust bag before emptying it into the bin.'

Schools needing a CO2 monitor to be provided with a canary

The means of monitoring ventilation and the spread of COVID is only one small, yellow bird away according to Government research. Should the bird turn blue and drop off their perch, it will explain why all the schoolchildren are blue and lying unconscious under their desks.

The classroom will be evacuated and designated as an appropriately sized office space or a 'spacious London apartment'. The students will then be moved to a smaller classroom to recover, but one with no annoying bird in it – or windows.

This cost saving measure will cut the expense of actual monitors and has no connection whatsoever with the fact the Education Secretary's best friend from Uni runs a Canary Farm. Meanwhile the new coalmine in Cumbria will be fitted with small primary age children, in cages. Should the children turn blue and drop off their perch...

Wedding guests bullied into giving cash not gifts with angry poem in invitation

'We can't wait to spend our special day with you,
But please let us give you a little tip or two,
Having you there on our wedding day,
Is all we really need, but please let us say:
We don't want your shite gifts
We want cold hard CASH you can shove all those b*llocks wedding gifts up your arse we don't want them if you're coming to eat and drink in 5* luxury at our expense the least you can do is give us £100 for the privilege you tight b*stards.
Carriages at midnight. RSVP to wewantcash@hotmail.com'.

The happy couple are planning a honeymoon in Barbados with their winnings where they want to thank their benefactors by posting a series of smug pictures on Instagram followed with #blessed. When they return, they are considering buying their first house so are already planning an extravagant anniversary party with a similar money extortion sub-plot.

Airline under fire for duct taping a passenger, switches to Pritt Stick policy

The airline in question has opted for a lighter touch by advising staff to use a zero tolerance Pritt Stick protocol, with additional Blu Tack if needed. In very serious cases, an escalation to a thorough plastering of troublemakers with Post-it Notes might be required.

This flies in the face of what decent, law-of-the-skies-abiding passengers actually want. One regular flier with more Air Miles than sense said: 'If I am on a flight and some nitwit tries to open an emergency exit, then blunt plastic cutlery ain't going to cut it. I want the crew to pile right in on them immediately and use a Jason Statham level of force. They can lash them with seat belts, put stuff stale buns in their mouths or stick a life vest up their bunghole - whatever it takes get 'em under control and shut them up'.

An unnamed budget airline which rarely deposits passengers anywhere near where they actually want to go has confirmed that any customer requiring restraint will incur an £80 surcharge for the duct tape.

PornHub to ban porn

'It's something we've been thinking of doing for a while,' said CEO Max Hardon. 'We think the idea of logging onto a computer, making sure your wife has left to visit her mother and then finding a video of that fetish she won't let you do is so cliche. We want to embrace new forms of explicit media, like full-on gardening videos or erotic needlework. It is our belief that we will thrive in this new world, and it'll only be a matter of time before all those other sites follow.'

This news was welcomed with dismay by sweaty-palmed users of the site. Regular visitor David Malcolm of Kidderminster Road in Truro (who requested not to be identified) said: 'This is ridiculous, how am I meant to get myself off now. My girlfriend left me two years ago and I can't afford an escort. I'll have to go back to buying FHM and... wait, that doesn't exist anymore either?! F*CK!'

Acting tips for the new football season

- Fall like a ton of bricks if an opponent's boot gets anywhere near a leg, rolling around on the ground as if the leg has been removed just below the hip. Subsequently getting up and running the length of the pitch in just under ten seconds

- If fouled – and following the above performance, the opponent gets red- or yellow-carded, adopting a rueful grin and trying to shake his hand

- Having finally been red-carded for a series of tackles which anywhere else would result in a jail sentence, leaving the pitch with eyes downcast and sadly shaking the head – think Mother Teresa

- Any measured, philosophical discussion with the ref must be accompanied with eyes widened, mouth open (and ideally spittle-flecked) and both arms held in the John McEnroe pose

- Generous applauding the home supporters after yet another home loss

- Ironically applauding the away supporters after an unprecedented away win

Prince Andrew appointed trade envoy to Love Island

Bringing a wealth of experience about private sex islands, the prince is said to have been ready to leave in an instant, having had his bags packed for a hasty exit months ago. He did insist that his new role would be covered by diplomatic immunity, anonymity on Tinder and an untraceable Search History.

Andrew will be solely responsible for the import and export of love to the UK, with his primary focus on emerging markets – 'nothing too old' he demanded. Unlike other Royals who have been accused of not working hard, Andrew promised to be very hands-on.

Man shaves after concluding his lockdown beard is more Lineker than Clooney

After four months of ensuring his face was blurry and poorly lit during Zoom meetings while he grew and trimmed and shaped his new look, a man has finally admitted defeat. However, he is not at all downhearted. 'My wife said getting rid of the beard took ten years off me so I'm going to grow it and shave it all off again at least twice more,' he explained.

Disgusting marine life found in ocean of beautiful plastic

'Our delicate and fragile microplastic ecosystems could be harmed,' explained a spokeswoman for the Institute of Secretly Getting Paid Shitloads by Fossil Fuel Interest Groups. 'If we don't see a significant change in our behaviour, we could be overrun with dolphins and shit. Everyone needs to come together and work hard to prevent that. Imagine turning your tap on at home and finding a blue whale in your glass.'

Patients who need blood tests asked to bring a bottle

While the NHS struggles to cope with a shortage of plastic sample bottles, one GP surgery in Walsall has asked patients to bring their own bottle: 'Avoid unwashed jam jars – as they could lead to a false diagnosis of diabetes. Food colouring bottles need a clean, as bright green blood is always a worry. Miniature whisky bottles can also be used, although if not properly rinsed beforehand they could lead to a false diagnosis of cirrhosis of the liver'.

Man dumps woman over inspirational wall art.

'As soon as I walked in, I saw a massive framed poster saying, 'May All Who Enter Leave as Friends'. I mean, really? Even the bloke who comes to read the gas meter?

'Above the sofa there was a big sign saying, 'Live Every Moment Like It's Your Last'. That felt like too much pressure to me - when I'm sitting on a sofa, I mainly just want to watch Netflix and eat Doritos.

'In the kitchen she had a sign saying, 'This Kitchen Is for Dancing', which struck me as being a recipe for indigestion, not to mention downright dangerous - you shouldn't leave a chip pan unattended while you go tangoing round the kitchen!

'Even in the bathroom there was a sign saying, 'Wash Away Your Troubles with Some Bubbles'. I don't like bubble baths. Most of my time in the bathroom is spent sitting on the toilet scrolling through my phone while I have a crap. I had thought Natalie seemed really easy going, but when I saw all those signs everywhere telling me what to do, I started to think that she's actually quite bossy.

The final straw came when I saw a sign above the bed saying, 'Sleep, Sweet Dreams'. No mention of sex at all - not even a little sign saying, 'Just A Quickie, I've Got an Early Start Tomorrow'. So as soon as we'd eaten the meal, I gave her the old, 'It's Not You, It's Me' spiel, and legged it out of there.'

When asked how she was feeling after the break-up, Natalie said: 'To be honest, I'm not too upset. All he ever wears are t-shirts with slogans on them like 'Just Do It', and 'Love Football', which made me think he's a bit immature. I texted my best friend to tell her and she sent me a meme which says, 'Be Strong Enough to Let Go, And Wise Enough to Wait for What You Deserve.' That's quite inspiring. I wonder if I can get that on a poster?'

Coldplay documentary shelved after background music segments hit 12-hour mark

The director explained: 'The problem was it became impossible to distinguish the short soundbites of music that fade in and out to provide gravitas and meaning to key moments in a documentary from the actual greatest hits of the band.

'We had a segment with Chris Martin struggling to complete the complex lyrics and melody in 'Clocks' and the music the editors placed over the top was Clocks. The band's drum kit falling over and needing to be Fixed Up...well you can guess the rest.'

'Segment music self-circularity is sadly increasingly common in pop', noted musicologist Peter McVeigh. 'For example, it is a little known fact that Keane have tried to split up a number of times due to falling royalties, only to be propped back up by the increased royalties from the segments of their 'Everybody's Changing' anthem that are inevitably played in montages where they announce they are splitting up.'

Ant and Dec added to list of proscribed organisations

A spokesman for the Department of Culture said: 'Something has to be done. Their brand of yeasty banter and faux blokiness has been allowed to fester and must be stopped. They have long outstayed their welcome and are becoming irritating beyond all belief.

'Their hopeless antics ought to have been curtailed years ago, but still, better late than never. And speaking for an utterly incompetent Government, it's nice to finally do something that can be applauded by all sections of the public.'

M&S to stop selling suits, almost 20 years after it sold its last one

In a recent poll, customers cited the top three reasons for why they might wear a M&S suit were - a funeral, a court appearance and a dare. Their last customer was a Malcolm Durrant, 57, who had purchased a particularly fetching three-piece beige suit, back in 2001.

The Head of Sales explained: 'We'd been holding out for a follow up sale. Therefore, when Mr Durrant walked back in, twenty years later, we thought we're back in business. All the staff were whooping and doing high fives. We thought we might even shift a pair of socks. So imagine our disappointment when he tried to return said suit, ridiculously claiming it had never been worn'.

Commented Mr Durrant: 'It hadn't'.

Bin collections to switch to once a year

CEO of French waste management firm, Merde explained: 'Fewer bin lorries on our roads means our carbon footprint and exhaust gas pollution will be significantly reduced. Yes, some squalor-related illness will reappear, but it will be a small price to pay when you consider the overall benefits to our environment. Anyway, we've got antibiotics these days so what's the problem?

There will be no more petty squabbles between couples over whose turn it is to put out the rubbish. They will simply adopt a system of husbands one year and wives the next. All those tiffs of the past will be consigned to the dustbin – when it's not full.'

Five Go Dobbing in the Neighbours

In other news...

Carrie Symonds gets second jab.

UK Afghan exit strategy "modelled on Brexit". More soon

Onlyfans reversal of porn ban greeted by one hand clapping.

Sexism at work reported by over 90% of lady-doctors.

Experts say gold coins found under St Pauls are first example of cryptcurrency

Duke of York refuses to comment on whether he had 10000 men

Sturgeon self-isolating, or as she prefers to call it "ultimate independence".

Extinction Rebellion in London. Rebellion extinction in Kabul. More soon.

City resigned as United re-sign Ronaldo

Medical team confirm winner of Paris 2024 Olympics stakeboarding 'not yet born'

Parents regret naming children Alexa, Siri and Cortana

Inventor of electric trouser press to be buried in coffin two inches deep.

10 out of 10 viewers preferred Sean Lock. RIP

Woolly mammoth urged to be more specific

Man in jogging bottoms arrested after appearing on no-fly list.

Man told by doctors he could drop dead relieved they were just being rude

Breakthrough: scientists finally identify 'the actual f@$k'

Burger sales treble after McDonald's announces they've run out of gherkins.

Students demand bigger loans to cover £10,000 COVID fines

EU behind plot to feed children claims Rees-Mogg

Oxford English Dictionary adds phrase 'zoom wank'

New TV satire show entirely for snowflakes, That Was The Woke That Was

British Olympic triple jump team coming on in leaps and bounds

Five Go Dobbing in the Neighbours

Sacked high jumper clears his desk

European Central Bank and English Cricket Board have thumb war over who keeps acronym

Fly still failing to take advantage of window of opportunity

New fifty pound note too heavy to lift

UK hydrogen power funding set to blow up

Sir Kier Starmer to be re-launched as 'Starmsy' to re-establish his street cred

Camels welcome straw ban.

Green light for Sizewell power station was initially 'a little off white'

Three men rescued from laundry device 'hung out to dry'

James Dyson speaks out against anti vacs campaigners.

Tom Cruise threatens virus: 'Come on then, pick on someone your own size!'

Anyone using the word 'granular' doesn't actually understand what is going on

Royal Navy to shoo British fish away from Europe & back to Britain.

Anti-democracy campaigners to elect new leader

Diet websites still asking customers to accept cookies

Man constipated on seasonings takes laxative just to pass the thyme

Johnson sets up committee to keep eye on unnecessary layers of Government bureaucracy

Struggling families urged to think of skipping meals as intermittent fasting

New monthly magazine 'What Virus?' advises best variant to catch

Man turning down fish with herbs reckons it's not the thyme or the plaice.

Five Go Dobbing in the Neighbours

Thanks to all the people listed below who have allowed us to reproduce their written work in this book.

A.Mantra	Adrian Bamforth	AlkaXS
Al O'Pecia	antharrison	apepper
Arthur Pyke	BangingOnAgain	Beau-Jolly
Benvoleo	Bobski	bonjonelson
Bookies Friend	Brigg AF	Camz
Chipchase	ChrisF	DailyMoose
Dan.F	Danny Soz	DavidH
Deceangli	Deskpilot3	Dick Everyman
Doctor Chutney	Dominic_mcg	Dumbing Down
Filthy Rich	FlashArry	FloraJardine
Frank Optional	Gerontius	Gibbet
Granger	Harry Palmer	Ian Searle
Iroquois Pliskin	Ironduke	ItsMeJack
Jack Nunn	Jack Reed	james_doc
Jeremynh	JETFAB	Jimmy Dodger
Joanne Starkie	JoF	Landfill
Lockjaw54	MADJEZ	Max Stars
Maxine Jones	Micca	Mick Turate
Midfield Diamond	Milo Shame	Mirthless Evil C
Mr Kerry T	Myke	nicharper
Nickb	Not Amused	OShaughnessy
Oxbridge	Paul L	Pdavies65
Ragmans Trumpet	Robowurzel	Rogerg
ron cawleyoni	Rowly	Sarah Tipper
Scribbler	Seymour totti	SimoneCleal
Sinnick	Sir Lupus	Smart Alex
Squudge	StanleyMizaru	Steve Blair
SteveB	StewartBarclay	SuburbanDad
Sugar Ray	Sydalg	thatwasbeast
TheNewsWalrus	Thisisalloneword	Throngsman
Titus	tonymc81	Trevor Rudge
Underconstruction	Vertically Challenged Giant	
Walter Eagle	Wrenfoe	Wrexfan

Also available from NewsBiscuit:

15 years of Typos – available from Amazon in eBook, paperback and hardback format

And finally...

First lunar restaurant lacks atmosphere.
UK jabless rate hits record low.
Covid test centres run out of tracing paper
Kanye's marriage goes West
Out of work fishermen 'swamping sea shanty market'
Football comes home; Priti Patel deports it
Film festival returns with Cannes-do attitude. More soon
Timpsons staff insist they are key workers.
Irony sirens sound as Boris tells country to 'be responsible'
The Guardian celebrates 200 ears.
US votes in most divisive election since the last one
Splinter group invests in new tweezers.

NewsBiscuit editorial team for Five go Dobbing...

Wrenfoe – editor, curator and task randomiser
Chrisf – editor and ticker maestro
Oxbridge – editor and full stop monitor supremo
Chipchase – editor and thumper of tubs
Throngsman – editor and formatter
Techguy – for letting all of the above access to the site

Artwork

Cover design – Wrenfoe
Cartoons - Mike Capozzola

Many thanks to all the biscuiteers who give their time, talent
and bank details for free to keep NewsBiscuit running.